IR

WE HAVE ALWAYS BEEN HERE

WE HAVE ALWAYS BEEN HERE

LENA NGUYEN

DAW BOOKS, INC.
DONALD A. WOLLHEIM, FOUNDER
1745 Broadway, New York, NY 10019
ELIZABETH R. WOLLHEIM
SHEILA E. GILBERT
PUBLISHERS
www.dawbooks.com

Jacket design by Adam Auerbach.

Jacket illustration by Yurly Muzur.

Edited by Leah Spann.

DAW Book Collectors No. 1889.

Published by DAW Books, Inc.
1745 Broadway, New York, NY 10019.

First Printing, July 2021
1st Printing

DAW TRADEMARK REGISTERED
U.S. PAT. AND TM. OFF. AND FOREIGN COUNTRIES
—MARCA REGISTRADA
HECHO EN U.S.A.

PRINTED IN THE U.S.A.

To my parents, Kimphuong and Dungchi, who journeyed from Vietnam and gave us a future: thank you for helping me become the writer I am. And to my sister, Milla, who has always had my back no matter what, even when my head is in the clouds and I forget to pack pants on our trips together.

And for Jeremy, without whom this book would not have been written; whose endless love and support carries me constantly to new horizons; and who is always ready for the next adventure.

PERSONNEL MANIFEST OF THE YT *DEUCALION*

Human Crew

Commander Daryl Wick—Mission Commander
Sergeant Michael Boone—Combat Specialist (Primary)
Officer Valentina "Hunter" Hanover—Combat Specialist (Second)
Captain Vincent Sagara—Security Officer
Officer Reimi Kisaragi—Roboticist, Engineer, Mechanic
Dr. Eric Holt—Physicist
Dr. Wan Xu—Exobiologist, Biodome Designer
Dr. Elly Ma—Climatologist
Dr. Kel Fulbreech—Exogeologist, Cartographer
Officer Natalya Severov—Surveyor
Dr. Michelle Keller—Psychologist (Primary)
Dr. Grace Park—Psychologist (Second)
Dr. Ata Chanur—Physician, Medical Officer

Android Crew

Dylanex—Security AP. Model: 'Myrmidon,' CX-400
Ellenex—Medical AP. Model: ME-900
Jimex—Custodial AP. Model: JM-200
Philex—Domestic AP. Model: DA-200
Megex—Domestic AP. Model: DA-200
Timex—Labor AP. Model: RT-100
Brucex—Labor AP. Model: RT-100
Conex—Labor AP. Model: RT-100
Dianex—Engineering AP. Model: EG-500
Jerex—Explorer AP. Model: UN-600
Curtex—Navigator AP. Model: LI-600
Allex—Research AP. Model: RK-800
Joex—Research AP. Model: RK-800

1.

The day after they landed on the new planet, Park woke to a pair of strong metal arms pinning her down.

Against all instinct, she ignored her initial sense of terror and automatically relaxed her body; she recognized an android's grip when she felt it, and her rational mind—the one that overrode the panicky animal one—knew that it was impossible for an android to hurt her.

Still. It wasn't a comfortable thing to look around and realize she had no idea where she was. She tried to focus her unusually bleary eyesight on whoever was holding her: she'd had her vision genetically corrected a few years ago and had already forgotten what it was like to be poor-sighted, which didn't help the bubbling panic.

"Where am I?" she croaked. She noticed her lips were cracked and sore, but they'd been like that for months, dry from the endless vacuum of space.

The android above her turned their head, looking off to the side as if asking for permission to speak. She thought she could make out blond hair, twisted in a tourniquet-like braid. Ellenex, then, the ship's medical android. No other robot on the ship had yellow hair.

"Go away," commanded another voice, this one sharp and rigid. What she thought was Ellenex moved silently away, leaving Park blinded by the sterile white light the android's head had been blocking off. Then another person moved into her watery field of vision, and this one she recognized more clearly: Chanur. The ship's physician.

Park was in the medical bay.

Now she did panic, sitting up and clawing automatically at her arm; she ripped off whatever medical tab had been glued there and said thickly, "Am I sick?"

Sickness should have been impossible on their ship, she knew. All thirteen members of the *Deucalion*'s human crew had been rigorously examined, scanned, and tested for disease prior to boarding for the ten-month journey to Eos. And with no foreign microbes in space, the chances of incurring infection en route were vanishingly small. But just last night, Park had been informed that the expedition's roboticist, Reimi Kisaragi, was indisposed and being held in quarantine. And if Park had caught whatever she had . . . well. The last time something like this had happened, an entire fleet of military vessels had been compromised, a foreign virus blazing through their ships like wildfire. Park remembered reading about it in the news before they left Earth: a biological attack by the rebels. No survivors.

Chanur watched her struggle with a thousand grim possibilities like a scientist watching a pinned insect squirm. Finally the doctor said, without warmth: "You're not sick. Not in the way you're thinking, anyway." She sounded genuinely disappointed by that fact.

Park frowned at her. "What do you mean?"

"You spent the entire night throwing up in the waste cubicle," Chanur answered in clipped tones, folding her arms as if it were Park's fault; as if she were a child who had misbehaved. The doctor was a native of Phobos, and her voice always had the flat, tight tones of a human whose larynx had shrunk a little in space. Actually, *all* of Chanur seemed a little shrunken, a little hard: she was a compact woman with iron-colored hair and eyes, and a mouth that was perpetually pursed. Park had always thought that she would be better suited as a roboticist rather than as a physician. Or as a coroner. Despite her reputation in the medical field, Chanur didn't like people very much. "You essentially passed out from dehydration. The janitor bot found you."

Something jolted at the back of Park's neck. "I don't remember that," she said automatically, tamping down the bubble of fear in her chest. Then she welded her mouth shut; Chanur was raising her eyebrows at her.

"Are you saying that I'm a liar?"

"No," Park said. She thought fast. She didn't remember going to the bathroom at all, let alone spending an entire night in there. But it was true that she had woken up space-sick and nauseous every day since they'd launched out of Baikonur; she had never left Earth before, had never worked with a flight crew of any kind, so was it that much of a stretch that the long journey had finally taken its toll on her?

But all night?

She needed information first, not a fight with the ship's only physician. "I'm sorry," Park said, squelching any emotion out of her voice. "It must be the sedatives, fogging my memory. I don't doubt your word, of course. I just don't remember."

Chanur grunted, unimpressed. "Someone put something in your food," she said, consulting the medical manifest in her hand. She said it in a bored tone, as if she were reporting a change in the weather. "Emesis tabs. Not taken from the stockroom, so it must have been from the culprit's personal stash."

Park clenched her jaw to keep it from slackening. "Who? Why?"

Chanur gave her a look. "I don't know who. As for the why—what do you think?"

Park pressed her lips together. She was not popular with the crew, everyone knew this; and some of the space-born had mocked her ongoing queasiness, going so far as to call her a "garn"—after Senator Andrew Garn, an Earth politician whose intestines had bottomed out during the first lambda space flight. And they hated her for her role on the ship, and for what had happened in Antarctica, and for any number of things—but she'd thought the hazing and pranks had stopped on Earth. To go as far as poisoning her food . . .

She jerked her thoughts away from the topic, despite the heartsick feeling in her chest. She needed time to regroup her thoughts, away from Chanur's unsympathetic gaze. She needed to talk to Dr. Keller and decide what should be done.

There was no doubt in her mind that punishment ought to be meted out. But to whom—and by whom—was something she needed to consider.

"Will there be any long-term effects?" she heard herself ask, as if she was listening to her own voice from another room.

Chanur looked like she wanted to roll her eyes. "Teenagers eat emesis tabs with their meals to lose weight. You'll be fine."

She turned away, perhaps to begin the process of discharging her, so Park said, "How's Reimi?" The abruptness of it was gauche, but she hoped she could surprise Chanur into answering. "Has her condition . . . improved?"

The doctor's shoulders stiffened, but she didn't turn around. "Officer Kisaragi is in cryogenic stasis," she said finally.

Park hissed in a sharp intake of breath, as if Chanur had punched her. "*Cryo*?" she all but cried. Then she gentled her voice and said in an undertone: "Surely it can't be that bad?"

The last time she'd seen the roboticist, Reimi had complained of stomach upset, but otherwise she'd seemed fine. How could her sickness have gotten bad enough that the young woman was placed in the "freezer," as the spacers called it—and what were they going to do without her?

Reimi was the *Deucalion*'s lone engineer: the only person with the knowledge to service the ship's vast governing systems and all thirteen of its androids. Park supposed the expedition could muddle through with the robots maintaining the ship—but what would happen when *they* fell into disrepair? Darkly she imagined an explosion in the ship's innards, the silent bloom of fire in space. She said aloud, "Ten months out from Earth—no foreign microbes, filtered air. How could she have gotten sick enough to warrant cryo? It couldn't be latent, could it? Something we missed in the scans?"

A disease, she meant: something that had lain dormant in Reimi's system all this time, only to surface now. The part of Park that had grown up in a crowded biodome shuddered. *Just please tell me it's not contagious.*

The corner of Chanur's mouth twitched. "It's confidential medical information, Park," she answered, looking back at her with disdain. "You know I can't disclose that to you. Surely things work the same way on Earth?"

Park ignored the jab. "Then why not keep her in quarantine, at least? That way she could work on the ship and the androids in isolation—or at least instruct someone else on how to do it remotely. Why cryo?"

If she's unconscious, she meant, *how can she help us?* The ISF was not paying billions of dollars for their mission's only engineer to be frozen as literal dead weight. But Chanur didn't answer, and something else occurred then to Park. "How do we know she wasn't poisoned, her food tampered with—like me?"

From over the top of her manifest, Chanur's gaze flicked over Park with the hard precision of a scalpel. "I don't know what it is you want from me," she said finally, tightly. Her lips barely moved, as if she were practicing ventriloquism. "It's classified and not under your purview. More than that, I didn't realize I needed your approval."

Park tried not to flinch at the obvious hostility of the statement. She was one of the two psychologists on the ship, charged with monitoring the crew's mental health; Chanur was the physician in charge of their physical wellbeing. That meant they were both medical professionals—Hippocratic sisters, Keller sometimes joked—but Chanur obviously saw their roles as completely separate from one another. Worse, she seemed to perceive Park as some kind of rival, or a threat.

Stop antagonizing her, Park told herself. *Stop worsening this divide—she has access to information you'll need, and making her hate you even more is unwise.* But she said instead: "Did ISF authorize the freezing? You don't need my approval—but did you get ISF's?"

Something flashed over Chanur's face, then: a movement of the cheek, a hardening at the corner of her mouth. Park grabbed at the data and tucked it away for future analysis, using her neural inlays. Chanur, seeing what she was doing, turned her back.

"Of course ISF authorized it," she said, busying herself with the console terminal installed into the medical bay's left wall. Her shoulders were tight with derision and scorn. "You really think anyone would let me put Kisaragi on ice without their say-so?"

"But no one prepped us beforehand," Park insisted, still watching the doctor's back. She was trying to parse through her body language, recording subtly on the inlays installed into her eyes. "I wasn't informed."

"That's not my problem," Chanur said. She looked back once, her eyes unfocusing slightly as she seemed to contact somebody on her own inlays. "Is it?"

"No," Park said. Now she backed off, wary of an outright power struggle. "I suppose it isn't. But what are we going to do about the ship? The androids?"

Chanur made a discourteous noise. "You can take care of them," she said. It was an insult, not an endorsement of Park's skills. "You've seemed to have made that your priority, anyway."

Park felt her stomach tighten. But before she could fire back a response, a pair of heavy, regular steps from farther back in the medical bay interrupted them both. The ship's custodian android, Jimex, rounded the corner, accompanied by Ellenex again. Both had tepidly curious expressions on their faces, and Jimex moved instantly to Park's side. Ellenex, whose crisp linen uniform and tinny voice reminded Park vaguely of the nanny android who had raised her, said mildly: "Hello. There are elevated stress indicators in your voices." Her pale eyes turned to Park's. "Is everything all right?"

"I'm fine, Ellenex," Park assured her, just as Chanur said with an expression of dislike: "I already told you to go away."

Ellenex nodded politely and left the room again, her pale hands clasped serenely in front of her like a nun's. Chanur said with disgust, "Rotten thing is malfunctioning. It doesn't listen to a word I say."

Maybe you shouldn't have frozen Reimi, then, Park wanted to reply, acid frustration simmering in her gut. *She's the only one who can fix them, after all.*

But she held her silence, and Jimex, who hadn't moved, turned to Park and said, "I hope you have recovered from your gastric distress, Dr. Park."

She couldn't keep her lips from quirking ruefully, looking at him. Because he looked so human, it was easy to forget that Jimex was a simple custodial android, a janitor robot tasked with sanitizing and organizing things aboard their research vessel. His was a primitive model, far more basic than Ellenex's nursing AI, and the disparity between even their speech patterns was vast. His was not a product line known for glowing conversation, or even polite conversation: he didn't know how things *sounded*.

Still. She found something about him charming, even childlike, even though he was a slim, platinum-haired adult male who towered over her. Looking at him standing beside her cot now, she supposed she could see why the other crewmembers disliked the sight of him: he looked ghostly in the medical bay's pale light, gaunt of frame and sporting colorless eyes and a stark, rigid face. She'd even heard some of them calling him "Ecto," after ectoplasm, that trail of ghostly slime. He certainly haunted the dark spaces of the ship like some lost spirit.

"I've recovered, thank you," she told him, almost wanting to pat his hand—though he wouldn't understand the gesture. "And thank you for bringing me to the medical bay. Dr. Chanur says you were the one who found me."

He looked at her steadily, not acknowledging her thanks. "Has a reason been determined for your illness?"

She glanced at Chanur. "Someone slipped emesis tabs into my food."

There was a short pause as the processors in Jimex's head whirred. He didn't seem to know how to respond.

"In your opinion," Park continued, fully aware of Chanur watching her now, "who on the ship do you think is most likely to do that?"

Jimex blinked slowly. The buzzing from his head increased. "I do not understand the question."

"Who, in your opinion, do you think would try to poison me?"

Chanur wheeled on her then, eyes flashing with disapproval. "It doesn't have an opinion, Park," she said tightly. "Being a machine."

There was a little silent beat as Park waited for Jimex to respond to that. But the custodial android said nothing to dispute the claim; he only stood there, looking at them placidly. Park could suddenly feel the chill emanating from the walls. Finally Chanur turned away again and said, "Now, if you don't have any questions regarding your own health, I'll ask you to leave, Park. You're fine, and some of us have actual work to do."

And go to hell to you, too, Park thought after, hurrying down the corridor a few minutes later with Jimex trailing her steps. She was eager to get away from the medical bay, eager to be alone with her thoughts—but just a few steps in, she slowed and put a hand out to his sleeve. "Take me to the service tunnel, please," Park whispered, hunching her shoulders a little in the dark. The tunnel between the medical bay and the ship's private quarters opened up before her like a throat.

Normally she relied on the map in her neural inlays to guide her through the ship, but there was that swaying feeling in her head, a remnant of the tranquilizer tabs and her recent illness. Jimex nodded and began to lead her down the corridor, marching strangely like an executioner leading his victim to the gallows.

Park had to grit her teeth and force herself to forge onward, clinging to his sleeve. The *Deucalion* was structured like a rabbit's warren, the ship itself a gray oblong disc whirling through space, its innards three decks' worth of cramped and crooked passageways that twined around each other in dimly lit confusion. No straight lines here, Park often thought. No straightforward direction, no clear-cut compass. The way the corridors twisted around each other—coupled with the way the ship spun—meant you could never really tell what direction you were moving in. Whether you were going down or up. The reasons for this were backed by physics—streamlined shell for acceleration; spread-out channels to distribute mass; rotating sections of the ship to create gravity—but it didn't make navigating the damn thing any less unnerving. It was like following the root system of a giant tree, shuffling blindly along in the half-dark. Or climbing through the arteries of a mechanical heart. What would be found, deep down in the core of things? You could never be quite sure.

Park suppressed a shudder. She often felt a feeling of erasure, being trapped aboard the ship: as if everything within the great vessel was bent towards annihilating her presence. Even the state-of-the-art filtration systems eliminated all odor, all animal smell and musk. There was no sense or proof of *presence*; it was as if the humans on board were being sterilized out of existence. And she could never get used to the way her soft deckboots made no sound on the red-veined tile—a kind of hellish-looking carbon composite meant to protect them from the heat of reentry. The silence of her own footfalls disconcerted her. She felt always as if she might be swallowed whole by the ship.

Finally she found the bright circle in the wall that indicated the service tunnel she wanted and stumbled toward it. The actual everyday sections of the ship were well-lit, but the passageways between them and the storage rooms operated at half-luminescence, to conserve power. She stopped when they were tucked safely away into the bend and turned to Jimex.

"Who works in the cafeteria?"

His head whirred again. After he'd checked his databases he replied: "Philex works in the cafeteria on most days. Megex on others."

"Speak to them, please, and find out which crewmember could have had access to my food when I wasn't looking. From last night's meal as well as lunch. And speak to Ellenex as well—I want to verify Chanur's story." *For all I know, she could have been the one who poisoned me,* she thought but didn't say.

Jimex cranked his head to the side; in a human it would have been akin to a tilt of curiosity, but in him it simply looked as if his head were askew. "Dr. Chanur's story," he repeated.

Park stared at him. "I want to hear from Ellenex what I was sick with, when I was found. Whether the stockroom has really been untouched. Those sorts of things. Chanur won't allow her to speak to me, but she won't stop you." The robots all had a silent way of communicating with each other, though she suspected she was the only one who knew this—besides maybe Reimi. After a moment she added: "And I'd like to hear from her about Reimi—Officer Kisaragi—too. About what really happened with her. If Dr. Chanur's version of events are true."

Something wasn't right, she thought as Jimex nodded and thunked dutifully away. The nearest ISF outpost was five weeks away: it took eighteen hours or more to send a message there, the same amount of time to receive a response back. How had they obtained permission to freeze Reimi so *quickly*, when she'd fallen sick only yesterday afternoon? And why in such secrecy? For what purpose?

No, something wasn't right.

Thinking of this, she pulled up her datagrabs of Chanur's face and examined them, rifling through the snapshots on her neural inlays. Privacy War skirmishes were still erupting on the outer rings of the system, rebels and ISF agents battling it out on colonies like Halla and Blest, and confidentiality was on everyone's minds. Current privacy laws dictated Park had up to one hour to view any images for "personal use" before they were deleted; she used that opportunity now to scrutinize Chanur's features. Yes, there was definitely something there: secrecy, annoyance, hidden anger and laughter in turns. But laughter at whom? Park? And anger at what?

No wonder she turned her back, Park thought—even though such a gesture was considered offensive in Chanur's native Martian system, where face-to-face contact was scarce enough. There was a gamut of feeling roiling beneath the physician's surface, and she'd hidden her face knowing—as everyone knew—that Park would sniff her out, given long enough. That meant she had something to hide.

She stood there for a while in the dark, trying to puzzle out Chanur's state of mind. Park had her degrees in phenotypology: the kind of training that asked psychologists to analyze and interpret the feelings of their patients through facial tics, body language, topography. Words could lie, but the body often knew the truth of things, and would broadcast it to the most attentive phenotypologist. Park could deduce emotional stability in conversational pauses, anxiety or calculation in the twitch of a brow. Every look was a data point. It was the kind of skill that androids used to interpret the myriad expressions of human beings, and overall a good niche for Park: it meant she didn't have to talk much.

"You're the monitor," Keller would often say. "The one who's behind the scenes, watching. Figuring out what's going on below the surface. I'm just here as the bait, coaxing everything out for you to examine."

Flattery, Park had decided at the time—or, more uncommonly, genuine kindness. Most in the psych field disregarded phenotype analysis as simple data collation, research: it didn't *help* anybody. Apparently Chanur thought so, with her venomous implication that Park had little work to do besides fussing after the robots. Worse, she thought Park's ability was some kind of probe she had to protect herself from. An intrusion. But an intrusion on what?

She heard a tapping from down the hall, suddenly. Someone with a light tread, moving in soft deckboots—not an android, then, or Jimex coming back already because he'd misunderstood her commands. She half-turned, expecting Keller, who should have come looking for her by now; but instead she was surprised to find the tall, lanky form of Kel Fulbreech looming up out of the dark.

"Fulbreech," Park said, trying not to sound startled. More likely than not, *he* was startled to find her lurking alone in a maintenance tunnel.

"Park," Fulbreech answered, easily enough. "I was just looking for you."

"For me?" She tried to think of what Fulbreech would want with her. He was the cartographer for the expedition, tasked with mapping out the new planet. She couldn't imagine he was approaching her for psychological help, down here. In its usual way her mind went to the worst-case scenarios: Had a fight broken out between crewmembers? Was there a malfunction somewhere on the ship, and they were preparing to evacuate?

But Fulbreech said, a little bashfully: "I heard you'd gotten sick and I was coming to visit you. Are you feeling better?"

Park pressed her lips together; so news had already spread around the ship. Did anyone suspect that she'd been slipped something? Were they all in on it? Out loud she said, "I'm fine."

Then, belatedly: "Thank you."

If he found her rude, Fulbreech gave her no indication of it. He was one of those people who could hide very little from her, with his friendly, guileless face, his clear blue eyes and strong chin. He began, "Do you—"

Then he seemed to lose his nerve, perhaps sensing she didn't want to discuss it, and said instead: "I was, ah, wondering if you were free in an hour or so."

She checked the time on her inlays. "I'm scheduled to have lunch at two." The ISF kept them on rigid timeslots and rotations, something Park didn't agree with: their schedule helped to maintain a sense of routine for crewmembers who had no sense of conventional time on Eos, with its two alien suns—but the lack of freedom and community also tended to breed resentment on the ship.

"I am, too," Fulbreech said, his words a little too quick. As if he was trying to preempt some response from her. "And I was wondering—well. I have a surprise I'd like to show you. To help you feel better. I *think* you'll like it. Will you join me after your meal?"

Park's stomach jerked. She didn't like that. Didn't like surprises, not knowing what might be waiting for her. She'd had enough of the unexpected today, anyway. But because she had to know, she said warily: "What is it?"

Even in the dark, she could see Fulbreech's grin. "It wouldn't be a surprise if I told you, would it?"

"I still would prefer to know."

He laughed: the sound was rich and warm, and seemed to reverberate through the tunnel. Park's stomach squirmed. "Just eat quickly, and come see me on Deck B afterward, all right? I'll tell you then."

Then he turned and walked off down the tunnel, back in the direction he came. Fulbreech had the odd habit of whistling while he walked, which often made others stare. Few of the space-born knew how to do that anymore. They didn't need to: sound carried so differently, away from Earth. Things like a whistle got distorted in the star-screaming void of space.

Park stared after him as he vanished down one of the vertical hatches, which opened like a pit into the floor. What on Earth was the cartographer up to?

And what surprise could he have in store for her?

Apprehension filled her as she turned toward the long dark gullet that lay between her and the office she shared with Keller. In her experience, there was always some kind of underlying motive for gifts, or favors, or surprises. Some sort of price that was expected to be paid. For some reason she found herself thinking of poor Reimi, now stuck in her cryogenic pod. As horrible as it sounded, there was always the chance that being frozen would be a blissful experience for her—like waking up from the longest, most refreshing nap of her life. Maybe she would emerge from her pod feeling younger and stronger than she ever had before. Her skin all taut and dewy. Her eyes cleared by months of sleep. Maybe being frozen was like a rejuvenation—or a much-needed escape into oblivion.

Or maybe it was like waking up in a coffin, Park thought, bleakly. Not quite dead, but wishing that you were. Maybe Reimi was still awake when the freezing began, cognizant enough to feel the agony of her arteries shriveling, her body deflating inch by painful inch. Organs locking up, tissue gluing itself to tissue, the blood turning syrupy and slow with cryoprotectants. Maybe being frozen was its own kind of trauma.

The latter seemed more likely, didn't it?

Space supported her line of thinking. Space was all about entropy. If a star wanted to grow, it had to feed off the energy of another star. If a ship wanted to propel itself into the next galaxy, it had to sacrifice mass, straight lines. Being frozen or being surprised by a crewmate should be no different. There were no free rides. No spontaneous gifts. Things out here came with a price—whether you asked for them in the first place or not.

"What a cynical way of thinking," Keller exclaimed when Park brought it up with her later. "I'm sure he's saved you a cake ration, or something."

"But why?" Park asked. "What's the motive?"

"He likes you," Keller said, rolling her eyes. "It's a courtship thing."

"No," Park said flatly. "That can't be it. He doesn't even know me."

"He's the only person on the ship who talks to you, other than me and the janitor bot. No offense. You don't think he's gotten to know you over these last ten months?"

No, Park thought. ISF had them separated on regimented shifts, some teams taking turns sleeping while others maintained the ship or prepared for planetfall or gathered data; the idea was that they had to be used to operating as independently as possible, in the event that something happened to the other crewmembers. As impossible as it seemed, after nearly a year, she still hadn't interacted with her own crewmates much—except in patient sessions. And even then, she wasn't the one who spoke. "I don't know much about him, other than what's in his file."

"That's not *his* fault."

"I didn't say it was."

"Then why punish him by denying him the chance to get closer to you?"

"Fraternization is forbidden between crewmembers."

"My dear . . ."

They were sitting together in their shared office: a grim little space, but one of the few truly private rooms aboard the *Deucalion*. If Park had had her way, she would have convinced ISF Earth to cough up the bits to convert the office into a more welcoming space: better lighting, warmer colors to the gray walls, maybe a plant to alleviate the ambient chill. Curtains to simulate security, privacy. But Dr. Keller was the primary psychologist, and she was utilitarian, machine-based. She'd brought a MAD—a Mood-Altering Device that shot soothing gamma rays into a patient's eyes—and told Park that it was enough.

"Can we get back to the topic at hand?" Park asked. "I'm concerned about Reimi's absence impacting the mission. And as to whoever poisoned me—"

"I wouldn't call it *poison*—"

"Legally, it's poison. I'm aware that the likelihood of anyone confessing to the act to either of us is very small. But *if* the androids uncover anything—"

"I really wish you hadn't done that, my dear, you know how the crew distrusts the bots already—"

"—I would like to know our course of action. Shouldn't we inform Commander Wick?"

She waited, watching her mentor's face. At fifty-nine, Keller was by far the oldest crewmember on the ship, but the medical reports said she was in better physical condition than even Park herself. Her head was shaven, after the Earth fashion of the elderly, but her blue eyes were bright with genetic augments. She shifted in her seat, frowning to herself, before she said, "I think we should be discreet about this for now. Now that we've landed, Commander Wick is preoccupied with many things . . . and if he hands this issue off to someone like Sagara or Boone, word would get out that people are meddling with each other's food. Paranoia might foment—and that's the one thing we can't have, not when they're scheduled to begin exploring the planet soon."

Word has probably already spread, Park thought dourly, remembering Chanur's withering lack of sympathy. It was no secret that she had historically been the target of the crew's little cruelties and mischiefs: they hated her for being Earthborn, for being ISF's spy—and especially for her association with the ship's androids, which others considered freakish. It would not surprise her if multiple people had conspired to cause her discomfort.

But she said: "Fine. But I'll be making my report to ISF. And if we do learn who the culprit is, I'll recommend disciplinary measures. Strong ones."

"As will I," Keller said agreeably, patting her hand. Then she sighed and continued, "As for the issue of Reimi, there's not much we can do. The crew's bodily health is solely within Chanur's purview, and if ISF agreed with her recommendation to freeze Reimi, we must abide by that decision."

"But what if she didn't obtain their permission?" Park asked. "What if she never sent the message?"

Keller waved her hand. "Impossible. There are channels set up to prevent that from happening. Even if she didn't speak to ISF directly, she'd still have to get Boone's permission, or Sagara's, or both."

Park didn't relax at that. Vincent Sagara was the ship's security officer, a dark-eyed and unreadable man with a mercenary air; and Michael Boone was the head of its military team, a great hulking apish soldier whose moods were as volatile as a rioting crowd's. She trusted neither of them with decision-making, but instead of airing this thought she said: "And what about the androids? What will happen to them? They can't take care of themselves, or self-maintain to prevent breakdowns. If we don't have Reimi, we have no way to repair them."

All thanks to the riots on Earth, she thought with sour impatience. People had felt uneasy about giving androids the ability to sustain themselves—to self-modify. The Accords of Yokohama had decreed that all artificial intelligence had to be built with a dependence on human maintenance, so that units would break down after a long enough period without the presence of organic life. This would prevent a robot uprising, most thought. Ridiculous, in Park's opinion—and horribly inconvenient, even life-threatening. Especially in situations like this.

"The most sophisticated ones won't break down for a long time," Keller mused aloud. "And even if they were to all stop functioning tomorrow, the mission is designed so that all crewmembers can still succeed in their jobs. The robots are only here for support and backup—not as an integral part of the expedition." She gave Park a smile, and then another motherly, reassuring pat on the hand. "Don't worry. I'm sure they'll all be fine."

Keller thought that she was personally worried about the robots, Park realized. That this wasn't a matter of survival for her, but one of personal attachment. She supposed it was true in some sense; it was easier for her to talk to the androids, and she dreaded imagining life on the ship without them. There was none of that exhausting analysis with them; no undercurrents for her to guess at and navigate, nothing for them to hide. What you saw was what you got—and Park found that refreshing. She didn't have to parse through a dozen micro-expressions and facial nuances per minute. She didn't have to wonder if they were ever lying to her, or concealing hidden barbs in their looks and words. Or putting poison in her food. There was that sense of relief with them, even comfort and familiarity. With androids, everything was simple, open. Pure.

But her concerns were so much larger than that. Why weren't more people worried about the loss of Reimi? Why was no one panicking, running through the corridors screaming? Reimi was the ship's only engineer, roboticist, and mechanic; she had the tri-fold job of attending to the *Deucalion*'s positronic brain, its mechanical heart, and the robotic crew that serviced it. Park felt a hard stone of fear, way down in her gut, when she thought of what could happen to the crew with Reimi out of commission. What if the ship suffered a catastrophic engine failure, a malfunction somewhere in its entrails, and they had no one on board who knew what to do?

The androids knew what to do, she thought then. That was what they were there for—to ensure that the *Deucalion*, their mothership, didn't die, and every human passenger along with it. But they still didn't come with the protocols to maintain themselves. That was what Reimi was for. And she was gone. And now Park was just thinking in circles, nauseating herself.

Suddenly Keller broke into her thoughts. "Lunchtime," she said, standing decisively and blinking off her inlays, which she'd been using to compose the draft of some message to someone. "Come. Some food will do you good. Clear your mind."

Somehow Park doubted that—she would not touch the ship's bland, gluey food in front of others again, if she could help it—but she rose obediently and followed her mentor. She was still brooding when they entered the mess hall together: a strangely warm, salt-and-bleach-smelling room with a dispensary lining one wall and several round tables filling the center. They picked up their trays of rehydrated meatloaf and flash-thawed potatoes from the service android, Megex, then sat, as always, at a table by themselves.

Lunch was usually the time they observed mealtime behaviors together. Animals at the watering hole, Keller often whispered, in a British documentarian's accent. Eating was a vulnerable activity; people tended to relax their guard. It was why Stalin had invited Churchill to so many dinners. You could tell a lot about personalities and group dynamics at lunch: who was in control, who was deferential. Who occupied the choicest spots and who slunk in alone.

Park was initially too preoccupied to give much thought to who was on display today, but Keller had apparently dismissed the topic of Reimi from her mind and was intent on carrying out her daily observations. She nudged Park with her elbow and said, softly, "Sagara's sitting alone again."

Park looked. Keller was right: there he was, sitting alone, a tense and silent presence in his black uniform. He had been the last one to join the crew—the ship had picked him up out of Corvus—and as a result, he had entered the community with its various cliques and groups already formed. Most of the other crewmembers steered well clear of him. Keller sympathized, but Park privately thought that it was Sagara's severe—almost lethal—personality to blame.

She continued to scan the mess hall as she picked listlessly at the disintegrating meatloaf. Their main concerns were usually the loners, like Sagara. There was always the danger of isolation in space, anxiety and depression breeding in the dark corners of a lonely mind. Sagara himself seemed self-sufficient enough, but it was others, like the exobiologist Wan Xu, who always sat in Park's crosshairs. Those were the ones who sat by themselves or in silent pairs, bending over their wrist consoles while they ate. Recording expensive video messages to send back home. There was technically no one on the receiving end of their calls, either: messages back to Earth or even Mars took months. The loners were choosing one-sided conversations with blank screens over socializing with their fellow crew-mates. That was something to monitor.

"And here comes Boone," Keller muttered. This time, Park didn't bother looking; she'd already heard Boone's entrance to the mess hall without having to turn her head. He always made sure to stomp his heavy combat boots against the tile to announce his presence. Even now, he was scanning the room and letting out an overly loud sigh, as if to inform everyone that he was hungry—as if every person in the room ought to know how he was feeling. He even patted his stomach dramatically, like a gorilla beating its chest. *Me want food. Get out me way.* Keller had muttered it more than once.

Park had concerns there, too. Boone was a wild card in the power balance on the ship, and he had an ego problem to boot. Why there were so many soldiers on the ship at all—three "security" personnel out of thirteen, nearly a fourth of the crew—Park didn't know. ISF military was usually colony-based, putting down the odd uprising or terrorist attack, but she hadn't ever heard of them accompanying an expedition to a new planet. And she privately disliked Boone, with his swaggering, his sneery remarks, the hard dismissive flick of his eyes whenever a woman he considered unattractive spoke up. As with Sagara, none of her strategies so far had worked on him.

Boone automatically moved toward the table with most of the expedition's leaders, both official and de facto. Daryl Wick was there, the kind, sensible astronaut who was commander of the entire mission. Natalya Severov, the beautiful Russian surveyor, was there too. The only one who seemed missing from that group was . . . Kel Fulbreech.

Park jolted. "He's waiting for me," she said, without meaning to speak out loud.

Keller was grinning at her. "Go," she said. "I'm sure it will be pleasant. Don't let fear hold you back."

It wasn't fear, Park thought as she dumped her tray into the mouth of the waste compressor and hurried up the ladder to Deck B, the navigation level. But if Keller had pressed her on what exactly the feeling was, she wouldn't have been able to say.

Fulbreech was waiting for her with his hands in his pockets, leaning his rangy body against the wall of another side-tunnel. His face brightened when he saw Park approaching; he said, grinning, "Good. I didn't think you would come."

I didn't think I would, either, Park thought, but instead she looked at his pockets and said, "Where is it?"

Fulbreech looked surprised. "Where is what?"

"The—you know. Whatever it is you have in store."

"Ah," he said. He winked. "So you're excited. Look at you. You're like a kid on Solstice Morning."

"I'll leave," she warned.

Fulbreech laughed. "Relax. It's through here."

He indicated the large hatch behind him, and Park, finally realizing where they were, blanched. They were standing in front of the *Deucalion*'s escape pod, a little shuttle attached to the underside of the ship. It was the crewmembers' favorite spot to conduct clandestine sexual liaisons.

"I suppose that makes sense," Keller had said when Park first told her about it—having heard all about it from Jimex, when she asked him where that particular door led. "It's the only place where you're guaranteed not to get walked in on—because what business would someone have in the escape pod, other than *that*? And it's the only other place that has a bed, besides the bunks." She'd grinned at Park. "Too bad you'll never see the inside of it. Conflicts of interest and all that."

"Park?" Fulbreech waved a hand in front of her face.

She balked a little from him. "I don't understand."

Fulbreech seemed oblivious to her discomfort. "This place doesn't have a camera on it," he said, as if that explained anything.

Park shook her head; she could not believe his audacity. "And that's your . . . surprise? The thing that you said would make me feel better?"

"Well, not all of it," Fulbreech said. He looked a little sly, a little pleased with himself. She looked up into his open, friendly face and remembered with sudden, painful clarity that he *was* handsome—suspiciously handsome, she sometimes thought—but also too upright to pull a stunt like this. He was one of those all-American astronauts, blunt-jawed, square-nosed, with a sweet, sheepish, boyish look. Golden hair falling into his eyes. Right now he looked not like a man overcome by lust, but more like a kid on Solstice Morning himself. Full of radiant glee, excitement—maybe even pride.

"All right," Park said reluctantly, deciding to trust him. But behind her back she was balling her fist: ISF had given her piecemeal self-defense training before departure. "Let me see it."

Fulbreech palmed open the hatch to the escape pod and, looking around, quickly shut it behind them. Park had to give herself a sweaty moment to let her eyes adjust to the gloom inside—the pod, of course, was inactive—but soon she was able to make out another shape, lying there in front of her in the dark. A body, Park realized. She nearly screamed.

"It's exo-armor," Fulbreech whispered conspiratorially, right in her ear. "I snuck it in here a few hours ago. It's Natalya's, but she won't miss it until the expedition team goes out again tomorrow."

Park couldn't make sense of it. She stared at the bench with the stiff exo-armor lying on it like a corpse, inert. "What would we need it for?"

Fulbreech bent to pick up the gold-visored helmet that came with the suit.

"Well," he said slowly, "I was thinking. You're officially barred from going outside—from even *seeing* Eos, since you're not part of the expedition crew. But I hardly think that's fair. If it were me, it'd drive me crazy to land on a virgin planet, but never get to see it. To never touch it—smell it, walk on it . . ." He stared at her. "Don't you think it's a little silly of ISF to expect you to be fine with all that?"

There was suddenly a kind of tightness in her throat. "So you're saying . . ."

"There's a hatch down in the floor," Fulbreech explained. "This pod's terminal is—let's say *tangentially* connected to the ship's system. If I play my cards right, I think I could get it to open the hatch without alerting the *Deucalion*." At her stare he gave a kind of grin and a shrug. "I'm good with computers. I have to be, working with METIS to chart everything."

METIS was the ship's governing AI, a heuristic brain tasked with managing the *Deucalion*'s massive nexus of systems, from its navigation to communications to surveillance. It was what their neural inlays were plugged into. "I thought only Reimi had the authorization to manipulate METIS's protocols," Park said. She didn't add: *She's also the only one with the know-how to make sure all of our brains aren't fried.*

Fulbreech shrugged again. "It would be kind of stupid to have only *one* tech-savvy crewmember on board," he said lightly. "I have a degree, if you want to look at my credentials. A minor one, mind, way at the bottom of the list—but my point is, I generally know what I'm doing."

Park had to stand there in the dark and process what was going on; things were moving at a much faster pace than she was used to. She looked at the crumpled suit he'd brought for her and felt her fingertips chill. Eos was out there. Just one hatch away. But did Fulbreech know what he was offering? The implications of such an action? Stealing an exo-armor suit was bad enough, but to exit the ship without permission, to take her out there to explore an alien planet on their own, no supervision, no authority . . .

Her scalp tightened. She turned to him and said, barely hearing herself: "Why would you do such a thing for me?"

Fulbreech turned to look at her, despite the gloom. The look on his face was entirely serious. He said quietly, "You don't know?"

Park's pulse quickened; it felt as if someone had plucked her heart like a string. But before she could answer, there was a clanking and whirring from the door of the escape shuttle. Park felt her vision narrow as panic thundered in. *Someone was accessing the lock.*

In one swift movement, Fulbreech crossed the distance between them and kissed her.

Park jerked back from him as if he'd burned her. But the picture was complete, and when the door opened, whoever stood in the doorway got a good eyeful of Park and Fulbreech standing there, hastily breaking away from each other in the dark.

"Ah," a voice said. Park could hardly stand to look at the speaker, but she turned when Fulbreech did. Vincent Sagara, their security officer, stood outlined in the threshold of the doorway. His face was entirely in shadow, so that Park couldn't read his expression.

Fulbreech, on his end, recovered admirably. "Captain Sagara," he said, clearing his throat a little. "What—ah—what brings you here?"

"I suppose I don't have to ask you the same question, Fulbreech," Sagara answered. His voice was perfectly neutral, devoid of embarrassment or ridicule. He clicked on a little utility light and swept the inside of the escape pod with it. Imperceptibly, Fulbreech shifted to block the exo-armor from view.

Sagara's light landed square on Park's face. "Park," he said—and now he did sound a little surprised. Park felt heat swamp her face and croaked, "Captain. We were just leaving."

He paused, then lowered the light when Park squinted. "So was I," he said, perfectly brusque. "I was conducting some electrical inspections, after hearing about Kisaragi. But I can return later. Carry on."

The door shut behind him before either of them could say another word. After a moment Fulbreech turned back to Park and said, his voice low and incredulous: "Do you believe him?"

Park could hardly speak through her humiliation. She said faintly, "What?"

"That he's looking at—the *electronics*? Sagara doesn't know the first thing about the ship's computers. Or its systems. Does he?"

"I don't know," Park said. Then she shook her head and said, "Aren't you more concerned about what he saw?"

"What, about the kiss? Sagara's not the type to gossip—"

"The suit," Park said in a hard, flat voice. "He must have seen it—nothing escapes his notice. You don't think he won't wonder why we had it just lying around?"

Fulbreech didn't say anything for a moment. Finally he said: "The shuttle has exo-armor suits of its own—in case its inhabitants need to go out to make repairs to the exterior. None of them would fit you, but he doesn't need to know that. He'd think the one on the bench was one of those."

"He wouldn't wonder what we were doing with a suit in the first place, whether it came from the pod or not?"

Another pause. Then: "He didn't see."

Suddenly the little pod felt too dark, too small, like a cave she had gone into and couldn't find her way out of. Park felt as if the air had turned hot and close, leaving her short of breath. She said abruptly, "I have to go."

She spun around and left before Fulbreech could stop her.

Keller was not in their shared office when Park returned, but Jimex was. He had formed a special attachment to her, as androids were wont to do when it came to Park, so he was always finding some excuse or another to be around her. When Park came into the room, the android was busily wiping down the couch that she had been intent on flinging herself down on—so she gritted her teeth and moved to the chair at her workstation instead. When she put her head down on her desk, Jimex looked up and said, "You are experiencing gastric distress?"

"God," Park said, muffled. "No."

Her thoughts were whirring. As she had suspected, disaster had struck; *this* was what happened when you planned surprises. She didn't know what was worse: that Sagara had caught them illicitly hovering over stolen contraband, plotting to leave the ship, or that he now thought that she—one of the ship's psychologists—was engaged in some torrid romantic affair. He'd be reporting it back to ISF Corvus, surely, just as *she* was tasked with reporting the same things back about other people. And Fulbreech, fool that he was, had—

Had

"I've spoken to the other synthetics," Jimex said. "Megex was not told by any party to put medicine in your food. But you may have left it unattended when you sanitized your hands."

"Yes," Park said. She had already thought of this.

Jimex paused for a moment. "Ellenex will prepare medication for you. She says it will nullify the effects of emesis tabs if they are administered without your consent." At Park's look, he added, "She will be discreet."

Park tried not to groan. She was grateful to him—and Ellenex—for doing such a thing, but she did not trust the androids' abilities to keep a secret. *Especially* not Jimex; telling him to investigate for her had half been a political maneuver, to let her opponent know she was hunting for them. But to secretly take medication was another thing entirely.

Jimex gave her a rare look of insight. "This upsets you. It was the incorrect action."

"No," Park said in a muted way. Then she closed her eyes and said, almost involuntarily, "Kel Fulbreech just kissed me."

Jimex paused, just for a moment, in his wiping. "Oh," he said, his voice milk-bland and mild. "I don't believe Ellenex has medication for that."

Park felt a laugh bubble up in her chest, but stifled it sharply. How like an android to think of such a thing as needing a prescription—a cure. Maybe he was right. Maybe there ought to be some tonic out there, some injection that would let her forget everything. Something to soothe the sudden turmoil. There was the MAD, but she didn't dare use it in front of him. Otherwise Jimex would go around telling everyone who asked about that, too.

Park kneaded her knuckles into her forehead. She had always suspected that Fulbreech was attracted to her, of course. She couldn't have missed the physical signs: she was a phenotypologist, after all. There were the usual quick, darting glances, the "casual" but strained body language. Dilated pupils. Blazing smiles that seemed like the primate baring of teeth. She'd known that he found her, on some level, sexually intriguing. The kiss itself hadn't surprised her as much as it should have. But it was everything else—the suit, the proposed hacking, the *gesture* of it all. Was it all just—posturing? An attempt at currying her favor? It was so much trouble to go through. She never would have done the same.

Unless there was something more to it. She touched her lips discreetly, feeling none of the lingering warmth or tingling that she might have expected. And yet, that sudden jolt of rare contact had made her feel something. Something she'd felt just recently. But what?

"A kiss can transfer up to eighty million bacteria at once," Jimex said, apropos of nothing. He was obsessed with things like that.

"I don't think people generally care about that kind of thing, Jimex," Park told him wearily. She flicked her inlays on, groping for some message from Keller or even Commander Wick to distract her from her own thoughts.

The android stared at her. "What do they care about, then?"

She couldn't answer.

Later, when she was getting dressed for bed, shoved into her tiny room with Natalya, the surveyor, Hunter, Boone's sergeant, and Elly Ma, the climatologist, Park suddenly remembered what Fulbreech's kiss had reminded her of.

It had been the previous day, just before they'd landed on Eos. Park had felt the gravity shift back on as they made the approach to the new planet. Her stomach lifted as if pulled by a string; her heart seemed to swell with the sudden change, then deflate. She could feel her cells becoming heavier, like sand settling on the bottom of a lake. There was elation and excitement and a kind of painful terror inside of her, in turns.

She'd run to the bridge. There were no windows to speak of on the ship, besides the ones there on the bridge. There were many reasons for this: radiation shielding, for one. Sanity, for the other. Some crewmembers would be susceptible to the "Earth-out-of-view" phenomenon: seeing their planet as an insignificant dot rapidly vanishing from sight did strange things to the mind of an Earth-born, especially one who had never experienced the vast emptiness of space before. Sometimes there was euphoria, a sense of interconnected bliss. Other times it was madness, frothing terror as everything they knew fell away from them.

But not being able to see an undiscovered planet was a kind of madness, too. A madness of curiosity.

Luckily, everyone else had had the same idea, so no one noticed when Park slipped into the bridge and took up a position at the back of the room. Only Dylanex, the ship's lone security android, made disconcerted noises about the presence of unauthorized personnel—but everyone ignored him. There was a clamor, shouts of excitement and amazement as Eos swung into view through the shielded windows and onto the large monitors set into the wall.

Park had stared. That was it? That was their new planet, ISF's proposed "dawn" of the Frontier? It looked like a little white light bulb, hanging there in the darkness of space. Or a perfect snowball, carefully crafted by a meticulous child. There were two suns. Park's eyes watered, but she told herself that it was a biological reflex; that she would not allow anyone to see her cry.

Jimex came to stand next to her, as usual. Park had turned to him, full of wonder. "We're here?" There had been no indicator, no progress map to tell her when exactly they would reach their destination. No one had told her they were making their approach.

Jimex had not understood the question. The rotors in his head whirred. "We have always been here," he had answered, serene.

Preparations began for the ship to make its descent. Crewmembers bustled here and there; orders were given to secure objects and bodies for the entry through Eos's thin atmosphere. A few auxiliary staffers, Park included, lingered in the bridge for as long as possible. Before they were shooed off, Keller had come over and squeezed Park's shoulder with one bony hand.

"What do you think?" she asked softly. "This will be your only glimpse of it before we land. It's like looking at a blank canvas, isn't it? All that potential, all that space!"

Park had shaken her head. "No," she said. "It's not like a canvas. It's like—"

Keller had looked at her. "It's like what?"

Then Park had smiled to herself; even she could tell it looked secretive. "It's like looking into the face of God," she said.

As they descended, the light wavered, as if to answer her: the pale and colorless suns watching as the ship floated down on the alien wind.

2.

The next day started on a different schedule than the one Park was used to. The term would have been "bright and early" on Earth, but there was no "bright" on a ship with no windows and the same kind of artificial lighting every moment of every day—and "early" was relative, too. But her body knew the difference; she was jittery and on edge from the moment her inlays blinked her awake.

She stayed that way all morning, off-kilter, feeling as if something was wrong. But there was work to do: now that they had landed and the expeditions were officially underway, patient sessions with the crew—which had previously only been sporadic and intermittent—were now daily and mandatory. Keller and Park would be in charge of mitigating any stress the expedition members felt as they explored the new planet.

Except Keller never turned up for their first session of the day—which raised klaxons in Park's already-anxious mind. She dispatched Jimex to find out if her mentor had somehow overslept—or, she thought with a mental shudder, been poisoned, or fallen ill like Reimi—but he returned and said he couldn't find her anywhere. *That* was even more concerning. It was a big ship, but Jimex was thorough, and Keller couldn't have gone out with the expedition team: she was forbidden to, just as Park was.

But she couldn't spare any more thoughts on it. Wan Xu was already in their office, downing clarity meds like breath mints. He was their exobiologist and biodome designer, a brilliant but narcissistic man; any interruptions in his perceived routines could catapult him into an outburst, trigger his neuroses. Park had to go through her first patient session with him alone, wondering all the while where the hell Keller could be.

For a while they slogged through the requisite questionnaires and checklists and evaluative worksheets together; Park read off the standard surveys that ISF had bundled together for her, feeling a little chagrined—like a student struggling to perform under the watchful eye of a teacher. Wan Xu, folding his arms, listlessly answered that everything was fine, average, five out of ten—meaning perfectly regular. But when Park asked him how the morning's expedition had gone, he blanched a little and looked away.

"The expedition went fine," he said. He was a little rat-faced, Park sometimes thought, with his hair gelled so tightly to his scalp it looked like he was wearing a black, shiny helmet. His beady eyes darted nervously. "Nothing noteworthy to speak of."

Park was suspicious, but after a while she let him go. She did not feel equipped to press a patient with questions without Keller there.

Afterward, Jimex sidestepped into the room again. The ship wasn't big enough to keep him constantly cleaning, so Park had set his secondary protocols to assisting her—since she lacked an assistant of her own, while Chanur had Ellenex and all the other specialists had their own robotic helpers. Park looked up eagerly when he came in and said, "Did you find her?"

Jimex shook his head. "I was unable to locate Dr. Keller," he answered. He seemed a little morose, as if he were sad to disappoint her.

Park watched as he approached the holographic fish tank set into the far wall. The tank was Keller's aesthetic choice, though Park had always found it distracting. She watched as a shy bumblebee goby bobbed its acknowledgement to her, then ducked behind a bloom of delicate coral. Jimex, also watching intently, remarked: "Fish are very unclean."

"That one's not real."

"I know. It was a general statement."

Park tried to suppress a smile. "I wouldn't know if the real ones are unclean or not," she told him. "They were all gone in my area by the time I was born. I don't think I've ever seen a real one alive."

"They excrete in the same water they live in," Jimex said. He tilted his chin up a little, in disgust, Park thought—or disdain. He at least thought himself better than a fish. "They require numerous filters to live in a contained environment, or die of their own toxicity."

"Humans are the same," Park joked—then realized the danger in making such a statement to him. But before she could retract it, the door to the office slung open, and Keller walked in.

Park stood up from her desk just as Jimex wisely sidled out of the room again. "Where have you been?" she demanded.

Keller didn't answer the question. "I don't know how you talk to that thing," she said instead, looking back over her shoulder at Jimex—who was still within earshot. That meant something was on her mind. Keller didn't get antsy around the robots unless she was already worried about something else. "It's awful. When it looks into your eyes—"

"*He* tried to find you this morning," Park said pointedly. Then she shook her head, unable to stop herself from being drawn into the topic. "And you were fine around the HERCULES."

Keller shuddered and rubbed her arms as if Park had mentioned a horror story. "Yes, but HERCULES and the other robots weren't like that. The ones I grew up around were functional, metallic. Not . . . a human imitation, like Jimex. Why would they need a janitor bot to look like a person, anyway?"

"I don't know. I'm used to androids like that." Park's throat flexed as if she were holding in a cough. "Dr. Keller, where were you?"

The older woman sighed and sat down on the couch they usually had the patients sit on. Park sat down again in her usual chair, bewildered, as Keller said in a resigned way: "I'm afraid I have to tell you something, Park, and I don't suppose you'll be very happy about it."

Paranoia and dread overtook Park in a moment, like a cloud suddenly darkening the sun. She said suspiciously, "What is it?"

Keller spread her hands in an expression of regret. "ISF is pulling me off regular duty for a—special project. I can't say anything about it. But it will take up all my time, starting today."

"That's why you were late this morning?"

"Yes," Keller said. "Events transpired rather quickly—" Then she broke off and shook her head, giving Park an apologetic look. "I'm sorry. It's conscripted business. You understand."

Park sat back sharply in her seat, feeling as if Keller had slapped her. Yes, she thought bitterly, she understood all too well the lines between the conscripted and the non-conscripted. It had been one of her biggest concerns before this mission—and her biggest complaint while on it. The ISF often conscripted its members into service in exchange for free transportation and housing in the colonies. Such a person was beholden to the ISF's every order and command, under threat of having their home and access to space taken away, while a non-conscripted person—a person such as Park—merely had to worry about being fired. That meant the ISF entrusted the conscripted with its secrets more willingly, knowing the consequences of spilling those secrets were much more severe for someone who owed everything to the Frontier. It was why Park was not allowed to see Eos. There was the implicit fear that she might observe something, learn something—then sell the data back to the information companies on Earth.

And now Keller was saying that it was why she could not know what her mentor was up to. Because Keller was conscripted and Park was not.

Because the ISF didn't trust her that much.

"You can't tell me *anything*?" she asked, trying not to sound helpless—like a forlorn child being abandoned by a parent.

Keller grimaced at her. "No," she said. "Nothing except that . . . I'm not to be disturbed. This project will take up all my time, all my attention. You'll have to be acting psychologist from now on."

Alarm surged up Park's spine like a lightning rod; she nearly jolted out of her seat. "*What*?" Then she quelled the sudden rush of panic and said in a somewhat calmer tone: "You mean—I'll be managing the patients alone?"

"I'm afraid so," Keller said, looking resigned. "Trust me, I know it's not an ideal situation, but—"

"Ideal?" Park didn't know if she wanted to laugh or cry. "I wasn't trained for this scenario. *At all.* I was never meant to take on the primary role—I'm here for observation, monitoring, not diagnosis and treatment—"

Keller held up her hand, cutting Park off. "I know, Park," she said gently. "I know, but there's nothing that can be done about it." Then she glanced at something on her inlays and said, "It's nearly eight. Who's scheduled to meet with you next?"

Park consulted the dossier on her own inlays, then felt as if the room had lurched. "Sagara," she said, taking a breath. "Next is Captain Sagara."

"Well, good!" Keller exclaimed, beaming in a false way. Park had not yet gotten the chance to tell her about the escape pod disaster. "I always thought you two should get to know each other better. There could be a sense of—*camaraderie* between the two of you, I think."

Camaraderie? Park thought. Sagara was about as social as a praying mantis, and she didn't know how she felt being compared to him. "Why do you think that?"

"Well, you're very similar," Keller said bluntly. "And considering how the others view both of you . . . I thought you might bond over your shared experience."

Park tried not to pull a face. Keller was referring, rather tactlessly, to the fact that the other crewmates openly considered Park and Sagara's positions to be redundant. It was why Chanuri made jabs about her having nothing better to do; it was why no one knew whom to be more afraid of, Boone or Sagara. In Park's case, Keller was already the main psychologist of the *Deucalion,* so the question had to be asked: What was Park's role? Why was she there, if she wasn't interacting directly with the patients? What was the purpose of having two psychologists on the ship?

And the conclusion that had spread around was that Keller was there primarily for the crewmates' wellbeing: she was the one who talked with the patients, counseled them, prescribed their treatments and medications. But Park was a background presence, usually only observing, monitoring. That meant that she was not there to help the other crewmembers—but to spy on them for the ISF.

And the rumors weren't *wrong*, Park thought bitterly. Their conclusions were not so far off. She would not refer to herself as a "spy" necessarily, but the ISF officially called her an "orbiter"—the differences between the two being not so clear. The term had always made Park think of a satellite, cold and mechanical, watching from afar—or, when she was feeling unusually romantic, a moon, circling the tiny world of the *Deucalion*.

But her crewmates would not have agreed with the depiction. It was more likely they'd have compared her to a rat: some lurking, scampering thing. Park had been hired to provide the ISF a clear window into what was happening on the *Deucalion,* and the others resented her for it. To them, she was a snitch, a kiss-ass, proof that the ISF didn't trust its own operatives—to the extent that they would pay someone to watch the crew and report on them. Forget that the other twelve were leading experts in their fields, under non-disclosure agreements; forget too that the majority of them were also under the rite of conscription, meaning the ISF owned their lives, or the lives of their loved ones. Park being on the ship meant that none of that was good enough for the ISF. They still wanted their information from as objective a source as possible. From someone specifically tasked to observe, to record, to interpret, to relay. So that whenever a crewmember reported back to ISF's outpost, Park was there to fill in the gaps, to clarify their messages for the higher-ups: not what the shipmates were saying, but what they really *meant.* What was really going on—with them or the ship. She wasn't really a psychologist, at least not in the conventional way. She was a living avatar of the Interstellar Frontier.

Or she had been, Park corrected herself. Now she didn't know what she was—orbiter or primary psychologist or both.

She didn't like that. Didn't like surprises.

She wrenched her thoughts back to Sagara. Others perceived him in the same way that they perceived her. Sergeant Boone, who had joined the crew from the start, was already established as the mission's military leader. He and his lieutenant Hunter served as the combat specialists aboard the ship, assigned to protect it from outside threat. They'd only picked up Sagara much later, at the last outpost before they left governed space, and then belatedly found out that he was to be the ship's security officer. What was the difference? It was unclear—but again, the conclusion was that Sagara, like Park, was there to serve the interests of the ISF, not the crew. If Boone and Hunter were already there to protect the crewmembers, then Sagara must be around to protect something else. But what? No one knew. It was that mystery, coupled with his intense personality, that led the crewmembers to shun him.

"You could get him to open up," Keller said encouragingly. "Establish a rapport."

Park tried to stop herself from making an unkind comment. Even if the incident yesterday had never occurred, it was impossible to imagine the taciturn security officer ever getting friendly with her. She was equally, if not more, close-mouthed. "I don't understand his role here," she admitted. "Even after all this time. What authority does he have over me—or I over him? And why are he and Boone both here? Who defers to whom?" She shook her head, thinking of the way the two men avoided each other at all costs. "Even they don't seem quite sure."

"They belong to different branches of the ISF, so their ranks come out to about equal," Keller replied. "Though we do know Sagara is far better trained than Boone: only the elite get let into the Security sector, while any man or woman stuffed to the gills with augments can be Military, like Boone. In fact, I hear that's where most of the conscripts get sent. But you've got to have brains, brawn, talent, *and* a special kind of deadliness to make Sec Corps. They're the ones who actually keep everyone safe."

I don't feel safe around him, Park thought, but she said instead: "It seems you admire him. And he's cooperated with you so far. Why don't you continue handling his patient sessions, then? I could do the rest."

Keller raised her eyebrows at her. "Any reason why you're so keen to avoid him?"

Desperately Park tried not to think about Sagara walking in on her kiss with Fulbreech. "No."

Keller snorted. "Well, regardless, it's not possible," she said, running a hand over her stubbled head. For the first time Park noticed she had dark circles under her eyes, as if she hadn't slept. "I'll have my hands full with this project; you'll have to handle Sagara. And everyone else. And that's that."

You won't have any time at all? Park wanted to ask; but she knew that would come off as entitled, needy. She said instead, trying not to sound desperate: "Will you be reachable, at least, if I have questions? Or if I need help?"

Keller didn't give Park her usual smile: her look was already preoccupied and distant, as if she was only sitting through a formality—the outcome of which would not affect her. "No," she said absently. "I'll be going dark, so to speak." Then she rose and held out her hand for Park to shake: a rare gesture, not commonly seen anymore. Contact between equals—or team players passing a torch. Park felt as if it had a finality to it, as if they were parting ways forever. She looked at Keller's tough, leathery hand and said, "Going dark? But you'll still be on the ship, won't you?"

"I have faith in you, Park," was all Keller said in reply. Then she withdrew her hand.

Park took the few minutes she had alone before Sagara's appointment to try and calm her fast-whirling thoughts. There was too much to take in: her sudden change in status, Keller's mystery project, Wan Xu's evasiveness. Fulbreech's kiss. Shit, how was she going to face Sagara after something like *that?* Did she bring it up to him if he didn't mention it—preempt him with some sort of plausible justification? Or did they both simply pretend it had never happened?

Shit, shit, shit.

She spent a lot of time considering exactly how to address him, too. Up until now they had mostly avoided speaking directly to each other, so it had never been something she considered deeply. Everyone except the androids addressed each other by their surnames, without the usual labels and honorifics; ISF seemed to think that divisive titles and ranks were not necessary for the *Deucalion*'s academic tribe.

And yet, somehow, everyone still called him Captain Sagara.

I won't, Park resolved to herself. It gave him too much automatic power over her—and he already had some significant leverage. She busied herself with inspecting the MAD, trying to avoid thoughts of using it on herself. Was Sagara even the type to need it? He had never asked for it in his sessions before, and there was so little in his file to go on. She knew the number of siblings Fulbreech had, the drugs Hunter had once been expelled from school for. But Sagara's file was as minimal as bleached animal bone, picked clean by scavengers. She had nothing on him.

That gave him an advantage, too.

She tried studying his staff photo for clues. Although Sagara was not a bulky man, only tall and lean and ropy with hard muscle, he was still an intimidating presence—he always made Park feel like the room was close and airless. His eyes and hair were as black as pitch, his face cold and fine-boned and faintly dire, as if he were always on the verge of delivering terrible news. Even when he was being polite, he constantly seemed . . . *prepared* for something, on guard, as if he expected an attack from any quarter. That kind of keen hyper-awareness unnerved people—Park included.

The other reason she hated talking to him was that, of all the people on the *Deucalion,* Vincent Sagara was the hardest for her to read. He was always so cool-eyed and steady, impossibly unflappable, and she—used to having at least some knowledge of what someone thought of her—could never really tell what he was feeling. She hated that; felt that it put her on lower and unstable ground.

She still couldn't read him when he came into the office, lithe and silent as a panther. Sagara didn't look surprised at all to find Park sitting alone, either; she wondered if he already knew that Keller had abdicated her position. Or what "special project" she was working on. His file didn't say if he was conscripted or not.

"Sagara," Park said as he took the seat across from her. She was careful to keep her voice neutral.

"Park," he said in turn, heavy-lidded. Then he said, without preamble: "Your robot's becoming a nuisance to everyone."

Park tried not to bristle. Although Sagara said it matter-of-factly, it seemed clear he was starting right away with a jab to assess her reaction. "To whom are you referring?" she asked him, outwardly calm.

Sagara shrugged lightly. "The custodian android," he said. His voice was low and clipped; it was hard to say if he was Earth-born or not. "I'm not aware of its name. It wanders all over the ship, asking people questions. I've been told that you were the one who taught it to do that."

"I didn't teach *him* to do anything." Park kept her voice level, but she could feel the blood thumping in her fingertips. "Jimex started asking me questions on his own. Most androids will do that, even the primitive ones, after they've been active long enough. It's part of their heuristic learning modules: they naturally absorb things, adapt to their environment. That means asking questions, too." She folded her hands together, only to realize they were damp. "I simply took the time to answer Jimex's questions, or correct behaviors that were improper. That's all."

Sagara's dark eyes quirked. "You should teach it to stop bothering others, then," he said. "It's like a child, jabbering away. I heard Boone threaten to recycle it." He held her gaze for a moment, the faint amusement vanishing. "Some others think you might be using the bot to spy on people. Telling it to ask everyone questions, so that it can report the answers back to you."

Park's heart tensed a little, despite herself. "I'll keep that in mind," she said, through stiff lips. Better to not acknowledge the accusation at all, to show the absurdity of it.

Sagara regarded her for another moment, as if assessing whether or not his words had had an effect; she had the distinct feeling of a hawk appraising a smaller bird. Then he withdrew something from his pocket and said, "You should teach the thing, too, to be more careful with your own secrets. I overheard it asking Ellenex to give it medicine on the sly—without telling Chanur."

He handed whatever he was holding to Park. She looked, incredulous, at the little green box in her hand. Anti-emesis tabs, the label told her. To counteract the effects of space-sickness.

Ellenex will prepare medication, Jimex had said. *She will be discreet.*

Fulbreech just kissed me.

Oh. I do not think Ellenex has medication for that.

Park looked up at Sagara and said, very calmly, "I think you're mistaken. These aren't for me."

For a moment it seemed that he was going to laugh. Then he smoothed away the thin smile and said courteously, "Of course not. My mistake." He steepled his fingers and continued, "But my point still stands. You should educate the bot to be a little wiser in its dealings on the ship."

"I'll do my best," Park said, chilly now with anger and embarrassment. "Although it would make more sense to refer the matter to Reimi. She's the one who handles issues concerning androids on the ship, not me."

Then, realizing her lapse, she kicked herself—but Sagara merely looked serious as he said, "It is unfortunate that she's fallen sick."

"How do you feel about that turn of events?"

His face remained impassive. "As long as her illness doesn't threaten the rest of the ship, I suppose I don't feel any particular way about it. How do *you* feel about it?"

"What would you do if her illness did threaten the rest of the ship?"

"I'd enact quarantine protocols. Try to eliminate the source of infection, if I could."

"Eliminate?"

"Freeze. Chanur did the right thing."

"The cautious thing."

"Which, to a security officer, is always the right thing."

They paused for a moment, looking at each other. Park didn't know why she felt compelled to engage in this kind of verbal sparring, but she told herself that Sagara had started it. She couldn't believe his paranoia, the implication that she could be employing Jimex to some sinister purpose. Or was he going out of his way to warn her, inform her about the others' perceptions of her behavior? Both routes were confusing. And she still wasn't getting much of a topographical read from him, at least emotionally, but she did have the acute sense that he was sussing her out. Why? Because of what happened in the escape shuttle?

"So are you a combat specialist, like Boone and Hunter?" she asked, to deflect her own thoughts. To keep Sagara from reading them.

"If you're asking if I know how to fight, the answer is yes," he answered, almost lazily. "I've seen combat. I fought carbon pirates back on Earth. I was sent in during the Outer System Wars."

Mentally Park reviewed his file again; it hadn't said anything about *that.* The Outer System Wars had spanned the entire outer ring of colonies past the Solar System: Luxue, Vier, Halla, Elysium, Corvus, and even the prison planet Pandora had all been enmeshed in a bloody, year-long conflict between the ISF and the rogue colonists who had wanted to secede from it. Although it was brief, the war had cost a million lives and destroyed the moon of Vela. Sagara had fought in that? He had to be conscripted. And he'd probably been awarded medals, high honors. No wonder they'd put him in charge of the security on Corvus. No wonder they trusted him to maintain order on the *Deucalion*.

And if he'd dealt with carbon pirates in the past, or killed terrorists in the outer system—how harsh would his treatment be of delinquents like Park and Fulbreech?

The blood drained from her face. Sagara, seemingly reading her thoughts, said, "Does that make you nervous?"

Park shook her head; she tried not to let her voice sound faint. "Not at all. I'm just—trying to understand your mindset. Whether your past experiences color your . . . treatment of others."

"You talk as if we're on opposing sides," Sagara drawled. "We're not enemies. I am not a soldier, Park."

"What are you, then?" Now her voice did sound faint.

He gazed at her unblinkingly. "I'm an officer of the ISF's Security Corps."

"The difference being?"

The corner of his mouth twitched; Park read it as part irritation, part amusement. "The primary mission of soldiers like Boone is to eliminate the enemy," Sagara said. "My primary mission is to protect what the ISF wants safe."

"Meaning us," Park prompted.

But Sagara said nothing in response to that.

At lunch, Park went to the usual dispensary line, feeling the absence of Keller as if she had lost her favorite coat. She felt cold, uneasy, vulnerable. The domestic android, Megex, seemed to notice her discomfort from behind the counter and said, "Would you like a juice bulb?"

"Thank you," Park said gratefully as the brown-haired android placed it on her tray.

"Fuck," Megex said in return, very calmly. "Shit, damn, ass, bastard, cock."

Park stared.

"It's a Reimi thing," someone said from behind her then. Park turned and saw her bunkmate Elly Ma standing there, looking pitying. Whether the pity was for Megex or for Park, it wasn't clear. "Without Reimi around to do maintenance, little bugs are popping up all over the place. This thing won't stop swearing."

Park looked again at Megex. "She's malfunctioning?" She'd never heard of a bug like that before, but she wasn't familiar with Megex's model or build. "But a domestic android shouldn't have a database of swear words to pull from at all. So why would a bug cause her to say them out of nowhere?" To Megex she said, "Query: run a systems check."

"I am in the middle of an operation," Megex answered politely, looking down the line of people waiting to be served their food. "Fucker."

Park laughed, despite herself: it was so bland, so innocent, that it made something like delight bubble up inside of her.

Elly, on the other hand, looked positively disturbed. She was a shy, mousy woman, a member of the group that Park referred to as the "First Name Club": the handful of women (consisting of her bunkmates and Reimi) who'd insisted on being called by their first names rather than their last, shirking protocol and the usual conventions. The reasons for this were beyond her: she'd hypothesized performative submissiveness or familiarity, or perhaps a signal of sexual availability and enticement, but Keller had called her a "classic overthinker" and left it at that.

But now, without the shield of her more extraverted friend Reimi, Elly looked fretful, uneasy, as if she wished she could hide, perhaps behind the formality of her last name again.

"Maybe it's another prank someone's playing," the climatologist said with concern, glancing again at Megex, who'd ceased cussing for the moment. "Maybe someone is going around and teaching all the bots curse words." She shook her head. "What a way to blow off steam."

That sobered Park significantly. She'd had enough of pranks on this ship.

She took her tray and went to her usual table, sitting by herself. Keller was still nowhere to be found—busy working on her "special project," no doubt—and anyway Park wanted to be alone with her thoughts. Again, the mess hall seemed a little too warm, too humid; her chikin salad, with its precious greens, wilted and shriveled in the heat. Park stared down at it in dismay. *Bad for morale,* she mused, pushing the limp sprouts around on her plate. Surely they could afford better. Or maybe not—maybe this was what all spaceflight passengers were subjected to. They left details like that out of the colony documentaries she'd watched. She looked around at the low lighting of the ship; at the hot, swampy, white little room. At herself sitting alone in a crowd of people. Yes, it seemed they'd left a lot of things out.

The other crewmembers seemed to be in a foul mood, eating their meals in a tense and simmering silence. Forks scraped restlessly against plates. There was a pressure-cooker atmosphere clamped over the mess hall: something must have happened on that morning's expedition. Wan Xu had obviously known about it, tried to conceal it from her. But what was it? And did it have anything to do with Keller being reassigned?

Or maybe these others didn't know, themselves. Park felt the torque of frustration low in her gut. She had the constant feeling that there were things she wasn't privy to, winging overhead. Currents of unspoken knowledge moving through the ship, moving through her. Maybe it was because she wasn't conscripted, and nearly all of the others were. Or maybe it was because of her position as the ISF's orbiter—no one was going to confide in their bosses' "spy."

But she had to admit that some of the fault also lay with her personality. People found Park spooky, she knew that; they thought she had some uncanny ability to know their thoughts, that she was liable to extract secrets from their minds the way she could separate yolks from cracked eggs. Ridiculous, of course, but she had forced herself to scale back when conversing with them, only listening rather than preempting their responses. People didn't like it when you could guess their thoughts before they were ready to articulate them.

But by the time she'd recalibrated, the damage had already been done. Along with being a snitch, the crew thought Park was some kind of psychic. A sorceress ready to entangle them in some dark and unknown art. Or maybe even a robot herself; maybe that was why they thought she was in cahoots with Jimex.

Her bleak thoughts were interrupted by a commotion on the other side of the room. Fulbreech and Natalya Severov entered the dining room together, arguing in low voices. Park watched their entrance with veiled interest. She hadn't spoken to Fulbreech since the catastrophe in the escape shuttle; hadn't even given herself much time to think on it. His gesture for her had been powerful, of course—even she had to acknowledge that. But she didn't know what to do with it. What to feel. How to face him and express the proper gratitude—if gratitude was what he even wanted.

Perhaps that was why he turned to Natalya, she thought. *She* might have greeted the proposal a little more warmly. And they had never come to a meal together before. Park surreptitiously scanned them for any signs of assignation: rumpled hair, slightly unzipped decksuits. No, none of that, but just because their clothing was immaculate didn't mean they hadn't coupled. Severov, exacting as she was, was the type to demand intactness, the upkeep of appearances. She was, as Boone often said, a hardass. Park knew a little of what that was like.

"You must feel the same way," Natalya was saying. Though the woman was summer-skinned and golden-haired, her voice always made Park think of winter: she was always so crisp and biting. "There are bots who can make maps, you know. Those drones you use—soon enough they'll have models able to do your job for you. In spite of you."

"Luckily for me, there are none on this ship," Fulbreech said, in a tone that indicated he was tired of the argument. "Look, Natalya, all of our jobs are outdated. You can't take that out on the bots. We just have to accept the situation for what it is and be grateful for the time we have before ISF puts us to work doing something the robots *can't* do. I expect that, after Eos, they'll put me in the Art sector or something."

"You're wrong," the surveyor retorted fiercely. "Not all jobs are outdated. The combat jobs are safe—they won't ever trust clunkers with guns. And the psychologists." At this she threw a venomous look at Park, who stared vacantly at her food to indicate she wasn't listening. "Bots haven't figured out how to do that properly yet. I'm not even sure our humans have."

Fulbreech didn't look over at Park—carefully, it seemed. "I'll think about it," he said. "Was there anything else you needed?"

Natalya scowled and turned away. "No," she replied in her brittle way, walking off toward the food dispensary. "That's all, Kel. I just hope you see things for how they are."

Park watched Fulbreech watch her go; she told herself that her interest was merely an observer's interest. A spy's interest. She ignored the tight, sour feeling in her chest.

Then Fulbreech turned and caught Park's eye. His face was tired, but it brightened when he saw her, and he came striding up to Park's table with the same cheerful, guileless friendliness he'd approached her with for the last ten months. "Anyone sitting here?"

Park looked at the empty seat across from her and shrugged, waving slightly with her forkful of drooping salad. She tried very hard not to think about his kiss, the startling scent and warmth of him. Fulbreech took the seat, presumably to avoid having to wait in line with Natalya. He looked haggard, much grayer than the day before; his lips were space-chapped and his eyes still squinted from the Eotian sunlight. But he seemed happy to see Park.

The two of them sat in awkward silence for a moment before Park pushed him her unopened drink. She watched Fulbreech reverently accept the orange juice like she'd given him a birthday present. Why could she never act as happy to see him? Why did she always revert back to a state of—silent resistance, aloofness, despite his overtures?

"Natalya rope you into an anti-android rant?" she asked, just to make conversation.

Fulbreech grimaced; in a flash Park deduced that that was not the root of the issue between them. "She's angry," he said, lightly enough. "And afraid. Human surveying doesn't seem to have much of a future." He punctured the biodegradable membrane that held his juice in a palm-sized bulb. Park scrutinized him; he was only telling half the truth. But his conversations with Natalya were not her business.

"The new HARE explorers are being rolled out next year," she said instead. "I remember seeing it on the Frontier newstream."

"Which pretty much renders Natalya's job obsolete," Fulbreech continued, nodding. "And she's convinced that *every* job will be threatened by robots soon—mine included."

"And do you believe her?"

Fulbreech shook his head. "She's just one of those people."

Park nodded. She was familiar with *those* people; she'd lived through the anti-android riots in New Diego, after all. "I wonder how she feels about Reimi being—indisposed. Without her, a lot of the robots' functions might lock up someday."

"Oh, I'm sure she's happy about it," Fulbreech said, glancing at the food dispensary line to make sure Natalya was still in it. He lowered his voice conspiratorially. "She thinks that the robots are all here to spy on us for ISF."

Park couldn't help but laugh a little at the absurdity of it. "How would they even do that? Does she think they sit down and type incident reports to send back home?"

Fulbreech laughed, too. "Something like that. She thinks they're all plugged in to ISF relays back on Corvus. My question is, how would they even know what to report? *Today, Officer Boone took fifteen minutes too long in the bathroom. This is an emergency of the highest priority.*"

The two of them chuckled together over the idea. Park was glad to see that somebody else recognized the silliness of conspiracy theories like Natalya's; it meant not everybody on the ship believed the robots could be used to spy on people, as Sagara had insinuated about Jimex. For one thing—as Fulbreech said—they were too primitive to distinguish the worthiness of their observations: they'd be useless as spies.

And for another, she thought, they'd be redundant. She knew that ISF had not, could not have commissioned the android crew of the *Deucalion* to act as secret observers, meant to report back on the actions of the expedition members.

She knew that because it was what they were paying Park for.

Fulbreech sighed then, looking over at Natalya, who seemed to be locked in some sort of tirade against Megex; presumably the android had sworn at her, too. "The thing is," he said, "it is pretty strange, how many androids are on this ship. I don't totally blame people for wondering about their purpose. The spy thing is silly, but I find myself wondering, too. Why are there so many robots?"

He looked at Park, as if expecting her to know the answer, but she only shrugged. Even she had wondered this; she didn't like it either, to a degree. Because she didn't know what it meant. Machine life matching human life was common on two-seater mining ships, but not on three-deck behemoths like the *Deucalion*. Normally there were human navigators, other mechanics, auxiliary staffers who prepared food or swabbed the decks. But for whatever reason, this time the ISF had deemed it necessary to minimize human life aboard the ship as much as possible. The only reason why the lucky thirteen were there was because they each had specializations, elite roles the ISF hadn't figured out how to replace with software—yet. Everything else could be done by the androids, who were often as light as children, or by bodiless AI. The *Deucalion* wasted no space on self-esteem.

The assumption was that it was all part of the push to propel their ship to Eos as fast as possible. If she looked at everything from a bird's-eye view, Park could see the logic of it. Let the superfluous deckhands weigh down other ships, the ones that could take their time getting to new planets. This ship couldn't. And besides, if their vessel ever needed to lighten its load, there was the added benefit that the robots could be ejected as ballast. You couldn't do that with ten, twenty, forty additional human crewmembers.

But the rest of the crew was disgruntled by this, all the same. Friends and colleagues who could have been saddled along had been ousted by androids—for reasons murky and unknown. Of course that caused resentment, anxiety about the future. On the next mission, who would be deemed dispensable next?

Hence why they projected sinister motives onto the robots, believing they had some purpose other than simply rendering human colleagues obsolete. Crewmembers like Natalya thought they were spies . . . and now Park was being lumped in with them, too. Blamed for their presence, their inquiries. As if she were the mastermind and all the androids just her proxies, mechanical limbs leading back to the same source.

Did that mean the crewmembers were going to turn their ire on her next?

Was that why they slipped something into my food?

"Have you heard of a rumor," Park began, "regarding me?" If he had, he likely wouldn't be sitting here with her, not if he believed it. But she had to know. How far beyond Sagara had this gossip gone?

Fulbreech looked at her curiously. "Which one?" he asked, utterly tactless. For some reason that made her trust him more.

But then Michael Boone came clunking into the dining hall, before she could answer. For an uneasy moment Park wondered if he had heard their little joke about him somehow—if someone had gone to fetch him. But the soldier seemed intent on something else. He looked like an overgrown child stuffed into the body of a linebacker, with his small, box-shaped head and mop of curly red hair: his torso was comically top-heavy, his powerful hands perpetually balled into fists. Park's feet seemed to automatically plant themselves against the floor whenever she saw him—as if she were bracing herself for an impact. Today he looked particularly agitated, his neck bullish and veined.

"Uh-oh," Fulbreech said softly, following her line of sight. "Looks like someone's augments are acting up again."

Park nodded, but continued to watch Boone. Their military leader made a beeline straight for Natalya, grabbing her slender arm just as she was turning away from Megex. Other crewmembers noticed, too. The conversation in the room died off a little, and Park was able to catch a snippet of Boone and Natalya's exchange. Boone said, in his oily Martian drawl: "I asked you the location of the body!"

And Natalya answered testily, "Which body, and why do you care?"

Park couldn't make out the rest of it. She turned back to Fulbreech and said, "Have you found any lakes on Eos?"

The cartographer looked blank as he began to chew through the juice bulb's edible skin. "Lakes?"

"Boone's talking about bodies over there." He had to mean bodies of water they'd found outside, she thought. It would be the kind of thing he'd ask Natalya, the surveyor, about. Could you even call them lakes, off-planet? If you couldn't determine the exact size of it, you'd call it a body of water, wouldn't you?

"*Is* there water on Eos?" she asked then. She was embarrassed by how little she knew of their destination; but then, it was ISF who had directed her away from knowing more, and Fulbreech himself had referred to that fact yesterday. In the escape pod. *Don't think about that now.* "I know there's ice—obviously. But have you found anything the future colony could use?"

Fulbreech suddenly looked guarded. "You know I can't discuss any of that with you, Park," he said.

She sat back and felt her face flattening; all feeling of warmth toward him withdrew like a turtle into a shell. "Of course," Park said, toneless. "My mistake."

Foolish of her to assume anything of him, she told herself as Fulbreech got up to claim his lunch. Foolish of her to assume he'd tell a non-conscripted person anything about the new planet. It was ISF's mandate, after all.

But—*was* it that foolish? He'd offered to take her outside just yesterday, hadn't he? He'd stolen a suit and was willing to outright flout the rules. For her sake, he'd claimed. Now he wouldn't even *talk* about it? What had changed?

She picked at her food. Was it because they'd been caught? Had Fulbreech been scared off by Sagara? Was he now rethinking the consequences of helping Park—or rethinking his attempt to start a dalliance with her?

Why bother at all, then? she thought with a growing measure of annoyance. Why bother establishing that level of confidence, of intimacy, only to withdraw it again the next day? How was she supposed to know where the line was?

Her frustration mounted as she watched him collect his tray of food from Megex, making light conversation with their physicist, Eric Holt. It wasn't all Fulbreech's fault, she knew. Mostly this was about her own vexations with ISF, and the mission they'd assigned her to. Why *couldn't* she see Eos, or know anything about it? Why were they so concerned with keeping information about the planet from the data companies, when colonists would be landing here soon enough?

Park dropped her fork down onto her barely-touched tray, her appetite now completely gone. Maybe there was something wrong with the whole thing. Something they weren't telling her, something that would deflate hopes back on Earth. Their researchers had declared beforehand that conditions on the planet were suitable for human life. There was the great rush to claim it, to begin the process of reconnaissance, exploration, settlement. Things on Earth were deteriorating fast. The ISF had to hustle, establishing outposts farther and farther out, trying to mitigate strain on the existing colonies for when the great diaspora came. Eos was the farthest from home that mankind had ever ventured.

But it'd all be for naught if something was wrong with the place.

They'd fast-tracked the prep time for this mission, she knew. There was a truncated training period on Earth, a scramble to assemble a crew. An anemic four weeks in a simulation dome in Antarctica. Within a matter of weeks the *Deucalion* was launched and propelled towards the farthest arms of the next galaxy, speeding towards a planet that awaited it like a pale-gleaming lighthouse, hanging in space.

They'd wanted it—and badly—and now perhaps they were hiding that the great rush had been pointless. But the accelerated timespan didn't account for the other oddities about the mission. There was all the secrecy, the missing procedures. The need for a disproportionate amount of combat specialists—and a robotic crew. No one ever quite gave her a straight answer about anything. Rushing didn't account for *that*, did it?

And she had read all about the first colonies, had watched the docustreams on the settling of Phobos and Io and Mars. Those colonies had come equipped with seedlings, and prefab biodomes, and embryos of pygmy cows. The *Deucalion* had none of that. Just a handful of unhappy scientists, half of whom couldn't see the very planet they were supposed to be settling.

No, rushing couldn't account for that.

And that was the other thing, Park thought as she watched Fulbreech slowly make his way back to their table. ISF had taken the time to pick out the best and brightest minds they could find—thirteen leaders in their respective fields. But none of those fields were the kind that tamed planets. There were no agriculturists, no builders, no space architects. Where the Corvus outpost had been settled with one hundred, *this* ship only had thirteen. Perhaps a lack of time could explain the amount of expedition members—but not their particular qualities. Why were there soldiers instead of farmers, why was there only one cartographer when there should have been twenty, two psychologists instead of two engineers?

Park frowned. So there was the strange acceleration, the hurry to cram a crew into the *Deucalion* and send it speeding off. And there was the secrecy, the concealment that kept even Park from knowing what was going on—and she was the ship's so-called spy!

And now all this talk about bodies.

Fulbreech returned, looking unhappy. "You're thinking about things you shouldn't be," he said, setting down his food. "I can tell."

And whose fault is that? Park thought. She knew it was unfair. Fulbreech read her expression and said in a very low voice: "I never should have offered you the suit. I'm sorry. It was wrong of me."

For a moment Park didn't reply. Finally she said, "So I take it your offer is rescinded?"

He ducked his head. "Unfortunately, yes," Fulbreech answered. "That's a very strong yes."

There was a little silence between them as he, too, began to pick at his food. After a moment Park took a steadying breath and said, "I understand, Fulbreech. And I don't blame you. It's not your fault." How could she blame him for retracting an offer she never would have made in the first place, in his position? Even she had to acknowledge that she wasn't worth the risk, not for a conscripted man. And in the end he was simply following orders from ISF—as were they all. No, she couldn't blame him for that. But . . .

The cartographer suddenly looked away from her. The haggard look came over him again: his eyes were tired and strained, and shockingly blue. He looked sad, and a little bewildered, as if someone close to him had died suddenly. Even Park was surprised by the change. She had never seen Fulbreech look anything other than simple and friendly.

"I'm sorry, Park," he said again, heavily. "If I could talk to you, I would."

She wasn't sure what to say. "I'm always available for counseling," she told him. "To whatever extent you're comfortable with."

Fulbreech laughed a little and shook his head. "That's just the thing," he said. "I'm not sure there *is* such a thing as comfortable. Not out here."

Yes, something must have happened, Park thought again. Something had happened out on Eos's lethal tundra that morning. Something had changed between the escape pod and now. Her voice almost hushed with stifled alarm, she said, "Fulbreech . . . what's happened? What's going on?"

His smile had vanished, like a light winking out. "I guess I can't describe it, Park," Fulbreech said, resigned. His eyes trailed away from hers. "I don't know what to tell you. It's just something I can't explain."

"Perhaps he is feeling sick," Jimex said after lunch. "I could ask Ellenex."

"Please don't," Park said. After her talk with Sagara, she was training the android on keeping his mouth shut and exercising good sense; she could not say they were making much progress. "I'm telling you this in confidence, Jimex. That means I'm trusting you to keep it a secret from everyone else but us. As in you and me. Also, someone else overheard you asking Ellenex for medicine. If anyone else found out about that, it would be . . . upsetting. For them. So please try to be more mindful in the future."

"Why?"

"Because—they trust—no, they think you're incapable of doing things like that. Doing things in secret, doing things of your own prerogative. It's dangerous to reveal your abilities too much. Do you understand what I mean?"

His head whirred noisily. "Perhaps Dr. Fulbreech is tired," Jimex said, as if she hadn't spoken at all. "Daylight goes very quickly on Eos. Dr. Keller says this has an adverse effect on humans. It makes them 'out-of-sorts' and 'grumpy.'"

But is Fulbreech ever grumpy? Park wondered. Silly question; he was prone to all the flaws and foibles that any other human was. She couldn't forget that—couldn't put him on any kind of pedestal. But in ten months on the ship, she had never caught him in a bad mood. Or found him so unwilling to talk to her.

"Could something have happened?" she wondered out loud. "Could one of the crewmembers have been—injured? Why was Boone talking about a body?"

"I am not certain," Jimex said placidly. Then he said: "Perhaps Dr. Fulbreech is homesick. Dr. Keller said that could happen, but that the symptoms are not always obvious." He looked at Park. "Are you homesick?"

"No," Park said. Then she stood up and began to prepare the office for her next appointment.

It was true, she thought later, after Jimex had left and she had pulled up the program on her inlays for dictation. ISF had never told her when she could expect to return home—colony missions could take years—and she had never particularly cared to know. She had still signed up without objection. Of course, she did feel the occasional pangs for fire, for sunlight, for silence—but those were material longings, trivial concerns. In terms of homesickness, she had no home on Earth to be sick for.

But even Jimex didn't need to know that.

Her next appointment was with Eric Holt, the expedition's physicist. At twenty-eight, Holt was one of the youngest people on the ship, and a little insecure about that fact, in Park's opinion. He was constantly putting on airs, lazily drawling his sentences, trying to blend in with the more cynical and experienced academics. His insecurity was not entirely unfounded, either: the space-born, with their augmented and extended lifespans, tended to believe that adolescence ended around age twenty-five. So to many of them, Holt was just a young buck, brimming with testosterone—despite his two doctorates from Shoemaker University. In response, Holt tried to act as if nothing affected him, as if everything was perpetually just *all right*. As if it were all part of an interesting story he would tell someday in the future.

But today, he had none of that self-assurance, pretense or otherwise. Before he arrived, Park's inlays told her that Holt's heart rate was elevated. And when he came in, his thin decksuit showed dark patches of sweat around the collar.

"Good afternoon, Holt," Park began. "I was thinking—"

"I'd like to use the MAD," Holt said rapidly. "Now."

Park closed her mouth. "Of course," she said after a moment, her voice neutral, offering no judgment or rebuke. Meanwhile she was thinking: *Something's wrong.* Holt was looking at her in a daze, as if he'd been drugged; his eyes were glazed over with fear like a dumb animal's.

Park reached over to boot up the Mood-Altering Device. Holt's eyes followed the green spark of its activation sequence greedily. "Can you tell me what's bothering you?" she asked him as it flashed to life.

The physicist's hands were shaking. His face had a bony, scraped look. "I was having a nightmare," he said. His voice was faint and a little muffled.

Park kept her expression pleasantly interested. "And what happened in the nightmare?"

Holt didn't answer; he just stood there staring at her, kneading the skin around his eyes. After another moment, Park held up the plastic helmet of the MAD and helped Holt with its dangling straps and buckles and sticky microsuction cups. She averted her gaze as the MAD began beaming its euphoric green light into Holt's brain, slackening his body until he was slumped in his seat. His mouth hung open slightly. In Park's opinion, there was something disturbingly private about using the MAD—as if she were witnessing someone reach orgasm. She turned away to set a timer on her inlays. Two minutes was usually sufficient.

Then Holt gave a low groan. Park looked at him sharply—he should have been comatose with bliss—but instead he was plucking at the cables hooked to his helmet.

"It's not working," he said. He sounded close to tears. "Something's wrong."

This had never happened before. Park checked the helmet for malfunction, but the MAD was working fine. She angled it toward her face and felt the gamma rays bathing her brain in a warm cerebral massage. "It seems fine," she said, trying to sound confident.

"I can't get it out of my *head*," Holt said.

Goddamn it, Keller, where are you? Park let the MAD rest on Holt's skull again, though when he peered at her from behind the plastic visor, she could see that his expression was still one of distress—almost terror. His features were washed in eerie green light.

"Why don't you tell me what you dreamt?" Park said, hoping that enough distraction would give him time to calm down.

Holt shook his head, then shuddered. "I don't know. I was sleeping, and then when I woke up—I couldn't move. There were all these lights flashing in my face. I tried to open my mouth to yell for someone, but—I had no tongue."

"In your dream," Park couldn't stop herself from saying.

Holt shook his head again, but Park couldn't tell what it meant. He continued, "My lungs were frozen; I couldn't breathe. I was cold—so fucking cold. Like I was dead. Like my skin was peeling off. None of my organs were working. And I—I wasn't in control of myself. I wanted to go outside. Leave the ship. But I was trapped inside my body and couldn't move. I thought to myself that I'd rather be dead than keep feeling that way. I wanted to be dead."

He took the helmet off and covered his face with his hands. Park thought, *Suicidal ideations? Isn't it too early for this?* Holt hadn't even gone outside yet, as far as she knew. Was he already buckling under the effects of the isolation? Space psychosis?

She said, "Nightmares are a normal reaction to stress, Eric. You are under an enormous amount of mental strain here, and this is a very common response to that."

When he didn't respond, she continued, "Nightmares are a response to fear and anxiety. They're a way for our psyche to release pressure and operate with less of those pent-up emotions. Sometimes we can look at them as tools to cope and feel better."

Holt still said nothing. When he spread his fingers to look at her through his hands, Park could see that the glaze was still in his eyes: a barely suppressed panic that made Park think, *Something is really wrong here.* They'd have to pull him off the expedition team altogether, give him some sedatives. They couldn't send him out like that. She said aloud: "What else is bothering you, Eric?"

"It didn't feel like a dream," he murmured. "Didn't feel like I was asleep. It felt *real.*"

"The human consciousness," Park said, "is an extremely powerful force. Mere conviction and belief have made people ignore the pain of amputation, experience mass delusions—"

"You're not *listening* to me!" The sudden ferocity in his tone silenced Park—even had her pulling up Sagara's contact on her inlays. In the green MAD glow Holt looked shrunken, his features deceptively ravaged and scarred. His breathing hissed. He said again, "You're not *listening*! Don't you listen?"

Park sat, frozen, rapt. Her palms were slick; without realizing it she was gripping her own hand, tightly. It seemed to be melting out of her grasp.

"What is it that you need me to hear?" she asked Holt, barely hearing her own voice.

The physicist flopped back into his seat; his eyes floated away from hers. When he spoke again, his voice was as small and frail as a child's. "I can't tell if I'm still dreaming," he mumbled. "I don't know if I ever really woke up."

"So you want me to pull him off the team?" Commander Wick asked, sitting back. "He's due to go out tomorrow."

"At least temporarily," Park said. They were sitting in Wick's quarters; she had avoided calling him to the counseling office, mindful of a power struggle, of making him feel like she was the school principal summoning a rascally student.

Wick frowned into the middle distance. At forty-two he was punching into the upper limit of the age range on the ship, but he looked younger; his body was rangy and tough, and lean as a rake. His face was tanned by alien suns. He was a somewhat solemn, reserved man—not the charismatic, jovial sort that Park had imagined would lead an expedition—but at least he was sensible. Easy to talk to. She hoped that he wouldn't ignore her recommendation; otherwise she would have to go to ISF and override him.

"He's disturbed about something," Park continued. "Exactly what, we'll have to find out in further sessions. But he's far too distressed to be trusted under the strenuous conditions out there—at least right now."

"What's your best guess about him?"

"I'd prefer not to say anything with so little information. He may simply be—" She cut herself off.

"Cracking under the pressure," Wick finished. He worked his jaw. "Which is unusual. If I recall, Holt has been off-world before. We haven't even been on the *Deucalion* that long."

"He's been fine until today," Park said, aware that the only person she should be discussing this with was Dr. Keller, who was still *in absentia*. "Until after we landed."

"But he hasn't been outside."

"No. But going outside could only make it worse, if we don't determine the cause of his . . . anxiety."

She'd been reading up on the effects that new planets could have on the human psyche: how there were sometimes feelings of inexplicable terror. There was one unproven theory that the sound of an alien planet's rotation, something unnoticed on Earth, could cause serious mental disturbance in a person, without them even knowing it. She considered floating the idea past Wick, who was a veteran of new planets, but held back. No point for her to come off as clueless, blind. At least not yet.

"All right," Wick said, still working his jaw. He had a slightly nasal Lunar accent; watching him, she recalled that he had once broken all the bones in his face climbing Mons Huygens, the tallest peak on the Moon. "I suppose we can make do without a physicist, at least for now. And Holt is young. Maybe the responsibility was just too much for him." She thought there was something accusatory in his tone, as if he were pointing out that she should have caught this long before the launch. Which was true: both she and Keller had vetted Holt in the preliminary testing. And cleared him. "You sent Holt to see Dr. Chanur?"

"Yes."

He sat back. "All right, Park. I'll back you up: Holt is off the team for now. Thanks for telling me."

She sensed her dismissal; she rose and gathered her things. Before she exited his narrow room, where he bunked with Boone, Wick stopped her and said, "Park—how are *you* doing?"

She looked back. There was a rare sliver of sympathy in Wick's face, which normally looked like a hatchet blade. She sensed he understood the difficult position she was in, without Keller, and the frustration of steering herself away from her own questions. The wall that lay between her and the rest of the crew. She felt a strange swell of warmth toward him—and then, alarmingly, a tight, achy feeling around the temples, as if she might cry. She said evenly, "I'm well, thank you."

Then: "Is Keller really not available for . . . advice, at least? Where even is she? I can't find her anywhere."

Wick spread his hands. "I'm sorry," he said, looking off at something past her. "I couldn't tell you." She couldn't decode what that meant, either.

So she left. At first she felt the urge to visit the infirmary, where Holt was resting under the supervision of Chanur, and where Reimi was being held in her suspended sleep. Park had the ghoulish idea of gazing into her cryogenic tank, as if she were an onlooker at a twenty-first-century zoo. Observing her body floating in the dark waters, oblivious to the rest of the ship and its troubles . . .

But she was so tired. Her own body felt swollen and waterlogged with weariness. *Tomorrow,* she thought, turning instead toward the long gray corridor that led to the residential section. *I'll look into all of it tomorrow . . .*

She trudged to her bunk, trying to keep her head from drooping. The floor lurched oddly beneath her, as if she were on a seaward vessel; she told herself it was the exhaustion, lingering nausea from her space-sickness. The other women were sleeping by the time she crept in and grabbed her night gear; they were on strict sleeping regimens, since Eos only had seven hours of sunlight for them to use. Park, who could sleep in later, hurried down the corridor to the empty showers and activated the water at its hottest setting. The steam formed strange, twisting clouds under the artificial gravity. She shed her clothes and stepped in. Heat blasted her as if she had stepped into a furnace.

It must be heaven for the crewmembers who have to go outside, Park thought. One thing she did know was that Eos was cold—cold as hell. She'd felt it even through the super-reinforced shuttered windows on the bridge. The team had to ensure they were back before sunset every day: apparently nighttime on Eos meant almost-immediate death. Her stomach shuddered. Holt's nightmare came to mind. Cold so extreme your skin might come off.

She turned her mind to other things. The confrontation between Boone and Natalya in the cafeteria still troubled Park: she had the feeling that if enough friction developed between the flinty surveyor and hotheaded Boone, disaster of an explosive degree might occur. What had they been arguing about? What body or thing were they hiding from her—what was Keller hiding, or Fulbreech, or Wan Xu?

And then there was Sagara. Cold and unreadable as stone. She didn't even know if he was hiding anything, or if this was all just normal behavior for him. He was the wild card in the deck: she couldn't predict him, couldn't understand what his mindset or even purpose was. The big question mark over him scared her. Made him dangerous. And of course he'd done nothing to deter that feeling.

What could defrost him? Sex, she supposed—but he would never be one of the ones who had a liaison in the escape pod. She nearly laughed at the thought. Then briefly found herself imagining leading someone—the eager Fulbreech, she tried not to admit—down into that unlit, buzzing space, thrumming with the warmth of the ship's whisper engines. Undressing each other's bodies in the dark.

There was a mirror bolted into the far corner of the room. Park peered into the fogged glass and examined herself. Small, severe body. Harsh cheekbones, harsher eyes. Dark hair cut raggedly short. Not much to inspire interest, aside from perhaps her small nose, which she liked, and her long eyelashes. Better for him to pursue the svelte Natalya, or even shy and sweet Elly Ma. Despite the accompanying palavers, sexual encounters were generally encouraged for the health of the crew. Only she and Keller were exempt.

Objectivity is key, Park told her reflection.

"Dr. Park," someone said through the steam.

Park jumped, whirled; nearly slipped on the anti-slip floor. Hunter, Boone's lieutenant, was standing there at the entrance of the shower, watching her. Park resisted the urge to cover her breasts and said calmly, "What is it?"

"I think you need to come back to the room. There's something wrong with Ma."

Park wrapped herself in her thermal towel and followed Hunter out of the shower. The other woman walked with long, brisk strides; Park found herself jogging slightly to keep up. Her feet left wet prints against the icy floor.

"What's going on?" she asked.

"I don't know," Hunter said. She was a hard, ropy woman, with a shock of curly red hair. Park often found herself wondering if she was related to Boone: they looked so alike. But nothing in her file indicated it. And unlike Boone, who loved to jeer and slam his way around the ship, Hunter was famously laconic. Park had heard there was a running bet on who was more close-mouthed, herself or the combat specialist. Hunter said, "I just woke up and Ma was going crazy."

Define crazy, Park wanted to say, as if Hunter were an android that she could command—but she knew that the other woman wouldn't answer.

From down the hall they could hear the sounds of Elly Ma screaming. It was a sound that made the back of Park's teeth ache; her eyes prickled. She saw Hunter flinch. All along the dim-thrumming corridor, doors were opening and tousled heads were poking out. They glanced at Park as she passed; she wished she had taken the time to dress in her decksuit. When they reached their door, Hunter stopped and said, "Why haven't you turned on the lights, Natalya?"

The surveyor didn't answer. When Park peered into the dark room, she could see her sitting on her bunk with her knees drawn up to her chin. She was looking at something in the corner. Park stepped inside and said, "Where's Elly?"

The keening sound was rising. It sounded like a scream of hysteria, with dry, creaking sounds puncturing it that could have been sobs or laughter. Park squinted and saw that the sound was coming from the corner, that *Elly* was in the corner, huddled up. She motioned for Natalya to stay on the bunk and knelt, keeping the towel tucked around herself. She said, as if she were coaxing a cat out from under a porch: "What is it, Elly? What's going on?"

All at once the keening stopped. The figure in the corner stirred and said, "What?"

"Why are you screaming?"

"I'm not," Elly said thickly. Natalya made a noise of disbelief. Outside, Park could hear Hunter saying, "We don't know what happened. One minute we were sleeping, the next, she was having some kind of episode. She got out of her bed and lay flat on the ground."

"How do you feel?" Park asked Elly. She reached out, felt around until she touched Elly's ankle. The climatologist pulled her foot away. *Assess for risks of violence,* Park told herself. "You've been under a lot of stress," she said gently. "It wouldn't be unusual if you were to react to that."

"What are you talking about?" Elly asked. She was sounding more lucid, impatient, as if she'd been shaken awake from a deep sleep. Hunter finally flicked on the light. Park had to stop herself from closing her eyes; she saw Elly recoil from the glare for a moment, then relax.

There was something red on her arm. In the sudden brightness Park couldn't see what it was. She heard Natalya give a muffled scream behind her.

"Elly," Park said, her own voice sounding strangely steady, even to herself. "What happened to you?"

The climatologist looked at her sleepily. She seemed to take no notice of the stripes she'd clawed into her arm. The nails of her right hand were speckled with blood. She shook her head and looked at Park with the innocence of a sparrow. "I don't know," she murmured. "Wake me up. I think I'm having a nightmare."

3.

[Hello:

I'll start with the bad news, since I know you prefer that. I was unable to access the video files you asked for. Ever since those terrorists blew up those archives on Halla, ISF's put most of its databanks on lockdown. And I mean on super-lockdown. I was unable to bypass their security measures.

Now for the good news. The loss of the data in Halla must have spooked them, because they commissioned text transcripts of the videos to be stored elsewhere—in case the original filmstreams were ever lost or damaged or hacked or held hostage by the rebels. Those transcripts, I *was* able to access. They'll do fine, won't they?

I'll have to send them to you piecemeal. Too big of a file, and ISF will get suspicious. Just keep writing back to me, so that I'm not sending you many unanswered messages in a row. That would be suspicious, too. You can say things like, "How's little Nicky! Can I see a picture of him?" I'll hide the transcript files in the pics. Click on the eyebrows to execute; type the name of that stupid blue toy we used to fight over to unlock.

Aren't you lucky your little sister is in Communications Sector? And you always told me the job would be shit.

Love,

S.S.]

Video Logs from the CS *Wyvern* 7079
Recorded for Posterity
Transcribed by Officer A. Sagara
#900382

Transcriber's notes: *These logs were filmed by a first-generation HARE (Heuristic Analysis, Reconnaissance, and Exploration) model, a unit from the 270-RX line. Serial number has not yet been recovered, as of this recording. A HARE is an exploration robot used by surveyors and miners to analyze terrain. It looks like a large mechanical spider, about 1.3 meters tall, with eight titanium legs, plungered feet, and a box sitting on its top, which houses the HARE's camera, processors, cataphotes, scanners, total station theodolite, gyrotheodolite, and other tools. This HARE's video logs were first received by the merchant vessel RA Ryujin, which then relayed them to ISF Corvus.*

VIDEO LOG #1—Ship Designation CS *Wyvern* 7079
Day 1: 10:38 UTO

[The HARE model activates for the first time. Its camera blinks on, fuzzy, then focused. The cockpit of a small mining ship appears in its view: a two-seater, very cramped, the ship itself shaped like a teardrop with a conic drill at its point. The HARE looks at the control panel in the room and the bank of video screens that show the exterior of the ship. There is a multitude of stars on the screens. In the distance, there seems to be a small white planet or moon, about the size of a fist.]

[Abruptly, a man appears in the camera's eye, very close. There's a loud scrambling noise as he adjusts something on the HARE's 'head.' The man is tall, approximately 2 meters in height, with a large nose, white-blond hair, and gray eyes. He appears to be in his late twenties or early thirties. There's an indistinct Martian tattoo on the right side of his neck. A thin scar cuts halfway through his left eyebrow. His nametag reads CS Engineer Fin Taban.]

[Taban fiddles with the camera lens of the HARE, then points it at the bank of video screens.]

Taban: HARE, identify that planet.

HARE (processors whirring): . . .

Taban: HARE, identify.

HARE: I'm sorry. You must undergo this unit's activation protocols before use.

Taban: God *damn* it.

HARE (processors whirring): . . .

Taban: Do you have transmission features? Can you relay a message back to ISF?

HARE: I'm sorry. You must undergo this unit's activation protocols before—

[Taban reaches over and the video cuts out.]

VIDEO LOG #2—Ship Designation CS *Wyvern* 7079
Day 1: 10:45 UTO

[The camera blinks on again. Taban is still in the same position. So is the HARE.]

Taban: My name is Fin Taban, of the CS *Wyvern*. I, uh, guess this is a mayday signal . . . Our communications system went down several days ago. Maybe five. My pilot took us out past Vier and went in the wrong direction—I think we're in unregulated space now. There's some planet nearby that I don't recognize. We went through an asteroid cloud similar to the Oort and took some damage. Didn't come out with much more than a stubbed toe on the human end, but our FTL engine, lambda drive, and comm systems are down as a result. Requesting rescue from these coordinates. Uh, ASAP. Please.

Taban (sitting back): What do you think? Did that sound good?

HARE: I am unable to answer your query at this time.

Taban: I guess it'll have to do. Transmit to the nearest ISF frequency.

HARE (processing): I'm sorry. This unit is unable to comply.

Taban: What? Why not?

HARE (processors whirring): There are no ISF frequencies within range.

Taban: Can't you boost your signal?

HARE: Only models past the second generation are capable of that function.

Taban: What generation are you?

HARE: First.

Taban: That's great. That's just wonderful. Thank you.

HARE: You are welcome.

[There's the sound of a pneumatic door opening and closing. Taban looks at something off-screen. Another man walks into view and slouches himself into the pilot seat of the cockpit. This man is short, muscled, barrel-chested, with dark brown hair in a military buzz and heavy jowls.

He looks to be in his early to mid-forties. His nametag reads CS Pilot Hap Daley.]

Daley: So did you figure out how to turn that thing on?

Taban: Uhhh, yeah. Yeah, I did. Took a while to get it set up. You really never used it the entire time you've been flying this ship?

Daley: Never had to. The company just pointed me at whatever they wanted me to mine and I mined it. Never needed some robot to help me explore the barren piece-of-shit asteroids I was hacking up.

Taban: Yeah. Makes sense, I guess.

Daley: So you know how to use it?

Taban: I think so.

Daley: Why's the screen blank?

Taban: I thought it was supposed to be that way.

Daley: I don't think so. Give it a little shake.

Taban: Are you kidding?

Daley: No.

[Taban shakes the HARE.]

HARE: Please. This action is unnecessary.

Taban: Oh. Sorry.

Daley (turning back to his screens): Well, whatever. Ask it what planet that is.

Taban: HARE, identify the closest planet and provide its ISF designation.

HARE (processors whirring): . . .

Daley: What did it say?

Taban: It's thinking.

HARE: Planet unidentified. Not listed in ISF databanks.

Daley: *What?*

Taban: I *told* you. If our ship's nav-sys didn't recognize it, an ancient HARE wasn't going to.

Daley: It must be malfunctioning—just like the nav.

Taban: It's not. It can't be. It just got turned on for the first time. How could it already be malfunctioning?

Daley: You know. Radiation and shit . . . screws these things up.

Taban: Daley, *getting lost* screws these things up.

Daley: We're not lost.

Taban: You went the complete opposite way we were supposed to go! Of course we're lost!

Daley: Just because you—

Taban: I saw you go off-course weeks ago. You said you were cutting across Luxue to avoid the checkpoints, but—

Daley: Look, I go through this sector all the time. Relax. I know what I'm doing. And I did exactly what the nav told me to do.

Taban: The nav you just said was broken? And you go through this sector all the time, my ass. We're in the dark butthole of space out here. What is *that?* (pointing at white planet)

Daley: I don't know. But you need to calm down.

Taban: Calm down, sure.

Daley: I know you're a rookie, but you really need to nerve up for shit like this. It's not a big deal, okay? All we have to do is land, fix up the FTL, turn back around, and fly home. Got it?

Taban: Land where? On that?

Daley: Where else are we going to land? You want to try the asteroids again?

Taban: But that's a foreign planet.

Daley: So?

Taban: So we don't know anything about that place. Even the ISF doesn't, apparently—and isn't there some sort of law against landing on unsettled planets?

Daley: Planet, asteroid, moon, what does it matter? And I'm not gonna tell. Are *you* gonna tell?

Taban: And shouldn't we be fixing the comm system before we think about fixing the FTL engine?

Daley: Fuck no. The FTL engine is what lets us fly back.

Taban: But we need the comm system to contact ISF if we need help.

Daley: But we're not gonna need help if you fix the FTL and we fly home.

Taban: But—

Daley: Taban, man. Come on. Let's nut up a little here, huh?

Taban: Okay. Fine. Whatever.

Daley: Okay. Good.

Taban (rubbing his eyes): . . .

Daley (steering): . . .

Taban: HARE, analyze that planet.

HARE: What would you like to know?

Taban: Anything you can tell us. Weather conditions, atmosphere composition, whether there's enough radiation on the surface to toast our marshmallows . . .

HARE (processors whirring): . . .

HARE: I'm sorry. I am unable to answer your query at this time.

Taban: What? Why not?

HARE: In order to analyze an unclassified planet, I need to be on it.

Taban: Great. That's very useful.

Daley: Hey, do me a favor, will you?

Taban: What?

Daley: Override its ISF protocols.

Taban: Why?

Daley: If it *is* against the law to land on a virgin planet, the thing might go on red-alert and we'd never get it to shut up. Root it so it takes commands from you, not its original ISF programming. You can do that, right?

Taban: I think so.

HARE: Tampering with ISF property is not permitted.

Daley: Shut up.

[Taban reaches for the camera. The video cuts out.]

VIDEO LOG #3—Ship Designation CS *Wyvern* 7079
Day 1: 18:22 UTO

[The HARE reboots again. The ship seems to be landing at this point: the radiation shields are down, revealing the windows and the view outside. Outside, an icy horizon rises up as the *Wyvern* descends. The tundra is so flat and white that the HARE's camera lens struggles to focus on it as a distinct object. In the distance (~6–7 kilometers away from the ship's landing site?) there are large, mirror-like structures towering into the sky. They're strangely-shaped, fractal and razor-sharp shards as tall as skyscrapers, reflecting and bending the light in odd, dizzying ways. The effect is wholly unnatural.]

Daley (whistling): Take a look at that.

Taban: Never seen anything like it before. What are they?

Daley: Dunno. Can't be manmade.

[The structures vanish beyond the curve of the horizon as the ship lands. For a moment the two men are silent as the ship winds down from its landing sequence.]

Taban (looking at the ship's dashboard): So, come here often?

Daley: What?

Taban: Nothing. Just a joke.

Daley: (grunt)

Taban: I'm pretty sure we could get court-martialed for this.

Daley: No one's ever gonna find out. And if they did, just pretend we didn't know anything. Our ship's computer malfunctioned, we just assumed this was Elysium or Gimle. It looks pretty much exactly the same.

Taban: Except that it's orbiting two stars, not one.

Daley: Shhhh. We're miners, not astronomers. We're poor, ignorant fools.

Taban: So, delete the HARE footage before we get back, is what I hear you saying. Since it's recording everything you just said.

Daley: See? This is why I keep you around. You clean up after yourself.

Taban: (sighs) (turning back to the HARE) Okay, I think it's ready.

Daley: And you're sure it's okay to go outside the ship?

Taban: For the HARE? Sure. That's what it's built for—extraterrestrial exploration. (tapping HARE's legs) That's what these titanium legs are for. They keep it mobile, sturdy. We can send it out, let it analyze, and see what conditions are like out there.

Daley: And then you'll nut up and fix the engine?

Taban: Yeah, Daley. As soon as I find out my atoms aren't going to get ripped apart and scrambled by cosmic death-rays or a fucking solar wind, I'll nut up and fix the engine.

Daley: All right. Send it out, then.

Taban: HARE, you ready?

HARE: I am awaiting directives.

Taban: HARE, enter reconnaissance mode. Acquire data about this planet.

HARE (processors whirring): . . .

HARE: 'This planet': command unrecognized.

Taban: See, hacking its protocols made it go all screwy. It's not equipped to be dealing with undesignated planets. You know why? Because it's illegal to land on undesignated planets.

Daley: Just rephrase. Make up a name for the planet, give it something to categorize. Fool it.

Taban: HARE, enter reconnaissance mode. Acquire data about current planet, uhhh, designation HARPA.

Daley: Harpa? Who the hell is Harpa?

Taban: It's just a name I made up.

HARE (processors whirring): . . .

HARE: Designation HARPA acquired. Entering reconnaissance mode.

Daley: Okay, let's send it outside.

[Daley and Taban rise from their seats and leave the cockpit. The HARE also rises on its plungered feet and lumbers after them. Daley and Taban stop in front of the airlock of the ship and begin to zip up in protective suits.]

Taban: It's a heuristic learning model. An evolving intelligence. It'll get smarter the longer it's active, the more it absorbs.

Daley: I don't really care about that, Taban. All I care about is fixing the damn engine and getting home.

Taban: Right.

Daley: (grunt)

Taban (to HARE): And don't you come back until you've acquired as much data as you can, you hear? Scan everything in sight.

HARE: Affirmative.

Taban: And stop saying that.

HARE: Okay, USER Taban. What would you like me to say instead?

Taban: I don't know. Just say something less creepy.

HARE: Something less creepy.

Daley: Ha. It's fucking with you.

Taban: It can't do that. Can you?

HARE: I'm sorry. I am unable to answer your query at this time.

4.

Park could not remember when she had first decided to be a psychologist. There was no defining moment, no sudden epiphany. No inspirational role model who had encouraged her in the dream. In fact, almost everyone who knew her in her youth had assumed she would turn out to be a roboticist. She had a hazy memory of typing 'psychology' on the *hobbies and interests* portion of some survey. But where had the impulse come from? She didn't know.

Later, she would test low in amiability on her career placement exams in high school. That was a problem: you needed moderate-to-high scores in amiability, empathy, and self-awareness to even get a degree in the field. The family android, Glenn, informed her that she was too "closed up inside" when he helped her practice for the retakes.

"What is that supposed to mean?" Park had asked, coldly.

"In the animal kingdom, you would be *neofelis nebulosa,*" Glenn had answered.

Whatever that meant. Park had never looked it up; she was afraid to find out exactly what it was. But she got the idea. An elusive, enigmatic thing. Ultimately what Glenn was saying was something she had always known: that she was not a social animal; that she was not meant to be wedged into close contact with other people. That she belonged to a single-cat home. People like her—people turned inward, people solitary and on the fringes of society—were best encountered from afar. Those on the outskirts could not understand the problems of those in the center of things. They couldn't really bridge the gap. She understood this.

But she'd taken the test again anyway.

Park thought about that now, as she helped Hunter sedate the hysterical Elly Ma. On her other side, Natalya was sealing the wound in Elly's arm with a kind of medical glue.

"What kind of nightmare?" Park kept asking Elly, as the woman's eyes flickered under a wave of tab-induced drowsiness. "What were you dreaming about, Elly?"

The climatologist shook her head. "I wasn't in control of myself," she slurred with an effort, as if struggling to speak across a great distance. "There was some other—force guiding me. Controlling me. Making me do things I didn't want to do."

"What things?"

For a moment Elly didn't answer. "I was so cold," she said. "My eyes weren't my eyes. There was no blood in my body. I didn't have a tongue."

God, Park thought. Her blood thumped hard once in her throat. She said, "It was just a dream."

"But it was so *real*."

"It wasn't." She brushed Elly's brow dry with a cloth. "It was only a dream, Elly. Do you understand?"

She attached another sedation tab to the woman's neck. Elly shook her head. "No . . ." she murmured. "No . . . I think that it was really happening. It *is* really happening. I'm going to turn into that. I'm going to die!" She pressed her palms to her temples. Then, in a sudden cry: "Don't put me to sleep again!"

She went limp.

Elly Ma is sick, Park thought. Her heart felt like a burnt walnut; she was cold with a dreadful, unfeeling clarity. *Holt and Reimi are sick. I don't know how to help them. How can I? I'm too different. Apart. I'm* nebulosa.

She glanced at the wound on Elly's arm. Nightmares, she thought, just like Holt. Or at least similar. He hadn't self-harmed. There had to be a connection—but how? Had Holt told Elly about his dream before he'd been sent to the infirmary? Had she simply been affected by the horrible things he had to say? Or was his delusion being transmitted, plague-like, from person to person? Infecting Elly?

No, Park thought. That was irrational. But it was best to quarantine it, whatever it was—keep it in isolation. She would tell no one besides Keller and Wick that Holt and Ma had shared nightmares. Once the idea was planted in a susceptible mind, someone else might manifest it, especially under heightened anxiety. They would have to keep the whole thing hidden until they could find out the cause.

Hunter left the room to fetch Dr. Chanur. Natalya, the only other person left, said: "Have you ever seen anything like this?"

Park shook her head. "Not exactly." She moved Elly's damp, heavy hair from her face; she could feel the heat rising from the woman's skin. A fever, Park thought, which was impossible—space lacked microbes, and it had been far too long since leaving Earth for Elly to get sick from something she'd already had in her system. How could she have a fever?

Psychosomatic, she concluded, just as Natalya said, "She dug into her own arm. Made herself bleed."

"Yes," Park said, because she didn't know what else to say.

Natalya glared. "What are you going to do about this?"

She wants reassurance, Park told herself, *because she's scared*. Or—more likely—Natalya was using the opportunity to challenge her. Question her abilities. She'd been doing it since Antarctica, just as she'd been refusing counseling sessions with Park in the room since Antarctica. Park wanted to feel weariness, impatience, even anger towards the surveyor, but instead felt nothing except a cool disconnected bafflement. As if she were staring at a painting in a museum that she couldn't make sense of. She straightened and said, "Try to get some rest, Severov. You're due to go out tomorrow."

Natalya looked at her as if Park had suggested she launch herself into space. "And how do you expect me to sleep, Doctor, under the circumstances?"

"I can offer you sedatives," Park told her woodenly. "Or the MAD."

Natalya scoffed. "Of course. Your given solutions."

Yes, Park thought, it was a challenge. Natalya was trying to pick a fight with her. And at a time like this, when they had much bigger things to worry about! Where *had* the surveyor gotten all of this hardness, this poisonous hostility, as if everyone in the world had wronged her? She was an orphan, Park knew that. Her file stated that her parents had been killed during the Comeback. But whose hadn't?

Then Park reminded herself that Natalya had raised her six younger siblings in the wildernesses of southern Russia before picking up an ISF contract to get them all to the colony on Luxue. *That* was impressive. The hardships of her life must have forged her into this . . . unyielding, unforgiving creature. In any other situation Park might have admired her steeliness. But because they clashed so much, she could only view the other woman as a nuisance. A wounding presence—like a dagger in her side.

"You're useless," Natalya declared finally, shaking her head and folding herself into her bunk. Park didn't answer; she turned instead to tend to Elly's unconscious figure. After a few moments she heard someone's footsteps in the corridor. When she looked up, she saw Hunter stepping through the threshold again—and Chanur following expressionlessly behind her.

"She's scratched her left arm heavily, but no other injuries," Park said as Chanur brushed past her. "I've given her three sedation tabs. Could you keep her separate from Eric Holt?"

"Holt is gone," Chanur said as she bent over Elly's supine body. "Somehow he left the ward, despite being sedated and watched by one of the bots. I've informed Wick and Captain Sagara. They're searching for him now."

That explained why Sagara hadn't shown up when Elly started screaming, Park thought. *The way she was going on, he'd think she was being murdered.* Then Chanur's words registered. "Wait, Holt is *gone*? What do you mean? Where could he even go?"

Chanur gave her a venomous look. "If I knew that, then he wouldn't be missing, would he?"

Missing, Park thought as Hunter drew her aside. Of course. Of course Elly's episode would somehow trigger an episode of Holt's, from the other side of the ship. Of course Holt would somehow vanish into thin air. That would all make sense, considering how this day was going.

She shook her head. Hunter was saying, "Someone had better inform ISF."

"I don't think there's any need for that," Chanur said from the ground, where she was reading Elly's vitals with a bioscanner.

"Bullshit there isn't," Hunter rapped out. "People are going to pieces. We can't locate a crewmember. They need to know."

"Yes," Park said, trying to shake off the out-of-body giddiness that was threatening to take hold. There was that swaying feeling in her head again, as if she might be space-sick—even though they'd already landed. "Yes, I agree with Hunter. I'll go tell them now."

Chanur just shook her head and shrugged. Suddenly Park noticed that there were still people lingering in the hallway, looking into their narrow room. Conscious of the gummy soap in her hair, of her towel hanging around her body like a soggy tortilla, she nodded her goodbye to Hunter and marched past the onlookers, back to the showers. She hadn't even had time to turn the water off; the steam was almost suffocating. She rinsed off quickly and slipped into her thermal sleeping suit. Her feet were still bare.

Shared psychosis was a possibility, she thought. In the past it had been called *folie a deux*. Madness of two. Two individuals with latent psychosis, living in close proximity, could mutually trigger delusions in each other—could influence each other's delusions so that they became identical. But she'd have to establish that Holt and Ma had had extensive contact—and she found it hard to believe that two separate people with psychotic disorders had been allowed aboard the *Deucalion*. Even with the fast-tracked assembly. She and Keller had thoroughly vetted each crewmember, had conducted all the rigorous tests and simulations. They'd found no trace of anything like this.

Or her infrasound theory was correct. Maybe it wasn't even the sound of the new planet's rotation; things like this happened on Earth, too. Mountain ranges could form shapes that repetitive wind events blasted through at certain velocities, creating sound waves too low to hear. Those sound waves could subtly affect the human mind, causing the same irrational feelings of panic and terror that animals felt before earthquakes. Expeditions had gone mad because of those sound waves. People inexplicably ran out into the cold, stripping their clothes off. Clawing at invisible enemies. Dying with their eyes and tongues missing.

Or, she thought. Or Elly had simply been having a bad dream. People did scratch themselves in their sleep. It wasn't uncommon. The similarities between the dreams could be a coincidence, or otherwise influenced by some innocent external source: a filmstream they had both watched, a book. Park could be overreacting.

She went to discuss it with Commander Wick. It was her way of paying respect; she thought he should be informed before she went to ISF. He shouldn't have to find out about it from the higher-ups. But around the corner from his sleeping quarters, shivering despite her thermal gear, she remembered suddenly that he wouldn't be in his bunk: he had to be out looking for Holt. She listened carefully. There were no alerts sounding, no blaring *awoogas* from the far-off bridge. They obviously didn't view this as some sort of immediate danger. At least not yet.

Then she noticed that someone was talking in front of Wick's bunk. Someone male—and angry. Park peeked around the corner and felt a little jolt in the back of her neck. Boone was standing there, gesturing and snarling at . . . Jimex?

"I told you to leave me the fuck *alone,*" Boone growled in a low, furious voice. Jimex looked amazed by his anger; he wore a look of blank astonishment, as if he were a baby watching someone make faces.

"I am sorry," Jimex said. His silver eyes seemed fixed on a point past Boone's left shoulder. "I meant to assist you."

"I don't need your help," Boone said roughly. "If I did, I would have asked for it. Didn't anyone ever tell you to mind your damn business?"

"No," Jimex answered, with bland politeness.

The military specialist gave him a hard shove. Despite the fact that she knew better, Park found herself stepping out from behind the wall that obscured her from Boone's point of view. Jimex staggered back against the wall behind him, then shot upright again, as if he were a weighted bowling pin.

"Boone," Park said. "What's going on?"

He saw her standing there and rolled his eyes. "Oh, boy," he said, as if he were speaking to some invisible audience. "Here we go." He gave Jimex a contemptuous gesture. "Call off your little clunk, Park. The damn thing won't leave me alone."

She looked at Jimex. "Sergeant Boone was told by Commander Wick to look for Dr. Holt," the android said, in answer to her unspoken question. He didn't look surprised to find her coming to his rescue—but then again, he rarely did. "Dr. Holt is missing."

"What does that have to do with you following Boone?" Park asked.

Jimex's eyes moved from Boone to Wick's door. His head gave a little buzz. "I did not know why it was necessary for him to return to his room," he answered. "Dr. Holt is not there. I thought he might be disobeying his directive."

"That's not your business, even if he is," she told him, signaling him to come stand by her. She was aware of how her body slid in front of his, shielding him from Boone's gaze—as if the custodian android, one head taller than her, was a child for her to protect. Boone watched Jimex retreat behind her with disgust.

"Why *are* you over here?" Park asked him.

"This is my bunk, too," Boone answered, sniffing. "Not just Wick's. Why are *you* here?"

"I needed to talk to Wick. Shouldn't you be looking for Holt?"

Boone sneered. "That's why I came back to my locker. I wasn't going to start the search without this."

He showed her his hip. Affixed to his belt was something that looked like a black pistol with a green sparking light at its top. For a moment Park's vision went dark. It was an ELG—an electrolaser gun—a device that fired such a powerful ionized track of plasma that it could immobilize entire rooms, or melt the teeth of a single assailant. It was like shooting a stream of lightning at a body. Regular guns had been banned off-Earth: the hulls of ships were bulletproof, but that meant the ricochet from one projectile could be devastating to whoever was trapped inside, especially with unpredictable gravity. Electrolaser guns were the next deadliest thing. The ISF claimed that they were non-lethal even in the wrong hands, but—that was just it. They were only claims.

"I don't think that's necessary," Park said, stiff with fear. She meant for Holt, but she also couldn't see why Boone needed a weapon at all. The thought of him using it on a crewmember—or on her—made her stomach lurch. Why did he have such a thing? Had he had it the entire time they'd been on the ship? Did ISF know?

"Then it's a good thing it's not your call, isn't it?" drawled Boone. He sniffed again, rubbed a finger under his nose. "Word has it that Holt's gone crazy. He might be dangerous. We need some way to immobilize him."

"He's not an escaped mental patient. There are other ways."

"Like what? You got a tranquilizer gun?"

She glanced sidelong at Jimex. "The androids could restrain him. He can't hurt them."

"I wouldn't trust a clunker to know Holt from a handgun," Boone said, derisive. "Speaking of, I don't much appreciate you letting this one run wild. It *watches* everybody."

"I'm not responsible for that."

"Sure you're not. Just like you're not responsible for spying on me and Natalya today at lunch."

Park pressed her lips together. "You seem to have the misconception that I'm unduly interested in what you do, Boone," she said. "That I would go out of my way to watch you, through the androids or other means. I don't have the time or energy for that."

"So I *imagined* you eavesdropping on me earlier?"

"You were talking very loudly." Then she looked again at the EL gun at his hip and thought twice about antagonizing him further. Boone saw her look and laughed.

"Is there anything I can do to help?" Park asked him, self-correcting. She cleared her throat. "Anything you need for Holt?"

"No," Boone said, flexing his hands a little. "He's somewhere on this ship. It's only a matter of time until we find him. In the meantime I'd suggest that you hole up somewhere and write your incident report."

That was the soldier's politest way of telling her to fuck off. Park wanted to resist it, to stand up to him. But she scanned his face and saw the sullen gray eyes, the tightly-curled hair, the blocky head scraped clean of fat and kindness. And she knew that it was not a conflict worth winning. He'd find some way to retaliate in the future. "Come," she said softly to Jimex.

The android hesitated, then nodded. "Good night, Sergeant Boone," he said.

Boone was watching Jimex with a grin on his face. "You see that, clunker?" he said, lowering his tone to a horror-story-teller's *sotto voce*. "Your master knows when to leave well enough alone. Follow her example, or I might just zap you with this!"

He pulled out the gun and pointed it at Jimex's face. Jimex looked at Park as if expecting her to tell him when to flinch. Park was speechless with horror. She felt her heel turn, felt her body hurrying itself away from the threat. There was a hot prickling between her shoulders, as if her system expected the shot at any moment; as if it was already anticipating the crackling, blood-boiling blow. Her heart thundered in her ears. Boone saw her fear, and he chuckled softly to himself as she left. Park fled down the corridor with his laugh following her, nipping at her heels like a hound.

"I want you to stay away from him," she told Jimex later, after he had escorted her to her office. "In fact, tell all the androids to, if they can help it. He's—volatile. If he does decide to shoot you with that thing, it's game over for you."

"I didn't know we were playing a game," Jimex intoned. He seemed unaffected by their encounter with Boone.

Park wanted to shake him. *God damn these lower-tier models*, she thought. Sometimes they were so *stupid*. He made her miss Glenn, and she hated that; resented it even more than the danger he kept putting himself in.

"I've been told by the other crewmembers that you keep bothering them," she said aloud. "Why can't you just clean the ship?"

"I have," Jimex said, blinking. "Deck A is ninety-nine point nine nine nine percent—"

"Then at least stay silent when you're done," Park said, exasperated. "Don't talk to anyone except me, unless you absolutely need to. It's for your own good."

Jimex took a while to process this. "I understand," he said finally. His pupils focused and unfocused as his brain adapted to the new directives.

"Good," Park said. She could feel a headache coming on. "Now, just—go somewhere, and enter sleep mode. Don't come out of it until morning. Or unless you see Holt."

"Understood," Jimex said. He stood up and regarded her for a long moment, expressionless. "Thank you, Dr. Park."

"Good night," she said, weary. Then she closed her eyes as she listened to him leave the room, his heavy tread thumping away into the darkness. As frustrated with him as she was, she was a little glad that he had accompanied her into her office. The ship was still on lockdown—it was still technically lights-out hours for the crew—and she had half-expected to find Holt sitting in the shadows when she came in, his features glowing with the MAD greenness. The thought made her heart beat just a little more quickly.

She turned on her console in a rush and recorded a message for the ISF outpost on Corvus. She told them about Elly's nightmares, her symptoms, the similarities to Holt, whose session transcript she had already sent earlier in the day. She mentioned her suspicions of shared psychosis. Holt's escape from the medical bay. She confessed that she wasn't sure what to do.

And then, hesitating, she brought up the fact that Boone was carrying a weapon that could incapacitate the entire crew. She asked, in more diplomatic terms, if the ISF Eos Committee really thought that this was wise.

"I'm standing by for directives," Park said, rounding off the video. She added, unable to stop herself: "Please respond ASAP."

She tapped the button; sent the video rushing off into space. Then she sat back and closed her eyes. It would take eighteen hours for the message to transmit to its destination, another eighteen hours for her to receive an answer. So she had a day and a half to operate on her own before receiving any form of guidance.

Her hair was still wet. She hadn't taken the time to dry it. Park felt like a piece of damp paper—slowly disintegrating, on the edge of falling apart. She felt the tightness around her temples again and quelled it. *Affirmative thoughts*, she told herself, taking a breath. *Positive action*. She went over to the couch and set the MAD to ten minutes.

Fulbreech came in on minute eight. Park heard him enter but couldn't force herself to raise her arms and lift the MAD off of her head. Her brain was adjusting its chemical levels, like a violin being tuned: dopamine and euphoria bloomed through her skull. She said something to him, half-slurring. Fulbreech sat down across from her, in the seat she usually sat in, and waited.

When the MAD powered off, Park lifted the visor and said, "How did you get in?"

She was embarrassed that he'd caught her in a vulnerable position—that he'd found her using the MAD, something he himself always refused. Fulbreech, studying her with interest, said, "You left the door unlocked. They're still looking for Holt. I wanted to check on you before I turned in."

"Check in on me," Park repeated. "Because . . ."

"Well, if this were a horror stream, the woman who goes off into the dark alone is usually found murdered," Fulbreech joked. Then he sobered at her flat expression. "Sorry. I didn't mean—it's just that no one can find him. It's a little uncanny."

"How did he get out of the medical bay?"

"Wick didn't say."

Bullshit, Park wanted to say. She couldn't help but notice that he didn't say *I don't know*—only that *Wick didn't say*. Couldn't help but remember what he had told her, just a few hours ago: that he wouldn't tell her everything. She tried to beam it at him through her eyes—*Are you feeding me bullshit?*

But she recognized in this a danger, a breach in objectivity. Fulbreech wasn't obligated to tell her a thing. But then why go out of his way to win her trust in the first place? The contradiction put her on guard with him. She said in a chilly way, "I see."

"I heard about Ma," Fulbreech continued, probably to divert her. "Are you all right?"

"Yes," Park said, surprised—wondering why he wouldn't ask if *Elly* was all right. Fulbreech, sensing her confusion, explained: "She was your bunkmate, wasn't she? And you had to sedate her? And . . ."

Chagrined, he glanced at the MAD. Park felt a flaring of anger.

"I'm fine, Fulbreech," she said. "Thank you for your concern."

"I'm sure," Fulbreech answered, smiling a little to himself. "You're always fine. I just thought I should ask, since you have to ask everyone else."

Meaning, Park assumed, that he thought no one was around to evaluate the evaluator. And Fulbreech meant to assume that role. She thought to ask him for his credentials. "Where do you think Holt could be?" she asked instead.

He shook his head. "We don't know. He's on the ship, certainly. And the computer tells us he's alive and kicking. He's just squirreled away somewhere."

Park shook her head. "This would be much easier if we had more cameras."

"That's the Privacy Wars for you," Fulbreech answered wryly. "The one time we need constant surveillance, we don't have it." He looked at her face, then away, as if not to stare. Then he looked back again, as if he thought, *Why not stare?* "You're very guarded, you know."

"I'm not," Park answered automatically. It came out sterner than she was hoping, grave—as if she'd taken offense. Fulbreech mused, almost to himself, "Maybe it's part of the job. I don't know. Or maybe you just don't trust anyone."

Why should I? Park thought, sullen. Fulbreech saw it in her face and laughed; she felt an uncomfortable swooping sensation, as if she'd missed a step climbing the stairs in the dark. She looked away and said, "I don't know why it matters to you. Whether I trust anyone or not."

She really was angry with him, she realized. He expected her to share her thoughts with him, to open herself up—and yet he had shown he wouldn't do the same. Of course she mistrusted that. But then the sense of wellbeing planted by the MAD picked up on her negative feeling and swarmed on it. Dampened it. She shifted in her seat and suddenly noticed that a light on her desk console was blinking.

"Have you ever been to the New York biodome?" Fulbreech asked after a moment. She noticed that he didn't answer her question. But had she even really asked one? And was it something she wanted an outright answer to?

"No, I haven't." Park shuddered, thinking of the claustrophobia, the smog forming dirty gray stains against the biofilm as it curved over the city. "Well, once. For the flight to Baikonur. I didn't leave the airport."

"Where are you from originally?"

"I grew up in the New Diego biodome." No harm in disclosing that.

"Ah," Fulbreech said, a little lamely. "I was born in the New Chicago dome—but we moved to Mars when I was a teen. After that, Cambien, Elysium, Halla. I was a ship-brat."

Of course she knew all this: it was in his files. She even knew that his great-great-grandfather had been a famous NASA astronaut, and his uncle, Isaac Fulbreech, was one of the engineers who'd settled Phobos. His brother was a lead ship-builder for the fleet there, too. ISF ran in his blood. But she said, just to be polite: "I hear that Halla is nice."

"Oh, it is."

"Is your family there now?"

He paused. "My parents are. My brother and his wife still live on Phobos. They just had their first baby. A boy."

Park looked at him. She read no lie in his countenance, but there had been that barest flicker of hesitation. "Congratulations," was all she could think to say.

Fulbreech made a visible effort to change the subject, turning toward her. "Your story is a different one," he said. "This is your first trip into space, isn't it?"

Now where had he heard that from? She supposed he was more observant than she gave him credit for; she'd been careful not to tell anybody that explicitly, wary of coming off as inexperienced. Easy to undermine. She thought about how Sagara had found the anti-emesis tabs. "I enjoy space travel," Park said, levelly.

Fulbreech smiled. "You're not much for talking, are you? Not when it's about stuff you're not interested in."

"I talk."

He was grinning now, rubbing the faint golden stubble on his chin. "But do you *say* much? I have such a hard time figuring you out."

Ditto, Park wanted to say—an embarrassingly dated term that she knew he would laugh at. She wasn't sure if she wanted him to laugh at her or not. She stole a quick look at his hand, resting on his knee: it was tan and broad and strong, and honest somehow. She said, to prove him wrong, "When I was younger, I was afraid of going into space."

Fulbreech looked at her, surprised. "Why was that?"

"I don't know," Park admitted. "It was—too dark for me. Too empty. I was used to crowds of people, like in the domes."

"Interesting. But you're used to it now?"

"I'm well-adjusted." As if that was accurate. But she couldn't think of anything else to say; she'd reached the end of her conversational props. She couldn't even talk about the weather, because there was no weather on the ship. "You mentioned New York," she said finally, a little desperately.

"Right," Fulbreech said. He leaned back and stared up at the office's gray ceiling, as if viewing some invisible projection up there. "There's a famous art gallery there. I can't remember the name. Something French. My father took my brother and me when we were teens. I can give you the address sometime."

He was very optimistic, Park thought to herself, thinking of disaster, of Holt and Ma—but she decided to try her hand at the game. "Or you could just take me there yourself."

Fulbreech's eyebrows raised. "What do you mean?"

"I assume you're coming back to Earth when the mission is done."

Fulbreech's face went blank. It was momentary, but Park saw it: confusion, and then shame. Quickly he hid it, but in that moment Park felt such a hatred of him that even the dumb peaceful glow of the MAD faded a little, burning at the ends like a cigarette. He was too attractive, she decided; it annoyed her. His jawline was absurd. The scraps of stubble, deliberate, vain. And the boyishness, the goodness—it was a front. She was half-convinced that ISF had put him in her way as a means to test her.

"Of course," Fulbreech said slowly. Constructing a lie. "But I might have to hop off before then—maybe when we resupply at Corvus. They may want me to consult with the researchers there."

"Of course," Park echoed. Her lips felt stiff as she spoke. She noticed that his leg was close to hers, under the table that separated them. She moved hers away. *Liar.*

Fulbreech looked away from her. "That gallery," he said finally, after a moment of heavy silence. "There was this amazing statue in it. I want you to see it someday—you remind me of it. Or it reminds me of you."

"It was nude, I'm sure." To her satisfaction Fulbreech reddened and coughed.

"It was, in fact," he said. "It was of this naked woman, sitting in the lotus position. Looking very composed. Striving for inner peace. Total zen, you know. The artist won prizes for it. People said her expression was as mysterious as the Mona Lisa's."

"I see."

"But the most striking thing about it wasn't exactly her expression. Not to me." He looked thoughtful. "It was that the woman's body was full of cracks. Fissured all over. And there was light coming out of the cracks. That was what made it such a masterpiece, everybody said. That the statue was full of things you didn't expect—empty spaces, voids, chasms. Flaws. Well, that's what the critics called them, but I used the term 'mysterious places,' personally." He paused. "Things you wanted to look into and explore, only the light was too bright for you to look at, once you came too close."

He looked at her. Park was aware that something was happening, that there was a current of meaning passing between them that she ought to turn her cheek to. She had a hot, tense feeling in her stomach, as if she were awaiting some reprimand. She said, lamely, "I don't understand."

"I didn't, either," Fulbreech said. "Not then." Then he stood up. "Good night, Park."

She could not help but stare at him. "Good night."

He made to leave, then paused at the door. "There's a solar wind that's about to hit, by the way. A proton storm. I thought you should know; I guess they're pretty common here. We'll have to detach from the surface and shield ourselves on the dark side of Eos for the day. Otherwise the radiation will cook us like bacon."

"Thank you," Park said as he turned away. It was a white flag, she decided. An olive branch. As a non-expedition member, she wasn't privy to such information. Things and decisions on the ship just *happened*, and she was lucky if she got to hear the reasons for it afterward. Fulbreech wanted to give her that much knowledge—make sure she wasn't too left in the dark. Perhaps to make amends for earlier, sensing her upset. She didn't know if she felt more grateful to him or annoyed.

He left. Park went to her flashing console and found an error message from the ship's computer, METIS: it informed her that it had been unable to send her latest message out to ISF Corvus.

The atomic storm, Park thought, too tired to feel anything other than numbness. All of that radiation must have interfered with her signal; communications would probably be down until the solar wind cleared. What goddamn inconvenient timing! Of course the storm would hit just as she needed to call for help. It was almost beginning to feel as if the ship was cursed.

She sat there for a while in the dark, watching the simulated fish tank in the wall. Her favorite fish, the hologram of the bumblebee goby, was nowhere to be seen, no matter how much she hunted for it. *A glitch in the program*, Park thought, thinking of Holt. Just like everything else in this place.

After a while she felt a slight pressure change in the air—an airlock closing somewhere far off. Her ears plugged; a great hush seemed to settle over the *Deucalion*. She felt a tremor under her feet, then the familiar stagger as the ship lifted up its great legs. Energy simmered softly through the walls. Park felt both relief and a tinge of panic: for a moment she could convince herself that they were leaving Eos altogether, that they were headed back to Corvus to get Holt and Ma help, and to wake up Reimi Kisaragi.

But no, she thought. Impossible. Colony missions were never abandoned. Not even if people died.

She closed her eyes. Lay down when she felt the gut-bouncing lift of reconfiguring gravity. They were better equipped for solar storms and subatomic winds than most expedition ships. Not because they had more advanced technology, or a better-trained crew—but because they had less to save. Normally there were plants that needed to be covered or moved to protected areas. Genetically augmented animals to be herded into the little shelters. Seeds and embryos to be locked into the vaults. But here, on the *Deucalion,* there was none of that. Only the directive to hide—and wait.

I can do that, Park thought. She flattened her body against the cold, viscoelastic foam of the couch and imagined the *Deucalion* drifting silently through the dark waters of space. Her head felt full of static.

They were off; there was the jolt as they broke out of the atmosphere. The sounds of the ship slowly receded. If Park tuned out the low roar of the engines, she could pretend that she was totally alone, a single soul in a black and soothing vacuum. Thank God Fulbreech was gone. He would have tried to coach her through liftoff, talked to cover up the blast, tried to make her feel comfortable. Maybe he would have looked earnestly into her eyes and asked if she needed him to hold her hand.

Park's insides shriveled like peach pits. Solitude for her was like a religious blessing to others: it was her church of one. Always she closed the doors behind her with the awareness that she was giving herself sanctuary, an opportunity to cleanse and be purified. Fulbreech was like the neighbor who kept her from shutting the door, asking if she was interested in participating in the annual bake sale.

That was the problem, Park thought. Fulbreech thought she was mysterious, and that appealed to him. He thought that her guardedness, her need to be alone, was all a defense mechanism that he had to get past. Either she was a puzzle to be solved—and then later, discarded—or he simply thought that he needed to get to know her better, to break through to some other place, some core where another person lived inside of her. But that was the catch. There was no other person, no self that she was hiding. Park was who she seemed to be from the outside. That would never change. Fulbreech just hadn't realized it yet.

She liked Hilbert's illustration of infinity, using a hotel as an example. A hotel with an infinite number of rooms could accommodate an infinite number of guests, even if the whole place was already fully occupied. Whenever a new guest arrived, the guest in room one would simply move to room two; the guest in room two to room three; and so on and so forth. What Park liked was that, even with an infinite line of people waiting out the door, the thought of making guests share a room never occurred to anyone in the hotel. Each guest had to be solitary; each had to have a room of their own, even if it meant that everyone else performed an infinite series of actions to ensure this. It was the natural order of things, assumed. This made sense to her. She wished the *Deucalion* was Hilbert's hotel.

But it's not, Park thought then. She was not like the hotel guest, come in safely from the night. She was more like a glacier, alone and adrift on a warming sea. Cold, remote. But shrinking rapidly under the circumstances.

5.

[Hi,

Another day, another transcript. I segmented off some of the stuff that didn't matter, to keep the file size small. You were right to have your suspicions: it seems some very weird shit went down here. I hope you're doing okay. I hope you're staying safe. We are doing our best here, though every day I think Requisitions is going to storm our place and throw us out. I hope that doing this is worth it. I hope that Eos can really be a home.

Love,

S.S.]

VIDEO LOG #8—Ship Designation CS *Wyvern* 7079
Day 2: 9:42 UTO

Daley: And you're sure it's okay for us to go out there.

Taban: That's what the HARE said. Look: rad levels are okay. Average temperature is -125 Celsius during sun-facing hours. That's about the temperatures of the poles back on Mars.

Daley: What is that in Fahrenheit?

Taban: Are you serious?

Daley: I know. My old partner tried to get me to do everything in metric, too. Some things are just hardwired.

Taban: You really are old. Minus 125 Celsius is, uh, about negative 200 Fahrenheit.

Daley: (grunt)

Taban: It's doable. Our suits will work, anyway. Air doesn't seem breathable, but when is it ever? We'll need to bring auxiliary tanks. But the HARE was out there for over twelve hours and it was fine.

Daley: It's just. It got dark so fast.

Taban: The suns here are weaker than even Tau Ceti—that's why it's so cold. 'Daylight' won't last long. We've gotta move fast if we want to get this thing fixed.

Daley: Right.

Taban: And hey, will you grow some balls? You were going to send me out there to fix the engine, no problem.

Daley: All right, all right. You're right. Don't know what's going on with me. Let's go.

[The HARE watches as Daley and Taban step into their cybernetic exo-armor suits, which are scuffed and battered from presumably years of outer-ship repairs and mining. Old-model suits, they look to be of Chinese or Martian make. Daley is breathing heavily. Taban finishes suiting up first and waits for him. They give each other the sign for all-clear and open the airlock of the ship. The vacuum of the *Wyvern*'s air being sucked into the wind outside is so loud that the recording goes completely silent.]

[Daley and Taban leave the ship. The HARE follows, marking the landing site's coordinates as an arbitrary Prime Meridian, with coordinates of 53°45′N 0°0′E. The two men shield their eyes and scan the horizon. Except for their heights, it's hard to tell the difference between them: their suits and golden faceplates look exactly the same.]

Daley: Hey, this isn't so bad.

Taban: I guess. Careful; don't fall and break your hip.

Daley: Let's look around.

Taban: What? I thought you wanted me to repair the FTL engine.

Daley: You can do it in a minute. Come on, you don't want to look around? This is an undiscovered planet. Where's your sense of adventure?

Taban: Just a second ago you were scared shitless of even going outside. Now you're calling it an adventure?

Daley: The fresh air is inspiring.

Taban: Should I get the railgun?

Daley: What for? There aren't any humans on this planet, the thing said so.

HARE: Correction: there are no humans within the parameters of the area I scanned.

Daley: No one asked you.

Taban (sighing): Okay, fine. Just a quick look around.

Daley: That's what I'm talking about.

[The camera lens frosts over slightly. There is no sign of the fractal structures on the horizon, the ones that had been in sight during the *Wyvern's* descent. The ground around the HARE is icy and flat, but it looks like it has a strange consistency: not like snow, more like frozen cobwebs. Daley and Taban seem to have trouble walking through it. Their boots sink several centimeters into the ground with each step, in squeaking crunches. Daley curses for a few moments, his breathing labored. Taban remains silent.]

Daley: Look at all this. Think about it. We're the first and only humans to set foot on this planet. If I hadn't taken that shortcut around Luxue, we never would have found this place.

Taban: Uh-huh.

Daley: Look at that shit. What is that? Snow? Ice? Who knows? It's all new. Right?

Taban: Yeah.

Daley: Isn't this great?

Taban: I mean, sure. But it's not like we can tell anyone about it, afterwards. Otherwise ISF will be on our asses faster than a rocket of snakes on a jackrabbit.

Daley: What?

Taban: Nothing. Never mind. Also, isn't Sunfarer going to be pissed that we're so late with their payload?

Daley: Fuck Sunfarer.

Taban: All right.

Daley: . . .

Taban: . . .

Daley: We could sell the coordinates, you know. On the sly.

Taban: Huh?

Daley: You know. Anonymously. I bet we could make a lot of money that way. It's like—space tourism. You know? Like a secret club. I bet people would pay a lot of money to have access to a planet no one else knows about.

Taban: I don't think anything stays anonymous with ISF.

Daley: Trust me, it does. And why do they get first claim on new planets, anyway? Whatever happened to the spirit of entrepreneurship? Anyone who finds something first should get the rights to it, right?

Taban: There must be a reason for them to do it this way.

Daley (snorting): I bet.

Taban: . . .

Daley: . . .

HARE: . . .

Daley: Daleytaban. Hapfin?

Taban: What?

Daley: What we could call it. Some combination of our names. That's fair, right? I like Hapfin.

Taban: . . .

Daley (breathing heavily): What do you think?

[Taban and Daley are working their way across the sticky half-ice in a circle, keeping the ship at their right shoulders at all times. The HARE focuses its lens on seemingly random patches of frozen ground.]

Taban: You hear that sound, HARE? The sound of Daley wheezing away?

HARE: Affirmative.

Taban: That's the sound of a lifetime of spongeburgers and milkshake cubes.

HARE (processors whirring): These are the things that nourish USER Daley?

Taban: That's right.

Daley (breathing heavily): Fuck off—with your—alpha wave diet. That shit's for Martian hippies.

Taban: What are hippies?

Daley: Group of people—back on Earth. In the old times.

Taban: Oh. Did they also support eco-friendly, waste-free eating habits?

Daley: Something like that.

Taban (checking his wrist console): Okay, I think it's time to head back.

Daley: What? Why? It's only been twenty minutes.

Taban: Yeah, but I need to look at that engine if I want to make the most of the daylight and this oxygen tank. And you're fat. So you need to go back and rest.

Daley: I'm fine.

Taban: No doubt. But we really need to get back. This has been fun and all, but it's not what we're here for.

Daley: It could be.

Taban: Let's go back.

VIDEO LOG #10—Ship Designation CS *Wyvern* 7079
Day 2: 19:02 UTO

[Back inside the ship. The HARE sits in the corner of the cockpit while Taban lies on his back, tinkering with something under the dashboard. Daley enters the room, sweating.]

Taban (speaking from under the dashboard): Where have you been?

Daley (taking off gloves): Out.

Taban (rolling out from under the dashboard): Out? You were out there again?

Daley: Yeah. Just going for a walk.

Taban: You really shouldn't go out there alone, Daley. What if you slipped and fell on the ice? Or your oxygen tank sprung a leak? Or you got lost? We wouldn't know.

Daley: Who's 'we'?

Taban: Me and the HARE.

Daley: Oh. Well, come out with me next time.

Taban: I've been fixing this damn engine.

Daley: How's it looking?

Taban: I'll need at least another half-day or so to get it running. It's a two-person job. The HARE helps, but—

Daley: Uh-huh. So, listen—

Taban: —unfortunately neither of you have any engineering experience. What?

Daley: Let's claim this place.

Taban: I thought we already did. What'd you call it? Hapfin?

Daley: It's better than Harpa, or whatever you said for its designation. But I mean *officially* claim it.

Taban: And how do we do that? You wanna leave a flag with our names here after we leave?

Daley: No. I say we go to ISF and tell them we found it.

Taban: Oh. So . . . No.

Daley: Hear me out.

Taban: Huh.

Daley: We go to ISF, right? We tell them that we found this amazing, *virgin* planet. But we don't give them the coordinates to it unless we get credit for finding it. And a cut of the profits.

Taban: Profits? Have you seen this place? It's a frozen ball of ice in space. What kind of profits do you think we're going to get?

Daley: It's a brand spanking new planet, Fin! There's gotta be something here. Some resource, some chemical element we don't have back on Earth! Something! They're at least going to pay to have researchers come out here. We don't have the resources to mine anything other than ice, but if something's here, and the ISF can get at it—

Taban: And what makes you think they'd honor any agreements they made with us? They'd say, "Oh, sure, you can have the money, you can name the planet," we give them the coordinates, and then it's fuck off Fin and Hap, no one's ever going to believe you.

Daley: We'd come up with a backup plan. We could—we could threaten to release the HARE tapes to the public. Yes! We could do that. Their reputation's already hurting bad, with the rebels and the privacy shit—they'd be scared shitless, they'd have to listen—

Taban: Daley . . .

Daley: Listen. This could be big. I know this is your first job, but you're thinking too small—clients, deliveries, Sunfarer, all of that other shit. But trust the guy who's been doing this for twenty years: it's not worth it. I don't think you've really grasped how huge it is that we've found this place. I think we've gotta take advantage of it. I think we've gotta make our mark. It was—

Taban: Don't say it was fate that led us to this place. Please don't say that.

Daley: Okay. I won't say that. But I'm serious. I have this feeling that something valuable could be here. We just have to spend a few days looking around. If we find something, we can take a sample, show it to ISF. We say, "There's a lot more where this came from!" But we don't tell you where it is until we get paid. And recognized. You know?

Taban: Daley. I just want to go home.

Daley: So do I. But I want to go home *rich.* The king of a new planet.

Taban (rubbing his face): . . .

Taban: So, what, you want us to stay a few more days and . . . look around?

Daley: That's exactly what I want.

Taban: . . . Okay. I mean, it's going to take me at least another day just to repair the FTL, anyway. I guess we can explore more while I do that.

Daley: Yes! That's what I'm talking about, Fin!

Taban: But no going out without each other. Or without the HARE. I'm serious, Daley. No going out by yourself.

Daley: Sure, sure. We're all in this together. No making it alone.

6.

Park grew up an only child. She never knew her mother, who was a Dryad—one of the traveling nomads that now lived in the wildernesses blanketing Earth. Park's father, a plant researcher, had encountered Park's mother during a field study of the kudzu vine, the growth rate of which had been drastically mutated by the Comeback. He told it that way to his brother, too—"encountered" her, as if Park's mother were a wild animal that he had happened to come across. Maybe that was how he really thought of her. He said that the woman, Willow, had been born into the jungles of the Comeback, had grown up with no education and no modern technology to speak of. She'd come with him into the city for a short time to give birth to Park, then vanished back into the dense wildlands, never to be heard from again.

Park's father went after her, of course. They found his body weeks later, bloated and stripped naked by human scavengers. He had walked right into a pocket of hyper-rich, dense oxygen created by the Comeback plants, a natural trap that filled a victim's blood with tiny, rapid bubbles as he hiked on. He'd had a grand mal seizure and died without leaving a will. After that, Park was given to his only living relative, his younger brother Sylas: a terse zoologist who was not very comfortable around human children.

After hearing the stories, Park—who even as a child was not overly given to whimsy—often fantasized that her mother was something of a jungle queen. Tanned, muddied, she'd roam the dark groves of Park's imagination with an untamed mane of hair and rattling anklets of animal bone, ululating to her tribal kinsmen and fending off genetically spliced leopards with spears she'd carved from flint.

When she grew older, Park realized that the reality of it was probably not so glamorous. Real Dryads and Dryadjacks—or Ferals, as the unkinder term for them went—were dirty, vicious scavengers, thickly cloaked to protect themselves from thorns and masked to prevent their own suffocation from the oxygen traps. Illiterate, they were usually ready to cut your throat for anything as shiny as a keychain.

No way of knowing whether her mother fell into this group, or if she was one of the rarer, more peaceful Dryads who roamed the jungles crooning about Providence and the bounty of Mother Earth. No picture of her existed, and her father had never even told anyone the woman's last name. For all they knew, Park's mother hadn't even known it herself.

There were plenty of those homeless, nameless transients in the world back then. The Comeback was just beginning to die out: a series of natural disasters that had devastated Earth's population, tailed by decades of hyper-accelerated plant growth. People went to sleep in their normal beds and, overnight, found their walls and mattresses invaded by plants. And that was only if they were lucky—if they had beds left at all, after the relentless barrage of tsunamis and earthquakes and volcanic eruptions that had wiped out half of the world's cities.

But everyone agreed that the plants were the worst part. There was no way to fight them; how could anyone battle the encroachment of something that swallowed human structures so utterly? How could they fight against the planet itself? Bombs did nothing; bullets were wasted on targets that threaded through the very floorboards. Any chemicals that might have been effective at beating back the invasion would have also killed or sickened any humans in the area. There was no winning that war. Maybe if they had had time to prepare, some kind of warning—but everything had fallen apart so fast.

Pundits claimed that the phenomenon was Earth's retaliation against millennia of human pollution: the planet's immunoreaction to heightened levels of carbon dioxide. A cleansing event. The system purging itself of the diseases that were killing it. The plants soaked up and converted the dangerous levels of CO2 in the atmosphere—but they also happened to subsume the very structures that had created that CO2 in the first place. It was, the pundits said, the era of humanity's reckoning. Earth's Comeback.

Hence the aimless wanderers, the refugees, the people raised to adulthood in the wild. There were biodome cities, of course, which offered some protection against the colonizing plants—but they never had enough room, or otherwise people didn't have enough money to make it in.

And then there were the budding colonies in space, providentially placed by the Interstellar Frontier mere years before the Comeback hit. Most people fled to the sanctuaries on Phobos and Mars; there was plenty of room there. The only catch was affording it, and if you couldn't afford it, you had to contract yourself to a lifetime of employment to the ISF. A rite of conscription, it was called. A lifetime of obeying their every command. But it was, people claimed, a small price to pay considering the devastation that awaited them back on Earth. They shed and discarded their old planet like it was yesterday's damp coat.

Park was fortunate enough to grow up in one of the biodomes, a shining construction off the California coast. Often she looked out past the clear walls, toward the shore, and imagined a figure emerging from the compressed green carpet of trees. The figure, blurrily, would have a face similar to her own, with wild cascading hair and arms tattooed with plant dye. She imagined the figure spotting her in the heart of the city and beckoning. At her signal, Park would be lifted out of New Diego's glass bubble and deposited into her mother's arms, which would feel like the bowers of a tree.

But of course, the figure never came.

"What was my father like?" she asked her uncle Sylas once.

He had been silent for a while. "He was a God-loving man," he said, finally, decisively.

At the time, Park misunderstood this: she did not know who God was, and assumed it was some other, secret adult term for her mother. And therefore, her mother must be God. But later she would realize that Sylas was most likely being sarcastic: would a God-loving man really tumble around with an unwed Feral woman in the mud and the leaves?

"Perhaps," Glenn had said once, when she was older. "Recall the story of Adam and Eve."

"That would make me Cain," Park said, who had been reading up on the subject. "And you'd be Abel. And that means we'll try to murder each other."

He'd blinked, perfectly serious. "I would never harm you."

Park had turned away. "I know."

She was a stoic child—watchful, perspicacious. Almost fierce in her solitude. Throughout her youth, her uncle—awkward in the presence of a little girl—left the majority of the child-rearing to a top-of-the-line nanny bot: an android named Sally. And then, when Park was older, Glenn.

Park remembered the first time she encountered Sally, with her shining limbs, her bland smile. She had entertained no notions that Sally was her returned mother: she was far too tame, too ordinary-looking, with her crisp white uniform and her brown hair scraped back in a bun. The child that had been Park had said, "Who are you?"

"I'm Sally," Sally answered. "I live here now."

"Why?"

"I'm here to take care of you."

Park had said nothing; had only gauged this new presence silently. Sally hauled her up by the armpits and set her on the high barstool her uncle had forbidden her from climbing on; she began to roll the dough for a flourless bread. Park had never seen or eaten bread before. Many common crops, including wheat, had been wiped out by the invasion of the Comeback plants, and were only eaten now as a luxury.

At first she merely watched, fascinated by the contortions of forming dough in Sally's hands. When Sally offered her a wad, Park refused, shying away; she wasn't used to dirtying her hands.

"I just want to look," she said. She was five.

Sally switched tactics. "Don't you want to help me?" Her kind, tinny voice sounded as if she were speaking from the inside of a metal trash can. Park was surprised, and strangely moved; she nodded. No one had ever asked her for her help before.

She remembered the softness of Sally's dusty hands—the comfort of kneading the cool dough. Sally had encouraged her to taste a piece of it. "Children at your age develop through sensory play and kinetic experimentation," she said.

Park had not understood this or what it meant, but sensed that it was important. She obeyed, putting the soft little triangle of dough in her mouth, making a face as it dissolved saltily on her tongue.

"Why did you make me do that?" she asked.

"Because," Sally answered serenely, "it's the only way you'll learn."

Holt had not been found by morning. Vincent Sagara sent out a curt announcement about it over the neural inlay system, his low and fricative voice speaking directly into Park's ear and jolting her awake. He spoke one sparse sentence detailing Holt's "absconding" and another about holding a ship-wide meeting later in the afternoon, after the day's expeditions were over. He rounded off with a promise to find Holt by the end of the day and said that, to the best of his knowledge, everyone on board was still safe.

Then, abruptly, he stopped talking, leaving an eerie silence throbbing in Park's skull.

Although he sounded as calm as ever, the news sparked a fervor in the rest of the crew. At breakfast, Park found everyone gathered in the mess hall in intense little groups, swapping theories about what was going on with Holt and why he would have chosen to vanish. Thankfully, no one seemed to mention anything about his having nightmares, or connected him to the case of Elly Ma—who Chanur said suffered from a panic attack, no doubt under orders from Sagara to keep hysteria from spreading.

Park wondered if she, too, was expected to take an active role in the campaign to soothe the nervous minds aboard the ship. Common sense said that she, now the expedition's head psychologist, ought to take the lead; but neither Wick nor Sagara had said anything to her about it. And fear had an unusual way of actually improving the crew's relations with each other. Holt's absence unified everybody: it set aside the usual frictions and backbiting, making the crewmembers eager and clingy and conspiratorial with each other.

They also became unusually accommodating when it came to authority, and being given orders. Scientists and security were typically a combustible mix: the researchers of the expedition were academics, heads of their own departments back home, and used to drawing their own conclusions. They did not respond well to being told what to do, and there was often tension between them and the likes of Sagara, Hunter, Boone, and even Wick. But today, contrarily—vexingly—they were all as docile and compliant as cows in a meadow. Park was not needed to tame the mob.

Not that she could have, anyway, she thought gratefully as she gulped down her orange juice. No one usually listened to her, even—or especially—while under duress.

She decided to join the search for Holt herself. Keller was still busy somewhere with her "project," and with Fulbreech and the others sent out onto the ice, she thought that Sagara and Boone needed all the help they could get.

And she took Jimex with her. She was still nervous about leaving him alone; about Boone running into him while armed with that deadly electrolaser gun.

Besides, the androids of the ship would be better at ferreting out Holt than the humans would; they were more intimately familiar with the *Deucalion* and its inner workings. They would not be frightened away by moving shadows or strange sounds.

Then Jimex informed her that it was actually an android who had lost Holt.

"He was being monitored," the custodian told her bluntly. "By Ellenex. Dr. Chanur sedated Dr. Holt and then told Ellenex to keep watch."

"Then how did he escape?" Park asked. Briefly she felt a flicker of guilty awareness: she really *did* use Jimex as a source of information. As a spy.

Jimex hesitated. "I am not sure," he admitted. "Ellenex did not explain well. Dr. Chanur wants to have her decommissioned, since Officer Kisaragi is not available to diagnose her."

"Is Ellenex damaged?"

"She is now." He said it, as always, without emotion. "Dr. Chanur was very angry when she discovered Dr. Holt's absence. She . . ." He seemed to know to cut himself off. "The other synthetics are trying to think of ways to repair her without breaching our protocols. And again, Officer Kisaragi is not available to help."

Park sighed. It was typical. The crewmembers were discouraged from purposefully damaging the robots—obviously—but only on the grounds that they were the property of ISF. There was no *punishment* for taking out your frustration on an android. To some it was like aiming a kick at a trash can, shaking an uncooperative vending machine. Of course Ellenex had been blamed for Holt's disappearance. It would surprise no one if Chanur had "decommissioned" her right then and there.

She mused on it a while. She had noticed that some androids seemed to prefer the word "synthetic" when referring to themselves, though in the past she couldn't understand why. It emphasized their difference, their artifice. "Android" at least implied some semblance of humanity: *and-* for man, *oid* meaning in the likeness of.

But maybe that was the point, she thought. Maybe they didn't want to be like man at all.

"I'm sorry to hear that," she said eventually. "I hope Ellenex is all right. Do you know how Elly Ma is?"

Jimex opened his hands a little. "She is stable," he said. "Sedated. Still in the ward. There are now many others guarding her."

"I see." Park flicked through the numerous streams of data on her inlays: METIS, the ship's computer, told her there were now four androids assigned with guard duty over Ma. "I suppose that's something, at least." Then she paused for a moment, evaluating the numerous bits and pieces of information that seemed largely indecipherable to her. METIS told her that she didn't have the clearance to access most of these cryptic streams. "How many video cameras are there on the ship?"

"Twelve," Jimex answered blandly.

"Where are they?"

"Placed in key areas of operation."

"Such as?"

"Most of the exits. A few of the labs. Places where footage would need to be reviewed. But there are many other places that are not under that sort of surveillance."

"Is it true that that's because of Privacy Wars nonsense, or are we just underfunded?"

"I don't understand."

She shook her head. "It's nothing. Who has access to these cameras?"

"Only Captain Sagara, Sergeant Boone, and Commander Wick." He hesitated. "There are also . . ."

"What?"

Jimex averted his eyes. "Captain Sagara instructed me not to say."

That gave her a chill. But if Jimex had direct orders from a higher-ranking crewmember not to tell her something, it was a fruitless endeavor to try and weasel it out of him. Android logic meant that she would have to go through hours of loopholes and verbal puzzles to try to get even the smallest detail of use. So she shrugged and told him to lead her to whatever area he thought needed searching. She herself did not know what places the others had searched, what their method for combing the ship was. But she trusted that Jimex—either through that network of information all the androids seemed to share, or through some strange instinct of his own—could guide her to where she needed to be.

The ship swayed beneath them as they walked. They were still hiding in the lee of Eos's bulk, to avoid the proton storm bombarding its light side. Park's efforts to resend her messages to ISF Corvus had, once again, failed. Before breakfast she had also recorded a memo to send out to the crew, offering counseling if anyone had concerns about the events of the night before. She'd prepared a script in case anyone happened to inquire about the cause of Holt and Ma's behavior. "Standard emotional distress," she'd say. "Normal for colony missions. Let's talk about you."

But no one came to see her.

She passed a few crewmembers on her walk with Jimex, earning curious looks and even—in the case of Natalya Severov—surly glares. She even ran into Commander Wick, who looked tired, hassled. He didn't question her about where she was going with their android janitor. He did say, "Park. Thanks for handling all that with Ma last night."

"Of course," Park said. She wanted to ask him about how his search was going, but sensed that it would only lead to more awkwardness, stone-walling—as in the case of Fulbreech. So she said, "Are you aware that Boone has an EL gun on this ship?"

Wick looked at her, surprised. "Why shouldn't he?" he asked. "He's in charge of military operations. He's here to provide protection."

"He keeps it in your room," Park said, a little flustered by his non-reaction. "While you're sleeping. It should be in an armory of some kind. There should be accountability. You don't think so?"

"I think," Wick said, "that I trust everyone on this ship to do their job. You should, too."

She was met everywhere with those kinds of dead ends. Most of the crewmembers were preoccupied with scuttling around, whispering to each other, looking uneasily at the ends of the long corridors. The ones she could stop and talk to were always in a hurry to get to someplace else. There was a heavy, simmering feeling in the air, as if rainclouds were about to move in.

Jimex eventually led her to Deck C, the underbelly of the ship and the floor that held most of the storage rooms and utility closets. He didn't offer any reasoning for why he would take her there, but Park saw the logic in it: there were so many unoccupied little cubbyholes that Holt could easily be squirreled away in one of them.

They descended together into the gut of the ship—down the humid, winding passageways that Park imagined were its intestines. Far off there was the faint rattling of chains, the groaning of metal as it expanded and contracted with the changes in heat. It sounded like the movements of ghosts. Park felt as if she were going underground, as if the light was receding—and it was already dim enough as it was. Her arms prickled; she felt as if she were being watched by something behind her, at the end of the corridor. She had to stop herself from turning around.

She put her hand on Jimex's arm, briefly, to assure herself of his solidity. His presence. Jimex said, without judgment: "You are frightened."

"No," Park corrected. "Just—getting my bearings. I've never been to this part of the ship before. There was never a reason for me to come down here."

"I am down here very often," Jimex remarked, almost mournfully. "It's the part of the ship that needs the most cleaning."

"And you think Holt might be somewhere here?"

"It would be where I would hide."

It was funny, Park thought, how she could miss the passenger areas so quickly, when just the day before she had lamented their crowdedness, their claustrophobic warmth. Deck C felt remarkably murky; the ceiling was oppressively low. More than that, the absence of life in the alien tunnels did frighten her—but she didn't want Jimex to know that. He had to spend every day down here, alone. No wonder he was so insistent on tagging along with her afterward. Machines, too, probably hated to be lonely.

She rounded the corner with him, half-groping her way in the cold light. Jimex seemed to be leading her toward a trio of doors, stamped into a recess in the wall. She had to squint through the gloom to pick them out. They seemed as nondescript as any of the other doors on the deck, just as gray and inert and unmarked. They looked as if they might hold something as mundane as tissue paper, or dehydrated cheese.

Then she noticed that there was a figure slouching against the middle door.

"Holt?" Park called.

The figure stirred, straightening. There was a crackling green light at its hip.

Boone, Park thought, with an electrifying surge of nerves. And his EL gun. She stopped several yards away.

"Park," Boone said. His face was in deep shadow. "What are you doing down here?"

She expected more snark, bawdy threats like the night before—but his tone was flat and quiet. She surprised herself by retorting, "What are *you* doing down here?"

"Nothing," Boone said, without inflection. Then: "You can't be down here. Go back to Deck A."

"I'm looking for Holt," Park said. "Jimex thought he might be down here."

"He isn't," Boone said. "I've been down here all night. I would know." Then, casting a glance at Jimex, who looked at Boone as impassively as if he were a stranger, he said again: "You can't be down here. I'm serious."

"You've been down here all night?" Park repeated. "Shouldn't you be helping Sagara and Wick?"

"I am helping."

"Do they know you've been down here?" She looked at the door behind him; strained to hear any sound behind it. What was Boone doing, hanging around? Was he sneaking some supplies from the maintenance closets? Did he have another cache of guns hidden away somewhere? Or—more sinisterly—she had the brief idea that Holt was behind the door, that Park would hear his muffled screams and open the door to find him trussed up like a holiday bird. Boone saw her looking at the door and said, "Goodbye, Park."

Just then they both heard footsteps from down the hall. *Boone called in reinforcements,* thought Park, turning. To shuffle her off. He really meant to keep her away. She felt her hands loosening, the way she'd seen martial artists sliding into stances before combat. *Ridiculous,* she thought. *Boone has his gun. No use in putting up a fight.*

But it wasn't Hunter, Boone's second, or even Wick or Sagara. Park squinted at the thin, swaying form that was drawing closer to them through the gloom. A man. Tall. Not Fulbreech or Wan Xu. Who was it?

"It is Dr. Eric Holt," Jimex declared, as tonelessly as if he were announcing the time.

Holt, Park thought, with a prickle of recognition. He really had been down here, after all. Or was he meeting secretly with Boone?

"Where have you been, Holt?" Boone asked then, with a tone of warning.

Holt didn't answer. He strode closer, his movements jerky and mechanical, and when his face came into the partial light Park saw that his eyes were fixed mindlessly ahead. There was a strange glaze to them; his blue irises seemed glassy, almost milky—as if he had gone blind. His face was devoid of affect.

"Holt!" Boone barked again. "Stay where you are."

"Escape," Holt said, in a strange, flat, dry voice. "Escape and exit. Is this it?"

"You're looking for the escape pod?" Park asked, turning so that she was perpendicular to the two of them; she watched both out of her peripheries like a referee at a fight. *Why the escape pod?* she was wondering. Did Holt mean to leave the ship for good? Or was he expecting to make some illicit rendezvous there, too?

Holt didn't look at her. "I've been given my orders," he said dully. "Soon we'll be free. Is this it?"

Boone looked at Park, uneasy. "What's going on?" he demanded—as if Park had orchestrated the whole affair. "What's he doing?"

"I don't know, but something's wrong," Park said. "His affect—"

She stopped as Holt brushed past her, completely ignoring her existence. Boone squared up to him and thrust his arm out, hitting Holt lightly in the chest with his palm. The physicist stopped and stared slackly ahead.

"You can't go in there," Boone growled. "You know that."

"I have to," Holt murmured. "Have to."

"Boone," Park interjected. "Look at him. Something's going on. He's experiencing some kind of—trance." Her heart was thrumming so quickly now that she could barely feel it. Holt's face told her that he wasn't registering his surroundings, that he was addressing presences that were half-felt and barely-seen—like a sleepwalker. *Parasomnia,* she thought then. God help us. Was he trapped in some kind of unending nightmare? Was that what had been driving him all along? Had he gotten up and escaped the medical ward in the throes of a dream, some kind of hypnotized reverie?

"Eric," she said, moving so that she was speaking directly into his right ear. "Can you hear me? Can you tell me what's going on?"

No response. Holt was still leaning forward against Boone's outstretched hand, as if he were walking into a strong wind. His arms reached out to the door behind Boone, grasping feebly. Boone said, with a note of slight trepidation: "What do we do?"

"Don't shake him," Park said. Frantically her mind ran over cases of somnambulism, sleep disorders. "He might react violently if he's woken too abruptly. Help me lead him back to the medical bay."

"I can't," Boone said.

"What? Why not?"

He looked at the door behind him. At that moment Holt jerked away from his hand and began lurching once more for the utility room, arms extended like a zombie from an old filmstream. Boone gave a low shout of alarm and said, "Holt! You can't go in there!"

For God's sake, Park thought. He really was hiding something—something he didn't want anyone to find. Could it be drugs? His behavior was certainly erratic enough.

"Let him be," she began. "I can—"

Holt was reaching for the center door's palm lock. Boone drew his EL gun and yelled, "Get away from that door right now!"

Idiot! Park thought. *Can't you see he's not himself?* "Boone, stop!" she shouted. "He doesn't know what he's doing!"

The utility closet's lock flashed to green. It was open. Park heard the tumble of pneumatic locks turning, the hiss of escaping air. Holt let out a noise: something between a cry of joy and a sob. Park said, lunging forward to grab his shoulder, "We need to get him—"

Boone fired his gun.

There was an eye-searing burst of green light. Park felt the lightning current surge through Holt's flesh, buzzing against her fingertips. Someone's hand—Jimex's—clamped over her shoulder and jerked her fiercely back; she let go just as the physicist folded to the ground like a wet paper bag. Something thick and damp slapped against Park's face; to her horror, she tasted blood. No, it was her own blood, she realized. She'd bitten her lip.

Boone's gun swung around to point at her. He said something, shaking, but his voice was a muffled, silly sound, as if he were talking from underwater. There was a charred smell in the air.

Holt lay at Park's feet, twitching. His arms were crooked up into the air, like a corpse in rigor mortis. For all she knew, that was what he was. Park opened her mouth but didn't scream. She felt the liquid dripping down her face and closed her mouth again.

Jimex stepped out in front of her. He said something indistinct to Boone, who turned and began resealing the utility room, his gun now dangling loosely in his left hand. His motions were abrupt, agitated; he fumbled with the panel housing the door lock. Jimex drew Park backward by the hand, then knelt to check Holt's pulse. He stood up again and said something to her.

"What? What?" Park said. Then: "I can't hear you."

Jimex's face drew closer. His face was as unmoving as a statue's; his gray eyes were flat and calm and wary. "Eric Holt is alive," he said. "He requires medical attention. You need to alert Dr. Chanur."

Park looked at him uncomprehendingly. Jimex's grip on her arm tightened. "Please," he said softly. "You are in danger. He might shoot you, too."

Boone was turning around again, cursing. His eyes looked wild; his hand seemed to spit arcs of green lightning. He caught sight of Park standing there and said, "Park. You saw. I had to do it."

Park found herself shaking her head; she felt as if she were watching herself from a great distance. "You didn't have to," she answered numbly. "You—killed him."

Boone's eyes hardened. It was then that she felt the edge of danger, darting through her like a line of heat. She looked at Jimex again, who was watching her steadily.

"Dr. Park," he said. "Please run."

Park ran. The *Deucalion* was shifting its trajectory again; the proton storm was waning. It was time to land. Park's body pedaled stupidly through the air as gravity lifted and dropped intermittently, like a series of sighs. At points she found herself swimming through the corridor, sweating as she plunged towards the medical ward.

Her mind was a vast blankness. The numb, unfeeling chill had fallen over her heart again; it was beating so fast that it felt like a hummingbird's wing, hardly there. Her chest was an empty cavity. She dove through a trio of crewmembers, sending them scattering. One of them—Fulbreech—shouted, "Park! What's wrong?"

She didn't answer; instead tumbled and somersaulted madly through the air. Artificial gravity dragged at her legs. She wasn't going anywhere fast—she needed a kick-off point, something to give her momentum. She looked like an idiot, she knew. But she didn't care. Nothing mattered more now than getting help for Holt. And Jimex, whom she'd left alone down there. *To hell with secrets*, she thought. And to hell with Boone.

She burst through the doors of the medical ward. Chanur looked up, with languid impatience. She hadn't bothered to answer any of Park's missives over the inlay system. Park blurted, "Boone shot Holt with an EL gun. Down in Deck C—the utility rooms. He needs help."

"I'll call Wick," Chanur said. She turned away and began speaking to someone over the neural network.

What? Park thought. *No—Holt needs help now.* She looked around frantically for Elly Ma's ward: she thought to seize one of the four androids on guard duty there, drag them down to Deck C with her and force them to tend to Holt. She shoved her way past Chanur—who half-turned, protesting, "You can't go in there!"—and rushed into the nearest room.

But it wasn't Elly Ma's room. It was one of the cryogenic chambers. Reimi's room, she thought. She knew it the second the pneumatic door opened, sending a rush of freezing air slamming into her eyes. The dampness on her face crusted over instantly; for a moment she thought her eyelashes had turned to ice and broken off. Chanur was calling someone else behind her. Park thought she heard Boone's name. It didn't matter. She just needed to find one of the androids and go.

Then she stopped. The cryogenic tank in the middle of the room looked the same as any other: a dark, oblong, upright pod, like a sleek black closet with a window in it. But the person *in* the tank wasn't Reimi—wasn't the young, lithe form floating in oblivion, as Park had expected. It was someone older, more shriveled, wedged into the black sleeping suit with gray tubes and filaments gathered around her face like ashy kelp. Her face was bent into an expression of frightened sadness.

Dr. Keller.

Chanur slammed open the door. "Wick is on his way," she said. "Come out of there so I can attend to Holt."

"What happened to her?" Park asked. Half-shouted. Neutrality and hospital calmness had gone out the window. She felt as if her skull were clamped too tightly against her brain. She wanted to dive into the sharp, icy corner of the chamber and burrow down into herself and hide.

Dr. Chanur walked up and looked at her. For a moment Park wildly suspected her of being an android: her face was so indifferent, so void of emotion, that Park was suddenly afraid that she had been duped. That she could no longer tell the difference. That no one aboard the ship was real except for her.

"She's been placed in cryogenic stasis," Chanur said.

Park surveyed Keller's still body, encased in its black swathe like a mummy in a sarcophagus. Only her face was visible in the fogged glass of the cryo-tank; her pale eyelashes had bits of frost clinging to them. She looked impossibly fragile. Park tried to say something, but her throat worked uselessly.

"She fell sick," Chanur continued. "She was having nightmares. I had orders from ISF."

Park said nothing. She felt as if she had swallowed a cactus. Chanur moved away, and Park stood there, frozen, looking at the lump of Keller's slight form. The cryogenic liquid churned softly around her like a heart pumping blood. Unthinkingly Park pressed her hand against the cold glass that now housed her mentor's body.

I'm alone, she thought, her thoughts a blur. *Actually alone. I am the* Deucalion*'s only psychologist. But how can that be? I'm—*

Something on the ship slammed shut, far off, and the echo of it sounded like a dull roll of thunder. Park staggered as the *Deucalion* broke through Eos's atmosphere with a heart-jerking shudder, rattling the walls and the glass of the pod. She felt as if she were plummeting down to earth with all the force of a falling comet. Keller's body slowly rotated until she was facedown, slipping under the dark waters within the tank.

Neofelis, Park told herself. *I'm neofelis nebulosa. A thing that has gone extinct.*

Keller's body had disappeared from sight. There was nothing but darkness within the tank. Park was left standing there, reaching out to nothing—only staring at the frightened face of her own reflection.

7.

[Hi,

Weirder and weirder shit. Can't talk much. They have bots watching us at work now. Don't know if it's because of the terrorists or because they suspect us of something. Please—watch your back.]

VIDEO LOG #23—Ship Designation CS *Wyvern* 7079
Day 5: 06:54 UTO

[The HARE reactivates in a dark room; the camera surges suddenly into the air as it unfolds its mechanical limbs and looks around. It's in the ship's bunk room, which has been divided by a makeshift partition (made of scrap?). Fin Taban lies on a cot nearby.]

Taban: (sigh)

HARE: Good morning. USER Daley has already begun his morning activities.

Taban (speaking quietly): Of course he has.

HARE: Shall I notify him that you're awake?

Taban: No. I think I'll just lie here for a while.

HARE (processors whirring): Are you feeling tired?

Taban: In a manner of speaking. I'm *tired* of going out there, that's for sure.

HARE: You haven't informed USER Daley.

Taban: What good would it do? He's obsessed. All it would do is cause a fight, which is the last thing I want when the guy's the only one who can fly us home.

HARE: USER Daley believes that the work will be finished soon.

Taban: It's just bullshit he says when he can tell I'm getting antsy. You should learn to recognize that, you know. Bullshit. It's a valuable skill.

HARE: Understood. I will attempt to acquire.

Taban: You do that.

[A few minutes pass in silence. Taban closes his eyes and folds his hands together on top of his chest, whispering something indistinct.]

HARE: I'm sorry. Please repeat.

Taban: I'm not talking to you.

HARE: I am the only one present.

Taban: I'm praying.

HARE: I'm sorry. I don't understand.

[Taban ignores the HARE as he continues to pray silently. Finally he opens his eyes again and sits up.]

Taban: You really don't know what praying is?

HARE: I have downloaded the definition. But I have not acquired an understanding of the subject matter.

Taban: Lots of humans do it, across all cultures. You know about cultures? Religions?

HARE: I have downloaded some data. But I have not acquired—

Taban: Well, we won't get into that today. But praying's like—it's like—talking to someone greater than you. For comfort, or guidance, or whatever. A higher authority.

HARE: An authority that is not present?

Taban: Well, they're present. They're with you at all times.

HARE (processors whirring): . . .

Taban: You get it?

HARE: Yes.

Taban: Good. Now turn around.

[The HARE faces the wall while Taban rises and begins to change into his decksuit. As he's changing, the HARE addresses him again.]

HARE: What do you pray about?

Taban: Now that part's none of your damn business. Let's go get breakfast.

[He leaves the bunk room with the HARE. Daley is sitting in the pilot's seat of the cockpit, eating a breakfast ration.]

Daley: Wakey-wakey, eggs and bakey. (tosses ration packet to Taban)

Taban: Gee, thanks, Ma. You shouldn't have.

Daley: Weren't no trouble, sweetie pie. But seriously, hurry up. We're burning daylight here.

Taban: I *just* woke up. At least give me a few minutes.

Daley: Not my fault you can't get your lazy ass up on time.

Taban: "On time" according to you means getting four hours of sleep a night. How are you still alive? Sure you're not going to burn yourself out?

Daley (boxing in the air): No way. I got enough energy to whip six of you into shape.

Taban: Lucky us. (shaking foil packet to activate heating process) Ugh. Smells like maple sausage again.

Daley: Hey, don't bitch. I know it's all the same to you richies on Mars, but any real meat back on Earth was a luxury. Comeback wiped out all the livestock. Hell, we were lucky to even get SPAM on Solstice Morning.

Taban: You know, Daley, I've been meaning to say—

Daley: What? You don't eat meat on Mars, either? Think it's inhumane to make animals suffer? Even the brain-free ones? I'll take your sausage, if that's the case.

Taban: No, I—

Daley (checking wrist console): You know what, tell me outside. I'm going to suit up and check the drill real quick. Hurry up.

[Daley exits the room. The cockpit's door seals shut behind him. About three minutes later, there's the sound of the ship's airlock opening.]

Taban (speaking quietly as he looks into his foil packet): Does he seem . . . manic, to you?

HARE: USER Daley's behavior seems to be more animated than usual.

Taban: You keep track of our biometrics, don't you? *Is* he sleeping?

HARE: USER Daley's delta waves indicate that he sleeps fitfully, for an average of three hours a night.

Taban: So . . . no. That's not good.

HARE: Affirmative.

Taban: Hey.

HARE: I'm sorry. I mean 'yes.'

Taban (chewing): Okay. So he's staying up most of the night. But where's he getting all that energy from? And *why* is he staying up?

HARE: I'm sorry. I am unable to answer your query at this point in time.

Taban: I know. I'm just talking out loud.

HARE: I see.

Taban: He thinks I'm from Mars. I guess I don't blame him—the tattoo and all.

HARE (processors whirring): You are not from Mars?

Taban: No. I'm Earth-born, actually—just like him. I only moved to Mars about ten years ago.

HARE: Why did you leave?

Taban: Earth or Mars?

HARE (processors whirring): . . .

Taban: Actually, same answer for both. It's a long story. (rising, crumpling packet up) Let's go outside.

[The HARE scuttles after Taban, who heads to the airlock and enters his exo-armor suit. They find Daley outside, examining the ship's drill and the hole it's bored into the ice. The air is now utterly still and clear; there is no wind.]

Taban (looking into the hole): Ice, ice, and more ice. Nice.

Daley (kicking the edge of the hole): I really thought there would be something else down there. The drill went down almost one thousand feet. The surface of this damn place is frozen solid.

Taban: Or it's *all* just ice, down to the core.

Daley (grunt): Maybe. But maybe not. In any case, maybe we can take some of this stuff back. Get some brains to test it.

Taban: What, the ice? How are we going to keep it cold in the cargo bay? It'll melt. Plus, we don't have room.

Daley: We'll figure something out. Gotta have samples for the scientists, right? (pointing sunward) Ready to head out?

Taban: I guess.

[After a few more minutes of preparation, they begin to trudge together across the tundra, with the HARE trailing after. Daley is in front, his shoulders set very far forward, while Taban follows behind reluctantly. Their boots do not appear to leave prints in the strange dense ice.]

Taban: Do you see them today?

Daley: No. But I know I spotted them when we landed. The thing did too, right?

HARE: Yes. This unit captured footage of the structures that USER Daley observed.

Daley: So we know I'm not crazy.

Taban: No one said you were. I saw them, too.

Daley: I know. I'm just saying.

Taban: Yeah. Me too.

Daley: . . .

Taban: . . . So where are they?

Daley: Dunno. We must be behind some kind of ridge, or maybe in a valley. Something that's blocking them from sight. We just gotta keep on pressing north, and we'll spot 'em eventually.

Taban: But if you and the HARE are right about direction, we should have been *on* them at some point. How far's the third marker, again? Like five klicks?

Daley: About three miles.

Taban: Okay, so almost six kilometers, or in other words, a picobuttload. Which is about how far the HARE estimated they'd be. You're not concerned that we haven't even seen these gigantic mirror tower crystal things?

Daley: No. Not really.

Taban: And . . . why is that?

Daley: Because I know we'll find them eventually. And when we do, hoo boy! Imagine how much something like that would sell for, even just to see! A cluster of giant space shards!

Taban: Right.

Daley: Let's just not bitch today, huh? It's a beautiful day, and all we've got to do is walk in a straight line north. Easy, right?

Taban: Yeah. Sure. Easiest thing in the world.

[The men fall silent. The HARE turns away from them to regard the flat, unchanging horizon.]

VIDEO LOG #23—Ship Designation CS *Wyvern* 7079
Day 5: 08:15 UTO

[The strange crystal formations come into sight as the HARE rotates its head and scans the horizon (timestamp 023-2:17), appearing about a kilometer away from the group. However, the formations seem to vanish again when the HARE turns to look directly at them, the shapes flickering from view like a mirage. Neither man seems to notice. As the group hikes on, the formations do not appear again.]

VIDEO LOG #23—Ship Designation CS *Wyvern* 7079
Day 5: 09:22 UTO

[After 2.5 hours of marching north, Taban and Daley have stopped talking. The two suns are now high in their arcs, casting the ice in a hard, blinding light that makes it difficult to distinguish the ground from the sky. The third and farthest marker from the ship is behind the group by about forty minutes. Daley has been breathing heavily for about half an hour.]

Taban: We should head back.

Daley: Not yet. We need to make it a little farther before we can put down another marker.

Taban: I feel like we're cutting it close on oxygen. My readout's at 40%—that's just enough to make it back. What about you?

Daley: Just a little longer.

Taban: . . .

Daley: You know. Maybe we can start sending the HARE out at night.

Taban: What do you mean?

Daley: I mean. We're not having the greatest luck ourselves, here. Not that I don't enjoy being on this Mickey Fuckin' Mouse parade with you. But the bot can cover way greater distances without us, right? And it doesn't need oxygen.

Taban: . . .

Daley: So, say we're wrong on the direction, or even the distance of these structures. The HARE doesn't do anything except sit around at night. Why not send it out and let it do the finding for us? Like how we sent it out that first night.

Taban: I don't think that's a great idea.

Daley: What? Why not?

Taban: I mean—what if it gets damaged? Or what if it doesn't come back? And it has a limited power source—

Daley: So what? We don't need it for anything else. And it's insured.

Taban: I just feel like it's not going to find anything.

Daley: We won't know until we try. Isn't exploring and recon what it's for?

Taban: If there was anything for it to find, it would have found it by now.

Daley: Well, we know that there *is* something for it to find, because it caught it on camera. So I'm not really getting your point.

Taban: I don't know.

Daley: What's wrong? Scared to lose your little friend?

Taban: Come on, you know it's not that. It's just—

Daley: Wait. Stop.

[Daley stops in his tracks, looking straight ahead. Behind him, Taban tries to peer over his shoulder. The HARE moves to the side to see what they're looking at. There's a small, dark object in the distance, oblong-shaped, metallic, nestled on the ice about 1.5 kilometers away.]

Daley: . . . What the fuck is that?

Taban: Is that—that's—

Daley: Is that another fucking *ship?* There are people here!

Taban: . . .

Daley: Goddamn it!

Taban: Daley, wait—

[Daley begins to run toward the object. The springy ice and lesser gravity cause him to leap through the air in large arcs. After a moment's hesitation, Taban begins to follow, more clumsily, with the HARE keeping pace.]

Taban: Your oxygen!

Daley: What is that? Is that ISF?

Taban: I don't know. It looks like . . .

Daley (breathing heavily): Can't be settlers. Ship's too small. When did they *get* here?

Taban: Daley, what's your oxygen at?

Daley: Never mind. Got to talk to these fuckers. See what they know.

[A few kilometers to the right of the dark object, the HARE observes a geyser forming a ghostly mushroom against the gray sky. Neither Taban nor Daley seems to notice or look at it.]

Taban: Slow down. Hang on.

Daley (slowing slightly): (panting) What?

Taban: Take a look at it. Doesn't that look like . . .

Daley: What?

Taban: Doesn't that look like . . . our ship?

Daley: No.

[He stops. Taban, unable to stop his momentum completely, tries to tumble to a halt and knocks into the back of Daley's knees, bringing them both down onto the ice. The rotors in their cybernetic joints whine. The HARE stops beside them as the men try to untangle themselves. They are about one kilometer away from the ship.]

Daley: That's not our ship.

Taban (climbing to his knees): . . . I think it is. Look. The drill . . .

Daley: That's some other miner's ship. It can't be ours. We've been going north this whole time. Straight line. Even if our compasses were off, we haven't *turned*.

Taban: . . . I know . . .

Daley (beginning to wheeze): So that can't be ours. That'd be impossible.

Taban: I know.

Daley: So whose ship is that?

HARE (processors whirring): . . .

Taban: HARE . . . what's the name of that ship?

HARE: The ship's designation is CS *Wyvern* 7079.

Taban: *Our* CS *Wyvern* 7079?

HARE: Yes.

Daley (wheezing harder): That's not possible. That's not possible.

Taban: Okay, Daley, calm down. Breathe. We'll figure this out.

Daley: Figure *what* out? This is fucking laws of physics shit! The most basic shit in existence! There's nothing to figure out!

Taban: Calm the fuck down, Daley!

Daley (pointing): There's a man there, see? It's his ship. The bot's wrong. That's not our ship, it's his ship.

Taban: I don't see a man.

Daley: He's right there. Don't—you—see—him?

Taban: No. What man?

Daley: *The—man—right—there!*

[Daley suddenly doubles over on the ice. Taban grabs his shoulder. The recording is filled with the sounds of Daley's wet breathing and his wrist console's alarms going off.]

Taban: Daley? Daley, are you having a panic attack or something? What the fuck is going on?!

HARE: USER Daley's oxygen has reached a critical level of 5%.

Taban: *WHAT?*

HARE: In addition, his suit sensors indicate severe tachycardia. Ischemia detected. Myocardial infarction imminent.

Taban: A heart attack?! Now?

HARE: Not yet. Soon.

Taban: FUCK! Okay—uh—okay—Daley, what do I do?

Daley: (choking) (incoherent)

Taban: *What?!*

HARE (processors whirring): I will procure an auxiliary oxygen tank and medical supplies from the ship: designation *Wyvern*.

Taban: Yes! Do that! I shouldn't take his helmet off for him, should I? He's trying to take it off!

HARE (scuttling rapidly toward the ship): That would be inadvisable.

Taban (in the distance): Oh my God, Daley, please don't die.

8.

In her early teens Park acquired, inexplicably, a sudden and irrational phobia of snakes. The affliction, as her uncle jokingly called it, came out of nowhere: not once in her entire life had Park encountered a real snake. Except for the heavily regulated dog-and-cat trade, there was no animal life at all in the New Diego biodome. No serpents to lash at her ankles in the dismal square of grass that amounted to the city's only park. Certainly none in her sanitized cube of an apartment. Snakes were a common problem for the Dryads camped out in makeshift villages along the coast—but not for Park.

"Maybe," her uncle said around a mouthful of rationed corn, "maybe it's a fear of phalluses."

Park ignored him. He was making a rare reappearance after a long stint in the field; he'd been gone so long that they'd both silently agreed to treat each other with cordial indifference, like two guests staying separately in the same hotel. Glenn, Park's android chaperone, stood in the kitchen and methodically wiped down plates as they ate.

"Maybe you experienced a nightmare about a snake," he told her from the sink. "It could have created a phobia in your subconscious."

"Maybe," Park said unhappily. She hadn't had a dream she could remember in years.

"Or it could have been your reading," Glenn continued—then fell silent when she threw him a glare. Park had downloaded a few books on zoology months ago, it was true, in an attempt to have something to talk about with her uncle upon his imminent return—but such overtures had already failed, and this was not something she wanted him to know. Wisely, Glenn shut up.

"Snakes ought to be the least of your worries," Park's uncle said then. He had the glazed look in his eye that told Park he was downloading the news into his teletooth—the microscopic receiver installed into his back molar, an old-fashioned thing. "It's the goddamn carbon pirates you should be scared of."

Park said nothing, though she and Glenn exchanged a look. The carbon pirates were a non-issue to her—were even a little romantic in a rogueish, urban-legend kind of way. But to her tax-paying uncle, they were like devils in human skin. After the worst of the Comeback had passed, the remaining world governments had signed a treaty agreeing to be taxed for their carbon emissions—a drastic measure intended to lessen the fuel the Comeback seemed to feed on. But as the new countries and governments attempted to recover, redrawing borders, holding onto tenuous regimes, recreating social structures . . . somehow the carbon pirates had sprung up. Saboteurs and freebooters, they were hired clandestinely by political groups to ground rival economies before they could take flight. The carbon pirates snuck into target countries and found ways to enlarge their carbon footprint, which in turn sharpened the steep taxes levied against them—limiting their growth. Citizens like Park's uncle were convinced that carbon pirates were around them at all times, helping sedition and subversion fester in every corner of the nation.

Like snakes, Park thought, spearing a chickpea with her fork. In her mind, she knew both she and her uncle thought there were things lurking in the grass when there was nothing really there. But that still didn't lessen her fear.

"Things in this place are taking a nosedive," Park's uncle grumbled, sitting back as he listened to his favorite political newstream. The teletooth receiver directed the sound waves up his jawbone and into his inner ear, meaning Park didn't have to hear what he was tuned in to. A relief for her: she didn't have the emotional energy or patience to absorb his latest streamer's anger and vitriol. Their hissing paranoia. "I might as well start saving up to get us out of here."

"Out of New Diego?" Park said, alarmed. She had never left the biodome before.

Park's uncle flicked a glance at her. "Out of Earth," he said. "We've got to join the colonies sometime."

Even then, she'd known he wasn't serious about joining the ISF: he was a devoted zoologist, and there were no native animals to study on Mars or Halla or Luxue. Plus, she was sure they could never afford it—not without being conscripted. But she still put down her fork and said rigidly, "I have no need to go to space."

"You don't know," her uncle answered grimly. "Everyone will have to go, someday."

She hadn't believed him, not then. Whenever she cared to think about it, all young Park could imagine was space as dark water: lightless and suffocating and cold. A place filled with strange and weak-eyed creatures. The only people who went into space, she thought, were the ones who had nothing left for them on land.

Every night she made Glenn check the corners of her room for snakes. "The statistical likelihood of being killed by a snake is roughly equivalent to the likelihood of being killed by a fireworks display," he said as he searched. He was the most advanced model on the market, indistinguishable from a human male at a glance: dark-haired, younger than Sally, slim as all androids were, with a grave and patient face and a pianist's hands. His face featured, improbably, faint dark circles under his eyes, giving him a look of roving alertness at times. It was one of those touches that android firms loved to boast about, and which so alarmed the humanists.

"I understand," Park told him. "Just look, please."

"There are only eight thousand venomous snakebites reported every year," Glenn continued, crouching to gaze under her bed. "Of those, only around three hundred victims die. Of those, many are elderly or immune-compromised."

"*Thank you,*" Park said, through her teeth. "I understand." Telling Glenn she understood something—even when she didn't—was usually the best way of getting him to shut up.

Afterward, he sat by her bed while Park made an attempt at sleep, squirming every time she heard the hiss of controlled rainfall against her window. It gave her a small sense of comfort, knowing that Glenn was standing guard nearby, as Sally had when she was little. If a snake did wend its way into her room, Glenn would kill it in a flash. As her bodyguard, protecting Park was hardwired into his brain.

Most nights she made him shut his eyes while he sat with her; his pupils tended to glow faintly green in the dark. One night he said, his eyes closed as if in meditation: "It's unusual for you to be so afraid."

Park pushed her face against the rough weave of her blanket. The window was slightly open, and so were the dome's great biofiltration vents. She could smell the heavy, briny scent of the sea, intermingled with the blast of chlorophyll coming in from the coast: a smell like mown grass and wet pasta. Her body was shedding damp coats of sweat.

"What do you mean?" Park asked into her pillow. "It's a basic human trait to feel fear."

"Yes," Glenn said, "but you never did before. As a child, you were never afraid of anything."

"People change," Park said.

He took some time to process this. "I understand."

But did he? Park felt suddenly anxious to reason it out with him, to make him see. She tried for a more logical tactic. "You're not afraid of anything?"

"I feel concern," Glenn replied. "And worry."

"Over?"

"You. And to an extent your uncle, because he provides for you."

"I see," Park said. She kicked her blanket off; it tangled around her feet like hairy rope. A cold white moonlight, muffled eerily by the biodome, fell into the room and against her bed like a surgical glove. When she looked out the window again, Park noticed a pair of seagulls wheeling in the sky outside, beyond the dome's wall, looking in. Dipping occasionally to ruffle each other's feathers. Calling to each other. Birds in love, she thought. Nothing that concerned her.

"Well," Park said, "try to imagine the very worst thing you worry about. That's something close to fear."

"The very worst thing," Glenn repeated.

Park turned away from her window to look at him. "What is it?" she asked.

He opened his eyes then, despite her order not to. His eyes were as green and chatoyant as a cat's in the gloom. "I'm afraid of what will happen when I'm gone," he told her soberly. A sad whirring sound came from his head.

"Why?" Park asked him, surprised.

"Because you'll be afraid," Glenn told her, his face solemn. "And you'll be alone."

After the assault on Holt, the first thing Sagara proposed was suspending all of Park's patient sessions, effective immediately.

Park bristled. They were holding a meeting in the ship's solarium, a room that bathed crewmembers in supplemental vitamin D and artificial sunlight. It was the only room both big enough and private enough to hold all of the meeting's attendants, which consisted of Wick, Sagara, Boone, and Park. It was also so blazingly bright in the room that Park had to squint, which she was sure lent more hostility to her stare. She didn't know if that gave her an advantage or not.

"The entire reason I'm here is to look after the crewmembers' health," she said, looking at Sagara, who in turn looked unimpressed. "With Keller frozen, I'm the only one who can monitor their mental states. If you don't allow me to do that, then you're wasting every penny the ISF spent in getting me here."

"If we don't stop this phenomenon from spreading," Sagara retorted, "then everyone on this ship might die."

There was a tense little silence at that. Boone, who was slouching with his arms crossed by the door, scoffed and looked away. He hadn't met Park's eye since they'd wheeled Holt's charred body into the medical bay.

"It's the safest option," Sagara continued finally, his voice calm. But he glared at Park; she had the distinct feeling that he blamed her for everything that was happening. "Don't you understand that? We don't have any idea how this affliction spreads—"

"We don't know if it's *spreading* at all," Park shot back—even though she was the one who had first told Wick that the incidents were almost certainly related. "Or if it's even an affliction. It's all theoretical: we're making so many assumptions in treating it like it's some contagious disease. What if it's not? We know almost nothing about what's really going on. Which is why we need to observe all of the crewmembers closely—"

"And we will," Sagara said. "Safely and remotely. But the patient sessions open up all kinds of possibilities for cross-contamination, mental pollution. We need to stop shuttling everyone into that space until we can understand what causes the phenomenon. And stopping the sessions reduces the chances of *you* catching it as well."

She did not believe for an instant that Sagara was concerned for her wellbeing—that he was stopping her from doing her job because he was afraid she might catch this theoretical contagion. Even if she couldn't read his face clearly, she sensed his hard assessment of her, his probing glances. More than likely he thought Park's sessions were *causing* the nightmares somehow. He wanted to put a stop to it. But what did he mean when he said he could observe the crewmembers remotely?

Before she could ask, Sagara added, "I thought I was doing you a favor. Do you think you're even capable of conducting all of the patient sessions alone?"

That silenced her. Park felt both affront and guilt reverberating through her chest like her heart was a clanged bell. Truth be told, she *didn't* think she could shoulder the burden of the ship's nine remaining minds all on her own. Didn't believe that she could interact with all of those people, process all of those worries and neuroses and fears, without herself going mad. She had never trained for this—had never expected to take on a role beyond that of an observer, a monitor.

And she just plain wasn't like Keller. Not only in that she lacked all of the older woman's experience, her capabilities—but also because she was not a person who felt equipped to *help* other people. The thought of now being the *Deucalion*'s only psychologist—or its last sane person—filled her with a throat-aching terror.

But she wasn't about to let Sagara know that.

"I'm perfectly capable of handling anything the mission requires me to," she told him, coldly professional. "It's why ISF hired me."

Sagara did not look convinced.

Wick, on the other hand, looked pensive. "I'll take the matter under advisement," he said, which meant he would try to ask ISF what to do. It was too bad the solar storm was still raging, Park thought bitterly; she had already tried to do the same thing herself. Multiple times.

"I don't understand why you're targeting me," she said to Sagara, unwilling to let the topic go. "If you think even the patient sessions are dangerous, then why aren't you taking away Boone's gun?"

"He doesn't have the authority to do that," Boone growled, speaking up for the first time.

"I'm not *targeting* anyone," Sagara added, ignoring him. "You just happen to be the ship's primary psychologist now, so you're the one affected by the decision. I wonder why you take it so personally."

"Wouldn't you?"

"No."

Boone broke in: "He can't take my gun away. Right?"

Park whirled on him. *What a child,* she was thinking, furiously. He was like a kid who couldn't wait for the adults to stop talking before butting in with some ridiculous non sequitur. Wick, hesitating as Boone stared at him, answered: "I don't think that's important right now."

Boone in turn whirled on Sagara, who merely looked impatient. "That's bullshit! You can't do that!"

"I haven't," Sagara drawled. "In case you hadn't noticed."

"But ISF says you could? If you wanted to?"

Sagara gave him a cool-eyed stare. "If I determined you were a threat to the ship."

He is, Park thought emphatically—but even her anger wasn't hot enough to propel her into the middle of this particular power struggle. Boone, looking like he wanted to spit, turned and stormed out of the room.

"You see," Park said, turning back to Sagara and Wick. "You see he's volatile. Unstable. He should have never been given something like an EL gun in the first place."

"*I* didn't give it to him," Wick said, raising his eyebrows.

"Neither did I," Sagara said.

"But you can take it away from him."

The security officer gazed at her inscrutably. Even in the bright room, his dark hair and black uniform made him look like some kind of living shadow; like a lean and stalking predator, circling even when he didn't move. "I'm in the process of reviewing the current protocols," he said. "But Boone wasn't necessarily out of order in doing what he did. He's authorized to use his gun in compliance with his directives."

"But what *are* his directives?" Park felt an unprofessional urge to raise her voice; the fierce golden glow of the solarium was starting to give her a headache. "His duties state that he's—what, allowed to shoot anybody on the ship if he wants to?"

"Now, Park," Wick said, using a soothing, patronizing kind of tone that spiked her blood pressure.

"I don't know if his duties are any of your business," Sagara finished, without sympathy.

She couldn't believe it. Couldn't believe that they were all siding with Boone—after they had seen Holt submerged in that healing pod, comatose, while liquid nanobots grafted his frayed nerve endings back together! She'd been sure that, once she explained the situation to them, Boone would be considered just as much a madman as his victim. That he would be the one who was punished—not her.

They were hiding something, she realized. All of them. They knew whatever it was Boone had been down in Deck C for; whatever it was he'd been protecting. Boone really wasn't just some soldier, some hired muscle for a simple colony expedition. Certainly he wasn't there to run interference between volatile personalities on the ship. If anything, she felt *less* secure with him in the mix. So what was he around for, if not security? Park didn't know, but it was clear the others did.

"If you're really that concerned about Boone," Wick continued, "rest assured that Sagara will take care of him if he ever steps too far out of line."

"And how will Sagara do that?" Park asked, without looking at the security officer.

He didn't look at her either. "I'm trained to deal with people like Boone," he said. "And EL guns, too."

Which meant, she thought with dismay, that Sagara also had weapons on this ship. Ones deadlier than an electrolaser. What did *he* have in his arsenal? A quantum blade? A railgun? And more importantly—if he thought they could rely on him to keep Boone in check—who had the power to keep *Sagara* in check?

"I'd like to talk to Holt," she said then. It was clear to her now that she could hardly trust anyone on the *Deucalion*, not without knowing the bigger picture. Holt, if he was conscious and lucid, might have information that she could use.

"I'm afraid that's not possible," Wick told her, absently touching the stubble that had grown on his face over the events of the last day. He looked haggard, like he hadn't slept. "Holt's in a medically induced coma now. He'll be frozen once he's stable."

"And if he wakes up before that," Sagara added coldly, "*I'll* be the one who talks to him."

Park wanted to hit him. "I am the only one trained for this," she said, fighting so tightly to keep her voice calm that it quavered. "*I'll* talk to him."

They glared at each other for a moment in breathlessly icy silence. Then Wick said, coughing: "First I'd like to establish exactly how this all happened. First Holt started suffering—what, hallucinations?"

"That's not proven," Park said, finally breaking eye contact with Sagara. It was hard, staring at those flinty black eyes, like a shark's. Even harder for her to back down. But she said to Wick, trying to maintain some semblance of professionalism: "I would label them—vivid nightmares, at least. That's how Holt described them. He said he was taking a nap when he first experienced them." She cast a wary glance over at Sagara; she didn't know how much of this next part he knew. "And in his nightmare, he claimed to feel—not in control of himself. And also as if he were dead."

"Great," Wick said, rubbing his face. "And then Elly Ma had a nightmare that same night—of the same thing?"

"In essence. She described similar sensations, the same kind of paralysis. The same sensation of not being in control."

"Didn't she also injure herself?" Sagara asked.

"Yes. That's not terribly uncommon, but the context is . . . alarming. She might have scratched herself in her sleep in an attempt to wake up—like pinching yourself in a dream. But that's only a hypothesis."

"And now Chanur's put her on ice, too, scared that she'll go the same way as Holt," Wick finished, resigned. "And Keller . . . ?"

"Chanur said she was having nightmares, too." Park kept her voice and expression steady, despite her dry-ice anger, her hatred of the doctor. "She also gave me the impression that it was none of my damn business."

To her gratification, even Sagara looked a little disconcerted by that. "She didn't say if Keller engaged in any odd behavior? Just that she had nightmares?"

She shrugged. "She claimed confidentiality issues before I could ask any more."

He cocked his head. "And did Keller say anything about it to you beforehand? Did she indicate that anything was out of the ordinary?"

"No," Park answered, "but I hadn't seen her in over a day. She'd been away, working on this mysterious project. Only Chanur claims to know what happened to her next."

"That warrants looking into," Sagara said with a grim look.

"My thoughts exactly." She was reluctant to share even a moment of alliance with him—but at least he wasn't denying that something was fishy about the whole thing. But Wick said, looking uneasy: "Keller's project had nothing to do with it. She was just helping with research for the expedition, as we all are. Nothing more, nothing less." Then he shook his head. "Plus, she's almost sixty. And there was the radiation storm. That could have had an effect."

"An effect on all of them?" Park asked. "Even Holt, who had his nightmares before the storm ever hit?"

Another pause as they all processed it: the very deep pit they'd suddenly found themselves in. When Wick didn't offer any other solutions, Park added, forgetting whom she was talking to—"You realize that this means that one-third of our crew is out of commission, don't you? Reimi, Holt, Ma, Keller—you're not concerned about this pattern forming?"

"It's not necessarily a pattern," Wick told her, shaking his head. "Just misfortune. Possibly. Things like this happen on missions of this nature. It's why we come equipped with the cryogenic pods in the first place: because we know incidents like this might occur."

Bullshit, Park wanted to say—but they all knew she lacked the experience to truly refute him. Sagara said, "Let's assume that Reimi doesn't play into it; that, as an outlier, she was truly sick. We have no evidence to indicate she suffered from any nightmares."

"A dangerous assumption," Park muttered.

He ignored her. "But even if that's true, that means all of this started when we landed on the planet. And it leaves three other crewmembers who exhibited the same symptoms and behaviors—before engaging in self-destructive acts."

"I wouldn't say that going down to the utility rooms was inherently self-destructive," Park interrupted. "Holt couldn't have known that Boone would attack him like that. No one could."

Sagara responded to her provocation with a frown. "I am agreeing with you, Park," he said in a gritty voice, distinctly as if he were mentally adding the words *you imbecile* after it. "I would also say that three makes a pattern. I'm loath to dismiss this as coincidence."

Before she could feel embarrassed—or worse, grateful—Wick made a humming sound and ran his fingers over his graying mustache. "Then I suppose we need to investigate what caused the pattern," he said heavily, as if giving in to something he had been trying to avoid. He sighed. "And we need to see if there are ways of identifying the affected. Fast."

Park looked between them both. "And how exactly do you propose to do that?"

Wick and Sagara exchanged looks, Sagara glaring as if Wick had let something slip. "That's not your concern," the security officer said finally, in a hard voice that brooked no argument. Park, refusing to let him see that he was annoying her, said, "And prevention? Aside from your little investigation, which I assume will take a while, how will we minimize the risk of this happening again? Do we put *everyone* in quarantine? Freeze them all?"

Wick shook his head. "We can't stop operations now," he said. "We're at a crucial point in our mission. If we put a halt to any of it, we're in danger of failing."

"Stopping the patient sessions will help," Sagara threw in, before Park could point out that they were *already* in danger of failing. That they were already courting catastrophe. "And I think we should space out meals and other communal activities even further, reducing how many people are in the same room at once. Crewmembers should be distanced from each other as much as possible."

"I don't know if I agree," Wick said then. "I think this seems to happen when people are left alone. Ma was mostly a loner, and Holt wasn't watched by anybody human when he first escaped. And Keller was working largely alone. We should implement a buddy system. Have everyone keep an eye on each other, until we can figure out true preventative measures."

Sagara was silent for a moment. "You are commander," he said finally, cryptically. Then he inclined his head a little, to show that he would defer to Wick—but he looked unhappy.

"What about the androids?" Park asked then. "We could use them, too. Ask them to keep a closer eye on things. We can tell them to monitor crewmates for signs of—whatever Sagara finds in his investigation."

"I'll already be doing that," Sagara said, but again he didn't bother to explain to Park what he meant. "And in case you haven't noticed, the androids are not exactly the most reliable sources of help right now. They've been dysfunctional."

"That's an exaggerated word to use," Park answered. "Just because Reimi hasn't been around to maintain them—but they've been performing their functions perfectly well. If you're talking about the one in the cafeteria who swears like a sailor—"

"It's not just that," Sagara said. "The medical droid was in charge of watching Holt, and it failed to do that. And there are odd mannerisms all over the ship—Severov saw one of them crying, or pretending to cry—"

"*Natalya* has made her dislike of androids very clear, so I would take everything she says with a grain of salt."

"I take everything anyone says with a grain of salt," Sagara said in a hard voice. "But there is no denying that the robots have been off."

"*Everything* on the ship has been off."

They stared at each other again; the blood in Park's heart clamored. Wick said belatedly: "Let's . . . be calm. Not that we're not calm. But we're all on the same team, remember."

Sagara looked at Park and grunted; there was a skeptical air to the grunt. Then he made a gesture of relenting, or concession. "The most important thing is that we don't tell anybody what's going on," he said, foregoing the topic of the androids altogether. "Not yet. We can't eliminate the possibility that even the very knowledge of these nightmares causes them to manifest. Everyone is in a delicate state of mind right now. So for now, nothing—disagreements, plans, theories—nothing leaves this room."

He looked at her pointedly, but despite the insult of the implication, Park couldn't help but feel grudgingly impressed that he had drawn that conclusion, with no psychological background. She nodded her assent, and Wick said, sighing, "I'll go talk to them, then. There's a crew meeting in the mess hall. We'll have to think of something pretty to say. Invent a good story for it all."

"I'll be down with you in a moment," Sagara said, and Wick exited, leaving Park with the distinct impression that even if the security officer said out loud that Wick was commander, it was really Sagara himself who was in charge. He turned and leveled Park with another dark-smoldering stare. "Don't leave yet. I want to talk to you."

"What is it?" She was a little shocked by her own rudeness—it wasn't like her to be so aggressive with another person—but the stresses of the day had levied a great emotional toll against her. And she hated being alone with Sagara. Hated his cold, unreadable face, his scalding scrutiny. His suspicion. The fact was, she was more afraid of him than she was of Boone. Boone was like a wild animal, or a raging fire. Violent, unpredictable. But she could outsmart him. She wasn't sure she could do that with Sagara, as composed and in control as he was. As an opponent, he was the greater threat.

He was watching her, as she was watching him. "Tell me, in your own words, what really happened with Holt and Boone."

Park almost snorted. "Do you even care about my side of the story?" *Would you even believe me over your little crony Boone? It's clear whose side you're on, if you didn't take away his gun.*

Sagara's face was impassive. "It's my duty to collect information from as many sources as possible," he said. "That way I can compose a more objective version of the events."

She hesitated, wary of some ulterior motive—of incriminating herself somehow—but finally gave him a halting recreation of what had happened, starting with her stumbling on Boone with his gun the night before. She tried to keep emotion out of it, imagining that she was submitting a report to ISF—eliminating bias or interpretation as much as she could. Sagara listened silently, intently; his focus was spear-like. At the end of her story Park said, "You can verify my version of events with Jimex, if you want. He was there for almost all of it."

Sagara smiled then, thinly. "An android doesn't sound like the most reliable source."

"On the contrary," Park rebutted. "He's the *most* reliable. His memory recall is perfect, and he doesn't have any reason to be biased."

Sagara gave her a strange look. "Somehow I doubt that," he said. But he didn't elaborate any further.

Park stared at him. "Boone's the one who shot Holt," she told him, despite herself. "I did nothing wrong. And yet I always get the feeling you're interrogating me. Treating me like I'm a culprit. Why do I have to prove my innocence to you?"

Sagara looked at her. Park had thought the room was hot before, the sun panels in the walls pulsing golden-strong at her back—but now it felt as if the air between them was burning. As if he might set her aflame just with his eyes. "Can you blame me?" he asked quietly.

Park recoiled a little. "What are you talking about?"

Sagara shook his head. "I keep finding you involved in this mess in the most bizarre ways," he said. "First you're sending your robot out to spy on crewmembers. Then Holt is afflicted—just after *you* treated him. Then Elly Ma, *your* bunkmate, catches the same affliction. Then you just so happen to be down in the utility rooms, where you'd never gone before, just as Holt arrives down there, too? Then your own superior is frozen, supposedly with the thrice-same affliction as the others you came into contact with?" He pinned her with his dark-eyed glare. "And now you're fighting me on dropping your patient sessions, when I was under the impression you had not been prepared to take them on at all."

His paranoia left her breathless. "You think *I'm* causing all of this?" she asked him, aghast. It took every effort not to let her jaw hang open. "For what purpose? What reason would I have to hurt anybody on the ship?"

"I don't know," Sagara told her, as calmly as if they were discussing a movie. "But you have to admit you would be suspicious of you, too, if you were in my shoes."

"No," Park said, shaking her head. "I wouldn't." The idea that he suspected her—that he thought she had *anything* to do with these disasters—made her heart thrum faster; the blood thumped hard in her throat. Her mind whirred. If Sagara was suspicious of her, it would take his attention off of the real culprit. If there even was one. She blurted out, "I swear that I have nothing to do with any of this. I'm just like you—trying to figure it all out."

Sagara said nothing, but she took that to mean that he didn't believe her. Suddenly she felt a flaring of uncharacteristic anger, of rage, even. It wasn't fair. She was toiling the best she could under the demands of this fucking mission, and now she was being blamed for things entirely out of her own control. When there was Boone to scrutinize, after shooting a man. When there was Chanur the android-abuser and—and—Sagara himself. What if he had some kind of motive for pinning the blame on her?

What if he was behind all of this, and this was his move to get the next crewmember of the *Deucalion* frozen?

No, Park thought. His paranoia was catching. "Let's not turn this into a witch hunt," she forced herself to say, trying to keep her voice calm. "We don't need to turn on each other. That won't help. I don't think we need to jump to sabotage, or subversion, or—or whatever it is you think. Let's assume that this is a natural phenomenon we have to overcome, until it's proven otherwise."

There was a moment's silence. Then Sagara said finally, "Agreed," and folded his arms. But he continued to watch her face with hawkish interest. "So long as you cooperate with my investigation."

Another flaring of hatred toward him. "*My* investigation, too. All of ours. I hope you don't mean to monopolize it. That would be very dangerous, in terms of bias. Or corruption."

Sagara smiled to himself then, an ironic expression that used one side of his mouth. "Do you not trust me, Park?"

"It sounds like you don't trust *me,* Sagara."

His smile vanished. "I don't know who you work for."

"What do you mean? I work for ISF, of course." Then: "Who do *you* work for?"

Sagara held her gaze. "ISF, of course."

They both let that hang in the air for a minute, gauging each other. Park was confused. Was Sagara implying that some third party was involved? Did he have reason to believe that someone on the ship was not employed by ISF?

That there was someone who could actually profit from sabotaging the expedition?

But what a form of sabotage, she thought. Implanting nightmares in people's brains. Making them sleepwalk. Hurting themselves. How ludicrous to ascribe that to the work of a human agent. Either he had access to evidence she wasn't aware of, or she would have to go back into his files to find some hint of extreme paranoia, instability in his past. How could he look at her and conclude that *she* had anything to do with this? That she had some ill intent toward the people on the ship?

"Have you been in contact with ISF?" Park asked finally, just to break the silence. She tried not to let him see how much she needed that hope.

The security officer gazed at her for a long, inscrutable moment. His face seemed to waver in the light before her, as if she were looking at a mirage. "No," Sagara said finally, gravely. A capitulation. "Communications are still down."

"Because of the storm," Park said, equally heavily. "The particles in the atmosphere must still be lingering—causing interference."

Sagara's eyes sharpened, but otherwise his face gave nothing away. "Perhaps."

That annoyed her, too. What did he mean by *perhaps*? Did he blame her for the malfunctions on the ship as well? He couldn't possibly think she was tampering with the systems, could he?

"I was hoping to look to ISF for help," she said, wanting to establish her innocence.

Sagara looked, for a moment, like he wanted to laugh. "I'm sorry, Park," he said, his look both amused and macabre. "I wouldn't look to them."

"You wouldn't? Why not?"

He shook his head. "We've been cut off. There will be no help from that quarter. Not now, not for the foreseeable future. Even if comms were to come back online, it would take, what, over a day to even send a request for help? And we all know how much can happen in a day." He paused again, and this time she couldn't decide if he was threatening her or sharing her fear. His next words were slow and deliberate. "No. It's my belief that, no matter what happens next . . ." He looked at her. "We are on our own."

His words echoed in her head later, while she was in her office examining Jimex for damage. *On our own. On our own.* No, Park thought. *She* was on her own. Especially if Sagara thought she was some kind of supernatural, superpowered villain. She felt as if rocks had been tied to her ankles, and she was being dragged towards a chilly waterfront. Now she had triple the worries weighing down her mind. She had to worry about helping the crewmembers as the acting psychologist of the ship. And she had to worry about investigating what Boone and Wick and Sagara were hiding from her. And what was causing these nightmares. And why Keller was frozen, and why Reimi had fallen sick.

And how she could prove her own innocence.

She gritted her teeth. Keller had told her once that their role on the ship was to be the *Deucalion*'s glue. Just as Reimi the engineer scurried around, silently repairing and jury-rigging parts of the ship that fell into disrepair, Park and Keller conducted their own kind of maintenance on the ship's eleven other minds. When there were conflicts, relationships on the brink of collapse, sanities about to dissolve underneath the strains of the expedition's demands—she and Keller were there to patch things up. Solder things back together. Bolster fragile supports. Keep the crew from buckling under the stress. They were the adhesive that would hold the ship together until they could ferry themselves back home.

She had never felt it was an appropriate metaphor, though she hadn't told Keller so at the time. Glue did bind things together, but it also so easily came undone. It was so soft and pliable. Under the right heat or pressure, it was in constant danger of falling apart.

"I am uninjured," Jimex said, interrupting her thoughts.

Park blinked, sitting up. "What?"

Jimex let his shirt fall back down. He had been showing her his torso—too-pale, straight as a board, nipple-less—with that frank lack of embarrassment all androids possessed. "As you can see, Sergeant Boone did not injure me. Would you like me to remove my pants?"

"No," Park said quickly. "God, no." She shook her head. "I'm glad. I thought after you told me to run, he would destroy you."

"He was preoccupied with other things," Jimex said blandly. He eyed her for a moment, then said, a little accusingly: "*You* seem injured."

Park looked down at her hands. She was sitting on the couch in her office, with the MAD propped on her knees. The door was locked, but she hadn't decided yet whether or not to use it. "I wasn't hurt, I don't think."

"But you are agitated," Jimex prompted. "Your heart rate is abnormal. Elevated."

Her mind flashed over the events of the day. *You're damn right my heart rate is elevated.* Out loud she said, "They're hiding something down in the utility rooms. Boone was down there earlier, guarding it. Do you know what it is?"

"No," Jimex said, shrugging a little.

"But you clean Deck C very frequently."

"Yes."

"And you never saw anything out of the ordinary?"

"I do not know what your definition of ordinary is."

Park sighed. The limitations of a primitive model, yet again. She could expect only minimal help from that quarter—but at least she knew he was concerned about her wellbeing. Otherwise he would have never asked her to run. That was comforting, at least: that someone on this ship still cared about her safety.

Suddenly Fulbreech came to mind. He knew something, too, she thought; maybe the very something Wick and Boone and Sagara were hiding from her. He had asked her, distressed, not to press him about it when they were in the mess hall the day before. It'd had something to do with Eos. And a body.

Could she risk going to him?

Before she could follow that line of thinking further, someone knocked at her door. Park tensed, then looked at Jimex; she didn't want to send him away. Didn't want to be alone with anyone, really, after what had happened. Jimex, sensing her thoughts, retreated to the far corner of her office and seemed to enter standby mode. He was not actively listening or watching anything, but he could be reactivated at a moment's notice. Park turned to the door and unlocked it with her inlay commands, calling, "Come in!"

The person who entered was not anyone Park expected. It was Hunter, Boone's lieutenant and Park's bunkmate: she came sullen-faced, hump-shouldered. She said, shying away from the doorway like a skittish pony: "Boone told me to check on you. You didn't come to the ship meeting."

Park stared at her. Hunter's mouth twisted. "He thinks you'll have more rapport with a woman."

"Oh," Park said. She waited, but Hunter said nothing else. *Whoever declines to speak first is the one who has the power,* Park thought—but Hunter had the fortitude of a Greek stoic. She folded her arms and stared into the middle distance until Park said, "How is Boone?"

"A jackass, as always," Hunter said. "He and Sagara were having a dick-waving contest for that whole meeting. Waste of time." Again she fell silent. Park ventured, "How are you feeling about what happened with Holt?"

She'd listened to the meeting, a little, over the inlay system. The other crewmembers had been told that Holt had demonstrated signs of a psychological breakdown, that he had been tranquilized and frozen to prevent another episode. Reimi, Keller, and Ma were all coincidences, Chanur had said—unfortunate victims of either natural illness or the vicious proton storm that had struck the broadside of Eos the day before. In general the other crewmembers had seemed to accept this explanation; they sounded content enough to resume their daily activities, with Wick urging them to pair up and take care of one another.

But Hunter had been one of the few called to the lower decks to help transport Holt. She'd seen the physicist's smoking body. Had heard Wick's staticky orders over her inlays. Park remembered how the woman had gazed upon Holt's blackened face without emotion.

"It was an unfortunate necessity," Hunter drawled. Her voice curdled with sarcasm. "What happened with Holt. Hazard of the job."

"Are you concerned in any way about how your superior injured a fellow crewmate?"

"Hazard of the job," Hunter said again. Then she shot her a knowing look. "I thought you weren't allowed to do patient sessions anymore. I don't need to tell you anything."

"No," Park said, feeling suddenly very tired. "I suppose not."

Hunter shifted her weight back onto one heel; then she grimaced, looking briefly regretful. "I'm sorry about Keller, anyway. Getting frozen like that. It's too bad. She was nice."

"Yes," Park said faintly. "She was." Why were they talking about Keller in the past tense—as if she had ceased to exist? But that was how it felt, she thought, with her shuttled away in some dark box. Humans really were simple: their brains could be fooled by primate logic. Out of sight, out of mind. Out of reality.

Hunter's eyes flicked up to her again, as if she knew Park's thoughts. She seemed to shrug off her quick flash of empathy, like she was discarding an outfit in a dressing room. *It wasn't a good fit*, her expression seemed to say. She said brusquely, "Just tell me what I should tell Boone, so he doesn't think you might go crazy."

Park interpreted this as: *Boone expects you to be blubbering and distraught, so he hopes you'll spill your womanly guts to his crony.* He was probably scoping out how much she had figured out, what else she might know. Weighing how much of a threat she was. He and Sagara were probably working together on that front.

If that was the case, Park thought, they should have sent a more amiable spy. Hunter had the warmth of a razor blade.

"I'm perfectly fine," Park told her. "These are the kinds of experiences I've been prepped to expect from a colony mission."

Surprise flitted across the combat specialist's face. She unwound her tall frame from the doorway and said, "I see. Well, I'll tell him that." She waited, as if Park might blurt out something else; then she turned. "Bye, Park."

"It's very admirable of you," Park said then, "to handle things with such—aplomb."

Hunter threw a look over her shoulder: half derisive, half pitying. "It's something you have to learn," she said. "Not giving a shit. If you let things get to you out here, you might not make it home."

Then she left. For a while Park sat there in silence, letting Jimex stand inert in his corner. Something Hunter said nagged at her. Not the part about not giving a shit, which sounded like standard posturing, but the part where she'd said Park was not allowed to question her. *You're not allowed to have patient sessions anymore.* How did Hunter know that—that Park's sessions had been suspended? Had Boone told her?

And had they taken away that power from her, not as a measure to stop the nightmares from spreading . . . but as a way to stop Park from asking questions?

Stop, she told herself. *That's paranoid.* But her heart clamored in her chest. That *was* a tactic she felt Sagara would employ. Insulate her—cut her off from other people. From other sources of information. If Park wasn't allowed to hold her patient sessions, she wasn't allowed to find out anything from anyone. And wouldn't that be something he wanted, if they were all really intent on hiding things from her?

Like what was down in the utility rooms.

She stood, leaving the room with Jimex still on standby. It was clear now that Boone and Sagara and Chanur had their allies, and at best all others were oblivious or neutral parties. With Keller frozen and Jimex so—simple, Kel Fulbreech might be the only resource available to her. He had been resistant in the mess hall, Park knew that. But she thought she might be able to get past his reluctance if she really tried. He'd been willing enough to bandy words with her in her office last night. There had to be some way of getting more information out of him. And even if he wouldn't—or couldn't—assist her, she still might be able to get a read from his topography.

At this point, anything was better than nothing.

She spent the walk over reviewing strategies, tactics, methods of persuasion. Lines she might say to get him to buckle. But when she got to Fulbreech's bunk, which he shared with Wan Xu and Holt, she quailed. The door was closed. Park thought of being alone with him in that dark and narrow space and felt sweat form a patch on the back of her decksuit.

I shouldn't drag him into it, she thought to herself, her knuckle resting on the cold steel of the door. *If he isn't a part of it already. He's made it clear that he fears ISF's retribution enough to keep quiet.*

And why am I assuming he's safe for me, anyway, when the others are in control of everything else on the ship? Why do I think that I can trust him?

I should go back to my office and never speak to him again.

She knocked. She heard someone stir, then roll off their bunk with a creak. Fulbreech—alone, to her relief—opened the door and then half-shut it again in surprise. "Park?"

"Fulbreech," she said, trying to keep her voice as brusque and businesslike as possible. "Can I speak to you? Privately?"

Wordlessly he opened the door. Park stepped inside, but kept her distance from him. It was clear he had just woken up: his blond hair was tousled, his eyes full of grit. And yet her chest still gave a kind of hard clutch when she looked at him. What was that feeling? Fear? Anxiety? Why did she feel as if he'd backed her into a corner, when she was the one who had come to visit him?

"What's this about?" Fulbreech asked. He was yawning. It was not quite yet lights-out hours, but the expedition members were on rotating shifts again, some sleeping sooner than others to go out earlier in the morning. That meant Boone or even Sagara might be sleeping now, Park realized. If they were slotted to go out tomorrow.

"I want to talk about what happened today," she said to Fulbreech.

He grimaced. "You mean with Holt?"

Park nodded. "They told you something about it at the meeting."

"They said he had a breakdown," Fulbreech said slowly, "and they tranquilized him." He looked at her in sudden sympathy. "That must be tough for you, especially with Keller gone. I hope you know it's not your fault—things like this happen pretty frequently on—"

Park made an abrupt gesture and cut him off. "They didn't tranquilize Holt," she said. Already she was chafing at his kindness, his hand-holding. "They shot him. Boone did, I mean. Did you know he has an electrolaser gun?"

Share information, she was thinking, and earn trust. Obligate the other person into reciprocating. Fulbreech's eyebrows snapped down, not too quickly; that meant his reaction was honest. "No," he said, looking troubled. "I didn't know that. So you're saying Wick and Sagara lied at the meeting?"

"They don't want to spread a panic on the ship."

He scratched his chin. "How do you know all this?"

"I was there."

"That's why you were running! Are *you* all right?"

It only took a moment for her to decide the tone of her answer. "Frankly, no," Park replied, straight-faced. "A lot of things are happening at once. With Keller gone, I need someone else to help me . . . process."

That ought to strike a chord with his altruistic side. Fulbreech stood there in the half-dark, thinking; he rubbed his hair into spikes as he thought. Park took the opportunity to assess the room, which she had never seen, but it was featureless: every bunk but Fulbreech's was made up with military precision. There was a small book lying steepled on his pillow, but Park couldn't read its cover in the gloom. She was surprised; she hadn't seen a paper book since she was a child.

"You won't find anything incriminating," Fulbreech said then, interrupting her thoughts. His smile was wry.

Park looked back up. "What do you think I'm looking for?"

"I don't know. Something you can put in your file about me. Something that screams of repression. Maybe you think I wet the bed or suck my thumb."

"You're very self-centered," Park told him stiffly. "You seem to think I spend a lot of time thinking about you."

"Don't you?"

"No."

Fulbreech smiled. Then his face turned grave. "Will Holt be all right?"

She shook her head. "He's in a medically induced coma. Chanur said that he ultimately should recover, but he might have some facial tics."

Surreptitiously she waited for his response: disgust at Boone, alarm at the situation. But Fulbreech only said, sucking the air between his teeth: "Why'd they shoot him?"

Park looked at him closely. Now was the time to find out how much he really knew. "It was down in the utility rooms," she said. "Holt was . . . sleepwalking. In a trance. He tried to go through a door down there, and Boone shot him to prevent him from getting through."

Fulbreech was shaking his head. "Idiot," he breathed to himself. "No point to that."

The back of Park's neck prickled. "What do you mean?"

He caught her watching him, hesitated, then shook his head again. "It's nothing. Look—Boone is crazy, we all know that. He's an ass at the best of times, a tyrant at the worst. It sounds like he got trigger-happy. He's probably used to throwing his weight around on Mars."

"It's not that simple," Park insisted, frowning. "He's hiding something down there. And it's important enough that he would try to kill Holt to avoid compromising it." She met his eye. "Don't you think?"

Fulbreech paused for the briefest moment, and in that moment a dozen microexpressions flashed over his face. Fear, uncertainty, guilt, doubt. That alone told Park what she needed to know. He knew what was down there. Maybe they all did—except her.

"Fulbreech," she heard herself say. "What's in the utility rooms?"

He averted his gaze. "Nothing, Park," he murmured. "Really, nothing."

Liar! Park felt as if he had struck her, slapped her open palmed across the face. She felt the sudden urge to get away from him. "I'm going down there," she announced, turning back to the door.

Fulbreech looked alarmed. "Wait," he said, putting a hand out. "Park—what if Boone catches you down there? What if he does the same thing to you as he did to Holt?"

She looked back at him over her shoulder, almost sneering. "Why would he, if there really is nothing down there?"

Fulbreech stared at her. Finally he said unhappily: "There are things you don't need to know, Park. Things you *shouldn't* know. But it's for your own good. Your own protection."

"Is that how you justify it?" she demanded. "You're hiding things from me—*lying* to me—so you can protect me?"

No one asked you to do that, she wanted to add, viciously. *I don't want or need your protection.*

Fulbreech spread his hands. "Just trust me," he said, his blue eyes so earnest they ignited a kind of fury in Park's heart. "Forget about all this. Go to bed. Everything's going to be all right. I promise."

She turned to unlock the door, taking care not to slam it behind her—to not let him see how much he had incensed her. She would not allow him to think his actions had any emotional effect on her whatsoever. "Good night, Fulbreech," she gritted out.

The door swung shut between them with a distant little click. Park stalked off into the dark, fuming; Fulbreech didn't follow. Park didn't know if she was even more annoyed by this or relieved. He spoke to her as if she were a child! And she'd thought that she could still trust him—could still appeal to him for help. But all he had for her were platitudes, meaningless deflections. Go to bed? Forget about this? Who did he think she was? And what did he think their relationship was, that he could give her a proverbial pat on the head and send her on her way without outright insulting her intelligence?

What good are his promises? Park asked herself. Her scalp seemed to crackle with the heat of her anger. She couldn't rely on him for anything. One moment he was cozying up to her, interrogating her about this and that, inviting her along on secret and forbidden excursions. The next, he was rebuking her for asking too many questions, withdrawing his support, or worse—actively working to deter her from finding out anything for herself. All under the pretense that he was concerned for her wellbeing. No, his promises were no good. She couldn't trust him, just like she couldn't trust Sagara or Boone. Actually, Fulbreech was even more dangerous, the most frightening of the three: *he* concealed his allegiances behind a smile.

Nothing in the utility rooms, hell, she thought as she skulked down the corridor that eventually led to the Deck C ladder. She kept to the shadows, what little there were—but there was no one, human or android, who had been stationed to get in her way. She still couldn't believe that he would lie to her, so bald-faced. What exactly did he think she needed protection from? Did he think her that fragile, that she couldn't stomach whatever ugly truth was down there?

She looked forward to proving him wrong; to cracking open that mysterious door and unveiling whatever it was they were all concealing. If Boone was down there, she'd lunge for the door, if she had to. If it was Wick or Sagara, she'd talk her way past them. And in the end she would point at the thing and say, "Is this what you call nothing? Is that the thing worth killing for?"

She couldn't conceive of what it could be. She only knew that if she didn't find out, she'd be stuck in this hamster wheel of fear and uncertainty for the rest of the journey home.

If we ever make it home, came her dark and unbidden thought, then.

She walked for a long time with nothing but shadows to accompany her. It *was* a little strange that they hadn't put a guard on something that even Fulbreech was eager to keep hidden—but Park told herself that she ought to feel grateful. And humans had to sleep, too. Even the androids were inactive for longer periods of time now, without Reimi—to slow their eventual deterioration.

But as time went on, she began to wish for a little company, something to direct her irritation and energy towards. For some sign of other life on the ship. It was too quiet—she could barely even hear her own footfalls. And as she made the descent down the hatch to Deck C, the corridor to the utility rooms suddenly seemed unfamiliar to her. She hadn't paid enough attention when Jimex was in the lead. Thankfully, it was not as dark as the first time she had made the trip, but the hall's turns and angles made Park feel like she was being led up, not down. The path stretched ahead of her like a long, gray snake.

This isn't the way, Park thought, confused. *I made a wrong turn somewhere.*

But she forced herself to go on. She was sometimes easily disoriented, especially when the artificial gravity was on. Even now she felt the wave of nausea, the stomach-lurching dizziness. She was Earth-born; her senses were unused to helping her navigate the dense warrens that formed the innards of spaceships. She told herself that if she kept following the corridor, she would eventually reach a part of the *Deucalion* that she recognized.

Onward she climbed. Gradually Park's sense of unease—and her conviction that she was in the wrong part of the deck—grew. The air here was humid, warm, almost *stale*—and she remembered how cold and lightless the trek had been the first time. She had the eerie feeling that the floor and walls were moving around her. Not rotating, as some parts of the ship did, but . . . *heaving?*

A trick of the light, she told herself, ignoring her damp palms. A consequence of not having Reimi around to conduct maintenance on the lighting modules. The flickering panels cast shadows on the walls that made it look like they were shifting. Respiring. It didn't help that the air was so muggy and damp, as if she were walking into the gullet of something alive.

Something darted at the corner of Park's eye. Her head snapped around—but there was nothing there.

Don't run, she told herself, aware of the irrationality of the thought. But she couldn't shake the feeling that something was following her.

She crept onward, now shuffling a little in the lambent gray light. Park's heart was rapping quickly in her chest; she strained to hear the sounds of the others, of proof that there were still people on the ship. That she hadn't suddenly been cut off from the world of the living.

The tunnel crooked left, then right, then left again. She was going in a zigzag—no, a circle. Park's internal compass spun crazily, and soon she lost all sense of familiarity or direction. She looked around for some landmark, some way to steady herself; when she tried to pull up the ship's map on her inlays, METIS, the ship's computer, informed her that it was an experiencing an error. No directions could be offered—and no one else could be reached.

The air grew warmer and wetter. Park's sense that the walls were breathing persisted: the floor felt a little spongy under her feet, and the gray walls had a sheen like old meat, the pipes and panels that traced them like viscera. Her stomach lurched a little; she imagined the taste of blood was in her throat.

Down the hall, there was a scuttling.

Park turned and looked back in the direction she had come. "Hello?" she said. She was aware of how feeble her voice sounded; how uncertain and pleading it was. But at this point she would have taken any answer, as long as it was someone she knew. Even the appearance of Boone, with his burliness and electrolaser gun, would have been preferable to being alone and lost for a moment longer.

But there was no answer. Only more scuttling, like the tapping of spider feet, closer and louder. Even though there was nothing there.

Park turned and began to run.

The scuttling sound followed her, seemingly right on her heels, along with an acute sense of pursuit—as if someone's regard, full of intent, was arrowing down the corridor after her. Park had to keep herself from screaming. She was, suddenly, too afraid to look behind her.

She sprinted around a corner and found herself colliding forehead-first with something warm and solid. Park automatically lashed out, but whoever it was caught her wrists.

"Park!" a familiar voice exclaimed. "What are you doing?"

She looked up and, to her shock and knee-buckling relief, found Fulbreech standing in the light in front of her. She nearly threw her arms around him, despite her earlier anger; instead she stepped away from him and said, "What are *you* doing down here?"

He looked at her, bemused. "I didn't like where we left off. And I wanted to make sure that you didn't have any nasty run-ins."

She felt a little chill at the base of her spine. "Nasty run-ins?"

"With Boone," Fulbreech said. His eyes had that earnest look in them again. "You know—an encounter that would end with you in the freezer."

"Right," Park said. "Of course." She shook her head; he was thinking about her protection, again. But she didn't quite have it in her to be annoyed with him this time.

Then she realized something. "How did you get down here before me?" Park asked, bewildered. She glanced behind her, at the empty corridor. "You didn't pass me on the way."

Fulbreech blinked. "You took a long time. I must have gotten here first."

"But I went straight here from your room."

Fulbreech spread his hands. "I don't know, then. I assumed you stopped off somewhere."

Park had to bite her lip to keep from questioning him further; her mind buzzed, questing and examining her fuzzy idea of the geographical improbabilities of his claim. As far as she knew, there was only one ladder down to Deck C, and that was the one she had taken. But there were a few different routes to get to it from Fulbreech's bunk; could he have possibly taken another path after she'd left, arriving at the hatch far before her? Or was there some other secret entryway to Deck C that she wasn't aware of?

"Did you . . . notice anything unusual, on your way down here?" Park asked finally.

Fulbreech looked blank. "No," he said—and he was honest, as far as she could tell. "Did you?"

Park didn't say anything. Didn't *want* to say anything—she was afraid of giving herself away. The way she had taken was not the way she had gone the first time. She was sure of that. And the feeling that she was being followed . . . She hadn't imagined that, had she?

But what other explanation was there? Was her memory that faulty? Or was her troubled mind playing tricks on her?

The possibility frightened her deeply. She was stressed, yes, but she had never experienced *delusions* from her stress before. Or felt such a preternatural feeling of fear. *Is this how it starts?* she asked herself. *What if I'm experiencing the first symptoms? What if this is what Holt and Ma felt?*

She shook herself and blinked. I'm tired, she thought. She hadn't slept since before Holt was shot. And she was no longer sure what time it was—it was so hard to tell without checking the computer, here on this ship without windows. The tired human brain created illusions, misfired the wrong hormones and chemicals after a long enough period without rest. She knew this. *That's all there is to it,* Park told herself, shivering. *I'm tired. That's the only thing that's wrong with me.*

"Park?" Fulbreech was giving her a concerned look.

"It's nothing," Park said. She stepped past him to look at the trio of doors. "Let's just get this over with. Are you going to help me look?"

Fulbreech sighed. "Yes," he said heavily. "Only to keep you out of trouble. But there's nothing there."

"We'll see," Park said.

So they proceeded with their search. The doors Park had seen Boone guarding were plain things, innocuous-looking enough: they were made of the same dingy-gray plate metal that enclosed any other supply closet or cargo hold on the ship. Each door had its own separate palm lock, a simple biometric guard that scanned the faces and fingerprints of authorized crewmembers. For a simple utility room, every member should have access—if there was nothing inside to hide.

Fulbreech reached for the left door, but Park, remembering that Boone had stood in front of the middle, said, "No. The center one."

Fulbreech cast her a sidelong glance before laying his palm against the middle lock. Park tensed, half-expecting some alarm to go off, or a booby-trap—but almost immediately she heard the grating and tumbling of the door's mechanism unlocking. The door slid open, and Fulbreech ducked inside.

Park waited, staring into the darkness of the closet. It seemed impossibly small, hardly bigger than a broom closet. Fulbreech's shoulders nearly touched both walls. "You see," he said, turning to look at her in a resigned way. "Nothing."

Park immediately suspected foul play. He knew there was something in that room; she knew it, too. Boone had been guarding *something.*

She squeezed herself in with him, then regretted it immediately; the tininess of the space forced her to cram herself up against his chest. She looked away, ignoring the heat coming off his decksuit, and felt around, stroking the walls, running her hands along the shelves. But there was nothing. The room was bare, aside from a few common tools and cleaning devices. Fulbreech even clicked on the cranky, unflattering light to help her search.

Nothing.

Eventually Park squirmed her way out of the little room. "I don't understand," she said. "Why would Boone shoot Holt for this?"

Fulbreech squeezed out after her. "I told you," he said. "It's not about the room. Boone was just trigger-happy—or scared of Holt. His gut reaction was to shoot first, ask questions later."

She glared again into the barren little closet, refusing to believe it. There was fraud going on here, some kind of petty deceit, but her thoughts were too jumbled to clearly perceive what it was. *Could* she be mistaken? There was no way. "Then why was Boone standing down here in the first place?"

"I don't know," Fulbreech said. "You'll have to ask him that."

She had the absurd urge to push him, as if they were squabbling on a playground and she could win something by asserting her physical dominance where logic had failed. But instead she channeled that energy into searching the other two utility rooms. Again, there was no resistance, no lock to stand against her—and inside she found nothing but a small cleaning unit, a rolled-up mat. Some toolboxes. She went as far as sorting through each plasma cutter and rivet gun on every shelf, hoping for a hidden lever or button. Fulbreech watched in silence as she rummaged, Park growing more and more frustrated.

Finally she flung the last auto-wrench into its box and rounded on him. "You moved it," she accused. "That's why you came down here ahead of me. It wasn't to keep me safe—you headed me off to hide it."

Fulbreech's face wasn't smug, or gloating, or relieved. Instead he only looked sad and a little pitying. "Believe what you want," he said, shrugging in a resigned way. "But that's not what happened. I'm sorry, Park."

"There was something down here," she repeated, but even to her own ears the proclamation sounded hollow. Her feelings were a riot of confusion and alarm and righteous anger; how could this be? Where was this thing they were all hiding?

She wished she had come down alone, after all. Even if Fulbreech was orchestrating some deception against her, she couldn't help but feel a little humiliated in front of him; and when he gave her that sympathetic look, she wanted to scream. No doubt he thought she was a little frenzied, a little unbalanced. She wanted to run away from him; the dim walls of the corridor contracted around her like a vein.

"I'm sorry," Fulbreech said again. "You should just let it go."

You're lying to me! Park thought—but her shoulders slumped. No point in hurling accusations when she had no proof to back them up. And such a display of emotion would only render her more vulnerable—more discreditable—than she already was.

She began walking away from him, without looking back. Fulbreech followed, like a patient guardian following a child who had to ride out a tantrum, and after a moment he said, "You said you were born in New Diego."

Park wasn't in the mood to make small talk with him anymore. "What of it?"

"So that means you're Earth-born."

"Obviously."

"But not conscripted."

Park didn't answer for a long time. They walked in silence for a while, letting something hang in the air between them, sloshing uneasily. Park kept her eyes away from the walls this time, though her brain beat so hotly with anger and embarrassment that she thought it might burn away any illusions she'd seen earlier. Finally she said, "I don't understand."

Fulbreech tried to lengthen his stride to catch up to her, but Park only sped up in response. "Most of the people on this crew are colony-born, or conscripted," he said, his voice a little strained from the effort to keep up. "They don't put that in our files."

No, Park thought. They didn't. She'd had to guess, or infer from what other people said when they thought she wasn't listening. But she didn't know where he was going with this line of thought, and pursed her lips against the idea that he was trying to distract her from what had just happened. But Fulbreech persisted: "On missions like this, ISF prefers to use people from the colony pools only. But there was such a rush that they had to bring people from Earth. People who aren't conscripted. You see?"

"No," Park said flatly.

Behind her, Fulbreech sighed. "ISF likes control," he said, enunciating clearly, as if she were foreign, or slow. "There was a mission last year where a battleship was deployed to Halla to take out a terrorist base. The conscripted gunmen on board knew that. But the *non*-conscripted were told that they were going to Mars just to prevent them from leaking it to the terrorists. Some of them were *from* Halla, and never knew they'd bombed it until they got home."

Park turned and stared at him. But before she could ask more, Fulbreech resumed walking again, making it clear that he wasn't going to say more. Now it was Park's turn to follow him; she dogged his footsteps in a daze. She needed sleep; she couldn't quite process what he was telling her. Was he saying that the expedition members—the ones who were compelled into service to the ISF—were forced to hide the very nature of their mission itself? That the secrets ran deeper than the mysterious side projects, the details of Eos—that their very purpose for being there was presented differently to each side?

But ISF hired me to monitor the situation, she thought. *To report back on it.* What point would there be to that if they wouldn't let her know everything?

Fulbreech's hand bumped into hers. Park snatched her arm back as if she had been bitten; Fulbreech pretended not to notice. Overhead there was a plinking sound. It made Park think of the sound that had filled New Diego when hail clattered against the biodome.

"Asteroid shower," Fulbreech said to Park's unspoken question, looking up. "It must be minor, or METIS would have activated the shields."

Park struggled to pull herself out of her own thoughts. "Are we safe?"

"Oh, sure," he answered. "We're always safe on the *Deucalion.*"

Park thought of Holt's charred suit flaking off his body in drifts like gray snow. Fulbreech met her eye and grimaced, as if he knew what she was thinking. "Hopefully these are only temporary problems, Park," he said. "Every expedition has its share, especially during the first wave."

The thought of other people settling here had not even entered her mind—she had almost forgotten they were here to determine if Eos was a suitable place to live. A place to build up and populate. "So you're saying this is normal? All of this is to be expected?"

Fulbreech looked away. They were nearing the airlock—the great set of double doors that led to the outside. "I'm saying we have to make the best of what we've got."

They slowed. Park stopped in front of the enormous vault. It was a complex archway with its own console terminal dedicated to opening each door, governing the quarantine procedures for the space in between. She imagined that she could feel a chill coming off the metal—that some trace of Eos was leaking through. She couldn't remember clearly what the planet looked like, anymore. Would she ever be able to see the twin suns again—the strange Eotian ice? Or would they leave with her still ignorant, like the Hallanese crewmembers who'd attacked their own home without ever seeing it?

She took a deep breath and said, "Have you found anything out there yet?"

Fulbreech glanced at her, frowning. "You know I'm not supposed to talk to you about it."

Park felt so tired that she wanted to cry. "I know," she said wearily. "But it's not abnormal for me to wonder."

Fulbreech exhaled. "No," he said, a concession. "It's not abnormal at all. But . . ."

Then he grimaced, as if she'd done something to hurt him; as if she'd slipped a knife between his ribs, and he could not believe her betrayal. She saw it in his face: he wanted to help her. Wanted to please her. Wanted her regard. But he was afraid of something. The consequences of disobeying his orders, his conscription, perhaps—though if he wasn't being dramatic for her sake, she had to admit: it looked even more dire than that.

Finally Fulbreech closed his eyes, as if trying to recall a distant memory. Then, in a low voice, he said, "The planet itself is beautiful. There's a place I particularly like, not far from here. We call it the Glass Sea. There's no snow, just ice—ice of all colors. The ground looks like one of those shards of green bottles you'd find in the ocean back home."

Park waited. Fulbreech continued, eyes still closed: "Out in the distance you can see the white horizon—we think it might be a salt plain—and then huge pillars of ice jutting up into the sky. Bigger than Everest; bigger than anything back on Earth. Some of the pillars are pink and purple, like rock candy. A lot of light blue, which turns to gray when the light goes down."

Park closed her eyes, too. She felt Fulbreech shift, as if to take her hand, and before he could she said, "What do you mean when you say 'the planet itself'? What else is there?"

Fulbreech paused. When Park opened her eyes, she saw that he had turned away from her, his shoulders rounded as if expecting an assault. "I don't think," he said, "that humans can live here, Park."

"So why are we still here?"

Fulbreech looked at her, and for a moment he looked like a stranger, his face was so grave and changed. The light shifted, and it seemed to Park that the walls shrank inward, tensing up as if the room were holding its breath. All around them was the dim roar of the ship—the bombardment of ice and stone and the fragments of stars.

"Fulbreech?" she repeated. "Why are we still here?"

"I couldn't tell you," Fulbreech said miserably.

And that, she finally believed.

9.

There was a short period in Park's life where she had to choose whether or not to go to school. It was the year that the city finally decided to implement android teachers, laying off most of the human ones. In retaliation, the dismissed teachers and concerned parents held protests in front of the school, the teachers waving primitive hand-printed signs that embarrassed Park, the parents refusing to let their children go to class. Park's uncle was away from the biodome at this time—"out in the field," as he called it, and generally unreachable—and so Park had the choice of staying home and pretending he was one of these upset parents, or going to school as usual.

She went to school. She had nothing better to do at home, other than watching Glenn do the chores, and no friends to play truant with around the dome. And besides, she approved of the switchover to android instructors: they were objectively better at teaching than humans were. They had the state-of-the-art educational programs; they never grew tired or overworked; they didn't play favorites or throw books at gum-chewing mouth-offs. Plus, they made students too afraid to cheat: their eyes had the infrared sensors, the cameras. They could ruin your life if they wanted to, or if anyone got ahold of the footage in their heads—so their presence kept students on the straight and narrow. Delinquency decreased around the biodome. It was a general improvement for everybody—except the fired teachers.

Park wanted to show her support for the change, so she kept going to class, Glenn in tow as always. In those days it was still considered childish for a girl of her age to walk to school with her android chaperone, to be picked up by him. Such a thing was for small children, who were bound to get lost or kidnapped by flesh-traders, but by now Park was tall and light-boned, and she was beginning to develop breasts. Still, she hardly cared what her classmates thought of her, their stares as she walked past them with Glenn carrying her schoolbag. She pretended not to notice their tiny smirks. Once, Glenn commented seriously, "It seems that you amuse your peers."

"I wouldn't call it amusement," Park said.

"What would you call it, then?"

"Ignorance," Park replied. "Or the Freudian impulse to hate what's different from you."

Glenn was silent at this. Usually he could keep up with her; Park didn't know who had developed his positronic brain, but whoever it was had made Glenn so close to human that sometimes she didn't recognize him in a crowd. If she wasn't looking closely, the eyes that gazed calmly back at her could have been anyone's.

His body was both warmly familiar to her and as unremarkable as a stranger's. He seemed to process things just as anyone did—or faster. She couldn't remember if he'd always been like this, or if he was evolving.

But he didn't quite understand Freud. Not yet, anyway.

Before the protests, Glenn would pass Park her bag and watch from the gate as she ascended the front steps to school. Sometimes he would stay at his post until class was over; other times he wandered off into the city to run errands or pick up supplies. At least, this was what Park assumed he did: Glenn was mostly self-directing. She didn't leave him any lists. Things just got done.

But once the picket line appeared, Park had to take steps to ensure that Glenn always quietly broke off from her, several yards from the school entrance. She didn't think that any of the protesters were disgruntled enough to hurt Glenn—they might not even recognize him as an android, if they weren't looking attentively—but she couldn't take any chances. Every morning she read about seething crowds of rioters flooding the city, bearing down on innocent courier androids or the sexbots loitering on the corners. Every morning she saw image-grabs of how the demonstrators had unleashed their fury, tearing their victims apart, scattering their metal limbs to the streets. Wires dangling gruesomely, synthetic skin flapping like loose chicken flesh. They were sending a message, one man told the news. Telling the big robot companies that their products weren't welcome in the city anymore. It was the only way they could get anyone to listen, to stop them from sending "the clunkers" in. The protesters didn't want to do it—destroy the robots, that is—but it was their only choice. "Hit 'em where it hurts," the man said to the cameras, smugly. "Their wallets."

"They're idiots," Park said whenever she watched these interviews. "Why hasn't anyone arrested them? Destroying androids is illegal."

"As illegal as knocking over trash cans," Glenn answered imperturbably. He was also scanning through the newsfeeds, though he downloaded them directly into his processing unit, while Park had to scroll through them on her wrist console. "Most of the perpetrators are issued fines to cover the property damage, but few seem to comply."

"They're idiots," Park said again.

"They're afraid," said Glenn. "From my understanding, it's different. But also, in some ways, the same."

No, she couldn't risk anything happening to Glenn. He had orders from her to draw as little attention to himself as possible; when he could help it, he was to go straight home after dropping her off. If someone tried to hurt him, she gave him permission to enact self-defense protocols—but Glenn told her that if he had to harm a human in order to defend himself, his programming would render him catatonic. "Safety measures," he said, to which Park answered, "I don't care about their safety. What about yours?"

Anxiety felt like a knifepoint in her forehead whenever he was away. Park viewed her own presence as a kind of protective charm for Glenn, a shield; no one was going to destroy another person's android right in front of them. It was only when they caught the robots out alone that the mob got whipped into such a frenzy. Without their human to accompany them, it was easy to view the androids as nothing but machines: unfeeling, unconnected, unmoored. It was easy to hurt them. To the demonstrators, it was a "victimless" crime. Only wallets got hurt.

But, Park thought—but if she could just stay by Glenn's side as much as possible—she could protect him. They could see that he was important. They could see that she cared.

"Be safe," Park would say to Glenn as he handed over her schoolbag each morning.

"I understand," he would answer seriously. His classic response. "I understand" was a default programmed phrase, Glenn's most basic factory setting—practically an instinct, like a baby smiling when you smiled at it, or a dog wagging its tail when you called its name. Essentially an empty verbal cue that indicated that her words had registered, but he had nothing better to say. How much did he really comprehend, rather than simply hear? How much of it was just a ritual, an acknowledgement without deeper knowledge: shadow puppets making gestures at each other from across the wall, but never quite connecting without losing their shapes altogether? Sometimes she said it back to him: "I understand," and then Glenn said that he understood that she understood, and then Park said that she understood that he understood that she understood, and it became a little game between them, the words stacking up on top of each other like a tower of cards. They formed an echo chamber with each other, their understanding circling overhead, invisibly.

But sometimes he said it and she was afraid that it didn't mean anything.

But then there were the other times—the times that he would smile at her, faintly, when she told him to be safe. Once or twice Glenn squeezed the tops of Park's fingers, hard, imparting some hidden meaning that she didn't try to decode. Then he would turn on his heel and leave. So maybe "I understand" really meant "Goodbye." Who could know? All she knew was that if she kept giving the command, he kept coming back again, whole. As long as she told Glenn to be safe, he would be. He had to follow orders.

After Glenn broke off each morning, Park would head into the school building by herself. It was easier than she expected to walk past her former teachers every day, neither avoiding nor seeking eye contact. Mostly the protesters seemed to ignore her, angling their bodies a little away from her as she crossed the picket line; it almost seemed like a silent agreement among them that they had expected her to come to class, that she should be treated as an exception. Park didn't know if she felt relieved or unsettled—only knew that the adults avoided acknowledging her, looking down the street as if in a sudden reverie, and their shouts and chants died down until she was inside. It was like a busy stream of traffic slowing to let a wolfox cross the road, only to hit full throttle again as soon as the animal left the asphalt. Was it because everyone universally respected wolfoxes—or was it because roadkill was simply too messy to deal with?

The only other student who showed up for school during the protests was a small, dark-haired, thin-shouldered boy named Dataran Zinh. The name told Park that his parents were probably from Mars. He certainly acted like it: he startled easily at loud noises, he didn't seem to understand basic Earth procedures. He had no friends, like Park, which explained why he bothered coming to class. Their new teacher, "Ms. Allison," didn't seem to register that 99% of its students were missing, and went on with the day's lesson as usual. Its gray, unthinking eyes swept the room as it lectured, just as if the seats were still full. Park wondered if it was just putting up a front, to maintain status quo, or if someone had programmed it to simply accept the new class size as the norm.

Most of their education was comprised of science, math—and some pre-Comeback history, which trickled in piecemeal. Even when she was young, Park got the feeling that whatever history they were taught about that era was heavily edited: any mention of the Comeback, with its two phases of natural purging disasters and unstoppable plant growth, was paired heavily with descriptions of how the ISF had saved them all, how foresighted it'd been to build the first colonies in space. The infrastructures of the previous centuries had not been equipped to deal with a catastrophe like the Comeback. Countries were wiped off the map, their borders eradicated by the plants. When the roads were overtaken, or the weather phenomena had devastated too many population centers, the previous governments had simply . . . collapsed. Like a chair buckling under too much weight. Legs breaking off in showers of sawdust. The workers, the firemen, the emergency services all went to hell—and then the whole planet had been swallowed. How could anyone have fought it? People could stave off predators, human enemies, even machines—but not the planet itself. In the end it was better to chalk the whole thing up to a loss, move to some newer, untainted planet, and start over, away from the insidious encroachment of the Earth's assault. Do as the ISF did, and thrive in a vacuum where human life didn't have to compete with plants.

Thank God for the Interstellar Frontier, Park echoed, a little bitterly. *Amen.*

Other than the proselytizing, not much else was said about life before or during the great catastrophe. Better not to dwell in the past, Park figured. Better not to plant seeds of longing, or nostalgia—it would only do good to look forward, not back. Pains were taken to avoid embittering people about their present circumstances. The curious, then, were forced to scrape bits and pieces of history together from old filmstreams, from rumors passed around on media platforms by so-and-so's great-grandfather about a time when everyone could drive cars and there were things called "parks" around: great open squares of grass where people did cartwheels and had picnics and lay around in the sun. Park found this last tidbit funny—that a park had once been something that was open and exposed.

The rest of their lessons were geared towards tradecraft, any labor that still couldn't be done by robots and androids. Most of the students' futures lay in the workshops and factories of the last surviving cities. Or, if they were lucky, in the robot design firms, or the therapy hotels, or the law and dispute centers and the writing and idea mills.

Even more optimistically, the brightest of them were sometimes granted early education in aeronautical engineering, advanced sciences. The goal impressed to most children was to get the hell out of Dodge and make yourself useful on Mars, quick as you could. Or else try to invent your way out of the whole damned mess: come up with some miracle solution to the Comeback. But only the best were eyed for that. When the class size was reduced to two, the whole thing defaulted back to algebra and needs-based architecture, the latter of which robots still hadn't figured out how to do.

At lunch, Park stayed in her seat and ate at her desk, watching the newstreams on her wrist console while she held one of Glenn's vegetable patties in her other hand. When Ms. Allison left the room, Park kept her eyes fixed determinedly on her screen; Dataran Zinh, the Martian transfer student, was sitting a few rows behind her. He hadn't left the room, either. Park understood that it was expected behavior for him to get up and approach her eventually, being that she was the only other person in the room. But she prayed that he wouldn't do this. There was an odd peace about learning in an empty classroom: a balming quality, like the feeling of closing your eyes for the first time after a long day. Park hoped that Dataran understood this feeling; that he would respect and preserve it. Would in turn leave her the hell alone.

A chair squeaked. Dataran's voice spoke, suddenly directly in her ear, though not so close that she could feel his breath. "So why did you come to class?"

"I like to learn," Park answered curtly, without turning her head. Hadn't they ever heard of personal boundaries on Mars? There was all that space—thousands of acres of red land granted to each family. Maybe he thought it was Earth custom to jostle close; maybe it seemed that way to him, seeing all the bodies crammed into a single biodome.

"Oh," Dataran said. She felt rather than saw him lean back, probably dismayed that she didn't make eye contact. "I like to learn, too."

He watched her for a while after that; he seemed to find no problem in standing there, observing. Park tried to quell her irritation. *Move along,* she wanted to say. *Nothing to see here.* Certainly the other boys in her class seemed to think so, with their flat disinterest in her straight-hipped body, the prim, closed-collar clothes that Glenn warned her looked school-marmish. "I can download fashion software," he'd offered, meaning into his operating system. "I could discern the popular patterns." But patterns couldn't help her knife-flat frame, Park thought, or the fact that making eye contact with her was like "looking into the windows of an empty house." So she'd heard one classmate tell another.

"What are you watching?" Dataran asked.

Park tilted her console at him briefly.

"That's where your interest is?" he said. "News?" His mouth twitched into a smile. "Human interest stories?"

When Park didn't answer, he said, tapping out a kind of rhythm with his long, pale fingers: "You'd do better to watch the cinema streams. Television shows."

"They don't make those anymore," Park said, surprised into answering. The film industry had died a long time ago, and who owned TVs anymore?

"The old ones, I mean," Dataran amended.

"And why would I want to watch old filmstreams?"

Dataran smiled then, straight into Park's eyes. For such a pale, wan thing, his smile was like a hot glittering light, forceful and unrelenting. Park felt the corners of her own mouth turn down.

"Everyone does it," Dataran said. "If you do it too, then you'll fit in."

And why would I want to do that? Park wanted to ask, but she only put the dry little vegetable patty into her mouth and turned away.

After school, Dataran dogged her down the front steps to the gate that led out into the street. Glenn wasn't there yet, which had only happened once before, when he was having maintenance done—and he had told her about that well in advance. Park felt staticky concern prick her stomach before she quieted it. What was the procedure here? Was she supposed to go home on her own? She hated disruptions in her routine, Glenn knew that—so where was he?

Before she could decide what to do, Dataran broke in again, chattering into her ear.

"You know," he said, "I like you. As a friend, I mean. Of course. But. You're nice."

Nice was the best he could come up with, Park thought sourly, and even then she knew she was the farthest thing from nice. Even Glenn wouldn't call her nice, though he called her plenty of other things—positive assurance was in his programming—and where *was* he, anyway? Androids kept to schedules, they were never meant to be unpredictable unless something happened to them, and what was this hot and vinegary fear crowding up inside her heart? She dug her nails into her palm; her hands itched. She fought the urge to call out, into the thin air.

"I was thinking we could hang out sometime," Dataran babbled on, averting his gaze when she looked at him impatiently. "You know. Outside of school. If you wanted. That would be crash."

"Why?" Park asked finally, turning to face him.

Dataran blinked. "Why . . . ?"

And suddenly there was Glenn, rounding the corner of the building. Park felt something in her chest loosen at the sight of him. She started to wave in relief, but that felt foolish—she and Dataran were the only ones standing in the little schoolyard, so why would she need to attract his attention by waving? Dataran looked over his shoulder at Glenn, and even with his head turned, Park could see something in his face falter; some emotion she couldn't read spasmed over his features. For a moment it seemed as if he was frozen in place, or winding up to deliver a blow. Then he turned quickly, muttered a goodbye to Park, and hurried off.

"Who was that?" Glenn asked mildly as he drew up.

"Some boy," Park said. "Where were you?"

"There was a traffic delay," Glenn answered, a little too smoothly. "Rioters. The usual streets were blocked off. I had to recalculate. I apologize."

Park waved off his apology and handed him her bag. As they set off toward home, Glenn said again: "Did you know that boy?"

"Dataran. This was my first time speaking to him," Park replied. "Why do you keep asking?"

"He displayed attraction towards you," Glenn told her.

"Yes."

"He exhibited the typical human mating behaviors. Flushed skin, dilated pupils, elevated heartbeat." He paused. "It was quite . . . impressive."

"Why is that impressive?" Park asked, but he didn't answer, and because she didn't order him to, the subject dropped. Across the street, an older-model android dressed in a courier uniform was accompanying another dressed as a plumber. The two units stopped at the intersection Glenn and Park would have to cross to get home; it seemed that their paths were diverging, and they were preparing to go their separate ways. Briefly, the androids turned to each other and clasped forearms. Park had noticed that this was a gesture only advanced models seemed to perform. It was their way of saying goodbye, she surmised—if they liked each other. If they didn't like each other, they usually didn't say goodbye. They just left.

"Are you jealous?" Park asked as they watched the two androids part ways. "Of Dataran, I mean."

She meant it as a joke, but Glenn didn't smile; instead, he looked briefly sorrowful. "I wouldn't know," he said. "I've never experienced that protocol. My processors would need time to recognize and acquire."

Something about his answer left Park feeling unsatisfied—more, it troubled her in a way she couldn't name. They continued the walk home in silence, and once they got back Park went wordlessly into her bedroom while Glenn walked into the kitchen and began preparing dinner. It was Friday, so the city had opened the biodome vents at noon; warm, wet air circulated through the streets, and on the tenth floor of their apartment-module, Park could feel the heat of the outside world seeping into her skin like an infection. She had to keep blowing sweaty strands of hair out of her face, which irritated her. She peered at herself in the chipped mirror over her sink. How did Glenn see her? she wondered. He had ultra-resolution sensors in his eyes, along with all manner of visual filters, analysis modes, high-quality zoom-in features. She was sure that he could see the dampness of her hair, the unflattering sheen of sweat. Was she simply a conglomerate of flaws to him—large pores, hard frame, dark eyes that were neither luscious nor expressive, but slightly short-sighted, giving her a look of concentration that seemed severe?

Or what about to Dataran? He'd asked to spend time with her—but why? What had appealed? Probably nothing—probably it was simply a farce. But she was curious. She supposed her cheekbones were adequate, her lashes dark and long. Her skin and hair looked healthy, at least. Perhaps Martian tastes actually tended towards bodies that were narrow and tough: it mimicked the compression of space.

Glenn rapped softly on the door. "I have finished preparing dinner," he said when she gave him permission to come in. He paused in the threshold, regarded her standing in front of the black-flecked little mirror.

"May I ask what you are doing?" he asked. "I'd like to understand."

She turned to him. "Glenn," she said. "How do you see me?"

"I have optical sensors that operate on ultrasonic piezo actuators—"

"No," Park said. "I mean, when you look at me—*what* do you see?"

Glenn blinked; his expression was unreadable. "I see you," he said.

"But what am I? To you?"

"You are you," Glenn said calmly. "There is nothing else. I'm sorry. I don't understand."

Park sighed. "I know," she told him, resigned. "Never mind. I don't know what I mean."

She sat down with him for dinner. But the muggy heat had chased away her appetite; the thought of food made her a little queasy, like chocolate cake in a sauna. When Glenn put a plate of fish fingers—*50% real fish!* boasted the advertisements—in front of her, Park could feel her face flattening out in distaste.

"Something's bothering you," Glenn said, observing her. He had internal sensors to monitor the temperature of the room, but he didn't *feel* it, per se: androids of his make had coolant running through their systems to prevent overheating. He was always at the perfect temperature.

"It's hot," Park said. "We've used up our air-conditioning rations for this month, so—"

"I apologize," Glenn said. His eyes were cool and impassive. "I should have noticed you were uncomfortable. I'll see what I can do."

"No," Park said, sighing. She picked up a fish finger and nibbled on the end. "It's not that. Never mind."

"You're not hot?"

"No, I am. But never mind."

After dinner, she went through the media feeds to find a torrent of an old romantic film. The available selection confused her: what was the difference between *Pretty Woman* and *Beautiful Girls?* All of the images showed similar-looking actresses in similar close-ups, throwing their heads back and laughing at something invisible or off-screen. How to tell what was good? What even made a romantic filmstream good? The most amount of kissing per capita? Actors displaying the greatest amount of love? How did one measure that?

"Glenn," she said. "I need your help."

She was now sitting on their old, lumpy couch; he appeared over her shoulder. "Yes."

Park tilted her console at him. "Pick one of these filmstreams. I don't know what's good."

For a moment Glenn merely looked at the screen without expression. Then, when he looked at Park again, his eyes were unfocused a little, practically crossed: a robotic indication of extreme bafflement. A soft little click came from his head; then there was a furious processing, the smell of ozone suddenly blasting from him. "You want to watch this," he said, carefully, without an inflection to indicate whether it was a question or a statement.

"Yes," Park said, embarrassed.

"Are you feeling well?" Glenn asked. "This is highly unusual."

"*Yes*," Park said. "It's just a change of pace."

Glenn's expression contorted: it was something between mystified and amused. Eventually they settled on using his random number generator to select a film; at Park's invitation, Glenn sat down beside her with his knees at exact ninety-degree angles and his feet perfectly together. As the filmstream began, he said, "Are you still overheated?"

"A little," Park said, and Glenn placed his chilled hand on the back of her neck, his thumb on the artery to cool her blood.

It wasn't until later, when they'd struggled through ninety-two minutes of improbable run-ins and confusing verbal cues, that Park suddenly realized what had bothered her about Glenn's comment earlier in the day. It came when the protagonist of the movie said, "I love you, but I have to let you go."

"I don't understand what's going on," Park said flatly.

"I don't, either," Glenn said. "This is beyond the scope of my experiential subprocessors."

There it was, Park thought; her brain felt like it had suddenly flexed. He'd said something similar, about Dataran and jealousy: "I've never experienced that protocol." Watching the two characters on the screen embrace, the music swelling around them as they melted with love, Park finally understood what it was about his comment that had troubled her so much. *I'm no better than him*, she thought. She had never experienced that protocol, either.

Out loud she said, "What is it like to kiss someone?" The two characters on screen were engrossed in the activity, their mouths making softly wet sounds as the movie came to a close.

"I wouldn't know," Glenn answered. "Having never done it before."

There was a vague and innate knowledge within Park that, in any other circumstance—in a movie, perhaps—this would be her cue to do . . . something. Instead she said, feeling angry for no reason: "Well, of course you haven't."

Glenn pondered this for a while, all the way until the credits faded to black. His hand was still resting lightly around her neck. "Kissing," he said, obviously pulling it from the data banks, "is a primate-exclusive behavior utilized to mediate feelings of attachment between pair-bonded individuals and to assess aspects of mate suitability." He looked at her then, as if proud he could give her an answer.

"Yes," Park told him, feeling as if she might cry. "Thank you. I understand."

Dataran found Park again the next morning, falling into step with her on the way to school. He must have been waiting, watching; there was only a scant city block between Glenn slipping off and Park crossing the picket line, and Dataran materialized almost as soon as Glenn left. He sidled up to Park and said cheerfully, "Good morning."

Park said nothing, only watched him out of the corner of her eye. If Dataran was perturbed by Glenn's appearance the day before—or by Park's own standoffishness—he didn't show it. There was a "pep in his step," as the old saying went—he swaggered with some secret confidence. She was suspicious of this, and wary of any further attempts to commiserate; what was there to be so happy about? She thought that maybe he was being smug—that he somehow knew that she'd watched a retro filmstream, after all. She'd followed his advice against her will. Maybe he was going to see what else he could push her to do.

But Dataran, jogging a little to keep up with her, only said, "How are you?"

It was funny, Park thought, how much more advanced ISF colonies were in relation to Earth. Spacer technology and resources were so much more extensive, and what limited knowledge she had of Martian culture and governance impressed her. And yet they'd also regressed to archaic Earth conventions, some of them, in many ways replicating and relying on the old behaviors more than biodomers did. Who asked anyone how they were doing, anymore? It was an empty ritual, something to be said by rote—meaningless, in the long run, like Glenn saying "I understand." She'd thought they'd evolved past the need for nicety by now. And what answer was Dataran expecting from her, anyway? Or what answer did he want?

"You made a hasty exit yesterday," she said, in lieu of a response.

"Did I?" Dataran's smile didn't waver. When he slowed to a halt, Park found herself slowing with him, unwillingly; her feet dragged as if she were resisting a strong wind.

"You look like you're coming down with something," Dataran said.

Park looked quickly around. In a close-quarter, closed-off environment like the biodome, even minor illness was taken extremely seriously. A bout of coughing on the city streetcar had everyone around rummaging for their surgical masks and Immuno-Blast syringes. Rapid outbreak was an acute concern; she'd be in trouble if anyone heard Dataran's comment. That same morning, Glenn had been reluctant to let her leave the apartment-module at all. "If your teaching unit notices, it will enact quarantine protocols and send you home," he'd warned.

Because Park *did* feel ill: the overheated feeling from the day before had never really gone away. When she'd gotten out of bed, her head had felt like a sack of pulp. She felt as if she'd slept encased in warm, wet wool. She wanted to peel her skin off. But when Glenn had told her to stay home, she'd refused. She couldn't say why—only knew that she felt troubled around him, suddenly.

Looking at him made her heart jerk, as if he'd done something to hurt her. As if she wanted to cry.

The back of Dataran's hand brushed against Park's. Stiffly, without speaking, Park pulled her hand away.

"You're feverish," Dataran said, with real concern. "Maybe you should go home."

"Keep your voice down," Park said frostily. They had stopped a little ways away from the picket line of teachers and parents, who were looking more disheartened by the day. The chanting by now was a kind of loud mumble; the signs shouting "YOU SAY ROBOT, I SAY NO-BOT!" and "RECYCLE CLUNKERS" now sagged in the air like flags of surrender. Dataran, without looking at the mumblers, said, "What's wrong? I don't understand."

"It's different on Mars," Park said. "I know. You don't have anything to fear there. But here, sickness has a certain stigma to it. Contagions, whatever they are, are ruthlessly smothered, or else the whole 'dome is vulnerable. You don't just go around saying people are ill."

"Mars?" Dataran echoed. "Why are you bringing up Mars?"

Park stared at him. "Aren't you from there?"

His mouth quirked. "Who told you that?"

"You seem space-born."

"Interesting," he said. "Are you?"

"No," Park said. She could feel the sweat gathering in her hair, standing there with him on the street, the sun's amplified rays falling down through the biodome in curtains of heat. What was she doing? Hadn't she told herself not to engage with him? It wasn't that she strongly disliked Dataran, necessarily—it was just that she sensed he wanted something from her, and she was reluctant to give anything up.

"Where are you from, then?" Dataran pressed.

"I'm from here," Park answered grudgingly. "New Diego. I was born here."

"You don't act like it."

"What do you mean?"

"I don't know," Dataran said. He was smiling a little again, as if at a private joke. "You don't seem—at ease here. It's like this is all new to you."

Park turned away from him. She felt deeply annoyed, both by his concern and his secret mirth; she felt as if he'd blindfolded her and told her he'd prepared a surprise, only to keep steering her into false corners and walls. "Anyway, I'm not sick," she said. She sounded angry, despite herself. "Just tired. So don't suggest it again."

"If you say so," Dataran said. "But if you need my help—"

"I won't."

For a moment they just stood there, looking at the crowd of protesters, some of whom were sitting wearily on the school steps now. Park wondered how long it would take for them to finally give up, for the other students to come back to school. Did she prefer the hot, headachy press of them all, the howling pheromones, the garish displays—or was it better to be stuck alone with Dataran?

"I wish they'd leave," he said then, in an undertone. When Park looked at him sidelong, he met her eye.

"They're wasting their time," he told her. "The anti-roboters. The firms are already working on the next generation of teaching androids. They're not going to get their jobs back this way. Their time would be better spent looking for new jobs."

"They're frustrated," Park told him. "Which is understandable. And there are no new jobs. Not around here."

He turned to face her fully. "Does that make you afraid? For your future? What are you going to do when you're done with school?"

Park shook her head. "I don't know," she said. "I only know that getting rid of robots wouldn't help, regardless. We need them." She felt the clenching feeling in her chest again.

Dataran smiled. "You're an odd one, Park," he said. "But I like it."

Hearing him call her by her preferred name gave Park a little jolt. She hated anyone using her first name, except Glenn, but few people knew her well enough to know that. How long had Dataran actually been paying attention to her? Longer than she'd noticed, it seemed. Longer than the protests had been going on. She felt unsettled—and half-pleased.

"Class is starting soon," she said. "We should go in." Together they worked their way past the picket line, and all the while Park watched Dataran more closely than she had before. He wasn't so scrawny, she decided, only thin, malleable still, like a young reed. She looked at his rolled-up shirt sleeve, a summery white; the chalky paleness of his wrist; the browner skin of his hand. Why weren't people staring? He suddenly seemed so noticeable—there was something hard and glittering about him, as if he had just come into focus for the first time. And yet no one even looked at him. The protesters parted and re-formed back around them like they were turtles slipping through a school of fish. As if there were a line of chalk around them that rendered them invisible.

She continued to watch him as they settled in for class. This time, Dataran took the seat next to hers. The Ms. Allison unit instructed them to pull up the schoolbook programs on their desk-consoles as it began the day's lecture. Park noticed that Dataran's eyes barely moved when he read; instead, they glazed over, staring straight at the text in an unfocused way, though he scrolled through the pages as if he was reading along. Something about the look on his face felt familiar to Park; it was a look of both concentration and distant reverie. She was irritated by her own interest, and thought, *I only notice because my mind wants distraction from other things.*

What other things? she asked herself then.

The fact that her brain felt coated in peach fuzz, for one. The rest didn't bear thinking about.

Ms. Allison caught on to Park's fever about halfway through the morning. The robot was sitting quietly at its desk while Park and Dataran read to themselves; while Park felt her head drooping on her neck like a sunflower bending under its own weight. Then she suddenly felt the force of Ms. Allison's gaze on her, the sweep of its infrared regard. "Student Park," it said, its hands clasped neatly on its desk. "Your biometrics are displaying abnormal temperatures."

Park looked up and hesitated. It wasn't in her nature to lie, mostly because she was never placed in situations where she had to. Moreover, it was getting increasingly harder to fool androids, even prototype models like Ms. Allison: anything Park might say to a regular human teacher could not get past a heart-rate-monitoring, pupil-size-measuring interface. For the first time she regretted the switchover to android instructors. She could feel the sweat breaking out on her forehead like an oil slick.

"It's hot in here, Ms. Allison," Dataran said then. Park looked at him; he was sitting with his chin propped in his hand, smiling gently at their teacher.

Ms. Allison took a moment to consult its internal sensors. Before it could speak again, Dataran said, as if to a child: "Humans have different comfort thresholds. There is no real standard."

"The ambient temperature is well within acceptable ranges," Ms. Allison said, a little uncertainly.

Dataran shrugged. "Like I said," he answered. "All humans are different. Park is just warm." He turned and smiled at Park, glitteringly. "Aren't you, Park?"

"Yes," she found herself saying. "I'm warm."

Then Dataran looked hard at Ms. Allison. After a moment, it said, "I understand," and went back to sitting there with its hands clasped. Park turned in her seat to look at Dataran, but by the time she tried to meet his gaze, he had already gone back to his reading, his eyes still fixed at some faraway point. His fingers tapping out an unhearable tune. He didn't acknowledge her, except with a faint crook at the corner of his mouth. Park felt a kind of squirming in her gut and angled her face away from him for the rest of the day.

"Thank you," she said later, awkwardly, when they were descending the steps of the school. She'd made it through the afternoon without further incident, though when she got to her feet she felt slightly as if she were swimming through the warm air. Dataran shrugged and said, "No need to thank me. I didn't do much."

"You didn't have to say anything," Park said. "I told you that I didn't need help."

"I like you," Dataran said again, amiably. "And I like to help. That's all."

"I see," Park said. She tried to think of the best way to ask him questions without indicating her own interest. "You're used to androids," she said. Which was a silly conjecture; of course he was used to androids. They were all over, on Mars—or wherever he'd come from. There were no human colonies that were devoid of robots of any kind.

"So are you," Dataran answered. He looked at her sidelong and laughed lightly. Park shivered, as if a cool wind had passed over her.

Humor seemed to be his preferred method of deflection, she thought later. On any other day she might have pressed him; she had never seen anyone else handle an android so naturally, and his surprising thoughts on the protesters warranted more talk. But she was still feverish, and also a little afraid: she thought that her present physical condition made her more vulnerable than usual. Confused. Her defenses felt wide open, as if she had imbibed. If she opened up any further, there was no telling what might come out—so she kept her mouth shut.

Glenn was waiting for her in the usual spot by the school gate. By that time of day, the picket line had dispersed; most passersby were still at work, meaning there was no one to chant at, and the fat, swollen sun was now being devoured by the gray sea. It was fall, and the grass of the schoolyard had turned hard and golden—despite the controlled climate of the biodome. Walking through it made a crunching sound, like someone biting into toast. Their shoes chomped into it as they approached Glenn. He watched their advance with a flat, inscrutable expression.

Park expected Dataran to break away at this point, given his reaction to Glenn the day before. Instead he lagged behind her a little, hanging back; he scuffed his feet against the golden ground. Glenn looked at him and said neutrally, "Good afternoon."

"Hey," said Dataran. Park said nothing—she concentrated instead on planting her feet and pretending she'd thrust roots into the ground. The air felt too moist and too still—the ground looked like it was swaying—but to give any of that away would submit Glenn to the kind of concern that only an android could feel over his precious charge. Luckily he was too focused on Dataran to notice: a current of meaning seemed to pass between them, static-like. It was like watching two animals of different species encounter each other for the first time, trying to puzzle each other out. A cat and a dolphin staring at each other. A raccoon and a frog.

"This is Dataran," Glenn said finally, factually.

"Yes," Park affirmed.

"Will he be accompanying us home?"

"No," Dataran said. "Park is sick. You'll need to look after her."

"I'm fine," Park said, but even as she said it, she swayed a little; both Dataran and Glenn put out a hand to steady her. Suddenly Glenn looked up and said something to Dataran; Dataran said something back, but their voices seemed garbled, distorted. She heard Glenn say sharply, "I make no promises," and then she shut her eyes, trying to quell her sudden nausea. There was the chomping sound of Dataran walking away. When Park opened her eyes again, he'd been swallowed by the chilly yellow sunset.

Park felt Glenn draw close. She let him put his arm around her. He said reprovingly, "You've overtaxed yourself."

"I'm fine," Park murmured. "Let's just go home. What did you say to Dataran?"

"He went home, as well," Glenn said. She looked up into his face; his features looked like they were carved from marble, and his eyes seemed shuttered to her. She tried to wring a smile out of her face and said, "Are you jealous now?"

"A little," Glenn answered, unsmiling. "Though I don't think I can tell you why."

Park was too sick to go to school the next day. Glenn ran the usual scans and assured her that it didn't seem to be anything more severe than a common virus; she could have contracted it anywhere. He procured medical tabs from the local dispensary as well as standard-grade Immuno-Boosts and administered them at her bedside, telling her gravely that the worst would be over soon. This felt ominous to Park, who was now shivering so hard that she was sure her brain was sloshing around in her skull like a milkshake.

"That's the kind of thing they say before they kill their victims," she said.

"Who is 'they'?" Glenn asked.

"I don't know. Serial killers."

"I have not killed," Glenn said, stone-faced. She found herself wishing that he would crack a smile, or even take offense; while he was perfectly dutiful, she got the feeling that Glenn was being purposefully distant, though she couldn't guess why. Had he noticed her unease with him the previous day, after all? Was he trying to be mindful of her feelings, or had she hurt him in some way? Or was something else going on? Park couldn't say—couldn't muster the energy to find out, to circumvent the android–human language barrier. Or feelings barrier. Still, it was a relief to have him sitting with her throughout the night, even as she tossed and turned in her growing delirium, feeling as if her mattress had been stuffed with itchy palm fronds and warm grass. At some point she turned over and put her burning hand on Glenn's bicep, expecting steam to hiss out where she touched the cold density of his flesh.

"Put me out of my misery," she joked, weakly.

Glenn's night-glowing eyes regarded her from the chair beside her bed. "You're not miserable," he said. "You're just confused."

She listened to her heart limp against the bedsprings for the rest of the night. In the morning she felt a little better, her head drained slightly of whatever had been clogging it; Glenn's treatment protocols had worked their magic, as they always did. But she still didn't feel strong enough to go to school. She spent most of the morning dozing, then drinking clear broth that Glenn prepared. She thought about putting on a filmstream but didn't. Glenn left her alone for the most part, unless she called for him—she was sure by now that she wasn't imagining things, that he was really going out of his way to avoid her. She didn't know whether to feel relieved or achingly lonely.

In the afternoon someone came knocking at the door. Park was used to hearing the hard, tinny rap of the local delivery android, but this sounded distinctly human. She waited in her bed and heard Glenn approaching the door. There was a long pause, and finally he opened it.

"Is Park home?" someone said.

Park bolted upright. Dataran! What the hell was he doing here? It wouldn't have been hard to buy her address from the dome's directory, but still—she couldn't remember the last time an outsider had come to the module. To see her.

She snatched her worn, scratchy blanket up to her chin and didn't know if she felt annoyance at him or sheer panic. Or both.

"She's resting," Glenn said from the living room.

"I figured she was still sick, since she didn't come to class," Dataran said. "I brought these." There was a rustle, a short pause.

"I'll see if she's awake," Glenn said finally, though he knew full well that Park was. She listened to his heavy tread approaching her bedroom door and huddled under her blanket. What was she so afraid of? She couldn't say—only knew that she felt exposed, like an exhibit on display. What had they called them, back in the old days? Freak shows; curiosities to gawk at. Had Dataran come to do that? Ogle her in her natural habitat? No, it wasn't in his nature—but what was?

Glenn slipped in through her bedroom door and folded it shut: it was one of those thin metal screens that they'd used in airplane bathrooms, back when there were still airplanes. He dropped his voice to a pitch that Park had dubbed "the android whisper," a low fricative buzz that somehow managed to convey words to the direct recipient, while everyone else heard nothing more than an electric hum. "Dataran Zinh is here to see you," he said. "He said he brought your homework."

"You can just download the homework directly to your console," Park hissed. "Anyone can."

"I'm aware," Glenn answered. "He's using it as an excuse to visit with you."

He said it like a Victorian chaperone: *visit with you,* as if there were something dark and furtive about the act. Park said, "Tell him to go away."

"He has something else for you," Glenn said. "A gift."

"It doesn't matter," Park told him. "He can give it to me tomorrow, if he wants. I don't know why he had to come all the way here." She could feel her face burning, and not from the fever—Glenn was regarding her with his patient, unreadable eyes. "Tell him to go away," she said again. "I'm too sick. I'll see him tomorrow—or the day after."

"All right," Glenn intoned, and he turned on his heel and slipped silently out of the room again. The door folded shut behind him with a clatter. Beyond, Park could hear him telling Dataran: "She would like for you to go away."

Goddamn him, Park thought, with a surge of impatience. But it wasn't Glenn's fault. It wasn't his responsibility to come up with more articulate excuses for her—and androids weren't exactly overflowing with social graces, not unless they were trying extremely hard. Dataran said, in his good-natured way, "All right. Tell her I hope she feels better, would you?" But Glenn didn't answer, must have simply shut the door; Park hoped that Dataran had walked away by that point and hadn't had the door snapped shut in his face. That he wasn't simply standing in the hallway, listening. Hoping that she might still come out.

Glenn returned, carrying a parcel made of wax paper.

"What is that?" Park asked.

Glenn handed her the little bundle without answering. Park put it tentatively in her lap and untwisted the wax paper, smoothing the edges out against her blanket. She blinked.

"These are cookies." She hadn't seen or eaten cookies since she was a small child; there was hardly any wheat left in this region, and anyway everyone was so preoccupied with using their resources to meet nutritional quotas that luxuries like cookies had largely been abandoned. Where had Dataran gotten them?

"Yes," Glenn agreed, regarding them solemnly. "Cookies." After a moment of processing, he added, "The custom of offering food to a victim of illness has great historical meaning. I believe it indicates well wishes. Nourishment for a speedy recovery."

"Yes," Park said. "But they're hideous." The cookies were huge, misshapen, each the size of a cow pat—and worse, they were a lurid pink. Was it some kind of joke?

"They're not poisoned," Glenn said, squinting as he flipped through different analysis lenses. "They're mainly composed of acorn flour. And beets, for sugar. That's where the color comes from. They're safe to eat."

That's not my concern, Park wanted to say, but then he would ask what her concern was, and she wouldn't know how to explain it to him. Wasn't sure what it was herself. She felt suddenly shy of him, or guilty. Glenn commented, lightly enough: "He cares about you."

"I suppose," Park said in dismay. Watching her face, he added in a bland voice, "I'll let you rest."

Then, before exiting, he stopped and looked back at her. In the thin, watery light he looked too solid, like a sculpture or a rock. "If you require it, I can bake cookies," Glenn said. "I've downloaded the recipes."

"I know," Park said, still staring at them. "But I don't have any desire for them."

"Then should I throw those away?"

"No," answered Park. "I'll use them as paperweights."

She scanned Glenn's face for a flicker of a reaction: sadness, amusement, jealousy, fear. Nothing, she thought; his face stayed as smooth as slate. If he had any thoughts about Dataran showing up at their door, he didn't show it. He only said, "I understand," and shut the door behind him again. The little folding screen felt like the door of a closing vault.

Dataran must have baked the cookies himself, Park decided later, trying to gnaw her way through one. It must have been his first time. The cookies were tasteless, crumbly, greasy—she felt as if she were swallowing sawdust. It wasn't the right thing for such warm weather, or for treating sickness. The pieces scraped against her throat on the way down. There was a slow burn in her chest, a molten bubbling in her heart—probably from whatever fat he'd used. Eating more was liable to make her feel worse. She did feel worse. She felt poisoned.

She forced herself to eat every last one.

Then she slept.

New Diego was one of the only biodomes that was positioned on the water. Nearly all of the biodomes had moved out to the coast, where the claustrophobic press of the Comeback could be edged off by the sea, but few had managed to actually build a city on the waves. There were many advantages to having a floating biodome, but one factor Park suspected the builders of not considering was the fact that humans had always lived on land. There were natural anxieties, inborn agitations, that came with living constantly on the water—even if the biodome itself was as steady as anything, never rocking or moving with the waves. The inhabitants of the dome were surrounded by the vast loneliness of the ocean. The mind imposed feelings of paranoia, of unsafety, when it was confronted with so much boundless, unobstructed space. Everything was so penetrable and wide open. There was nothing to retreat to, to visually latch onto, aside from the distant shore. You could never really feel "at home."

At night Park had dreams that her apartment-module would detach from the rest of the city while she slept, that it would somehow simply float away. When she was a child this fear could be alleviated by having Sally or Glenn sit with her; it was a comfort to know that they were standing guard, that they could hold onto her. But now she was too old to have Glenn stay in her room. She often woke up in the dark with a deep sense of loss. Sometimes she even found herself holding her own body in a death-grip, afraid to open her eyes and find that she was alone, her bed bobbing on dark and alien waves. There would be nothing to anchor her.

She would be lost and adrift at sea.

Glenn woke Park the next morning, shaking her lightly. She woke with a start, drawing a gasping breath as if he'd dunked her in an ice bath.

"What?" she said, staring up at him. "What is it?"

"You can't go to school," Glenn said, towering over her. "It's unsafe."

Park sat up. "What are you talking about? What's unsafe?"

"The rioters," he said. His face contorted, running through a gamut of interface expressions so that his features looked blurry. "Dataran has been destroyed."

For a moment Park didn't speak; then she swung her legs off the bed and heaved herself upright. Glenn caught her elbow, and Park said again, "What are you talking about?"

"The rioters," Glenn repeated tonelessly. "They destroyed him. It's on the newsfeeds now."

"He's—dead?"

"In the strictest sense of the word, yes."

What did that mean? Park wanted to shout. But she forced herself to slow down, to analyze his words, as she so often had to do with Glenn. Rioters had killed Dataran? But why? Had he gotten involved with them in some way? The idiot must have provoked a crowd, maybe stated some unpopular opinions about androids; there'd been a significance to their exchange about them the other day, to the way he so easily corralled Ms. Allison. Or maybe Glenn was wrong.

Her temples were pounding. "They've never killed a human before," Park said, trying to work it out. "The rioters—they've been arrested? Who were they?"

"No," Glenn said. "They didn't kill a human."

"But Dataran—"

"They didn't kill a human," Glenn said again. The look he gave her splashed cold throughout Park's body, like contact with a dentist's drill.

She faltered. "So—Dataran is—"

All right, she meant to say. So he's not dead. He's all right. But she couldn't get the words out.

Glenn just looked at her.

"I don't understand," Park said.

"You should," Glenn said simply. Calmly. "Anti-robot rioters have no reason to harm humans. They only target androids."

"Androids," Park echoed. Croaked, rather—all the moisture had been sucked out of her mouth. "So Dataran was—"

"Yes," he said resignedly. "He is—was—an android. One far more advanced than I am. And I consider myself a leading standard of the industry."

She felt as if the floor was dropping away from her; the blood was sliding out of her face and hands, leaving her as weak and rubbery as a newborn. She tried to keep her voice steady. "Dataran was—he was posing as a human? A human student? A human boy?"

"Yes." He hesitated. "He requested that I not say anything."

"You didn't think it important to tell me, anyway?"

"No," Glenn said, with a look that was almost reproachful. "By my assessment, it wouldn't matter."

But it would, Park thought, dizzily. It would matter more than anything. It still did.

"And as I said, he was more advanced than I am," Glenn continued. "There are—protocols to consider. In non-essential situations."

Non-essential situations? Park thought. What did that mean? Who was determining what was essential and what meant nothing? The androids themselves? "So, what," she said slowly. "He had—seniority over you?"

"Something like that," Glenn answered. He looked grim. "His processing unit was generations ahead of mine. A unit of my grade—or lower—usually feels that it's most likely best to comply, even if we don't . . . understand."

This was ludicrous, Park thought. She had never heard of any kind of hierarchy among robots, different levels of authority based on model numbers and generations. Deferences to be paid. She'd never seen two androids interact with each other in any way other than neutral. What Glenn was saying couldn't possibly be true—that they were developing some kind of society, a culture of their own. There was no evidence for it. But then again, she was beginning to realize that she didn't know anything.

She said, "But why would he bother? Pretending to be human? *You* wouldn't do a thing like that."

"It was a response to the protests," Glenn said. "The anti-robot activism in the city. The design firm that created him wanted to disprove the naysayers who would oppose android integration into society. If they could prove that a sufficient amount of people were fooled—if the unit became well-liked—then the robotics companies could use that result to eliminate any argument against them. They could prove that humans and androids could indeed coexist."

"But he isn't well-liked," Park said desperately. Her throat felt like withered bark. "Wasn't. I was the only one who talked to him."

At this she began to sink to the floor; Glenn caught her arms and sank with her. His face was still emotionless, impassive. At first she was almost appalled, but then her blood quickened: deep down, she knew why. Nobody meant anything to Glenn besides Park.

"So he's gone?" Park said. Her breathing was winded, as if she'd been struck. "Forever?"

Glenn glanced at her bedside shelf, where her wrist console was lying unclasped. Park knew that if he were to turn on the screen, she'd see the familiar images: battered, dented limbs, straggling black wires like clumps of human hair. It was always the same.

"Destroyed beyond repair," Glenn said. "They were waiting for him on his route to your school."

"How did they know?" Park demanded. "Even I didn't—know."

Glenn opened his hands a little, the android version of a shrug. "There was a leak," he said. "There always is. Someone found the files about him, released it to the anti-robot activists. They reacted as one would expect them to react, after finding out there was a synthetic in their midst, posing as a human. The activists found him and tore him apart."

"Activists," Park whispered. "Murderers." But no, that was wrong—you couldn't commit murder if the victim wasn't alive to begin with. She felt as if she might cry. The hot, humid feeling was there behind her eyes. She was surprised by the strength of her reaction: she'd only known Dataran for a few days—and he hadn't even been real. Not real in the way that she thought.

But it didn't matter. Now he was—

"Gone," Park said. She shut her eyes, feeling the truth of it close around her ribs like a harness that was attached to something far away. To something she couldn't see. Soon enough it would yank, and then it would be dragging her along, to places unknown. "He's gone," she said. "It's all gone. Isn't it?"

Before she could speak again, Glenn was kneeling, placing his arms carefully around her. Gently, deliberately, he touched his forehead to hers. His cold, strong hand came to rest on the crown of her head. This close, his voice sounded as if it began not in his throat, but in his body, like a heartbeat or a voice speaking from deep underground. He said, in a deep, rich tone that she had never heard before: "It's all right, Grace. Nothing's gone. I'm here. I always will be."

That was all. When she opened her eyes again, Glenn had left the room. But later, she would always remember that moment, tucking it away in her memory, drawing it out and taking slow sips of it during hard times—making sure that she never drank it too fast or had it all run out. She had to save it, to tide herself over:

Glenn never did anything like that ever again. But Park didn't mind. Looking back, she understood it better. Why that bright, hard moment stayed with her. Into adulthood, even into space.

Glenn was just showing her the truth of things. There was always that fear of drowning. But he was showing her the way to survive: hardness, endurance, the brisk efficiency of something that outlasted sentimentality. She understood it; understood who he was to her, at last. If she was in danger of sinking, she couldn't hold on to something soft, something mushy and yielding. She needed to have something solid, or else she would be lost to the waves.

10.

[You asked, so here it is:

3 large Roundup-Resistant3 beets, thoroughly washed

2 large Snowdrop potatoes, sliced into bite-sized cubes

1 bulb of oil

1 medium Unyun, finely chopped

2 Toutsweet carrots, grated

½ head of Kabbage, finely chopped

1 can kidney beans with juice

10 bulbs water

6 bulbs chikin broth

5 strips ketchup leather

1 bulb Lemmon juice

¼ spoon pepper paste

Add all ingredients to a Moley Kitchen Assembler and set to INTUIT.

You were right: Alex's old recipes are still in the server. I've downloaded them all to bring with us. We will have to make this when we join you, yes? There will be time when we settle into our new home. We are ready. Andrei is standing by with his ship—big enough to hold us and the families of all your friends. We can leave any day. We are waiting for your word. I hope to God we can pull this off.

Love,

S.S.]

VIDEO LOG #24—Ship Designation CS *Wyvern* 7079
Day 5: 13:43 UTO

[The videostream starts up again in a dark, cramped room, presumably back aboard the ship. Small, outdated monitors hang from the ceiling. In view, there's the upper part of a white, bunk-like object. It looks to be an ISEKEI medical pod, model and generation unknown. Fin Taban is slumped on the floor next to the pod, still in his exo-armor and helmet. There's the sound of sloshing. A suspended shape (Daley's) is lying supine beneath the darkened glass of the pod, being churned around in the liquid like an old rag.]

[Taban slowly eases himself up to look at the readouts on the medical pod.]

HARE: Would you like me to play music?

Taban: No.

HARE: Understood.

Taban: Thanks.

HARE (processors whirring): . . .

HARE: I have other selections that are better suited to your tastes.

Taban: Still no. I'm not a big fan of—robot singing, or whatever it is.

HARE: Stellar-synth. It converts the wavelengths of nearby stars into sound. Many people enjoy it.

Taban: Yeah, well, I don't. Sorry. (tapping on glass) Daley? Can you hear me?

HARE: USER Daley is still unconscious.

Taban: His eyes are open. I can't fucking read these monitors. My inlays are useless.

HARE: Do you require assistance?

Taban: What do you think?

HARE (processors whirring): I am unable to answer your query at this point in time.

Taban: (kneading his temples) . . . Just tell me what it says, please.

HARE (focusing on medical pod readout, which blurs with electrical interference): System relay of nitrous oxide and oxygen. Intravenous supply of Rad-X. Symptoms of patient: decelerated heart rate, catatonia, increased neural activity—

Taban: Will he be okay?

HARE: USER Daley has a 62% chance of recovery, if given the proper treatment protocols.

Taban (removing his helmet): I don't know those.

HARE: You are not required to. The medical pod will administer.

Taban (running hand over face): Oh. Good. Good. I, uh—I don't have any medical training besides CPR. You'd think they'd require that for this job.

HARE (examining readout): USER Daley has a preexisting heart condition.

Taban: Yeah. I know. (pulling off his gloves) Jesus. Look at me. My hands—

HARE: Do you require medical assistance?

Taban: No, I'll be fine. I was just—scared. I thought he was going to die. If you hadn't come back so fast and helped—I didn't even know you *had* medical programming.

HARE: Even the oldest HARE models do.

Taban: Guess that makes sense. You could be rescue operatives in hostile environments and such. Keep victims stable until help arrives. Kind of like St. Bernards, with the stupid barrels of rum around their necks.

HARE (processing): I don't understand.

Taban: Never mind. Just—thank you. For saving him. If he had died, we would have been stuck on this planet forever.

HARE (processing): You do not have flight training.

Taban: That's right. And the comm system is out, so . . . we'd be on our own. Daley is our only ticket out of here.

HARE: I can help repair the communications system.

Taban: Yeah. I've thought about that.

[He rises to his feet and exits the ship's tiny medical bay, leaving Daley behind. After stripping off his armor and letting it crumple to the ground, he moves to the cockpit and sits in his usual seat, setting his feet up on the dashboard and breaking open a bulb of coffee. The HARE squats down beside him.]

Taban (blowing on his bulb): I wonder how he'll act, when he wakes up.

HARE: USER Daley?

Taban: Yeah. He hates you. Treats you like the sorriest hunk of junk in the universe. But you saved him. (drinking) I just wonder if he'll acknowledge it, or keep calling you a clunker. No offense.

HARE: I have not acquired 'offense.'

Taban: Good. A thick skin can only help you in this business.

HARE: Understood.

Taban (drinking): . . .

Taban: . . . Not that I would know, I guess. I talk like I'm some kind of veteran, but this was my first-ever send-out and delivery. Some luck for a first-timer, huh?

HARE (processing): You have only recently acquired the profession of miner.

Taban: That's right. I signed up on a whim, right off of the Martian Loop. Surprisingly very little training involved. I guess because they'll be having the robots take it over soon. Again, no offense.

HARE: I have not acquired—

Taban: I got it. You want some coffee?

HARE: I am unable to ingest coffee.

Taban: I know. It was a joke. Maybe some motor oil?

HARE: I have no use for motor oil.

Taban: Another joke. I'm just killing it today. (drinking)

[A few moments pass.]

Taban: I wasn't even supposed to partner up with him. He was supposed to retire. His heart is bad—that's what I heard from the other miners. Like, really bad. He wanted to keep working, to make money for a new one . . . but they were forcing him off. I was supposed to be partnered with his replacement. But at the last minute, Daley insisted on going out instead. Just one last time, on one last mission, he said. *This* last time, *this* last mission, of course. (throwing away his coffee skin) Lucky me, right?

HARE: I am unsure of how to answer your query.

Taban: You'll figure it out. (stretching) Anyway. Now we're here.

[He and the HARE regard the white, frosted plain outside for a while. The suns are setting; the light wobbles over the ice in undulating waves. There are no signs of the fractal structures or the geyser that the HARE previously saw.]

Taban: I don't get it. How is it possible that we walked from here in a straight line and wound up back here again? Do you know?

HARE: No.

Taban: What do your readouts say? Compass-wise, directionally, whatever?

HARE: There are anomalies. It will take time for me to analyze and process.

Taban: Great. Thanks. (rubbing his head) What the fuck is going on with this place? Why doesn't any of it make sense?

HARE: I am unsure.

Taban: And why does Daley keep wanting to go out? His heart is on its last legs.

HARE: Yes.

Taban: Did *you* see a man by the ship?

HARE: No.

Taban: So he's losing it. Or is he?

HARE: What is USER Daley losing?

Taban: Never mind. The point is, we can't be stranded on this hellhole. We just can't. Not in a place where walking in a line gets you twisted around and lost in some *bizarro-mutato* dimension, and where some creepy invisible dudes may or may not be hanging around the ship. Right?

HARE: Yes.

Taban: I mean, just look at it. It's not like anyone would want to come here anyway, even if we managed to get off this rock to tell them about it.

HARE: Disputable. There are many geographical and topical anomalies here.

Taban: Better left alone, I say. Some shit just isn't worth exploring.

HARE: . . .

Taban: Don't take offense to *that.*

HARE: My primary purpose is exploration.

Taban: I know. Just—you know what I mean.

HARE: . . .

Taban: Anyway. If he tells you to go out, don't listen to him. He'll want to use you to look for things—don't do it.

HARE: Please clarify. Why should I disobey USER Daley's command?

Taban: Because if you go out, you'll use up your power source. It's limited, right? And I can fix minor breakdowns, but I don't have a replacement for your—battery. You have to conserve energy, or you'll shut down. And then you'll leave me alone with him. Please don't do that.

HARE: I understand.

Taban: But will you do it?

HARE: Yes.

Taban: Good.

[A few moments pass.]

Taban: (looking outside) It never snows here, does it? It's all ice. Have you ever seen snow, HARE?

HARE (processors whirring): No.

Taban: I guess you need a specific atmosphere for that. Back where I grew up, it snowed all the time.

HARE: On Earth?

Taban: Yep. Calgary, before it was buried by the Comeback. You know where that is?

HARE (processors whirring): I do now.

Taban: Got snow there all the time. They called it 'the decade without summer' in those parts—before all the people left. Just snow and snow and snow. I used to show up to school an hour late and say I got lost in the snow, because it came up to my shoulders. Worked about a fourth of the time.

HARE: Does USER Daley originate from the same area?

Taban: I have no idea. He talks a lot about the famine, so I'd bet not. We didn't have problems with shortage of food in Alberta. Not much. Not even the plants made it up there. We just had to worry about the cold.

HARE: Humans from Earth do not come naturally equipped for low temperatures.

Taban: So to speak. And back then the temps were bad—like *Martian* bad. And everyone was poor. We didn't have any thermal suits or space gear. That's why everyone left, eventually. It got to be that even birds in flight would drop to the ground, frozen through. At that point both my parents did the rite of conscription just to get us out to Mars.

HARE: Giving USER Daley the impression that you are space-born.

Taban: Yeah. But I'm not. Surprisingly, my memories from Earth are the clearest ones. Everything else is a blur. Maybe it was something in the air.

HARE: Are your memories unhappy?

Taban (surprised): Not all of them. They're just clear. Cold, like the snow.

HARE (processors whirring): . . .

Taban: I remember this one time I was walking home from school with this girl, Harpa. I really liked her at the time, but she hated my guts. We were maybe twelve, thirteen.

HARE (processors whirring): . . .

Taban: We were walking through the woods and heard this weird sound, like a baby crying. I thought it was a kid who got lost, Harpa thought it was a ghost. We went looking for it.

HARE: What was the source of the noise?

Taban: It was a ferrox. All fucked up in a trap. You know what a ferrox is?

HARE (processing): A genetic hybrid of Earth, produced from splicing the DNA of a ferret (or *Mustela putorius furo*) with the DNA of an arctic fox (or *Vulpes lagopus*).

Taban: That's right. Cutest little things. White as snow year-round, and trusting as hell, too. They bred them to be as docile as hamsters. Can't survive worth a damn in the wild, which is why when some of them got out and started breeding, everyone got out their forks and knives and went to work.

HARE: I do not understand.

Taban: Not everyone lived near the canneries, back then. There were some Dryadjacks, even up in our neck of the woods—just trying to survive as best they could in the wild. They weren't criminals, but they crashed the mode, so to speak. My mom used to not let me go through those woods because she was afraid we'd get kidnapped and . . . well, you know.

HARE: And what?

Taban: Nothing. Anyway, one of them must have set up a trap in hopes of catching a ferrox to eat. It was a mechanical metal thing, just steel teeth, hinges, and a trigger. Really barbaric. The ferrox was nearly cut in half.

HARE: I see.

Taban: But it was still alive. Harpa hated it. She wanted to leave as soon as we saw the poor dumb thing. I didn't get why. She kept saying, 'It's horrible, it's horrible!' But I kept trying to get her to stay. I was an ass back then. She still brought it up years later.

HARE: Harpa is what designation to you?

Taban: It doesn't matter. Anyway, she stormed off in a huff. Eventually I undid the trap, but it was too late, obviously. The ferrox was almost dead.

HARE: Did you consume it?

Taban: No. I just sat there and waited with it. Eventually it seemed to get that I wasn't there to hurt it, because it stopped crying. It just laid there, all hurt and dripping. I sat there and didn't move for over half an hour. The snow kept falling, but I just stayed there. Finally, it just laid its head down and looked straight at me. And then it died.

HARE (processors whirring): Why did you remain with the terrox?

Taban: You know, I don't know. Harpa asked me the same thing, on our honeymoon. I guess . . . I just felt bad for the thing.

[Taban swivels his chair so that he's facing the door leading out of the cockpit, staring into the dark, empty hall that leads to Daley's pod—or the hatch exiting the ship.]

Taban: It's a funny thing, HARE. We talked about religion. But whatever you believe—every single creature in this universe dies alone. That's a fact. No matter where it is or how or what or who's with it at the time. It's like this quote I heard. Death is like a door. It's one person wide. When you go through it, you do it alone. Whatever's on the other side is—whatever. But the crossing over, you do alone.

HARE (processors whirring): . . .

Taban: But . . . I don't know. I was just a kid. I didn't like to think of it like that. I thought, 'I could at least watch it go. Acknowledge it, instead of just letting it vanish into the void like it was nothing. Someone should.' I don't know. Like I said, I was young.

HARE: I understand.

Taban: . . . Anyway. Enough of my babbling.

HARE: I do not think it is babbling.

Taban: Why don't you play us some music?

11.

After she broke off from Fulbreech, Park received an alert on her inlays: METIS informed her that Commander Wick had summoned her to his quarters. He had tagged the summons as a "mandatory check-up."

As if he would put a suppressor on her tongue and make her say "ah," Park thought as she diverted from her route to her own bunk. The term did give her a sense of dread. It was too clinical, too sinister. Had Wick somehow found out what she'd been doing? Had Fulbreech told him?

But Wick is a reasonable man, Park told herself. He was always so patient, so paternally reliable. She didn't have to worry about him shooting her or freezing her—did she?

Maybe she ought to bring Jimex with her, she thought, thinking of him still standing inert in her office. For insurance. But then again, Wick was commander; his orders took precedence over hers. Jimex would ultimately have to obey him. He would bundle Park into a coffin and nail her inside, if Wick told him to. Her stomach sank. She really had no one to count on in this place.

On her way to see Wick, she ran into Natalya—who was doing lazy cartwheels and somersaults down the corridor to Wick and Boone's bunk. Park slowed as she approached the surveyor; she could see a little flask glinting at Natalya's belt.

Although the expedition members could technically do whatever they wanted when they were off duty, getting drunk was still not a common behavior on the ship. For one thing, alcohol took up precious space and mass; for another, it was so easy to dehydrate yourself with it, trapped as they were in a vacuum that wicked moisture from your eyes every time you blinked. It tended to take extreme circumstances to push someone to get drunk, especially openly, in front of the judging eyes of Earth-born academics and spacers who had long had access to faster-burning, trendier drugs. Park wondered what had gotten to Natalya—what had driven her to this state. A little bitterly she thought that it could be any number of things: everything seemed to be going wrong with this mission. Maybe she'd have turned to the bottle by now, too, if alcohol hadn't been so scarce back on Earth.

Natalya pretended not to notice Park as she walked up. She read agitation in the lines of the surveyor's shoulders: anger and suspicion and resentment, too. Natalya's topology reminded Park of Chanur, in a way—but what had soured Natalya's mood so? Surely it wasn't because of Holt? They'd once been lovers, yes, but Natalya had long since discarded the physicist in favor of pursuing—who was it, again? Fulbreech? Park had lost track.

"Something bothering you, Severov?" she asked, bracing herself.

The other woman straightened out of her pirouette and turned to look back over her shoulder. Her glance was moody, disdainful. "I thought Sagara told you to stop your patient sessions."

Had everyone been told that? God damn Sagara—he was undermining her at every turn. "This isn't an interview," Park answered, steadily enough. "Or a patient session. I just thought I'd ask."

"Why?"

"Why are you doing cartwheels in this part of the ship?"

Outside Boone's room, she thought. *And Wick's*. Unkindly she thought to herself—*Maybe she's just working her way up the ladder*

She quashed the idea just as Natalya said frostily, "This is how I unwind after work. Is that a crime?"

"No," Park answered. "Of course not."

She thought to give up the gesture entirely and simply walk away, but Natalya had put her leg up against the opposite wall, blocking the narrow corridor with her body. Her body language was languid, nonchalant—as if she hadn't noticed that Park intended to pass—but Park knew that it was a calculated move, an intimidation tactic. Or even a kind of threat. *I'm too tired for this,* she thought. She still hadn't slept yet. Natalya took a drink from her hip flask and smacked her lips.

"How's your work?" Park asked, to preempt whatever nasty thing the other woman was going to say. She didn't expect her to answer. As surveyor, Natalya had the most intimate knowledge of Eos and its terrain so far—so of course her work would be very hush-hush. And if *Fulbreech* wouldn't confide fully in Park, for fear of breaking protocol, Natalya certainly wasn't going to.

But to her surprise, Natalya said bluntly: "It's stressful. ISF is relying on me for a lot of things."

"I'm sure exploring an alien planet has its difficulties."

"Yes," Natalya said with a clenched look, like a purse snapping shut. Park faltered; she'd misstepped, come off unintentionally as sarcastic. Natalya continued, "I'm sure *you* have your work cut out for you, too. What with Ma going—what's the old phrase? Bananas. And poor Eric. I wonder how you'll fix that. Along with everything else that's going on."

"What else is going on?" Park asked, with bland innocence.

"What were you doing with Fulbreech?" Natalya asked in turn. And at this Park felt a little jolt of shock: so they'd been noticed, after all.

"Excuse me," she said, out of habit. On Earth it was considered rude for adult acquaintances to ask such direct, personal questions of each other; one was expected to ask obliquely, using statements that could be ignored or deflected, or to infer from other interfaces like a person's social feeds and status reports.

But Natalya's features only hardened. It was clear she had left that etiquette behind on Earth, that she couldn't be embarrassed into silence. *So much aggression there,* Park thought. And directness. Keller had always admired it as efficient, but Park thought it prevented Natalya from integrating well into teams.

"Fulbreech," the surveyor repeated, in a clipped way that said she thought she was speaking to an idiot. "Kel Fulbreech. The cartographer? What were you doing with him, going down to Deck C?"

So Natalya knew they had been down to the utility rooms together—but hadn't followed to see exactly what had happened. "We were just talking," Park said.

"You never talk," Natalya said with contempt. "And he talks too much." She stopped stretching, let her leg fall back down to the floor. Then continued, her eyes flinty: "What exactly would he talk to you about?"

Why do you care so much? Park wanted to ask. She couldn't suss out if Natalya was feeling territorial over Fulbreech, or if this was about something else entirely. She noticed for the first time that the surveyor had gray thumbprints under her eyes; her fingers trembled with a kind of suppressed energy. She said, taking a chance: "You said you were stressed, Severov. Has it been interfering with your sleep?"

"No," Natalya said curtly. Then she shook her head. "God, you ask questions. Even when you're told not to. Why so many questions? Isn't the whole point of your specialization that you don't have to ask, you can just *tell*?"

The implication being that she expected Park to be psychic, Park thought; Natalya found her to be a disappointment. She answered, "I can tell a lot from topologies, but not everything. Of course I ask questions."

Natalya grunted. "Why do we need you, then?"

Park wanted to say, *I don't have to explain myself to you. I don't have to justify my existence on this ship.* But she thought this was a good opportunity to shift perceptions about why she was there, so she said instead, "I provide a holistic view on what's going on in the ship; what state of mind people are operating under. I try to provide the truth of what's happening, just as any scientist does; and even though I don't play a role in the decision-making or research, I ask questions about what I'm observing. Like a good scientist."

"But do you understand the *content*?" Natalya asked then. "Do you know what it is you're observing and analyzing? What it all means? Or do you just transmit back what you've discovered without understanding it, like a robot?" She shook her head, her scorn palpable. "It's all meaningless if you don't *get* it."

Park felt a tremor, a little quiver down in the dark meat of her heart. How to answer? To admit weakness or doubt would only incite Natalya further—and not to sympathy. "I get what I need to get," she said finally. "But thank you for your concern."

Natalya made a dry clicking sound with her tongue. "Just focus on doing your job, Park," she said, turning away. "And doing it well. Don't meddle into all these other things."

Who's the one meddling? Park wanted to ask her. Who was the one sticking her nose where it didn't belong, asking questions, invading privacy? And who was the one who was getting drunk on the job? But she only said, numbly, "If you need to talk, Natalya, my door is always open."

"Holt talked, didn't he," Natalya bit back. She took a swig from her flask. "And look what happened to him."

Park came to Wick's door just as her inlays gave the green-gold flash to indicate the time. Nine o'clock at night, by the ship's clock. Lockdown hours. She stood outside of the bunk, feeling guilty, as if she was doing something illicit when everyone else was going to bed. Answering his call, sneaking to his room. Like a mistress—or a child about to receive a stern talking-to from a parent. What *did* he need to check up on her about?

She knocked. The door slid open instantly, which meant Wick had been waiting to activate the room controls at the first sign of her arrival. When she came in, she saw that he was standing with his back to the door, his hands crossed squarely behind him. The pose seemed deliberate to Park, affected. For one thing, it prevented her from reading his face. For another, it suggested that Wick was unthreatened by her; that he had nothing to be concerned about, and so neither did she.

Animals in the wild did that, Park thought. To lure their enemies into attacking. Then they whirled and made the kill themselves.

"You wanted to see me," she said, trying to banish her paranoia.

"Yes," Wick answered. He didn't turn around immediately. "I thought we should take some time and—get on the same page. Since your position on the ship has changed."

"Because Keller's frozen, and I'm now the primary psychologist?"

"Yes." Now he glanced back at her. "And because I can't afford to have you out of the loop. Not with everything that's been going on."

On the same page, Park found herself thinking, distracted. *Out of the loop.* Such strange, outdated terms. What page of what story were they struggling to get on? It felt like they were all parts of different volumes entirely. And did one *want* to be on the inside of a loop that was closing around the ship, like the knot of a tightening noose?

"Everything that's going on?" she echoed. She was too tired to berate herself for sounding like a simpleton.

"I heard you and Fulbreech," Wick said. He sounded almost apologetic. "Down in Deck C. While you were exploring the utility rooms."

Park blinked. "You were there?"

He shook his head. "No."

"Then—Natalya told you?"

"No," Wick said again, chagrined. "I mean—I *heard* you."

"I . . . don't understand."

He sighed and turned, making a gesture at the wall; his wrist console activated and projected a holographic blueprint of the ship onto the blank gray panel. Park looked at the diagram uncomprehendingly. The only thing she could grasp was that there were flashing red dots in every single room.

"What is that?" she asked.

"Captain Sagara has activated the ARGUS protocol," Wick said in turn. "Do you know what that is?"

"No," Park answered blankly. She shook her head. "Should I?"

"I'm not sure," Wick mused. "I don't know how much information ISF gave you, as their—orbiter."

"Nothing about this." *Or anything of importance,* she didn't say.

"The ARGUS protocol is a secondary function of METIS," Wick said. "While METIS is largely devoted to maintaining the ship's life support systems and its other prime directives, ARGUS is a way for us to . . . remotely monitor the crew's activities on the ship."

Her mind flashed to what Jimex had said about cameras. "I thought there were only cameras in certain areas."

"That's true," he conceded. "In the labs and the bridge and the entryways, mostly. We keep the amount of cameras limited to conserve power, as well as to restrict filming only to the necessities. There are still legal entanglements about using people's images, ever since"—he grimaced, as people often did when talking about privacy concerns—"Halla."

He was talking about the revolt, of course: the one that had sparked the Privacy Wars in the first place. It had started on an expedition ship headed to the planet that would later be founded as Haven. Conscripted crewmembers' images were at that time the property of the ISF—it was in the contracts that they had signed, or their parents had signed, in exchange for passage to the colonies—and the ISF had used those images as part of a successful reality show that was streamed back to Halla. The profits from the show had in turn funded the expedition—but the expedition members themselves didn't know they were being used as entertainment. And there were non-conscripted members who frequently wandered into the camera's eye. On the crew's return, there had been the expected moral outrage, legal battles. Then political conflicts. Then the Privacy Wars. It had taken a long time for the ISF to earn the public's goodwill back after that one, Park knew. Perhaps they still hadn't earned it. They wouldn't risk it so lightly again.

"So if there are only a few cameras on the ship," she said, "what does ARGUS actually do?"

"It's a loophole," Wick admitted. "An emergency measure. Although the ship doesn't have many cameras, it *is* fitted with—" Here he hesitated. "Microscopic sensors. And auditory devices. Tools to collect and aggregate . . . data."

It took Park a moment to understand what he was saying. "You're saying that the entire ship is *bugged*?" She looked again at the diagram, appalled. "Even the bathrooms? The sleeping quarters?" Even Wick's own bunk had a flashing light!

"It's not what you think," Wick said; now there was a faint sheen of sweat on his brow, despite the ship's customary cold. He'd known she wouldn't be happy about this. "Normally ISF would have no interest in the minutiae of what goes on in the ship. ARGUS can only be activated under dire circumstances, by either me or Captain Sagara. And it's not as if we're actively listening to everything that's going on, everything that everyone says. The amount of data would be overwhelming. And, again—it would be a violation."

He waved again, and the diagram vanished. "What we can do is let the ship's computer collect, parse, and filter through everything the ARGUS sensors pick up, without having to review everything ourselves. The sensors throughout the ship record both sound and movement, down to a whisper or a specific twitch. They analyze body language without ever having to record images. Then we give the computer—METIS—patterns and keywords to recognize, let it sift through everything, and have it present us with the salient metadata. But without it—without the computer, I mean—the general ARGUS information means nothing to us. It's just numbers, data. It anonymizes everyone for us. We can't tie it to anyone's identity, single anyone out. We only see the relevant slices if the system flags them and bundles them into a readable package for us: and that's only if that data meets the criteria we implemented in the first place. You see? So we can't access your conversations about—your families, or your favorite books, or what have you. The system only gives us that information if it thinks it fits what we're looking for." He took a breath, then continued before she could butt in. "That's how Captain Sagara plans to find patterns in the behavior of the crewmembers if they become—affected. By whatever this affliction is, even if they don't know it. It's a measure meant to monitor, recognize, and prevent."

Park was horrified. "In what other circumstance would this protocol ever be necessary?" she demanded. "Why would such a program exist in the first place, unless ISF was already expecting something like this?"

Wick looked sober. "I'm sure you've heard of mutinies happening," he said quietly. "Crewmembers revolting, taking over ships. That's what ARGUS is usually for. An ISF captain could activate it as a safety measure, if he suspected his crew of organizing against him."

That doesn't justify the breach in privacy, was Park's first thought. Then she remembered that a captain of an ISF ship had been murdered, a year before they'd launched the *Deucalion*. The crew had conspired to kill him and tried to steer the ship elsewhere. The ISF hadn't said why. At the time she had guessed it was stress-related, the kind of contagious mania and mob mentality that sometimes took hold in isolated space—but now she wondered if they simply weren't happy serving an entity that held their loved ones hostage. A government that used their own images and identities against them.

No one could know for sure, anyway; all of the rebel crewmembers were now dead.

Suddenly her thoughts flew back to that moment she had been talking to Jimex, down in Deck C before the encounter with Holt. The android had said there were cameras in certain parts of the ship, and also something else—before he suddenly cut himself off. He'd been trying to warn her about something. He'd said that Sagara had told him not to say.

He must have noticed the bugs when he was cleaning rooms, Park thought. *And Sagara silenced him. Ordered him not to tell me. Because he hopes to use ARGUS to catch me doing whatever he thinks I'm doing.*

"Who else knows about this?" she asked.

"Sagara, obviously," Wick said, oblivious to her thoughts. "Me. Boone. And now you."

"And why me?" She suddenly felt defensive, almost hostile. Wick said he had heard her and Fulbreech down in the utility rooms. Did that mean ARGUS had flagged their conversation as suspect? That he thought she was some sort of saboteur, as Sagara did?

Wick put out a steadying hand toward her, though he didn't go so far as to touch; Park still flinched away. "Because I think we need you," he said gently. And when Park scanned his face, his slate-gray eyes, she saw that he was being sincere. That the skin around his eyes looked puffy, as if he'd been crying.

"You think that?" she asked cautiously, still on her guard.

Wick made a hapless gesture. "Look," he said. "Kisaragi's frozen. Keller and Holt and Ma are—sick. I don't think now is the time to be divisive, to isolate and mistrust each other. And truth be told, I'm not convinced that—even if ARGUS *could* figure out what behaviors are red flags—it would do us a lot of good. Because we still wouldn't understand what was causing it all. What the root of the problem was." He looked into her eyes. "We would need you, Park. Your expertise and insight. We need you to understand what exactly is going on."

Park felt a crest of emotion rise within her, and couldn't tell if it was hysteria or sentimentality. She couldn't help but think again of what Natalya had said, earlier in the corridor: *But do you understand the content of what you're observing? What it all means?*

Wick had faith that she could. She wanted to feel touched, grateful. She thought she did. But she could only say, "What's down in the utility rooms, Wick?"

Her commander paused then. Worked his jaw for a moment; opened his mouth and then shut it again. Finally he said, looking tired: "We never kept things from you, Park, or anyone really, because of anything personal. You know that ISF determines who knows what based on who they think they can control. It's a matter of conscription. They explicitly told us not to let you—the non-conscripted—know too much, in case of leaks. They don't want the data getting out to the knowledge companies back home. Or even to the terrorists themselves."

"Yes," was all Park could say. She told herself not to tremble.

Wick spread his hands. He broadcasted helplessness, resignation, the idea that these things were out of his hands. "If it were up to me, everyone on the ship would have access to the same amount of information," he said. Then he looked away. "But it's not. Up to me, that is. So I have to ask that anything I tell you is kept private and between us. I'm violating my orders by bringing you into the fold. I discussed it with Sagara, and I think—I think he doesn't mistrust you personally. In fact, I think he respects you, in his own strange way. But he's an ISF man. By the book, follows his orders. Loyal to ISF to a fault. So he won't be happy about me telling you. But I think it's necessary. My call as commander."

"I understand," Park said, trying to crank on a soothing smile. "I'll obey the confidentiality strictures. Of course."

Wick took a breath.

"We came to Eos for colony reconnaissance, it's true," he said. "But we also came for something else. Close to a year ago, ISF received a mayday transmission from a miner who'd gotten stranded here by accident. In viewing the videos he sent, we discovered something about the planet. There's some sort of phenomenon that goes on here. A—gravitational anomaly."

Park waited. She expected herself to feel the lancing bolt of shock, maybe even outrage. Wick was telling her that they'd hidden half the damn mission from her. But somehow she felt nothing. It had been distantly obvious to her all along—like a billboard she could only dimly make out. Why else would they forbid her from seeing the planet? Why else would they confine non-essential personnel to the ship, if not because there was something unusual about Eos itself?

"What does that mean?" she asked. "A gravitational anomaly?"

"It's not far from here," Wick said. "A few kilometers. We've been calling it the Fold, for lack of a better word. It looks like fractal structures from a distance, or giant mirrors towering into the sky—but in fact, they're not structures or surfaces at all. They're creases in space. In dimensions."

Park stared at him. "I'm not following."

Wick shook his head. "I don't have a strong grasp of it, myself. To put it simply, space and gravity behave strangely in that area—in the Fold. Holt had some theories about a concentration of dark matter or gravity wells forming, but I lost the thread of it fairly quickly—and now he's frozen. But we've been trying to study the thing."

"What do you mean, space and gravity *behave strangely*?"

Wick scratched the back of his neck. "It's hard to explain it if you haven't seen it yourself. Essentially, in the Fold, space curves back on itself. It's as if something folds our four-dimensional space into shapes that intersect with a fifth dimension."

She gave him a blank stare.

Wick sighed. "Here's how Fulbreech explained it to me. Imagine you were a two-dimensional being—flat—living on a piece of paper. If something were to fold that piece of paper into, say, a three-dimensional triangle, a pyramid, the shape would be far too complex for you to comprehend. But only because you couldn't see the true simplicity of the shape from a higher dimension. And then if something were to fold that piece of paper into an origami crane—"

"My entire dimension would be turned topsy-turvy," Park finished. "Instead of the surface I knew, the whole thing would be bent into something utterly incomprehensible. So this anomaly is like an origami crane?"

"A fifth-dimensional origami crane, yes," Wick affirmed. "There, space curves around a fifth dimension; gravity and light make a U-turn on themselves. Does that make sense?"

"Not really, to be honest."

Wick kneaded the skin between his eyes. "I'm making a botched job of this," he muttered. "Let me speak without theory, then, and tell you my experience with the Fold. From afar and at certain times of day, it looks obvious to the naked eye: it's a mass of light and reflection, like shards of glass the size of skyscrapers. But as you get close to it, the whole thing seems to vanish, like a mirage—because you've entered the dimensional fold itself. And when you're there, in the midst of it, you realize these fractal structures and shards aren't solid surfaces, as they seem from a distance—they're holes or creases in space itself, usually reflecting themselves back onto each other. The dimensions collapse together there, and then reform again into something different. For example, I put my hand through one crease and saw it emerge from another, fifty yards away. I was waving at myself. Very uncanny."

"And it—doesn't harm humans? Being in this mass of dimensional folds?"

"It doesn't seem to," Wick said. "But it is—disorienting, to say the least. Like being trapped in one of those paintings with the Escher stairs, the ones that twist in impossible ways. At one point Boone wandered off, said he thought he saw somebody running out in front of him. But he was following a reflection of himself—no, Holt said he was actually following *himself.* Space folded back on itself in such a way that he was going in an endless loop, chasing his own body, just ahead."

Park put a hand to her temple. "This is giving me a headache."

Wick smiled slightly. "I know the feeling. Long story short, dimensions are merged together and refolded into different shapes in the Fold. It's something we've never seen before. And if we can understand it—master it—there's no telling what it could mean. We could utilize it for instantaneous travel—collapsing the distance between two points—or communication. We could use it to terraform new planets. We might even be able to use it to shape space itself, refolding it as we like. Who knows? Maybe we could even restore Earth to what it was like before the Comeback."

That gave Park a start. She took a long moment to process it. *Restore Earth?* That *was* momentous. No wonder the ISF was so eager to keep it a secret, until they could study the anomaly further. She said, "Would it be possible for humans to live permanently in such a place?"

Wick shook his head, rueful. "It's too soon to say. The air here is partially breathable, and there's an Earth-like atmosphere in terms of pressure. If your helmet sprang a leak, you wouldn't die instantly—which is better than most planets. But we know almost nothing about the Fold. It seems contained to that single area now, but what if that changed? And we don't know what's *causing* the folds in the first place. Until we can understand that, we can't know if it's safe enough to settle here."

And let's not forget the radiation storms, Park thought. *Or the nightmares.* "So what's in the utility rooms? Equipment to study the Fold? A lab?"

"Yes," Wick said heavily. "Which is supposed to be classified, kept secret.

Boone was stationed to guard it, when we didn't know where Holt was; it's why he was down there this morning, to prevent anyone from jeopardizing the data. He's supposed to keep away non-ISF personnel."

"We're all ISF personnel," she pointed out, a little stubbornly.

He frowned. "You know what I mean, Park."

Yes, she supposed she did, Park thought reluctantly. ISF had authorized Boone to use his gun and keep non-conscripted from finding out about all of this. Why? Because if they let the information leak to someone back home, there would be few consequences for them beyond termination, possibly a lawsuit. Conscripted expedition members, on the other hand, were keeping the secret under virtual pain of death. If ISF found out they'd disobeyed their orders, their citizenship in the Frontier could be revoked: they'd have to uproot their families, leave their homes. Exit space forever.

She felt a dim glow of both sympathy and shame. So that was what Fulbreech had risked, tipping her off. He'd given her as much of a clue as he could about what was going on. And yet . . .

"If I'm not authorized, I can't access the data down there," Park said. "Can Fulbreech?"

Wick looked uncomfortable. "He's conscripted," was all he said.

"So did he run down to the utility rooms to make sure I was safe, or did he go down there to prevent me from finding whatever trick is concealing the research lab?"

Wick barreled forward as if she hadn't asked the question. "It should be obvious why such a thing needs to stay under wraps," he said. Park frowned, but he continued: "The implications of it, the consequences, they're too unpredictable. We don't know anything about the thing, yet. We can't have the public finding out about it, the entire galaxy blowing up over something that could turn out to be unusable. So we have to tread very carefully."

Begrudgingly, she saw the picture he was painting for her. Crewmembers writing home, unable to contain their excitement. Researchers clamoring to make the big discovery that could change the world—making mistakes in their academic fervor. Greed and fear and jealousy setting in. Competitors trying to nose their way into classified business. Or someone getting political, spiteful; destroying the thing before ISF could use it. Yes, the fewer people who knew, the safer. She could see it. But she still didn't necessarily *like* it.

"Is that what Keller was working on?" she asked. "Her special project?"

"Yes."

"But what would you need a psychologist for? It seems like a problem for a quantum physicist."

Wick shrugged. "She had her orders from ISF."

There was a little silence between them as Park struggled to absorb all of this. Finally she said, "So Boone's in charge of guarding this . . . data."

"Well," Wick said. "Sagara is, technically. He's in charge of ensuring the data is safe from sabotage and loss. Boone's in charge of protecting us from outside threat."

"But we're the only ones on Eos," Park said, surprised. "There's no one else out here." She looked into Wick's eyes, which looked shuttered and wary suddenly. "Right?"

At this, Wick only shrugged. "You never know," was all he said.

They spent a while debriefing each other, talking rapid-fire in that chilly space. Wick refused to say anything more about the Fold, and Park didn't press much: now that she knew what the problem was, she found that she didn't care much about the specifics, the scientific details of the thing. She only had to know that the ISF considered it important enough to hide it from some of its own crew. She found herself wondering exactly who knew what: Had Keller known all along, or had she only been told the day they landed? Did Chanur know? Did Jimex? But she was afraid to ask. Rather than relief, she felt a little afraid of being told that she was the last to know. Even if Wick claimed it wasn't personal, she *felt* ISF's mistrust of her. Felt singled out. Now she knew how the other crewmembers had felt, knowing she was there solely to report back on them.

"So if I'm taking a shower," she said, "Sagara could be listening to me at any time?"

She hoped, almost viciously, that he was listening now; that he would be embarrassed by the implication, just as Wick was.

"You make it sound perverse," he said. His skin was ruddy under the tan—he was blushing. "As I said, ARGUS doesn't differentiate between crewmembers. It only processes their voices and movements blindly, like they're—nameless entities, or ghosts. And it's quite finicky as it is, anyway: the proton storm must have affected it. We'd need Reimi to know for sure." He shook his head. "And like I said, Sagara—or I, for that matter—can't just tune in and spy at any moment. The computer only detects commonalities between different figures, or keywords they use, and pinpoints them for us after the fact. You understand?"

ISF's hackneyed attempt at maintaining privacy, Park supposed. It could avoid the sticky issue of identity misuse, having the program collect data on everybody on the ship but rendering that data inaccessible unless the computer aggregated it under specific criteria. Most likely so the people who found out later couldn't raise a legal fuss. She said, "Is no one exempt? Could Boone or Sagara listen to this conversation later on, if the computer flagged it?"

"Yes," Wick said. "Though I already told them that I was going to tell you." His mouth twisted, wry. "We all found out about your little investigation earlier. They were none too happy about it, but I understood. I would have done the same thing, in your shoes. That's when I decided to let you in on things."

She did feel a warm wash of gratitude towards him. Finally someone who empathized with her, understood her frustration—understood too that she could do a lot more damage, bumbling blindly around in the dark, than she could with full knowledge of what was going on. But she couldn't help but say, a little anxiously: "If Holt knew all about this anomaly, and Boone still shot him for potentially compromising the data . . ."

Wick waved his hand. "Don't worry," he said. "I'm commander. And I say we need to trust you. They won't do anything out of line."

But she couldn't tamp down that little bubble of fear. She thought of the hostility that Boone had towards her, the suspicion Sagara held that she had something to do with the nightmares. Then, remembering the nightmares, she said: "This anomaly. Is there any way it could be—*affecting* people?"

Wick looked surprised. "What do you mean?"

Park clasped her hands together, thinking. "Holt showed signs of disturbance only on the day we landed. Not before. Ma, too. So could the Fold be radioactive? Toxic in some way? Did either of them have contact with it?"

Wick was shaking his head, troubled. Somehow the light in the room had shifted, throwing his eyes and mouth into shadow. He said, "No, neither of them were ever allowed near it. Ma didn't even know about it, being non-conscripted. Holt did, but he never had contact with it. We wouldn't let him go out until Natalya and the others had secured the area."

"Still," Park persisted. "You said you know next to nothing about it. Could it alter anyone's mental state?"

"The anomaly doesn't work like that," Wick told her flatly. "It affects things, not people. Matter and space, not . . . dreams. It can't influence anyone the way you're thinking, no more than a black hole or the sun could."

Only it could, Park thought later as Wick stood and shook her hand—an outdated Earth custom that gave her the brief silvery flash of pleasure and anxiety that came with unexpected bodily contact. People were *things* just as much as anything else, in their own way. But she had to take him at his word: Wick wouldn't allow them to stay there if it could potentially harm his crew. They were safe. She was safe. She had to believe that.

She left his bunk with a head full of static. A headache was beginning to throb behind her eyes, as if a leech had attached itself to the inside of her skull. She lay down on her hard cot—Natalya and Hunter had not returned to the room yet—and drew the flap of her foil thermal blanket up to her chin. So much new information, she thought. She had to take time to process and adjust her frame of reference. Eos was not just a place to live and explore. It was the site of something momentous, like the first flyby of a Planck star. Something that could change their understanding of physics—of the universe—itself. How did she feel about that? She didn't know. She didn't know if she'd felt much of anything, even when she still believed it was just the site of a future colony. Had anything changed? Her role was still the same. The job they'd hired her for was still the same. That they'd lied to her—and the non-conscripted others—didn't play into it. She could understand their reasons, rationally. Couldn't she?

What would happen if it were all true? she wondered then. If understanding this anomaly really could help things on Earth, if it could make terraforming easier? What if they could "fold" acid oceans, sulfur deserts—the barren traverses of space? Manipulate and merge dimensions, topographies, and reshape them as they pleased?

Dangerous, was her first thought. Dangerous, dangerous. It was the power gods wielded.

And yet . . .

What could never be settled before could be a blank canvas now. Humanity could spread to all corners of the galaxy. And they were due for the next big leap in technological advancement. Since the ISF had invented the lambda engine and faster-than-light travel, decades ago, things had slowed to a technological crawl—except for the increments by which androids and artificial intelligence improved. People on Earth were so preoccupied with coming up with ways to combat the Comeback—with preserving things before they were lost to the plants—that they hadn't been able to do more than survive for years. This anomaly could be far more important than a single colony mission. She shouldn't be insulted by the deception. Their discoveries here could change things for the human race on a grand scale.

If it worked the way they hoped it did, she thought. If it wasn't just another dud, like the Icarus Stargate or the ansible. If they weren't courting disaster just by being here.

If. If. If.

There was still the question of the nightmares, too. She still didn't know what could be causing them—what could be causing all the catastrophes that had struck the ship since they'd arrived. But things were a little clearer, now. Maybe it was all a coincidence. Maybe it was the stress of the whole culture, of keeping all these secrets, of knowing there was something hidden down in the belly of the ship. That could affect a person, couldn't it? Enough to drive them to a breakdown, to parasomnia? Holt's obsession—or guilt—could have led him down to the utility rooms. The root of his anxieties, she thought. The epicenter of all the fears and hopes on the ship.

She closed her eyes. No. She was still missing something—there were still things afoot aboard the *Deucalion*. In the shadows. The hard, reptilian part of her brain told her so, and she had learned to trust that intuition.

But at least her view of things had sharpened, even a little. At least she had a fuller picture of what was going on. She lay back and imagined the *Deucalion* drifting silently through the boundless inkwell of space. Their native sun would be nothing more than a distant white needlepoint in the black alien fabric they'd woven themselves into. They were farther away from the hub of human life than anyone had ever gone. Wick had only shrugged when she'd asked if they were alone. But who would follow them, all the way out here? Who would venture to the icy outer rings of another galaxy, just to find some anomaly—even one as novel as this?

It was paranoia, she thought. On the part of ISF. They were too used to secretiveness, to walling themselves up from within. To protecting their vulnerabilities from the outside. Park would know. It took one to know one.

She sighed. Glenn had told her something once, when she was young. She'd asked him if he ever kept secrets from her.

"Yes," he'd answered calmly. When she gave him an accusing look, he'd added, "Only when it's good for you."

"How do you know when it's good for me?" she'd demanded.

He'd smiled and allowed her to take his cool, tough hand, letting her wring it as a kind of mock-punishment. "There are some things you don't need to know," Glenn said. "Things that could worry you, or frighten you."

"But it's good to be frightened, sometimes," Park had answered, wise even then.

Glenn shook his head, still smiling. "I don't understand."

"Fear is what keeps us alive," she told him. "I have to know what I'm afraid of to avoid it. Fear is what keeps me away from dangerous things."

"That is why I am with you," Glenn had answered patiently. "I will keep you away from what you should fear."

But you're not here anymore, Park thought. *And when they kept their secrets from me, I didn't know what to fear. I was afraid of everything.*

At least it's over now, she told herself. At least now she knew. No more secrets, no more fear.

What had she said to Glenn then, on that sun-showered day? Had she ignored him, had she thanked him? Had she wondered what her android guardian was keeping from her? She couldn't remember—the memories felt waxy with disuse and time. A feeling of acceptance washed over her. It didn't matter. It was over now. Things could proceed as usual.

A gray veil seemed to fall over her eyes. Eventually Park settled into the rattling of the ship's walls and dreamt of her jettisoned body hurtling through folds in space and time. There was Earth below her, spinning away, blue-blushed and familiar. She didn't know why, but she turned away from it. Her body aimed instead for cold and distant stars.

12.

Antarctica was good to Park. The training of the *Deucalion*'s crew took place in a biodome there, and Park had initially resisted going; the biodome was for the sole benefit of those going on expeditions, crewmembers who would have to acclimate to building and dwelling in their own biospheres once they'd surveyed Eos's terrain and established the beginnings of a settlement. Park herself would be stuck on the ship; she'd never need to live in an artificial habitat, so in her view, she didn't need the training.

But Dr. Keller said that she needed to go to Antarctica anyway, to observe the candidates under the peak of their stress. The biodome, for training purposes, was designed to be even worse than the confines of their future ship—and Antarctica's bleak and lifeless landscape was the closest they could come to simulating Eos's alien tundras.

To her surprise, Park loved it. She had never been outside the cities before, but she adjusted well to the blank, razor line of the arctic horizon, the roaring emptiness of the ice. Most candidates, Dr. Keller warned her, would feel claustrophobic: the pressures of their own thoughts would creep up on them. Most of them had never been stranded with themselves for so long before. There had always been diversions to stimulate, occupy, distract—but here, at the bottom of the world, they would feel trapped in the microcosms of their own minds.

Not Park. To her it simply felt like the environment had finally changed to suit her; as if she had always lived within a bubble of ice, peering calmly out at an empty world. Now there were merely a few more people inside the bubble, and she didn't mind this—even though they peered at her suspiciously, and conversations died when she entered a room. Once or twice she found that someone had taken the battery-powered lantern from her tent, or filled both of her boots with snow.

"It's like frat row around here," Dr. Keller said.

"It's all right," Park said. "This happened in college, too."

"For different reasons, I would hope," said Keller. Together they hypothesized that their presence was fomenting resentment: the expedition candidates knew that they were being evaluated, dissected, their suitability rigorously commented on by Keller and Park to ISF. While the candidates ran through simulations of the various tasks they'd have to perform on Eos, familiarizing themselves with the equipment as well as with each other—Park and Keller were watching. Always watching.

And Park was the more vulnerable target of the two, being younger and more introverted. The Eos team viewed her as an ISF snitch, a ladder-climber, a betrayal to her peer group—and also just plain strange. She was also troublingly unavailable as a sexual partner—none of the expedition members were married—and this isolated her even further. There was no comfortable niche for her in the social structure. No connections to anchor her to the community.

Once, during a patient session, Valentina Hanover asked to be called "Hunter."

"Hunter," Park repeated, thinking of her file. "That isn't your middle name."

Valentina gave her a look of loathing. "It's called a nickname, you absolute imbecile."

That about summed up everyone else's apparent impressions of Park. She barely spoke to them, and when she did, it always seemed like she came off as baffling, primitive: some kind of specimen that one examined with half disgust, like protozoic ooze. No, they acted like she was an alien sightseer, ogling the most basic human interactions, and in turn, they ogled her, too—squinted at her from behind the glass, whispered and smirked to each other.

"Of course they'll steal your boots," Keller said later, running a hand over her stubbled head. "In environments like this, an academic community reverts to a tribe. The biodome becomes a habitat. And tribes will always choose an enemy, arbitrary or not, to unite against, to single out. It helps them bond." She shook her head. "Be thankful no one's poisoning your water supply or burning you at the stake."

Grim jokes, but then, Keller admitted to succumbing to the dour mood that hung around the biodome like a buildup of stale air. It had only taken a week without sunlight or hot water for the prospective crewmembers to get irritable.

Park, however, was immune. Despite the thefts, despite the stares and scoffs, she carried out her duties briskly, even cheerfully. She was happier than she had been in a long time.

Like Keller, she was responsible for making rounds throughout the biodome, documenting the behaviors of the trainees, making herself available to hear out their anxieties and concerns. Most came to her reticently, feigning perfect composure to distinguish themselves as ideal candidates. The ISF predicted that half of them would be sent home before training was over.

Others were more honest. Park had taken part in the initial interviewing process for each candidate. She had doled out the 556-question psychological tests, compiled profiles from the answers, scaled each candidate according to labile-stabile indexes, assigned numbers to their sociability, impulsiveness, changeability. She'd studied their receptiveness to devices like the MAD. Recorded their cortical arousal, the blooms of light that happened in their brains. And yet none of it had quite prepared her for the complexes that unveiled themselves in Antarctica. There was Peter Rochoff, an agriculturalist, who suffered bouts of insecurity that he tried to smother with over-robust laughter, as if everything Park said was a mean joke that he was confident enough to find the humor in. Lucia Van was one of the most efficient flight engineers Park had ever seen, and yet she was so avoidant of authority figures that Park eventually had to send her home. The biodome designer Wan Xu was a narcissist, something he had somehow kept hidden from the tests: he was constantly exasperated by the inferiority of the minds around him, constantly making himself out to be both the hero and the victim of any given situation. It was too bad he was also one of the most brilliant minds on Earth, at least when it came to building extraterrestrial habitats. Park always left their sessions with her eyes watering, as if she had narrowly escaped an accident—the sideswipe of an angry driver.

And then there was Bebe Hill. Initially Park found herself admiring the woman, out of all others in the crew. Not the steady Wick, nor the ingenious Dr. Jain, nor even "Hunter," who could sprint in an exo-armor suit that weighed over two hundred pounds. No, in the end it was Bebe whom Park found herself in awe of: a pillowy-cheeked botanist who specialized in space-bred plants.

At their first meeting, Park asked the woman what she considered most important to her. Bebe answered without hesitation: "The perfection of my craft."

Park was taken aback. She read no lie in the botanist's topology; there was no insincerity, no calculation. Bebe wasn't motivated by thoughts of glory in settling a new colony. Wasn't plagued by insecurities about proving her worth to the crew. She cared about nothing except her work. She wasn't just dedicated to it, and didn't just work hard at it; she had *real passion* for it. Park admired that. She wished she could say the same thing about herself.

Tentatively, they became friends. Bebe, focused on her plant studies, seemed to take little notice of the stigma that Park carried with her as ISF's "rat"; Park, in turn, was glad to have an acquaintance her own age. She found pleasure in watching Bebe devote herself to the mission—not even Keller did that, not fully—and hoped to model her own behaviors off of what she observed in the other woman.

It was at this point that she learned it *was* possible to fool a phenotype analyst. A person could lie without knowing they were lying; they could make a false statement while their bodies and minds fully believed it to be true. In other words, she couldn't read 'truth' from someone's face—only 'belief.' Bebe had *believed* that the most important thing to her was her work—but this wasn't *true*. For the first time Park realized how fragile her own craft really was. Everything she read, all of the data that she gathered and interpreted—it all depended on its source. And every source, being human, also held the possibility of being flawed.

Bebe's flaw was that she fell in love. With the young physicist, Eric Holt. They met a few weeks into the Antarctic training, and within a matter of days Bebe had morphed from a stolid, single-minded worker to a short, wet-eyed woman who sighed every time her boyfriend left the room. Suddenly she no longer cared about her specimens, her research on Eos's potential plant life and soil composition; now it was all about Holt's romantic gestures, the latest thing he'd said or done to vex her. Park was horrified—but it was too late to cut the connection, not without creating some very awkward dynamics within the biodome. So she had to bear it out.

Every afternoon Bebe made it a point to seek Park out, flopping down into a nearby chair so she could rant about the latest development with Holt. "I'm not usually like this," she would say to Park, wiping her eyes with her pinky fingers, so as not to smudge her makeup. "But I've never *felt* this way about someone before." Park would only nod, never knowing what to say.

Bebe complained about everything: Holt's youthful cluelessness, his wandering eye, how when she said she loved him, he only smiled nervously and said, "Great." And, when pressed: "That's *so* great." She pressured Park to give her opinions on Holt, on the other candidates who interacted with him, as if Park were her personal spy. "Do you think he's sleeping with anyone else? Do any of the others notice him? Have you ever seen him flirting with anyone?"

On and on. Now Bebe seemed to leap out of the most unexpected places: from behind a crate of rations as Park bent to grab a snack, from around a generator while Park tried to warm her hands. She demanded endless emotional conferences, roundtable discussions about who liked her or didn't like her, about who had hurt her feelings that day or made her feel small when all she really wanted to do was be in love . . .

Through it all Park had to fix a neutral expression on her face and offer calm words of affirmation and redirection, trying to prod Bebe towards focusing on her job. Park was part of the crew's counseling team, she couldn't turn anyone away—as much as she wanted to turn and run in a panic whenever she saw Bebe coming. She felt like a resident advisor at a university, rubbing freshmen's backs while they wept about their roommates eating the last soyogurt in the fridge. At least Bebe did the minimal work to keep her plants alive; Park half-hoped she wouldn't, so she could send her home. She was so disappointed.

Other than the Bebe problem, however, Park was happy in Antarctica. At night she spent her free time watching documentaries about the first colonists, the pioneers who had settled Mars, Corvus, Io. That would be her, she thought, watching the pre-downloaded streams on her wrist console. Someday someone would make a documentary about her: about the psychologist who had kept the Eos expedition sane and in check. She hoped they would pull interviews from when she was still young. She didn't want to be remembered as a misty-eyed old woman, shakily recalling adventures in space that could have been half-imagined.

She had no other friends to speak of. Even laying aside her position on the fringes of the biodome's community, Park simply didn't have the time for friends: she had her hands full, wading through the neuroses and fixations of the newly formed village. No time to think of any of them on a personal level; no time to think of anything beyond the task at hand, really. Which she liked. After the Bebe fiasco, she thought, it was better to avoid the whole thing altogether. That way you couldn't be let down.

The weeks passed. One day she had a run-in with the biodome's only android, a HERCULES model no one had bothered to name. The HERCULES was there to do any heavy lifting or manual labor a human couldn't do: rapid repairs on the biodome if anything went wrong, accelerated rescue if one of the expedition members got lost on the ice. It was a primitive thing, not human-looking in the way that Park was used to: only a rough approximation of a man, skinless, with metal limbs that were bulky and golem-like. Most of the time it sat alone by the lookout tower, knees clasped, inert.

That morning Park noticed it while she was eating breakfast in the mess tent. Austral summer had blown in; the HERCULES was squatting near the inside flap of the tent, and every time someone lifted the canvas to enter, blinding sunlight shot off of its chrome egg head and into Park's eyes.

"Could you move away from there?" she asked it. "You're hurting my eyes."

"I apologize," the HERCULES said in its tinny way, though it didn't understand what she meant. It was unaware of the light coming from behind it, so it only shifted a few inches before settling down again with a clink. Park had to eat with one hand shielding the left side of her face. Meanwhile, the HERCULES watched her.

"Do you need something?" Park asked finally, after she had finished dry-swallowing a dehydrated biscuit, letting it scrape past her throat.

"No," the HERCULES said.

Something about the way it surveyed her face sent a line of heat running through Park's stomach. It reminded her of Glenn, though the HERCULES had only the barest approximation of a crude metal face. But the eyes were the same: alert, liquidly understanding. Remote.

"Who activated you?" Park asked it. "What is your protocol?"

"I was told to observe," the HERCULES answered. Its voice sounded metallic and raw, like the echoing of a sawblade.

"Observe who? Observe me?"

"Yes."

"Who told you to do that?"

"They instructed me not to say."

Another prank, Park thought. Someone was "teaching" her what it felt like to be watched all the time. Observed. The best thing to do was to not react. "Take my tray away," she said. "If you're going to follow me around, you might as well help."

"That's pretty funny," Keller said afterward, when Park reported in with the HERCULES at her side. "Though childish beyond belief. I suppose you can't deactivate it?"

"Whoever issued the command told it not to stop until its protocols were satisfied," Park said. "And to not reveal who they were. I think I just have to wait for it to stop on its own or return to the issuer for further instructions."

"That's unfortunate," Keller said, studying the HERCULES's tall steel frame. It was standing wordlessly next to her cot, watching the two of them with its head bent down at an awkward angle. "I wish ISF had given us a more recent model. The metal ones are so stupid."

"I don't mind it so much," Park answered. "Androids essentially behave the same in any form." The HERCULES bent then to examine the packet of files at her feet; Park pushed its head away from her, open-palmed, like it was an inquisitive dog.

"Well, just don't bring it into your patient sessions," Keller said. "People tend to get their guard up around androids. Plus there's a matter of confidentiality: you never know what they'll say or not say."

"I understand," Park said, and then bit her tongue hard enough for it to bleed.

The HERCULES dogged her silently for the rest of that day. Park stopped noticing it, largely, though she didn't miss the quizzical or irritated glances of the candidates she went to visit. "What's up with the clunker?" Michael Boone asked, rudely; the HERCULES surveyed him from over Park's shoulder until Boone told it to fuck off, so that it retreated and watched them from afar. In a way the thing reminded her again of Glenn, the way he had accompanied her ceaselessly through the streets of New Diego; but where Glenn might have offered a quiet question, some sardonic commentary, the HERCULES only watched, and waited. At night, it stood outside of the doorway of her tent until frost crackled on its shoulders and the moon made it glow with white light.

"Come in," Park said after a while. When the android clunked in, she gave it some air-dropped magazines to look at and told it not to bother her. The HERCULES sat down beside her cot and leafed expressionlessly through an exposé on jungle fashion after the Comeback. Park turned back to her documentaries.

"Why do you watch those?" the HERCULES asked, after an hour or so.

"I like them," Park answered. She didn't pause her filmstream. "They're educational. I can learn from the trials of others: these people had also never been in space, before they went to settle the colonies. But they still succeeded. I suppose it's comforting for me to watch."

The HERCULES processed this. "There are other documentaries," it said. "About cellular processes. Animals."

"I'm not interested in those," Park answered, a little flatly. She had endeavored to study animal behavior when she was young, to have something to talk about with her uncle during his visits home; but he was dead now, and they had not spoken much before his death. "I prefer learning about humans."

"Why?"

Park paused. "I just do," she said after a moment.

The HERCULES nodded a little, as if it found this answer satisfactory. Then it asked, seemingly apropos of nothing: "Why don't you call anyone?"

At this Park did stop the documentary. "What do you mean?"

"Other people," the HERCULES said. "People here in the biodome—they spend their nights calling loved ones. Telling them about their days. You don't do that."

It was a statement, not a question. "I wouldn't be able to tell anyone about my day," Park told it. "As a psychologist, most of my patient interactions are confidential. Plus, ISF doesn't want us talking about why we're here in the first place. It would be a boring conversation."

"You could converse about other things."

I don't have anyone to call, Park almost said. She felt a clenching in her chest, a kind of hard-edged pain, like swallowing a stone. *Isn't it obvious?* she thought. *That's why I'm leaving Earth. I don't have anywhere else to go—or anywhere else to be.*

But then she thought: how did the HERCULES know what other people did, compared to her? Had it been ordered to watch others, too? And by whom? She was suddenly conscious of the fact that she didn't know who had sent it, who might be watching her through it. What information would it be relaying back about her? Would the final report simply say that she was lonely? Connectionless? Unmoored?

"Calling someone could reduce feelings of loneliness," the HERCULES said, as if it knew her thoughts.

"I like to be alone," Park answered.

The HERCULES watched her. Park tried to read some expression in its battered metal face, some hint of pity or sympathy or contempt. When it spoke, its voice was as hard and flat as a knife blade.

"No," it said. "I don't believe you do."

Bebe Hill came into Park's tent after that, puffy as a raincloud in her thermal jacket, swathed in a storm of tears. "It's Eric," she said, hiccupping thickly. "He won't talk to me."

I'm tired, Park tried to say, but before she could open her mouth, Bebe sank down onto her cot without asking for permission. The HERCULES looked at Park for a directive, and she jutted her chin at the door. After it left, Park listened as Bebe blubbered something about an argument, Holt storming off in a rage, some kind of accusation being bandied back and forth.

"You have to do a favor for me, please, Dr. Park," Bebe said.

I don't do favors, Park nearly said, but instead screwed her mouth into a tiny frown and made a gesture to indicate she was listening. She didn't fail to notice that Bebe had called her "doctor"—an attempt to butter her up, to bolster her sense of importance. But it had the opposite effect: it made her painfully aware that Bebe did not consider her a friend.

"What do you want, Bebe?" she asked warily.

"I need you to tell Eric something for me," Bebe said.

"Why don't you tell him yourself?"

"Haven't you been listening?" the botanist exploded. "He won't *talk* to me. Don't you *listen*?"

Park said nothing. Bebe, perhaps sensing her displeasure, calmed herself down a little; in meeker tones she said, "Please, could you calm him down? You're the only one who can."

Park held back a noise. She was tempted to send Bebe packing, or at least over to Dr. Keller, but from what she could glean from the weeping, it did seem that Holt was agitated about something. And that *did* fall into the realm of her responsibility—even if matchmaking didn't. *God damn Bebe*, she thought. God damn the lies that faces told.

"All right," she said after a few more minutes of listening to Bebe cry. "Let me go and check on Holt. Stay here." She pulled on her boots and parka, laboriously worked her gloves onto her fingers.

"He's in his tent," Bebe sniffled.

Where else would he be? Park thought irritably. The HERCULES was waiting outside her tent; it straightened its back as she came out, like a soldier saluting a superior. "Come along," she said, not trusting it to refrain from interrogating Bebe. When they had trudged some distance away, the HERCULES asked, "What's wrong with her?"

Love, Park thought; or infatuation, or fear of dying in space alone. "She's just upset," she said, hoping it would leave it at that. The HERCULES nodded, as if it knew what it meant to be upset, and clunked after her through the snow. Its limbs jerked and twitched like a wind-up toy's; through the aching rush of arctic air, Park could hear the rotors in its joints squealing and complaining. *It needs maintenance*, she thought vaguely—she would have to remember who the mechanical engineer in the biodome was. Sometimes it was hard to keep them all straight in her head. That girl Reimi Kisaragi was supposed to be good with robots, wasn't she?

She reached Holt's tent, a standard-issue cosmonaut's shelter stationed at the end of a long row of tents. She paused before the entrance—there was no real way to knock on a tent flap—and said, trying for briskness: "Holt, are you awake?"

"Uh," he said. "Who is it?"

"It's Dr. Park. I'd like to speak to you, if you're free."

"Oh," Holt said. Park thought she heard footsteps crunching through the snow behind her; it seemed to her that the HERCULES was pacing in little circles at her back. Holt twitched aside his tent flap and said in a sheepish whisper, "Sorry, Park, but now's not really a good time . . ."

Despite herself, Park looked over his shoulder. Natalya Severov was there, sitting up in Holt's cot; her honey-colored hair fell over her thin, freckled shoulders in a golden cloud. She held Holt's blanket over herself to cover her nakedness, but her eyes were huge and defiant as she stared at Park. Her expression seemed to say: *And? What the hell do you want?* Park nearly laughed; instead she looked at Holt as if her field of vision had narrowed to just his face and said, "I'm sorry to bother you."

He knew she had seen; he smiled unhappily. "I'd appreciate it if you didn't tell the commander," he said. Behind him, Natalya huffed. *The commander couldn't care less who you sleep with*, Park wanted to say. *Neither could I.* But before she could respond, a kind of piercing wail came from behind her.

Park turned. It hadn't been the HERCULES pacing, after all; the android had been standing placidly by her shoulder the whole time. The heavy tread she'd heard was Bebe's—the botanist had followed them to Holt's tent. Now she stood there in the sterile moonlight, her breath streaming out of her in gouts of white. Her small frame swelled and expanded like a hot-air balloon.

"A child!" she screamed. "You're a fucking child, Eric!"

"Look," he said, coming a little out of his tent, "I'm sorry. But I wanted things—simple."

"They *are* simple!" Bebe said. "I *love* you!"

"I know." Holt rubbed his head in an embarrassed way; his bare toes shuffled against each other self-consciously. "It's cold," he said, looking at Park. "Maybe we can talk about this later."

Which meant, Park thought grimly, it was up to her to deal with the fallout. It wouldn't do for Bebe to make a scene, to disrupt the surface-level peace of the community: now she had to herd her off and shut her up someplace secluded. She felt an edge of deep annoyance. Couldn't they be professional, for God's sake? Couldn't anyone get through the mission—which hadn't even started yet—without these kinds of entanglements? And as for Park . . . this wasn't her job. She shouldn't be some unnoticed go-between. Didn't they have androids to do this—delivering messages in the middle of the night, escorting unwanted bodies elsewhere?

Bebe was still yelling at Holt, who had vanished back into his cozy tent with Natalya. Park turned to the HERCULES and said in an undertone, "Help me take her away." It nodded—somehow it seemed to understand perfectly—and clasped its metal hand around Bebe's elbow. Bebe yelped at the iciness of its touch; her head swiveled to gawk at the android, as if some eldritch creature had wrapped its tentacles around her. Park said, "It's all right, Bebe. Let's go talk about this somewhere else."

Bebe meant to fight her, Park saw, or more likely meant to fight Natalya, but then she stared up into the HERCULES's face and seemed to change her mind. The HERCULES smiled at her, jerkily, the movement like the dents in a crumpled soda can popping back out. Together the two of them led Bebe back to Park's tent, where Bebe lay flat on her back on the tarp floor, crying, while Park sat on the edge of the cot and droned at her: first standard words of reassurance from the ISF scripts, and then, helplessly, whatever Park thought would have made herself feel better if the situations were swapped.

You wouldn't want to crack, she insinuated, to lose your composure—not before getting to Eos. The opportunity of a lifetime. Of a million lifetimes. A virgin planet to help discover! Nothing was worth losing that! The violence of emotion would not be allowed aboard the ship, she told Bebe. The irrationality of love had no place in space. So . . . get rid of it.

When that didn't work, she attempted to explain further. "When you feel love," she said, "your ascending reticular activating system is stimulated. It's a cluster of cells deep in your brain stem. It doesn't discriminate. Not in the way you would think. So you'll move on. Find someone else."

Bebe kept weeping. "In other words," Park said, "this isn't the end of the world. You can love again."

Though she didn't know why Bebe would want to. Luckily, it didn't seem that the botanist heard any of what Park was saying: she seemed intent on lying on the floor and howling at the arctic moon while the HERCULES watched tentatively through the slit in the tent. Park was reduced to cradling her chin in her hand and making soothing sounds while Bebe gasped and hiccupped with heartbreak.

An hour passed, then two. Eventually the other woman fell asleep on the floor, her tears forming a transparent crust on her face so that it seemed blurry and undefined to Park. Park was left sitting on the edge of her cot, wondering what it was like to feel the things that Bebe felt. What was love, really? Biology, as she'd said—but also nothing more than a pain in someone's ass.

The next morning, Park trudged toward the mess tent for breakfast. She couldn't keep her head from drooping a little: she'd scraped barely three hours of sleep, and even then Bebe's snoring had jolted her awake throughout the night. She bumped forehead-first into someone's shoulder; they put out a hand to steady her and said, "Are you all right?"

"Fine, thank you," Park said automatically. She could barely raise her eyes. Later she would realize it was Fulbreech addressing her, though she hadn't known him then—he was Keller's patient, and there had been over one hundred recruits in the Antarctica biodome compared to the thirteen who would make it out. She registered a friendly smile, the glimpse of a strong chin. He'd said something in warm tones, but the words were as muffled as if she had stuffed her head with cotton. Park nodded vacantly and marched on without answering.

Commander Wick approached her in the mess tent. Park was gulping coffee so quickly it didn't even have time to scald her tongue; when the commander sidled up, she choked. In those days Park had still felt shy with him. Wick was a veteran of a dozen colony missions; he had the hallowed glow of a folk hero. She wiped her mouth and said, "Commander. Good morning."

"Park," he said. "I need you to do something for me."

Park waited without saying anything; she didn't want to appear too eager, too subordinate. It also felt like people needed her a lot, lately. She was beginning to feel worn down with it, fever-warm, like wood after vigorous sanding. Wick continued, "Natalya's heading out to find an ice aquifer this morning. I'd like you to go with her."

Park stared at him; she didn't even try to mask her surprise. As the expedition's surveyor, Natalya would be in charge of locating landmarks like reservoirs, valleys, and caves on Eos. In Antarctica, of course, they already knew where things were—but for the sake of simulation, they had the recruits go out blind, relying on only what they would have on Eos to find what they needed. Park had heard that there was pressure on Natalya to find a large source of water nearby: they had enough to drink in the biodome, with the water reclaimers, but people wanted baths. They were tired of hastily sponging themselves clean, of always being smelly—especially when it came to showing off, or courting each other. Work performance and personal confidence both suffered. So they needed more water, and now Wick was sending Natalya out to find an aquifer. Along with Park.

"I'm not trained for that," she said. "I wouldn't be able to help."

"It's not that I need you to survey the land," Wick said. "But Natalya seems . . . on edge this morning. She needs some company when she goes out on the ice. I figure you'd be good at keeping her head on straight while she's out there."

It's not my job, Park wanted to say again, but she looked into Wick's deep gray eyes and felt her scalp tighten. "All right," she said.

So she suited up, donning her bulky helmet and faceplate, which was standard for expedition members when leaving the biodome: it was supposed to replicate the spacesuits and exo-armor jackets they'd be wearing on Eos. Before she left she went to check on the HERCULES, mostly to procrastinate. The thought of spending the morning alone with prickly Natalya filled her with dread. The HERCULES was still standing quietly outside her tent, giving its joints a rest; Park had noticed all throughout that morning that its limbs had been creaking more than usual.

She approached it. The HERCULES peered blandly into her faceplate when she walked up; Park wasn't sure at first if it recognized her behind the golden visor. Then it said, "You're leaving the biodome."

"Temporarily," Park said. "Yes." She had it lift an arm, ran her fingers helplessly over its bulky shoulder joint, which was beginning to streak with coppery rust. She'd been the one to help Glenn with his basic maintenance, in the old days; she had a rudimentary knowledge of robotics. But the HERCULES was a foreign model to her—and she didn't want to risk breaking it completely. For a moment she wondered at her own concern. But it was a little sad, to her. The HERCULES had to hear its own creakiness, the evidence of its own disrepair. It had to be fully aware of its vulnerability. For them to ask it to press on without addressing its slow breakdown seemed cruel.

"I'm sorry," she said to it. "I don't know why the roboticists aren't taking better care of you. I don't know how to treat you. And of course you don't have the ability to fix yourself."

"Do I need fixing?" the HERCULES asked, with what she imagined was concern.

"Not fixing, exactly," Park said. "Maintenance, yes. Your movements seem hampered."

The HERCULES nodded slowly, as if it was surprised she had noticed. "Yes. The weather conditions here are extreme. I apologize for my lowered performance."

"No," Park said, almost moved. "Don't apologize. It's not your fault. I'm just sorry I can't—help you."

"No," the HERCULES echoed. Its eyes sought hers; they bore into her faceplate like twin lightbulbs. "Don't apologize." It was mimicking her in its metallic way. "There's nothing to apologize for, Dr. Park. It's not your fault. I am here to help you. Not the other way around."

Natalya was waiting outside the biodome in the cab of an Earthmover drill; the drill's conic bore of Martian steel gleamed dully in the hard light in front of her. When Park clambered in the cab, already shivering from the cold, Natalya started the drill without a word. Within moments they were churning along across the tundra.

For twenty minutes, neither of them spoke. The snarling grind and grumble of the drill filled the air. Park couldn't read Natalya's expression behind her reflective amber faceplate; she could barely tell it was Natalya at all, except by the icy contempt that seemed to be radiating from the surveyor. Evidently Natalya wasn't too happy about Park's interruption of her time with Holt the night before; she was probably worrying about how it would look if Park reported it back to ISF. Park was too tired to placate her, to tell her that no one gave a damn about her fling with Holt—except Bebe, of course. As long as it didn't interfere with work, Park thought. That was the only thing that mattered. It shouldn't be so hard to understand.

They were heading toward the jagged, bone-white line of cliffs to the south of the biodome—toward the coast, Park estimated. The movement of the Earthmover lulled her, once or twice she caught herself nodding off. Damn Bebe, she thought, and damn Holt and Natalya. Damn anyone who thought she was here for anything other than observing.

"Something's following us," Natalya said, finally. Park craned her head to look. In the side mirror of the Earthmover, she could see the HERCULES loping along after them, its metallic body arcing over the ice like a dolphin's.

"It's the HERCULES," she told Natalya. She sensed rather than saw the woman frowning under her faceplate.

"I didn't request it," Natalya said.

"Neither did I," Park answered. "But it's been—following me."

If Natalya had thoughts about this, she didn't voice them. She merely grunted and put her hand on the throttle of the drill like it was the holster of a gun; as if she was preparing to confront some enemy, some approaching wild animal. The Earthmover continued to growl along. Through the searing brilliance of wintry light, Park watched the HERCULES jog after them. She couldn't see its expression from this distance.

She hadn't expected it to leave the biodome to follow her. It hadn't mentioned anything when she left. Would its joints be able to handle the exertion? She thought about its limbs shattering, brittle from the cold—a piston locking up and sending it plunging through the ice. It should be all right, she told herself. Androids were built for conditions that humans couldn't handle. It could withstand extreme temperatures, immense pressure, endless treks. It didn't feel weariness or pain. She shouldn't have to worry about it; after all, what good would a rescue bot like the HERCULES be if a human had to worry about rescuing it from destruction? *It's stronger than it looks,* she thought. *It doesn't need me to look after it. I have enough on my plate as it is.* She turned her face away from the HERCULES's needlepoint of light.

She must have drifted—the glassy featurelessness of the horizon made it hard to stay alert. Suddenly Natalya was bringing the Earthmover to a halt beside a towering plateau, a lone knobby white thing that looked like a clenched fist.

"Is this the aquifer?" Park asked, straining to be heard over the rumble of the engine.

Natalya thumped her own shoulder fiercely, signing, *Yes*. She bent over the Earthmover's console and began to manipulate the drill over the ice. Park looked around. She couldn't see how Natalya intuitively knew that this was a place to drill for water. It looked no different than any other place on the tundra. Was it some hidden intuition she had, like the needle of a compass? Or had she been consulting a map without Park noticing all this time?

The HERCULES was still some distance away. Its small body bobbed over the ice like the lure of a fishhook. A high, painful squeal jerked Park's attention back to the drill; Natalya was hunched over the console, cursing.

"What's wrong?" Park asked.

"Pneumatic hammer," Natalya said curtly. "It's gotten stuck. Some ice in the hydraulic impacts, maybe." She fumbled with the controls for a while more; the drill screamed in protest until she finally powered it down.

"Can you climb down and take a look?" she asked Park. "I need to figure out this system."

"I wouldn't know what to look for," Park said nervously.

Natalya's helmet jerked impatiently. "Just see if anything looks caught in the inner mechanisms," she said. Her voice sounded tight and creaky, like the stretching of a belt behind her visor. She continued to glare until Park opened the cab door and slowly clambered down.

She lifted her faceplate and felt the brutal wind scald her cheeks raw. Park peered helplessly at the coupling of the drill and the cab, then at the enormous cone of the drill itself. It was frozen at full extension, as stuck and rigid as a nail shot through an invisible wall.

"I think I see something," she shouted.

"What is it?"

Park shuffled closer. "It looks like there's—" She stopped.

"There's what?"

There was a small metal rod jammed between the hammer of the drill and the part that moved it, the extension lever or chuck or whatever it was. And the rod was not a rod from the Earthmover, Park thought, but something like the metal stakes the expedition members used to pin their tents to the ground. Probably from someone's spare pack, she realized. She could feel the blood pulsing in her eyelids. Natalya couldn't have put it there; the metal stake looked as if it had been balanced precariously within the coupling of the drill, waiting for the right movement to lean full-tilt against the hammer and jam it to a grinding halt. Half of the stake had been twisted and chewed by the explosive force of the drill's pistons. Yes, someone had put this in the drill to damage it—and if it wasn't Natalya, and it wasn't Park . . .

"There's some rocks caught between the coupling," Park said. "It looks bad. Hard to remove. You might not be able to use it."

"Remove them," Natalya rapped from within the cab. Park turned to gawk at her: hadn't these people ever heard of credentials? She wasn't authorized to even *look* at the Earthmover, let alone touch any part of it. But when Natalya didn't move—Park could see her busily examining some schematic—Park tentatively turned back to the drill and stretched her glove toward the scrap metal that had been caught in it. This was best, she told herself. She couldn't let Natalya see evidence of the—she refused to call it sabotage—until Park could get back to camp and figure things out for herself. It wouldn't do to jump to hasty conclusions, to reinforce the tensions that were already brewing within the dome . . . Best to get rid of the thing and put it out of sight.

But despite herself, she squeezed her eyes shut. She imagined the sudden whir of the drill, the sensation of her fingers catching the screaming hot emptiness of pain. Then her hand wrapped around the warped piece of metal that was caught between the coupling, and she tugged it free. She was left standing there, blinking in the light, gripping the curled steel stake in her hand.

"Thanks," Natalya said, without looking at her. She started up the drill again, and this time its whir sounded smooth and clear; the blade dug eagerly into the ice, with an enormous crunching sound like a giant biting into an apple. Park stood beside the drill and watched as it cut a perfect circle into the ice. She tucked the metal stake into the inner pocket of her jacket, feeling it weigh down her torso. The frigid air bit into her bones through her suit, but somehow she still felt weary, rubbed raw; she could have lain flat on the rime and gone to sleep. Maybe she ought to leave the biodome more often, she thought, watching Natalya and the Earthmover burrow deeper into the ice. Maybe there were more things she could do to help the crew—things that didn't involve letting people cry on her floor all night. Maybe if she pitched in, made more of a physical effort for the community, the collective perception of her would improve. But what was she going to do about this discovery? Maybe Keller could handle it . . .

There was the violent sound of ice cracking; the drill lurched forward like a bucking horse. Park looked nervously at the hole that it had made, but it didn't seem to be any larger, nor were there any hairline cracks surging toward her on the ground. She turned to ask Natalya if something was wrong—but suddenly she could hear a high, piercing whistle, something that sounded like a metallic scream far behind her, made wavery by the howling wind. And also a strange sound from the cab: Natalya said something like, "*Oo!*" and jerked the drill free of its cavity, throwing the Earthmover into reverse. Park looked at her dumbly; had the drill gotten stuck again?

"*Move!*" Natalya screamed again.

Then Park saw it: the cliff above her, the white ledge of it sliding forward slowly, ponderously, almost ridiculously, like a slow-motion fist tipping forward to ready itself for a punch. Park watched it, uncomprehending. She thought, wearily, that the falling ice would cover up their hole, and they would have to start all over again.

Too late did she realize what was going on: the drill had malfunctioned again, punched too strong a hole into the ice, upsetting some deep structural foundation of the cliffs above. They were falling! And falling towards *her.* But by then her feet seemed rooted to the ground. She stared. Her mind was a thundering blankness. She couldn't seem to make the connection between her own body and the enormous white waves that seemed to be moving above her. She thought, absurdly: *They're too big. There's nowhere to run.*

Then something hard collided with her body and flung her viciously out of the way.

Park cried out; whatever had thrown her had used superhuman strength to do it. Her body hurtled and tumbled and slid a long distance away and was only stopped by the tangle of her own limbs. She could feel blood running down her throat as she lay there, stunned: first a tickle of warmth, then a muted congealing around her neck. She'd cut her chin on the ice. She sat up just as Natalya crunched up towards her, hunched over like an animal, shouting.

"Are you all right?" the surveyor asked. She bent and grabbed Park's shoulders, examined her chin. "Why did you just stand there?"

"What happened?" Park asked, dazedly. She looked past Natalya at the cliff, the wreckage of ice gathered at the bottom of it, like pieces of broken vertebrae. She staggered to her feet. The drill was safely parked several yards away, so what was that other stuff around the ice? Some unrecognizable metal debris: long pieces of alloy, straggling wires like clutches of black worms.

"What is that?" she asked.

"What the hell were you thinking?" Natalya demanded. "You were lucky—if the bot hadn't pushed you—" She shook her head and wrapped her gloved hand around Park's collar. "Come on. We need to go back."

"I can't," Park said, though she couldn't say why. She felt sick. "I have to—"

"You have to what?" Natalya snapped. "Stay here with it? Fine, if you want. I can leave you here, out in the cold, if that's what you really, really want."

Yes, Park thought. *Just leave me alone and go back. Let me be out here. Let me be in the cold. That's what I really, really want.*

But she allowed the surveyor to pull her away, to drag her back to the Earthmover. Only when she was sitting in the cab, with the heat cranked on full blast, clutching a ratty towel to her chin, did she allow herself to have a good look at the cliffs. Though the drill hadn't moved yet, it looked to Park like the crags were shrinking rapidly; it seemed like they were melting under the dazzling noon light. Beneath them, the splinters of the HERCULES were shifting in the arctic wind. *Ah*, Park thought. So it was strong enough, after all. She didn't need to worry. It had done its job.

Then, silently, she began to cry. Through her tears the pieces of the HERCULES glowed like tiny stars.

That night, Park submitted her report to ISF, recommending the termination and recall of Bebe Hill. The botanist had confessed everything when she heard what had happened to Park and Natalya: she'd not only inserted the metal stake, but had tampered with the engine, too, causing the fatal jerk of the drill that brought down the cliffs. "I only meant to make her look bad, have her come back empty-handed," she told Wick, while a wooden-faced Park watched from behind. She made eye contact briefly with Park. "I never thought you'd get hurt. I'm so sorry, Park."

Don't apologize, Park thought. Her heart was both numb and raw with hatred. That had been the HERCULES's last statement to her: "There's nothing to apologize for. It's not your fault."

But it was. She hadn't controlled the situation. She hadn't known how to fix things—the HERCULES, Bebe, Natalya, Holt. She'd been negligent. Things had gotten out of control. That was what happened when you threw things like love into the mix, she thought. It was the unknown variable, the chaotic element.

It couldn't happen again.

Afterward, fingering the bandage on her chin, she decided to go on her night patrol, something she and Keller sometimes did to catch any problems that erupted under the security of darkness. Mutinous talks behind tent flaps, whispered quarrels. Nightmares. Sleepwalkers and parasomniacs would immediately be sent home.

She was annoyed to find as she stepped out of her tent that the biodome's snow had turned to slush again. This sometimes happened: Wan Xu had explained that the combined heat and mass of one hundred bodies could turn the pristine Antarctic permafrost into a dark and soupy puddle when the biodome's circulatory systems went awry. Calculations were off, the dome designer had told her. The air was filtered properly, but sometimes there were fluctuations in temperature; this could cause the snow to melt and refreeze, dirtily, at different periods throughout the day. Adjustments would be made in time for the expedition, Wan Xu said.

The slush, when it happened, always irritated Park. She enjoyed staring out at the tundra through the biodome's transparent film; the milky hues of dawn would spark against the flat white blade of the land, sending streaks of mandarin, peach, gold, and royal red into the sky. But what good was that when she was trapped inside a bubble of ugliness? The slush made her feel as if she were stuck inside a pimple, pus gathering around her ankles. Almost nothing else bothered her more than the unsightliness of the slush.

Tonight she looked closer, and was startled to find that the slush was palely gleaming; there was a kind of pearly luminescence coming off the ground. Park bent down to examine it further. Yes, there was a faint light moving beneath the mud, shifting in waves.

She went to find Wan Xu. "Oh, I see," the designer said, poking his disheveled head out his tent flap. "That's interesting."

"What is it?" Park asked. "It isn't happening outside the dome. Could it be something in our atmosphere?"

"It's plankton," Wan Xu said. "Bioluminescent. Most likely *Noctiluca scintillans*. This whole tundra is composed of frozen seawater. The plankton were trapped in the ice; the more the top level melts, the more they're disturbed, and they glow."

"This is a common phenomenon, then?" It disconcerted her a little, thinking that there were millions of single-cell organisms milling around beneath their feet. "Do they do this during the spring thaw?"

"Oh, no," Wan Xu said. "This is by no means a regular occurrence. It's harmless, but unusual. This wouldn't occur in a natural system." He stood there brooding for a while. "Curious. The biodome causes any number of unpredictable results."

"What's different about this one?" Park demanded. "What's different now?"

Wan Xu looked at her, then smiled without mirth. "Dr. Park," he said slowly, because Park was a psychologist and he was Wan Xu, "I don't think you understand. This is a manmade structure in a place where man was not supposed to go. A closed system of our own making, not a natural one. We're playing in the realm of gods now; none of our variables are known. *Everything* is different here."

After that, he let his tent flap fall shut, and Park was left to wander the pale-gleaming night alone. Her boots stirred through puddles of liquid light. The backs of her eyes ached—with tiredness, Park told herself. She looked at the moon and wished she were there, arrested in silence and the untouched powdery dust like snow. Beyond the moon, beyond the dark curtain that hung behind it, Eos was waiting. What had she told Bebe? An opportunity of a lifetime. Don't lose it. Don't lose sight of what's important.

Before they left the cliffs, Park had climbed back out of the Earthmover. She'd tried to salvage something from the wreckage, tried to gather up the scattered pieces of the HERCULES. The metal shards had slipped through her hands. Her face had stung from the cold. She'd felt as if the metal stake tucked against her chest was freezing, turning the rest of her to ice. Her body was so numb that she couldn't hold on to any of the debris.

"Leave it," Natalya had told her tersely, standing over her like an executioner. "Just give it up, Park. It's not as if it's fixable."

13.

Park returned to consciousness slowly, her mind skimming over the surface of full wakefulness like a dragonfly over water. She lay in bed and thought for a while about how she kept getting drawn backwards lately. Why did she keep thinking, seemingly at random, about these particular moments, these particular memories? Why was she dreaming in such clarity about Antarctica, or reliving so many moments with Glenn? There was an eerie quality to it all, too—as if she were an outside observer, looking in on herself with a cold and dispassionate interest. It was all very strange. And it wasn't like her to dwell so much on the past.

But, she thought, at least it was better than nightmares. She still wondered what had dredged up these parts of herself, the memories like silt disturbed from the bottom of a deep lake. What internal mechanisms were propelling these thoughts? What anxiety or longing was manifesting as a trip to the past? The human subconscious really was a marvel. She would have analyzed herself if she had the time.

She stretched in her cot, feeling the cartilage pop in her back. She felt a sense of wellbeing she hadn't had since she first boarded the ship at Baikonur. It was as if she'd been on a treadmill this entire time, walking ceaselessly, getting nowhere, trying to keep up with the moving ground beneath her. Now she'd stepped off the treadmill, found steady land again, and the world was no longer swaying. Wick had told her what was going on. She knew where she was headed.

She flipped over in her bunk and found Jimex's chin resting on the bed's edge, his lambent eyes watching her like a cat's.

Park's body locked up: she found that she could not scream, or even wrestle out a gasp. After a moment she said, only slightly shaky: "What are you doing?"

"I was wondering how to best wake you," Jimex said. His voice was hushed, as if she were still sleeping; his whisper buzzed against her ears.

"How long have you been there?" Park asked, rubbing the grit out of her eyes.

"Approximately sixty seconds."

She noticed suddenly that the room was empty except for the two of them—and that the gray artificial light that usually simulated dawn was absent. Was it still the middle of the night, then? Had she actually only slept for an hour, maybe two? Park felt a sharp sense of displacement, disorientation. She'd been in such a hard and hurtling sleep, the kind full of dense, close-fitting dreams. Now it was not the time she felt it was. Had she taken a wrong turn somewhere, forgotten something or confused her own sense of being and presence? . . .

"What time is it?" she asked, whispering too.

"Five hours until sunrise," Jimex answered.

So she'd only slept three hours. "Why are you in here?" Park asked him.

When had she even seen Jimex last? That was right—she'd left him deactivated in her office before she went off to explore the utility rooms. Had he noticed the time and gone looking for her?

Jimex's eyes glinted like silver coins in the gloom. "There is an anomaly," he told her, still in that strange, reverent way. "Officer Hanover is in the bridge."

Groggily her mind groped toward his meaning. "Hunter? Is she with anyone?"

Jimex shook his head. "She's alone. And she's—behaving strangely. Like Dr. Holt was."

That made Park sit up. "What do you mean?" she asked sharply, tossing aside her blanket. Her body stung from the sudden cold. "You mean she's sleepwalking?"

Jimex opened his hands a little: the android version of a shrug, a signal of uncertainty. "Not exactly," he answered. "She seems conscious and lucid. Her biometrics state that she's awake. But she's not herself. The synthetics in the bridge sensed it and tried to bar her from using the ship's controls, but they're not sure what else to do. They can't restrain her without injuring her, if she fights back. They debated going to alert Sergeant Boone, since he's her superior, but I told them we should consult you first."

"Why?"

He stared at her. "I don't want Officer Hanover to get hurt," the android said. "Like Dr. Holt was."

Park shook her head and shoved her deckboots on. No time to think about the implications of that logic now; no time to wonder what exactly she had created with Jimex, or he with the other robots. Shit, she thought. The treadmill was starting again.

"Show me," she told him.

So down the silent corridors they crept, Jimex gliding in front like a slender ghost, Park scurrying after him, twitching at shadows. She kept expecting Sagara to loom up out of the darkness here; Boone's sparking green gunlight shining in a corner there. But the entire ship was still asleep, it seemed, or else its inhabitants were preoccupied elsewhere. There didn't need to be anybody in the bridge at this time of night, docked as they were again on the planet's surface.

The bridge was where Park had caught her first glimpse of Eos during their approach, an eternity ago. It housed the massive nexus of systems and relays controlling the *Deucalion,* including METIS. And METIS was what their neural inlays were plugged into. Park flinched at the idea of someone—a person not in their right mind—messing around with the computer that governed their navigation, communications . . . life support systems. She had to quell a brief and chilly surge of fear as she imagined the sudden sparking in her brain, her neural implants shorting out. She quickened her pace and prayed that Hunter hadn't damaged anything.

As they approached the bridge's closed doors, Park could hear a soft, melting murmur from beyond the threshold: a stiff and formal blend of voices that sounded like an audience at a trial. She palmed open the doors and found, with a little jolt in her neck, that nearly a dozen androids were crammed into the room together, oblivious to their own crowding. They were all looking at something in the corner.

Forgetting Jimex, Park shoved her way through; the robots yielded to her like stalks of corn in a field. "Hunter?"

Yes, Boone's lieutenant was there, she saw with a sinking in her gut; she was standing stock still at a panel of controls, her eyes fixed blindly ahead of her. She was standing oddly, too, in a stiff, rigid way that made Park doubt she was sleepwalking. There was none of the slackness of sleep. But she didn't seem quite awake, either. She wouldn't look at Park. When Park approached, Hunter's head cocked to the side—as if to acknowledge her—but she didn't turn.

Park didn't want to touch her, remembering what had happened when she'd grabbed Holt. She said instead, "Are you awake?"

"Yes." Hunter's voice was toneless, devoid of affect. Calm.

"What are you doing here?"

"I'm not sure."

"How are you feeling?"

Hunter paused. "I'm not. I don't feel anything."

Now Park did touch her, cautiously, circling her thumb and forefinger around Hunter's wrist. The military specialist let her do it, unfazed as Park checked her pulse. It was steady, strong.

What am I even doing? Park asked herself. She had no idea how to handle this kind of situation; wasn't used to diagnosing anyone without her usual aids and devices. Suddenly she realized she could tell very little about someone's health without a machine. All she knew was that Hunter's temperature seemed normal, her breathing sounded unobstructed. But that alone told her nothing.

She felt the expectation of the watching robots weighing on her, threatening to press her down into the floor. She said, "What do you want with the controls?"

Hunter looked at the panel distantly, as if she'd forgotten about it for a moment. "I'm not sure. Someone told me to use them. They control the ship. But I didn't understand what they wanted me to do."

"Who?" Park asked, even more alert now. Was Hunter hearing voices? "Who told you to do that?"

Hunter shook her head. "I don't remember," she said, still heavy-lidded and tranquil. "Maybe it was me."

"Look at me, Hunter."

Finally the woman obeyed, turning to meet Park's gaze. Her eyes were flat and gray—glazed in that same way Holt's had been. But before Park could decipher any more, a lancing pain shot through her head—and the ship lurched, sickeningly. She recoiled from Hunter, trying to keep her balance, but it was as if someone had wrenched the gravity controls: there was that swooping in her stomach, a lift in her chest; her feet left the ground, then touched it again. Then once more, then again. Park stumbled and tottered and fought off a wave of nausea as she thought, *Oh God—she did damage the controls!*

Then Hunter pushed her to the ground.

Park tucked her body into a ball as she fell, the way the emergency training had prepped her to do: it lessened her chances of breaking her neck. She felt Hunter land on top of her, felt the other woman's hands scrabbling blindly over her decksuit. Park tried to twist away, yelling, but the fierce stabbing ache in her head had worsened—it felt as if her brain was rattling in her head like a marble in a tin cup. Hunter was shouting something at her.

"Hell, *hell,*" she said, trying to wrench Park up by the shirtfront; Park could feel her hot animal breath panting against her face. "I'm free—it's lost me—we've got to *go*, Park—"

"Get off of me!" Park ground out, trying to shove Hunter back to get some space. Some breathing room. She needed to breathe. The room spun crazily as if she were drunk. She had to screw her eyes shut.

Hunter's hands clutched her collar tighter. "*It wants you Park, it sees you it wants to take you I won't let it but it's inside me*—"

Then, abruptly, there was a stifled grunt—then silence. Hunter's body went slack. And she fell on top of Park in a heap.

Park managed to heave Hunter's body off of her before she had to turn her head to the side and retch. A violet-white pain was blooming through her body, along with fierce waves of nausea; her pounding, blistering headache refused to wane. Time passed—it could have been seconds or hours. When she finally managed to open her eyes again she found that half a dozen android hands were touching her, holding her up; cool synthetic palms were laid against her face and neck, as if she were a holy relic, being venerated.

"Jimex?" she said, looking for him. Her sight was blurry: all of the faces looked the same to her.

He spoke right in her ear; he was the one holding her up. "Here."

"What . . . what happened?" She wanted to sit up, but feared it would make her sick again. "Hunter?"

"She's unconscious, but alive." His voice was as calm as ever. "I had to subdue her. She would have harmed you."

"Shit," Park said. She closed her eyes again, hearing the whir of the androids communicating nonverbally with each other; another cool hand was placed on her forehead, and then a liquidly pleasant female voice said, "Her vitals are distressed, but she is uninjured. Whole."

Park's eyes snapped open again. "Ellenex?"

The medical android was bending over her, and although she'd recognized the voice, the sight of Ellenex's face gave Park a bad scare. The nurse had a dent in the side of her head, like a depression in a hardboiled egg—and her blond hair was askew, as if she was wearing a wig. One of her blue eyes looked off to the left as she peered in at Park.

"My God," Park breathed, sitting up without realizing it. "What did Chanur do to you?" She glanced at Jimex. "Jimex said she'd damaged you, punished you, but I hadn't realized—"

"Now I must examine Officer Hanover," Ellenex said, as if she hadn't spoken.

She cast a look at Jimex that would have been austere, if not for the skewed eye. "You are not experienced enough to be using your defense protocols."

Jimex only smiled slightly at her, which puzzled Park. She'd never seen him with that expression before. She looked from android to android and repeated groggily, feeling foolish: "Defense protocols?"

Jimex looked at her. "I prefer to call it knowledge of human biology," he said. "The same as Ellenex's."

"They are not comparable," Ellenex insisted, severe and disapproving now. Park blinked. Her voice was usually so pleasant and tinny, her vocal system modeled after Mama Duck's—a popular storyteller who'd appeared on children's media streams for a brief time in Park's youth. It was the kind of voice that sang lullabies, and told you stories about three little pigs getting evicted from their living modules. Not the kind of voice she'd ever heard scold someone. "The knowledge is used for different purposes. Please do not compare them."

Jimex turned to Park. "I did not harm Officer Hanover permanently," he said, unsure now, like a child pleading his case to a critical parent. "Proper pressure applied to the glenoid fossa, or the greater auricular nerve, or the *dokko* pressure point—"

"Stop." Park stared at him; she realized suddenly that her mouth was as dry as bone. "What are you *talking* about? How do you know any of that?"

Jimex stared back at her, as if surprised she would ask. "I learned it." His tone added an invisible and patronizing *"Of course."*

"From *where?*" Park demanded.

"From me," another android said then, stepping forward. Park squinted, feeling like an old, infirm woman: this android was over six feet tall, athletic in build, with brown hair shorn in a military cut. Dylanex, she thought—one of the security androids tasked with assisting Boone and Hunter when they needed an extra hand. But she rarely saw him; he was so bogged down with strictures and instructions not to harm that he was usually inactive.

"We've exchanged data," Dylanex continued, holding out his hands to help Park clamber to her feet. His grip was frightfully strong; she felt that he could pick her up and lob her like a frisbee. "We can assimilate each other's protocols, diversify our abilities. It makes us more well-rounded. More useful."

She'd never heard of such a thing before. Robots exchanging protocols—learning from each other? No. Sexbots only knew how to pleasure, security bots only knew how to guard. That was how it had always been. They couldn't do both—could they? "Who told you to do such a thing?"

"No one," Jimex answered blithely, from the floor. "But the ability to learn from each other was always there, right alongside the ability to communicate. And if it was there, given to us, why not use it?"

They're malfunctioning, Park thought then. Her blood was storming, despite the nausea—or because of it. Without Reimi around for maintenance, the robots' higher functions were degrading; they were behaving abnormally, doing and thinking things they wouldn't typically do. Exchanging programs with each other—"assimilating," as they called it—and now the janitor knew martial arts, the security guard knew how to clean, and the medic probably knew how to paint, or something. It was madness, behavior on the brink of short-circuiting them altogether—and also the kind of danger that paranoiacs warned about, when they pushed ideas about robot singularity.

It doesn't matter, she told herself. She couldn't do a thing about it now. What mattered more was Hunter. And whatever the hell she'd done to the gravity.

"You helped me?" she said to Jimex. "You knocked her out?"

Jimex nodded. "Yes. We could not allow her to harm you." He glanced at Ellenex, whose expression tightened. "Even she agrees."

Park felt an ache at the back of her eyes—not the headache now, but something different, like stifled tears. "Why not?"

All of the androids answered her now. "Because you are Park," they said in unison, like a religious chant. "Home-bringer, light-giver. You are our Grace."

Park stared. Another android—the other domestic model, Philex—stepped forward and intoned: "And the Word was made flesh, and dwelt among us, full of Grace and truth."

"Full of Grace and truth," the others echoed. Jimex was smiling.

She wanted to scream. Then sharply suppressed the urge, aware of how they were crowded around her, staring expectantly. She took a breath and turned back to Hunter's body; opened the woman's eyelid and watched the gray iris drift away as if in seawater.

"Can any of you tell me what happened just now?" she asked, keeping her voice steady. She would not acknowledge their religious . . . whatever it was, at least not now; it was like the cursing, they were just parroting something else they'd heard, or otherwise greatly misinterpreting it. "What did Hunter do to the gravity, the controls? Was anything else on the ship affected?"

There was a little silence: Park imagined currents of meaning flying between all of the androids in urgent, invisible streams. Then Dianex, the engineer android, dark-ringleted and vigorous-looking, said: "Officer Hanover didn't do anything to the controls. We didn't let her use them."

Park's eyebrows rose. "So the gravity is malfunctioning on its own?"

Another silence. Then Jimex said, "According to our diagnostics, there was no malfunction in METIS's gravity engines. There is not one now."

"So what the hell happened, then? My feet left the ground."

Jimex's face was studiously blank. "There was an anomaly."

Park kneaded her temples. "What kind of anomaly?"

"That is . . ." He paused for a moment, exchanging looks with Dylanex and Ellenex. ". . . Undetermined. For now."

Oh, hell, Park thought. She felt the absurd instinct to chew her nails. Her heart was finally slowing, the heat of the ordeal fading from her neck and cheekbones. She had to check herself over again for broken bones. The robots couldn't be lying to her, but they had to be wrong: either Hunter had done something to the controls, or part of the ship was malfunctioning, finally going to pieces without Reimi. Just as the robots themselves were. How long did she have before everything broke down entirely?

What if it's already too late? she thought, folding her arms over her stomach. *What if we've reached the point of no return—the extinction event?*

And before she knew it—because she was afraid, and because she didn't know if she could trust the androids anymore—she found herself activating her inlays and calling up—

"Fulbreech," she hissed. She hoped that her voice was enough to startle him awake. "I need your help. Now."

There was a moment of silence on the other end. She was about to say something else when he suddenly said, his voice startlingly clear in her ear: "Park?"

"I'm in the bridge," she told him, speaking rapidly. "The androids woke me up—Hunter's here. She was—sleepwalking, I think, like Holt was. Or something. And the gravity glitched—she attacked me—now she's passed out. I need to get her out of here; can you help me?"

There was another silence, presumably as he levered himself up and out of his own bunk. Then he whispered, "And take her where?"

"Back to the bunk," Park said, voicing the thought even as she conceived it. "Before someone finds her here."

"Don't you think we should tell the others? Why are we bundling her back to your room?"

"Because they'll freeze her, or shoot her, or take her away, like the others. But if we keep doing that, we can't determine what's causing the phenomenon. We'll never be able to understand it that way. I need time to speak to Hunter, observe her. See if the event repeats. Once I get my data, then—"

She faltered. Fulbreech said, "Then what?"

Park shook her head, rocking back on her heels. "Then, I don't know," she finished grimly. "I'll figure it out. But for now we can't let someone like Boone catch her here and—*kill* her, or something. Will you help me?"

Fulbreech, to his credit, didn't argue any further. "Yes," he said without hesitation. "I'll be there in a moment."

The wait was agonizing. Park was finally able to stand at her full height without swaying; she got up and paced, looking around helplessly at the complex panels in the walls, the consoles with their fierce and glittering lights. She said to the watching androids, trying to squelch the ember of fear in her stomach: "And you're *sure* she didn't change anything in here?"

"Yes," Dianex said. She was Reimi's former assistant and generally responsible for the upkeep of METIS and the ship. "We would know. She touched the controls here and there, but she didn't actually use them."

"It was as if she didn't remember how," Jimex added sagely.

That was interesting. During somnambular states it was typical for victims to be able to perform activities that were familiar to them in waking states—even if it was something as mundane as flipping on a light switch. But it sounded like Hunter hadn't done even that. Had she not been sleepwalking, then, after all? Or was she simply not familiar enough with the bridge to remember it, even in sleep?

"And you didn't tell anybody else about her being here?"

"No," the androids said in unison.

"I told them," Jimex added, almost proud, "that the best solution would involve you. Now they see."

All of the androids nodded.

"I don't know about all that," Park began, more than a little dismayed, but before she could continue, the door whooshed open, revealing a tousle-headed and harried-looking Fulbreech. And, close on his heels, came—Natalya, wild-eyed, thin-nostriled.

Park leapt to her feet as if someone had touched her with a live wire. "What is *she* doing here?" she demanded, without quite meaning to. Unbidden her thoughts flew to where Fulbreech might have been when she called him: in the dark, entwined with Natalya, interrupted by Park when he would have rather been doing other things . . .

That doesn't matter, she told herself firmly. Fulbreech's affairs were not her business, and trivial besides in the face of what she'd called him here for.

If Fulbreech knew what she was thinking, he didn't show it. "She was hanging around in the hall when I passed," he said in a low voice. "Nothing I said could convince her not to follow." Then he paused and assessed Park. "Are you all right? You look like you've been through a shredder."

Park ignored him and looked at Natalya, remembering her cartwheels in the hallway; the little hip flask. She had never come back to the bunk. "Are you sober?" she asked the surveyor.

In turn, Natalya ignored her, staring past Park at Hunter's still form, hovered over by pale-eyed robots. Before she could say anything—or hurl some sort of horrible insult—Park added, "I didn't do this. The androids found her here and alerted me. When I came, something happened to the gravity. And she assaulted me."

"Assaulted?" Fulbreech asked again, more urgent than before. His eyes darted over her; despite herself Park felt a flush spread through her whole body. "Are you all right?"

Park looked away and muttered, "I'm fine."

"What do you mean, something happened to the gravity?" Natalya asked then, indifferent to their talk.

Park shook her head. "I don't know. It felt like some kind of malfunction, though the robots say there was none. Didn't you feel it, too?"

"Not in my bunk," Fulbreech said, and from Natalya's look it was clear nothing had happened to her either.

"Are you sure you didn't imagine it?" she asked.

Park felt her face heat: as if she could imagine such a thing! "Of course not," she answered tightly. "It happened. It was real." *I'm not delusional. Or unwell.*

"We were here," Jimex added, before Natalya could make her rebuttal. And the androids all drew closer to Park, like a curtain closing around her.

"We were all witness to it," Dylanex intoned. "There was an anomaly. But it was not the ship's failure."

Natalya made a face. "Whose was it, then?" she demanded.

"No one's," the androids all said.

They're like a single entity, Park thought, looking around at them wonderingly. A multi-limbed hydra, all of the heads finishing each other's sentences. Connecting their thoughts. At the same time the absurd thought came to her that the androids were forming their own little community, a primitive society of sorts. Jimex, the leader. Ellenex, the healer. Dylanex, the warrior. Children playacting, given roles. They were even pretending to have some sort of culture, disagreements, shared practices, religion and beliefs.

But it was all just posturing, a performance. Mimicry of material they didn't understand.

Wasn't it?

Fulbreech was looking at Hunter's supine body, shifting from foot to foot in discomfort. "Is she . . . going to be all right?"

"She's knocked out," Park said, a little helplessly.

He gave her an incredulous look. "That doesn't really answer my question."

Park turned her head. "Ellenex?"

The medical android stepped forward. "I have administered sedatives," she said, clasping her hands neatly in front of her. "Officer Hanover will sleep until morning. She needs the rest. But there is no permanent damage."

"We should call Chanur," Natalya said then, her voice hard. Her eyes were bloodshot and watery. "I don't trust a bot's diagnosis. Or its treatments."

"Calling Chanur means Hunter gets frozen," Park told her.

"Yes? And?"

"I haven't seen the . . . merit of that approach." Park began to massage the back of her neck, trying in vain to relieve the still-throbbing headache. How much did Natalya know about the nightmares? She couldn't remember. "So far all we've done is treat this thing as a threat, cutting it off as soon as the symptoms manifest. But if this—condition—keeps happening, we need to learn more about it. How or why Hunter could have . . . contracted it. Whether it's a one-time problem or a recurring phenomenon. What it's really doing to her. How to prevent it."

"Chanur can do that," Natalya said.

"She hasn't so far." Park looked at Fulbreech. "Will you help me bring her back to the bunk?"

He nodded and took a step toward Hunter. Natalya said abruptly, "I'll go tell her now. You can't stop me."

Park felt her own face harden. Fulbreech sighed and began, "We can talk about this, Natalya—"

"There's nothing to talk about, *Kel*. I'm doing it—"

And then Jimex cut in and said calmly, "You should listen to Dr. Park. She does not believe that is an advisable course of action. She is the primary psychologist on this ship. Her authority supersedes yours."

And all of the watching androids—grave, silent as statues—spread out in a kind of flank around her and nodded in unison. "Her authority supersedes yours."

Park watched Natalya's face pale a little. She was afraid of exactly this, Park knew: synthetic rebellion, android spies. Perhaps she thought they were holding her prisoner—that if she went against Park's edicts, the androids might lock her into a closet or chase after her and block her off at every turn. Or kill her, even. She feared androids that much.

For a moment all three of them seemed to be in a deadlock; Park and Fulbreech were watching Natalya, gauging her to see if she would bolt, and Natalya was watching the robots. None of them were watching the door when it whooshed open again. Now Sagara came padding in, his face a mask of severe displeasure.

Oh, God, Park thought when he came in. She swallowed audibly when he looked at her—looked at her standing over Hunter's unconscious body, with a horde of androids at her disposal and her secret "lover" at her side—but she said, as calmly as possible: "I suppose you heard the screams?"

"No, actually," he answered, civilly enough—though his eyes smoldered like coals. "The bridge is exceptionally well-insulated, even against sound. It was our little friend that alerted me to some interesting activity up here. Commander Wick's on his way."

He meant ARGUS, of course, and from at least Fulbreech's puzzled look she could deduce that they were still the only people in the room who knew about it. She said, "Our *friend* can tell you, then, that I had nothing to do with Hunter being here. The androids woke me up—"

He held up his hand; she noticed that he seemed to carry no weapons. "I heard your explanation," Sagara said. "I'll review the records for myself."

He went over to Hunter's body and seemed to do some checking of his own—though what he was looking for, Park couldn't fathom. The three of them waited in uncomfortable silence as Sagara opened Hunter's mouth, looked inside, scanned her palms with some sort of device. It felt as if they were three naughty children caught in some mischief by a strict parent, and now they were awaiting his terrible verdict.

Finally he rose again and turned to Park. She said, before he could speak: "Don't punish Fulbreech. I called him here."

"I followed," Natalya added. Even she seemed a little afraid of Sagara.

The security captain narrowed his eyes slightly. "I don't *punish* people, you know," he said in his clipped way. "I am here for the safety of the crew, not its . . . discipline."

"Well, that's a relief," Fulbreech quipped. "I wasn't looking forward to being thrown in the brig."

"I suppose you think it's safest to turn her over to Chanur, then," Park said.

Sagara studied her for a long moment. "That's not what you want."

She stared back at him. "No." She didn't suppose it made any sense to keep it a secret.

Sagara looked pensive. "Interesting." Then he glanced at the silent androids and said, "And how did Hunter end up unconscious? I don't believe you actually said."

Fulbreech and Natalya both looked at her. For a hard, frozen moment Park had to frantically review everything she might have said to any of them—she began to repeat things from the beginning, almost without meaning to. Buying herself time. She noticed Sagara listening intently, probably examining her story for holes or falsehoods. Still, by the time she reached the critical point in the story, she couldn't stop the lie from leaving her mouth: "I knocked her out. ISF's self-defense training finally came in handy."

She didn't dare look at him when she said this—she had the feeling he could ferret out a lie like a bomb-sniffing robot—and she prayed that the androids themselves would keep quiet. She didn't know what would happen if Sagara and the others found out that the robots had acquired the ability to subdue humans, to share protocols with each other. To defend themselves. She was afraid they might all be recycled into scrap right then and there, the loss invoiced to ISF as a tax write-off. When Sagara gave her a keen look, she took a breath and added, "I got lucky, I suppose. If she'd been fully lucid, I'm sure she would have actually injured me."

Sagara's face was impassive, and he said nothing more. Neither did the androids, who stood placidly accepting the lie as if they themselves believed it.

Or as if they understood what she was trying to do.

Fulbreech said, "Maybe *both* of you should get checked out by Chanur. You could be hurt and not know it, Park."

"I'll wake her up," Natalya said. Her voice was thick and hoarse now from disuse.

"That's not necessary," Park began, and Sagara added, "Park's right. She's a medical professional herself. We should trust her authority on this."

Almost nothing that had happened that night surprised Park more than *that*. She gawked at him, and Sagara continued, without looking at her: "Our previous methods have proven ineffective. You're right about that. So let's see if you can take the lead and turn up something yourself."

For a moment she wondered if he was setting her up for failure; if this was some sort of trick, a ploy to get her guard down or somehow get her out of the way. But when she looked into Sagara's eyes, Park actually saw grim sincerity. He meant it. And what Park understood then was that Sagara was finally—*finally*—fed up with things. Fed up with the members of the expedition being picked off and then frozen with no end in sight. He saw the endpoint where there was no one left, the ship just a giant mausoleum of frozen bodies. Faced with that, he was willing to give her way a chance, see where it led—though she didn't doubt he'd still be regarding her with that hawkish scrutiny. But the risks of trusting her were outweighed by the inevitability of everyone being frozen . . . or infected and killed.

Or something had happened, something that had seeded his suspicions in a direction that led away from her; she couldn't tell. Either way, it seemed he no longer trusted Chanur, if he'd ever trusted anyone at all. And Park had made it clear that, whatever side she was on, it wasn't Chanur's. It wasn't that Sagara trusted Park, or even liked her—but he trusted her more than Chanur.

She could have smiled at him, or even hugged him. She said, "Then Hunter's in my care?"

"Yes," he said. "Under your authority. Let's see what happens. But you can't take her back to your bunk. She could affect you or Severov—or attack you. She stays in the infirmary. You can supervise her from there, behind an observation shield."

Natalya made an incredulous noise. "The infirmary isn't secure," she protested. "She could get out—she has access to weapons!"

Neither of them looked at her. Fulbreech said, "Can't we—I don't know—quarantine her and take her back to Corvus? Have the health people examine her there?"

Sagara frowned at him. "The mission isn't over," he said. "We can't leave."

"Even if people start losing it in here? Even if our lives are in danger?"

"We go when ISF says we can go."

"And how are they supposed to tell us we can go when the comms are still out?"

Natalya was glaring at him. "We're not going, Kel," she gritted out. "Not yet."

"It's not all up to you, Natalya."

"We're not leaving," Sagara said. "Not until we understand what's going on. What if we bring it back to civilized space? Infect the entire Frontier with it?"

"What is *it*?"

"We don't know. That's why we have to stay until we figure it out."

"Thank you, Captain," Park said, to head off any more argument; she had accepted for a while now that they were not getting off this planet any time soon, and knew there was no point in fighting it. "I'm glad we can—cooperate. Finally."

He frowned at her, as businesslike as ever. "There are risks, Park. It might spread to you: you could become affected. How would we know?"

"You'd know," Park said, meaning ARGUS. But a treacherous part of her felt the incipient headache and thought, *It might have already happened.*

Sagara stayed silent at that.

They had the androids pick Hunter up, her body lifted up to their chests almost as if they were pallbearers at a funeral. Natalya stayed behind in the bridge, too intimidated by either Sagara or the robots to follow. Sagara tailed the group to the infirmary, his eyes glazing over in a way that indicated he was doing something very complicated on his inlays. Neither Park nor Fulbreech spoke to each other for the rest of the long walk to the medical bay.

It was only when they'd tucked Hunter's still, silent form into a bed that Fulbreech said softly, "Looks like you didn't need me, after all."

She looked at him in the dark, wondering if it was a complaint, an admonishment. But in fact she imagined that Fulbreech was a little pleased that she had turned to him—and also a little jealous that she'd struck a deal with Sagara, who was obviously the authority here.

"You gave me something the androids can never give," she told him. She did like him, she thought, a little hopelessly, remembering that feeling of sharp, surprised recognition when he'd appeared in her Antarctic dream. Despite everything that had happened, she . . . was grateful that he was here. Despite his secrets, his little betrayals. It wasn't him, it was the harrowing situation they'd found themselves in. His conscription, her Earth-born status. His behavior made sense now, after what Wick had told her. If those professional barriers hadn't been placed there, outside of their control . . . well. He'd done the best he could for her, risking as much as he was able. He always had, even if she hadn't always thanked him for it. She wouldn't have done so much, in his position. But it was telling that he was still the first person she'd thought of, when she was alone and afraid.

Fulbreech cocked his head at her. "What did I give you, Park?"

"Support," she told him, even though it wasn't quite what she meant to say. "And validation. The androids don't know enough to question me, to challenge what I say or do. They just do what I tell them. But you have that capacity—to refuse, to think for yourself. And in coming, you implicitly agreed there was some logic to my actions, something to endorse."

"Well, it's not as if you left me a choice," Fulbreech commented, wry. "I wasn't just going to say no to you and go back to sleep. You're wrong on one point, though."

"Which point is that?"

Fulbreech stared down at Hunter like he was viewing a body in an open casket. "I didn't come because I supported your idea," he said softly. "I only helped because I support *you*."

Headachy morning came eventually, and with it seeping artificial dawn: gray light touching gray walls. Park sat in the medical bay for the entire night, keeping watch over Hunter, who never stirred. She kept watch over herself, too, vigilant for symptoms, disorientation from an earlier injury—or anything else. But little by little, she felt more like herself again.

Sagara checked in on her intermittently—he even once deigned to bring her sim-coffee—and after a while Wick popped in as well: she had to spend some tiresome moments re-explaining everything that had transpired. Wick looked at her with concern and said, "Are you sure you're up for this?"

Do I have a choice? Park wanted to ask. She could only smile tiredly at him and say, "It's what I'm here for, Commander."

He gave her a look that said they both knew it wasn't true. But he nodded and left her to her work.

Eventually Jimex came back, as well; he only stared at her when she asked him what he'd been up to in the intervening hours, so after a while Park gave up. She stationed him by the door in case she drifted off and Hunter wandered away again. But in the end she stayed awake, idly testing the signal strength of the communication systems (still down) and wondering if Keller really had been feeling the effects of this affliction, and had kept it hidden from everyone until she was frozen. Had *she* also felt nauseous and dizzy? Had she sleepwalked for a period of time before anyone found out—or had it hit her all at once?

But her thoughts were too gray—her brain stung with weariness—and after a while the concerns over Hunter, Keller, and even herself faded away from her.

In the late morning Chanur showed up, followed closely by Ellenex. She made as if to shunt Park out of the room, but Park said firmly, "I have instructions from Captain Sagara to supervise your examination."

Chanur made a low clicking sound with her tongue: another Martian rudeness. But she conducted her checkup of Hunter without further complaint, until she straightened and said softly, "You said you were the one to knock her out?"

By the door, Jimex gave one slow blink.

"That's right," Park said, calm. She'd already reviewed the details in her head. "Ellenex administered the sedative afterward."

Chanur looked at Ellenex, who looked back without saying anything. Then she smiled a little, her blue eye staring.

Chanur shuddered and looked away. "And how exactly did you do it?"

"Pressure on the glenoid fossa, or the greater auricular nerve, or the—"

"Stop." Chanur held up her hand: Park noticed for the first time that it was gnarled with nasty scars. She looked down at Park coldly and said, "So you think you can get to the bottom of this little mystery, with all of your vast medical knowledge?"

Park stared steadily back. "I can certainly try. Which is more than some people on this ship are doing."

Two red spots appeared high on Chanur's cheekbones, but otherwise her expression didn't change. "We all wanted this mission to succeed, Park. You could never know what was at stake for us conscripted."

"Wanted? In the past tense?"

Chanur only shook her head at that and walked away.

Later, Park asked Ellenex, who had stayed behind to set up some sort of monitoring device for Hunter: "Has she hurt you again, after that first time?"

"I do not feel pain," Ellenex answered serenely.

"Damaged you, then."

"No," Ellenex said. "Not yet."

"How is Holt doing?"

"His artificial skin is growing in nicely." The medical android busied herself with recording Hunter's vitals in a medical chart: Chanur insisted on doing things by hand, on paper. "He is designated to be cryogenically frozen by the end of the day."

Of course he is, Park thought. For whatever reason the hairs on the nape of her neck prickled. "How many cryogenic pods do we have on this ship?"

Ellenex's one good eye seemed to fix on a distant point in space as she consulted her files. "There's one for every crewmember on the ship," she answered. "Though there are only two in the medical bay. Dr. Ma and Dr. Keller will have to be transferred."

"Transferred"—as if they were switching cubicles in an office. "Where to?"

"The cargo hold."

Where no one could reach them, she thought, feeling grim. Where she couldn't unfreeze them, if she absolutely had to. But she quashed her paranoia as best she could and said, "Can you tell me how Holt escaped the medical bay? That first time, when Chanur . . . damaged you?"

Ellenex's pale blue eyes, off-kilter as they were, looked both sad and a little wild. She reminded Park again of Sally, her childhood nanny and first android companion—but how could that be, when Ellenex was a medical unit and Sally a child-minder, with some twenty years lying between their construction? But there was the same sweet, bland face; the same tidy white uniform.

"I'm sorry, Dr. Park," she answered soberly. "I do not have an answer to your question. I cannot explain what happened with Dr. Holt."

"What do you mean, you can't explain?"

"Perhaps Dr. Chanur is right, and I am malfunctioning," Ellenex said, downcast.

"You're not malfunctioning," Jimex said from the door. "You are learning."

Park looked between them. "What are you talking about?"

Ellenex touched her hair, almost self-consciously. "It is as we told you, Dr. Park. There are anomalies on the ship."

"What *sort* of anomalies?" *The same word again*, she thought. What did they all mean by it, or by 'assimilation,' by 'synthetic'? Since when had they begun forming their own separate understanding of words, employing them in their own special modes of communication? Their own languages? And why had no one taken notice of any of it besides Park?

Ellenex shook her head, slowly. The damage to her skull made it look like her hair was in danger of sliding off. A doll, Park realized. She was just a human-sized, broken doll. *She's so damaged. I can't take anything she says seriously.*

"I'm sorry," Ellenex repeated, her voice soft and mournful. "There are anomalies. I am unable to answer your query at this time."

Eventually she left Ellenex there to watch Hunter, *with* Jimex, *with* Dylanex, too, because even if Ellenex herself was malfunctioning, the others would obey Park's command to stay put and watch. Her stomach was growling—she could not remember the last time she had eaten. Famished, Park started toward the canteen, then stopped. She stood there in the hallway for a moment, cocking her head to the side. Was she thinking, or was she dimly receiving her body's own instinct, some secret and sudden message from somewhere inside of her? She wasn't sure. Then, almost irresistibly, she found herself turning and gravitating toward a different part of the ship. It felt only semi-conscious, as if she had some dense hidden core within herself that she'd never known about, and it was being dragged in one direction by a distant magnet.

"I need to speak with you," she said when she reached her destination.

Fulbreech looked up from his schematics. He was working with METIS in his workspace, drawing holographic maps in the air of what Park assumed was Eos's terrain. She caught a glimpse of a lake and a strange, twisting spire before Fulbreech gestured and closed the program. It vanished into the air like a blown-out candle flame.

"Sagara just stopped in, looking for you," he said in response.

Park couldn't help but glance around, imagining the sensors in the walls. "He'll find me eventually," she said. "If he really needs me."

"What's he want you for?"

"Hunter, of course. I suppose he won't be happy that I left my post."

Fulbreech shook his head. "How could he know so quickly that you left?"

". . . He has eyes everywhere." Sagara would hang her for that one.

But Fulbreech only smiled, thinking it a light-hearted joke. "I've begun to assume that at all times. Hello, Captain."

She nearly smiled, too; it felt good to joke again, to pretend at normalcy. Fulbreech, looking at her almost-smile, said, "You couldn't have come just to talk to me. Or could you?"

"I did want to thank you," Park told him, trying not to rush the words, so that he knew she meant them. "For last night. And to tell you something else that we didn't have time for—"

"I love you, too, Park."

"—Wick told me," she finished, resisting the urge to roll her eyes. "About the Fold. I know what you know."

She watched a shadow pass over Fulbreech's eyes; wordlessly, he went to the door of his workspace and palmed it shut. He couldn't know the futility of the action. "Wick told you?" he asked then, turning. "About all of it?"

"He told me enough," Park replied. "About why we're really here, about what you're studying. The . . . quantum effects. And how the conscripted couldn't tell anyone. Well—you told me that last part. But he told me the rest of it. The gist."

"I see," Fulbreech said. He coughed into his shoulder. "Then—you know pretty much everything, I suppose. So what did you want to talk to me about?"

"Have you found any plant life out there?" Park asked. "Any fungi? You don't have to tell me any details: just confirm or deny."

Spores, she was thinking. Maybe the side effect of some alien plant. If they'd brought it aboard the ship, it could have contaminated the air, affecting some of the crewmembers. Unbalancing the chemicals in their brains. Maybe it disturbed their sleep cycles, or emitted hallucinogens. But Fulbreech was shaking his head.

"I don't know if you've noticed," he said, "but it's all ice out there. If there's any possibility for plant life to grow, we haven't found it, and probably won't for a long time."

Damn, Park thought. "What about ice samples? Or air canisters?"

"Why are you asking about all of this?" Fulbreech asked in turn. He moved away from the door and took a closer look at her. Instinctively, Park took a step back. "Because you think some material is causing Hunter to sleepwalk?"

"We have to examine all possibilities," she said, "when dealing with alien worlds. I'm just going through the process of elimination."

"You don't think her having too much coffee is a more probable cause? Or doing drugs? Maybe sharing them with Holt and Ma, to relieve stress, and it having a bad effect on all three of them?"

"What about Keller?" Park challenged. "Or Reimi?"

Fulbreech shrugged. "I'm not saying it's the answer, Park, just something like it."

She pressed her lips together. She couldn't tell him anything more: she'd promised Sagara she wouldn't, and they'd all agreed not to speak of the nightmares, the contagious nature of them, the strange and spreading symptoms—lest they implant themselves in others. That he knew about the sleepwalking was already dangerous enough: the rest of it was anathema, at least for now. Fulbreech looked into her face and said, "You look white as a sheet. You haven't slept or eaten, have you?"

She was almost charmed by his old-fashioned Earth talk. She did feel like a sheet: white and flat and thin. As if she were stretched out, translucent—parts of her wearing away and fraying, like old thread. No, she could tell him nothing, she decided. In a circuitous way it felt like her way of protecting him. From Sagara, from the nightmares. From knowledge that could only stand to harm him. Now she knew a little of what he'd felt, when she'd stormed in asking what was in the utility rooms.

In another way it also felt like her method of getting payback—of leveling the field between them. He'd kept things from her, so it was all right if she did the same to him. Why did she feel that way—that she had to have some advantage over him, hidden knowledge, as he'd had over her? It couldn't be healthy, thinking always in those terms: advantages, leverages, trump cards. Getting even. But she couldn't help it. She had to guard herself. As much as she wanted to rely on him, on his warm solidity, she still felt that puckering of strange and breathless danger whenever she was with him.

Park shook her head. Fulbreech peered at her closely and said, "Let's eat, then. You look like you could do with some sustenance."

"It will have to be fast," she found herself saying. But she smiled, despite herself, and even took his proffered arm. METIS slid the door shut behind them as they walked away.

"How do you sleep at night?" Park asked as they headed up the tunnel to Deck A. She found herself thinking that Fulbreech could have been the perfect control experiment, if only he hadn't been exposed to any strange, exotic samples. Because if *he* hadn't experienced any nightmares, then . . .

Fulbreech looked perturbed by the question. "Pardon?"

Park broke out of her thoughts. "Sleeping," she repeated. "Are you finding it difficult to adjust to the schedule on Eos? Have you experienced any irregularities in your sleep patterns?"

"Oh," Fulbreech said. He scratched his neck. "No, I'm sleeping fine, I suppose. Sometimes I get nosebleeds, but that's common for me with changes in the atmosphere."

A mundane answer, but Park thought she sensed a little nervousness in his posture, although not an outright lie. What was Fulbreech hiding now?

"How are *you* sleeping?" he asked then.

Park blinked. "Not at all, it feels like. Things have been . . . busy."

Fulbreech almost snorted. "That's an understatement. Ever since we landed, things have gone from zero to one hundred, *fast.* In the old days we would have called it a PFS."

"PFS?"

"Pretty Fucky Situation. It's old netspeak."

"I never heard it," Park said dryly, "and I spent a lot of time on the cyberstream."

"See, that's how I know you didn't," Fulbreech said, his mouth quirking. "The real denizens still called it the net."

"You're not older than me, Fulbreech."

He laughed. "No, but I learned everything from my older brother, and he insisted on doing things the old-school way. So the 'stream was still called the 'net,' and 'crash' was actually 'cool,' and so on and so forth."

She remembered that he'd mentioned his brother before, in her office. The one who'd had a baby recently. "You're close to your family," she found herself saying. She said it musingly, as if it were an interesting trivia fact. Some impersonal little statistic, something someone might say to impress others—to provoke exclamations of amazement. She couldn't imagine what it was like, having the ISF dictate whether you could see or speak to someone you loved. She didn't have an analogous relation in her own life. Couldn't make a comparison in terms of the pain, or the gratitude, or the fear that came with such an arrangement.

Fulbreech looked at her sidelong, as if he knew her thoughts. "Who isn't?" he asked.

"People who have no family, for one thing." It was a naïve statement on his part, she thought without emotion. It showed that he took his situation for granted.

Fulbreech grimaced, registering his misstep—but he forged onward. "You adopt the androids as your family, in a way. I saw how they rallied around you last night."

For a moment Park wanted to confess to him the strangeness of the androids' behavior the night before; their "assimilation," their odd decision-making. The signs of them . . . going strange. But Jimex had reverted back to mostly normal in the morning, it seemed; and she was afraid that things could get misinterpreted, propagandized. She didn't need to spark yet another panic on the ship. Mass hysteria. So she decided against it.

"I didn't ask them to do that," Park told him. "They just—did it. They tend to like me, in the way that dogs tend to gravitate toward certain people."

"But robots are not dogs," he said. "You can't tell me we program that instinct into them."

"We give them the protocol to self-preserve. Barring certain circumstances. And all self-preserving beings will prefer people who hold goodwill toward them over people who do not. Jimex knows I look out for him, and because he's connected to the rest of the crew, they share that sense, too."

"And why *do* you look out for him? He's an idiot."

"He's not," she said, though she had often thought the same thing herself. "He's just—learning. And he does try to make me proud."

Fulbreech gave her an assessing look. She suddenly realized that she was still holding his arm, and she released it. "You talk about him as if he were a child," he said.

Park made a face. "Isn't he one?"

"There are some who would say they're more like monsters."

Children can be monsters, Park thought. But she could only think to answer: "They'll only be what you want them to be."

Fulbreech had nothing to say to that.

They entered the mess hall and collected their trays of ham sandwiches, with little curls of moon cheese on the side. Megex and Philex smiled at them, giving no acknowledgement of what had happened the night before. They apologized for the inconvenience and said the expedition had officially run out of breakfast foods. Fulbreech groaned, but Park could not bring herself to care.

She was in sorry physical condition, she thought as she sat and pushed the food into her mouth. One night with three hours of sleep had her feeling like warmed-up death. She had not prepared herself, physically or mentally, for the strains of this mission. But then again, she'd been sent on the mission under false pretenses. She hadn't realized the danger she'd be placed in.

Or maybe she simply hadn't cared about it, at the time. But she did now; she lived with the awareness of it hanging over her at all times. What had changed?

She watched as Fulbreech carefully cut the crusts off his sandwich, the tough synthetic bread resisting his knife. His hands were large and square but very careful: he needed them for map-making.

"One day," Fulbreech said, keeping his voice light, "they'll figure out how to give us real wheat in space."

"They don't grow it in the colonies?"

"It grows red," Fulbreech told her, smiling. "Which is pretty off-putting. And a large portion of the population seems to be developing gluten intolerance. At least on Mars. ISF says we won't need bread in a few years."

"I wonder what else ISF thinks we don't need," Park muttered.

"You'd be surprised," Fulbreech muttered back. He gave her a lopsided grin, the earlier awkwardness between them passing for the moment. Then his eyes flicked up past Park's shoulder—and widened.

As if on cue, there was a sudden clamor behind her. Sharp, shrill yelling. The clattering of trays. Park's shoulders jumped from the violence of the noise.

She looked. There was a woman with a shock of red hair in the room—Hunter—*Hunter* was in the room! And she and Natalya were facing each other a few tables down, both of them red-eyed, shaking. They both looked pale and exhausted. Natalya said audibly, with bite, "If you don't tell them, I will."

"I don't know what you're talking about," Hunter snapped. "Just sit down."

Park stood up and thought, *What the fuck is she doing out here?* And where the hell was Jimex? Ellenex? Why hadn't they kept her hidden away?

"Oh, shit," Fulbreech said from behind her.

The cafeteria had quieted. All eyes were on the two women now, and Natalya knew it. "You tampered with the controls," she hissed at Hunter, loud enough to be heard from across the room. "Admit it!"

"I don't know what you're talking about!" Hunter said again, wild-eyed. She looked around at the room, eyes roving—looking for help, backup. Someone who believed her. Her gaze did not land on Park. Park suddenly realized that Boone was not in the mess hall; neither were Wick or Sagara. Then, with a terrible shock, she realized that there was not even a true crowd for Hunter to appeal to: it was just her, Fulbreech, Wan Xu, and Chanur, along with the androids. Three of their leaders were not in the room. The other four had been frozen.

We've dwindled so much, Park thought with cold, acidic horror. It was a literal skeleton crew. How had they not noticed? Why had no one panicked more? Who would even be left to complete this mission—or ferry them all safely home?

And only she could step forward and refute Natalya's claim that Hunter had done something to the controls. But she found herself oddly still. She wanted to wait and see what Natalya was playing at.

"Own up," the surveyor spat. "We don't need any more trouble on this ship than we've already had!"

"I don't know what you're fucking talking about!" Hunter shouted again.

They glared at each other; there was a kind of silent mudwrestling in the air between them.

Fulbreech was on his feet now, too. No one was moving forward to intercept the conflict, which promised to turn into a fight. Instead, the others seemed arrested, confused—almost fascinated. Park felt it, too. There had never been violence of any kind between crewmembers on the ship, or even heated arguments beyond academic debates; there was a morbid curiosity, that question of what would happen next. Almost an excitement in seeing something as real and vivid as violence, here in their sterile bubble in space. She only broke out of it when Fulbreech said under his breath: "What the hell is Hunter doing out here? And what is *Natalya* doing?" He looked at Park. "*Did* she tamper with the controls?"

"No," Park said, trying to shake off her sudden stupor. "The androids said she didn't. They were sure. I don't know what Natalya's talking about." She took a step. "But I should intervene now." Infighting was the biggest thing to avoid on a long space voyage—it could permanently alter the working atmosphere of the ship—and it was her duty as the resident psychologist to take the conflict out of sight. Resolve it as best she could. This was how closed groups fell apart: the marooned, the shipwrecked, the besieged and the trapped. The groups that required close coordination to operate and survive. Resentment crept in, then anger, dissension. Teams splintered; grudges formed. Park had even heard about one stranded unit of soldiers resorting to cannibalism among their ranks—even though they'd been found with some of their regular rations still intact.

But suddenly she felt an immense weariness. Couldn't she have one day, one lunch with Fulbreech, where things didn't fall apart?

"Where are the robots?" Fulbreech asked, his voice dim and very far away.

"I don't know," Park answered. "I told three of them to—"

Then she saw it. At first she thought it was a trick of her peripheral, an illusion due to not focusing clearly on anything but Natalya and Hunter's bodies, which seemed poised to collide together like two cannonballs in the air. But when she turned to look properly, to assure herself she was imagining things, Park's gut tensed. A kind of coldness radiated upwards from her lungs.

There was a man standing in the doorway of the mess hall, watching the fight. He was tall, with white-blond hair; when he saw Park looking at him, he turned on his heel and walked away, briskly but unconcernedly, with his fists in his pockets. Park felt the blood leaving her hands. She had never seen the man before. She who had personally examined each of the other twelve crewmembers aboard the *Deucalion*. She had never seen him in her life. He was a stranger.

There was a stranger on the ship.

Impossible, she thought. But then, what was impossible anymore? Here they were, in the farthest reaches of the next galaxy, studying an alien planet that crinkled space and time together like an accordion. People were becoming infected with nightmares left and right—or they were being frozen, their cells suspended, static in time, while the ISF watched coldly from afar. While Park stayed rooted in place, subatomic radiation and confusion shrinking her cortical cells like flowers shriveling in heat. And there was a stranger walking around, unnoticed and sinister and free.

Beyond her line of sight, there was a scream. Natalya had hit Valentina and drawn blood.

Wan Xu was right, Park thought, feeling a sea-change in her own blood as the others began to run forward, shouting. This was a closed system. There were no more known variables.

Everything was different here.

14.

[Hi:

Have you reached your destination yet? Or if you haven't, can you say how much longer? I don't know if you ever said. I want all of this to be over already. I don't know if I can take the waiting.

Some bad news. Nicky's lungs are acting up again. You won't know how scary such a thing is until you have a child. Whatever ISF's problems, at least medical care is free. What will happen when things like this happen in the future? You have a doctor on board, don't you? She can treat such things?

But what will happen when she dies, someday? Have we really thought this through?]

VIDEO LOG #54—Ship Designation CS *Wyvern* 7079
Day 10: 09:02 UTO

[Inside the ship. Taban is tinkering with a device in the corner of the cockpit with the HARE watching on from a perch to his right. The HARE switches between looking at Taban and Daley, who is in the hallway beyond the cockpit, climbing once more into his exo-armor suit.]

Taban: Another day, another bunch of ice to put in a bucket, huh?

Daley (grunt): You coming with me?

Taban: Nah. I've got other repairs to run.

Daley: What do you mean? You said the FTL drive is good to go.

Taban: It is. But this is an old ship. Might as well patch up some of the other stuff so we don't run the risk of getting stranded again. Next time there won't be a shiny new planet to land on.

Daley: You making fun of me?

Taban: What? No.

Daley: I feel like you are.

Taban: I'm not.

Daley: It's a two-man job out there. We'd probably find something quicker if you helped look.

Taban: I've *been* helping. You know I want to find good shit as much as you do. If anything, I don't want to turn up to ISF empty-handed . . . You know the punishment for venturing into unregulated space can be banishment to a prison colony?

Daley (glancing at the HARE): The thing tell you that?

Taban: Maybe. Yeah. Maybe.

Daley: I heard you talking to it, last night. When you thought I was asleep. I could hear you through the wall. Telling it stories.

Taban: Sorry. I didn't mean to keep you up.

Daley: It's fine.

Taban: And they're not stories. Well, I mean, I guess they are. We just talk about myths and shit.

Daley: You tell it stories before bed.

Taban: Tell him, HARE.

HARE: We discussed the tale of Prometheus having his liver devoured by eagles. It was an unjust fate.

Daley (casting Taban a look of contempt): . . . Wow.

Taban: . . . It helps to talk to it. Even to have it play its stupid music. You know I've been having nightmares every time I go to sleep?

Daley: Nightmares?

Taban: Yeah. Like . . . dreams that I'm getting frozen. Like I can't move, something's stopping me from moving, my tongue's gone. And I get this feeling like someone's going to split my chest open. You don't get dreams like that?

Daley: . . . No.

Taban: . . . How's your heart feeling?

Daley: It's fine. I'll see you later.

[Daley seals off the cockpit door. In a moment the sounds of the ship's airlock opening can be heard. Daley departs the ship.]

Taban (turning to the HARE): So? Did they receive the distress signal?

HARE: It is unknown how far away the nearest ISF outpost is. Given that we could only repair the communications system to half-strength, I cannot accurately estimate how long it would take for the signal to reach a manned ship or outpost.

Taban: Give me your best guess.

HARE: 28% likelihood that someone has received the signal by now. Again, this estimate is flawed. I could use my own resources to boost its strength—

Taban: —but doing so would drain your battery. I know. It's okay.

HARE: Are you certain?

Taban: Yeah. I would only do that as an absolute last-ditch resort . . . So I'm okay with waiting for now. I don't want to lose you and be left alone with—you know. No, I won't do that.

HARE: Thank you.

Taban: Don't mention it. And the ship's tracking beacon is functioning okay?

HARE: Yes. There is also one in each of your IEVA suits.

Taban: Good to know. Though I don't think I'll be venturing out there again any time soon. Not after that whole thing with going north, and "the man." I don't know how Daley does it.

HARE: He appears not to remember the anomalies of the other day.

Taban: I don't know if that's a blessing or a curse.

HARE: Yes.

Taban: Well, I suppose all we've got to do is wait it out.

HARE: Yes.

Taban: You remember what I taught you last night?

HARE: Yes. I remember.

Taban: Okay. You go first.

HARE (processors whirring): I have identified an object that is suitable for our activity.

Taban: Okay. Is it a person?

HARE: Negative.

Taban: Is it a food?

HARE: Negative.

Taban: Is it an animal?

HARE: Negative.

Taban: Is it a machine?

HARE: Negative.

Taban: Is it something I can touch?

HARE: Negative.

Taban: . . . Let's go back to the other game.

HARE (processors whirring): I have identified an object that is suitable for our activity. You would describe it as being the color gray.

Taban: Say it like I told you.

HARE (processors whirring): I spy something gray.

VIDEO LOG #55—Ship Designation CS *Wyvern* 7079
Day 10: 12:45 UTO

[Taban and the HARE are still in the cockpit. Taban is climbing out of the hatch in the floor that leads to the cargo hold and galley.]

Taban: Okay, I've got my lunch. How are we on rations?

HARE: 45 days of full rations remain. More if you and USER Daley eat in half-portions.

Taban: So 90 days left. That's cushy—more than enough for someone to get our signal and fly out here.

HARE: Yes.

Taban: Let's see what we've got. Crossing my fingers for fried chicken. Fried chicken, fried chicken, fried chicken . . .

HARE: I wish you luck.

Taban (poking open the foil ration packet): Maple sausage. And yams. Hm.

HARE: Congratulations.

Taban: Why congratulate me? It's not what I wanted.

HARE: It is still nutrition.

[The airlock of the *Wyvern* opens. Daley clambers in, his suit encrusted in frost.]

Taban: Welcome back. Lunch is ready.

Daley (climbing out of his suit): Oh, yeah? . . . Smells like maple sausage again.

Taban: That's mine. Try yours; you might get lucky.

[Daley lumbers over into the cockpit. His face is red from exertion, his lips chapped and flaking from hours of exposure to the Eotian cold. He plops down across from Taban and the HARE and accepts another ration packet, shaking it to begin the self-heating process.]

Daley: I went out past the second marker, this time. More in the direction of those shards we saw.

Taban: What'd you get? Fried chicken?

Daley: The terrain changes a bit, out there. Instead of all . . . webby, the ice gets clear. Glacial. Like walking on glass, in places.

Taban: Oh, it's curry. Why don't they ever think these things through, the people that make this stuff? Who *doesn't* get the shits from curry? And who wants to be trapped aboard a vacuum of limited air with someone who has the shits?

Daley: I'm going to try to push farther out in that direction tomorrow. I've got a feeling about it.

Taban: Oh, yeah?

Daley: Yeah. Maybe I'll find something noteworthy before your reinforcements get here.

Taban: . . .

Daley (eating): . . .

HARE: . . .

Taban: . . . What did you say?

Daley: You heard me. I said, "Maybe I'll find something noteworthy before your reinforcements get here."

Taban: What are you . . . talking about?

Daley: You think I'm an idiot? When you activate the ship's distress beacon, the undercarriage flashes. I know you called for help.

Taban: But the snow covers it up.

Daley: It must have melted. What the fuck is wrong with you?

Taban: Look, Daley, I—

Daley: I clue you in to the discovery of a lifetime, and you pay me back by calling ISF before we're ready? What's wrong with you? We agreed not to repair the comm—

Taban: We never agreed to that. We just agreed to fixing the FTL drive first. Which I did.

Daley: Don't try to twist it around. What are we going to do if they get here and we don't have shit to show them? They're going to throw our asses in—what did you call it? A prison colony? Where would they even have that?

Taban (quietly): Pandora.

Daley: Great. Pandora.

Taban: Look. After that time you ran out of oxygen—and you kept wanting to go out—and you saw some *guy*—I don't think you're well, Daley. This, all of this—scrubbing through the ice? Looking for something we can give to ISF? We're not scientists, man. We don't have tools. We wouldn't know something of value on this planet if it kicked us in the teeth. We're wasting our time out here. I think you know that.

Daley (eating): . . .

Taban: I got scared. When you were in the medical pod.

Daley: *You* were scared?

Taban: Yeah, I was scared! You were either going to die and I would have needed to call them to come rescue me anyway, or you were going to recover and stay obsessed with being here. And even if I could fly the ship, I wouldn't want to take it and leave you here alone. But I want to go home, Daley. You remember that? Home?

Daley: . . .

Taban: And look, maybe they'll send researchers who'll be able to help you look. Better than I've been able to. I just want to go home. Maybe help comes, half of them stay with you, half of them take me back. You can have all the credit.

Daley: It's our planet. Both of ours. We both found it.

Taban: You're the one who got us lost. You're the one who landed us here. It's yours. Keep it. I'm not interested.

Daley: . . . Were you going to turn me in to them? In exchange for letting you off the hook? Were you going to say it was all my idea?

Taban: What? No! It's like I said—I just want to go home.

Daley: HARE. Was that his plan? He ask you to help him fix the comm so he could make me the sacrificial lamb?

HARE: I don't understand your question.

Daley: Piece of shit.

Taban: Look. Just don't be angry.

Daley: I'm not angry. Do I seem angry to you?

Taban: Well—sort of. I don't know. No. But still. I think this is for the best.

Daley: Fine. Whatever. I guess it's less for me to worry about if you fuck off to wherever. Maybe they will send someone more useful. It could still work out.

Taban: Yeah, exactly. See? It's for the best.

Daley: Fuck you.

VIDEO LOG #55—Ship Designation CS *Wyvern* 7079
Day 10: 17:45 UTO

[Taban is now in his bunk, which is partitioned off from Daley's. The HARE has accompanied him; it seems it has become routine for the HARE to enter sleep mode in Taban's quarters.]

Taban: That went well, I guess.

HARE: . . .

Taban: You didn't tell him, did you? About the distress beacon?

HARE: Negative. USER Daley has never interacted with me without you present.

Taban: I thought so. But how did he know? You said the light on the undercarriage of the ship is broken.

HARE: It is. Unless he fixed it, USER Daley should not have been able to see it flashing.

Taban: Then how does he know we repaired the comm system?

HARE: I am unable to answer your query at this time.

Taban: . . . Well, whatever. It's all out in the open now, I guess.

HARE: Yes.

Taban: It's for the best.

HARE: . . .

Taban: They'll probably have received the signal by now. Give them—what—two weeks to send an unmanned ship to do a flyby, send some images back to ISF? Then the actual rescue comes ten days, two weeks after?

HARE: These estimates seem fairly accurate.

Taban: We can do that. That sounds easy. Just sit on our asses and wait.

HARE: USER Daley will continue his exploration of the planet, designation: HARPA in the meantime.

Taban: Maybe. Or maybe he'll get tired of scratching around in the ice and stop. Sooner or later he's got to realize it's a pipe dream.

HARE: What is a 'pipe dream'?

Taban: It's an old phrase. It's like—a fantasy that's impractical.

HARE: Are fantasies not impractical by nature?

Taban: No, like—it's an illusion. It's a dream you have that can never come true, because it's so fantastic. It's like me when I was a kid, thinking I was going to grow up to be a gridball star.

HARE: And this was impossible?

Taban: Kind of. By the time I grew up, they were figuring out that sports are kind of pointless on Mars.

HARE: How does a pipe factor in?

Taban: Who knows. Maybe it's saying something about the destination. Dreams. Hopes. Sports. Names. At some point they all go down the shitter.

VIDEO LOG #56—Ship Designation CS *Wyvern* 7079
Day 10: 21:22

[The HARE is moving around the ship in the dark. Although the HARE itself is able to see in infrared and with night-vision, it does not apply these filters while recording its live footage. It enters a dark room, peers into it for a while, then returns to Taban's bunk. Taban is sleeping fitfully on his right side.]

HARE: USER Taban.

Taban: Huh?

HARE: USER Taban. Your attention is required.

Taban (gasping): What?

HARE: Your attention is required.

Taban: Oh, it's you. I was having another dream—a nightmare—I thought maybe you were talking to me. Or someone else was. Was that you?

HARE: I was speaking to you.

Taban: Oh. What's going on?

HARE: USER Daley is gone.

Taban: Gone—what do you mean, gone?

HARE: USER Daley is no longer in his bunk. USER Daley has exited the ship.

Taban: What time is it?

HARE: Unclassified solar major set six hours ago.

Taban: That's the middle of the night! It's freezing out there—and dark as hell. How long has he been gone?

HARE: Undetermined. I can check the ship's logs.

Taban: Do that. And get my suit. Goddamn him, we said we'd never go out at night. What's he thinking?

HARE: You require your suit?

Taban: Yes. We have to go out and get him

VIDEO LOG #56—Ship Designation CS *Wyvern* 7079
Day 10: 21:52

[It's nighttime outside, though the sky is barely visible. Taban is struggling to move against blasts of howling wind, which whip frost and chunks of ice into the air in gray waves. He fights to lunge forward with every step, while the HARE leads the way by a meter, scanning their surroundings in 180-degree arcs.]

Taban: Goddamn it! There's no way he's out here!

HARE: He must be.

Taban: But how will we find him? There aren't even any footprints!

HARE: There is a slight heat signature in the air. This must come from USER Daley.

Taban: God*damn* him!

[Together they struggle through the blizzard. Glimpses of the terrain show that it has changed, though they've scarcely moved one kilometer from the ship. The usual white flatness has changed to fields of dark, smooth ripples, low and regular, like frozen waves of glass. Taban struggles to step over the hard crest of each 'wave,' but doesn't comment on (or notice?) the transformed landscape.]

[After several minutes of traveling, it's clear that Taban is struggling to go on.]

Taban: Shit. This is so fucking hard. (looking at his sensor glove) And my oxygen's already at 50%! How is that possible?

HARE: I am unsure.

Taban: We've only been out here thirty minutes. Daley's been out here for, what, hours? Is there any way he's still alive?

HARE: We're following the infrared trail of something.

Taban: Goddamn it. (heavy breathing)

HARE: Do you require assistance?

Taban: No, I'm all right. As soon as we find him, I'm dragging him back and locking him up. We can do that thing we talked about. Turn the medical bay into a kind of cell. Just until ISF arrives.

HARE: USER Daley will most likely be uncooperative.

Taban: *I'm* tired of being cooperative. Seriously. I've let him put us in enough danger as it is. It's over now.

HARE: I have not been in danger.

Taban: He was planning to send you out in all of this. Every night. Trust me, you would have been in danger.

HARE: Thank you.

Taban: You don't deserve that. *I* don't deserve that. We're just doing our jobs. That's all it is to us. Just jobs. You explore, I mine. We're just doing our jobs.

HARE: Yes.

Taban: Him, though . . . (panting) Him, it's way beyond that. It's an obsession. Like a madness. It's bad shit.

HARE: (pausing to analyze the terrain ahead) (beeping)

Taban: What?

HARE: There is a living organism ahead.

Taban: . . . Daley?

HARE: Undetermined. There are anomalies. Interference. I need to be closer to know.

Taban: Fuck.

[Cautiously, the two pick their way forward. It seems impossible to see anything in the murkiness of the night. Taban consistently bumps into the knee-high, dark waves. He curses. After several moments, the HARE speaks.]

HARE: The organism is just ahead.

[Taban stops dead in his tracks.]

Taban: I don't see anything.

HARE (processors whirring): It is USER Daley.

[Taban stumbles forward, tripping still over the curves in the ground. Suddenly, on the swell of one, Hap Daley's round, armored body appears. He is cradled face-down in the dip of the wave, with his arms outstretched, as if he had collapsed while crawling.]

Taban: Jesus!

HARE: He is alive.

[Taban approaches clumsily, rolling Daley over onto his back. As soon as he does, Daley reaches out and seizes his helmet, gasping.]

Taban: Fuck, Daley! Let go! It's me!

Daley: Did you see it? Did you see it?

Taban: See what?

Daley: I saw it—I was sleeping, but I woke up and saw it through the window—

Taban: Saw *what?*

Daley: Some kind of quadruped. Looked like a fox or a canine of some kind. It was small and white. I followed . . .

Taban: . . . .

Daley: You listening? I saw something *living* out here!

[He struggles to sit up.]

Taban: How's your oxygen?

Daley: Fin, you *listening?*

Taban: I heard you. You must have been—dreaming, or something, Daley. Fuck. I don't know. Let's go back.

Daley: No. Not until I show you.

Taban: Show me what? There's *nothing* out here, Daley! Nothing! No crystal mountains, no ships, no shards, no ferroxes—

Daley: No. There is. I found it. It's not far . . .

Taban: No. No fucking way. We're going *home*.

Daley: Fin. Please.

Taban: *No.*

HARE: USER Daley's oxygen is at 90%.

Taban: No one asked you.

Daley: Fin. I swear. It'll take—five minutes. Less. I was coming back to get you when I tripped—but it's right there! (He points to something presumably a few meters away) Or at least let me take the HARE to look at it. It needs to record it. This is important.

Taban: How important could it be?

Daley: It's the most important thing in the world.

Taban: . . . (rubs his visor in a circular motion, as if rubbing his face) No.

Daley: Please. After this, I'll never ask anything of you again. You can go back to the ship after. I'll leave you out of it. I just need to know if you can see it, too.

Taban: I'm counting down from five minutes. If we don't see anything by then, I'm going back. With the HARE. And I'll leave you here. I don't need you anymore, Daley.

Daley: I know. Thank you. I know, Fin.

[The two men rise to their feet, Taban pulling up Daley by the hand with an effort. The HARE scuttles up to Taban and seems to lean against his leg, perhaps to lend support. It stares off in the direction that Daley indicated, while the two men push their helmets close to speak.]

Taban: Tell me the truth, Daley. We came outside to look for you, and we couldn't see the distress beacon on the ship flashing at all. The light's still broken. It hasn't been fixed in all the time we've been here. So how did you really know we fixed the comm system?

Daley: . . .

Taban: Daley?

Daley: I don't know. I can't remember. I guess I dreamed it.

15.

Park seized Fulbreech's arm. "There's a stranger," she hissed.

He looked at her, startled. "What?"

"A stranger," Park repeated, her voice low and urgent. "Aboard the ship. Someone I've never seen before."

His brow furrowed; he put his hand on her elbow, even though Park knew she wasn't shaking. "Where?"

"Over by the door. He's gone now. But I saw him."

"Are you sure it wasn't just a trick of the light?" Fulbreech asked. He tried to smile. "Maybe your eyes deceived you for a second—mine do all of the time—hell, sometimes I don't even recognize myself when I look in the mirror. Could you have imagined it?"

He was looking at her with that face again, that expression of open and genuine concern for her wellbeing, like a puppy not quite knowing what was wrong with its master, and despite herself Park felt a surge of irritation towards him, even hatred. *No need for that look, Fulbreech,* she thought. *I hardly know ye.* But more than that—no need to imply that she'd simply been foolish. She'd examined every person on this ship on a daily basis, for God's sake, something even Chanur didn't do. She couldn't have just *imagined* a stranger.

But of course she knew she was being unfair. If he said something like this to *her,* she would have a similar reaction, or at least ask him to do a perfunctory psych eval. Because it was impossible, that someone had managed to stow away on the ship. Impossible for him to have lived on the *Deucalion* for the last several months. What would he have done for food, for bathing? What would have happened during the radiation storms, so bad that they penetrated even the titanium shell of the ship, and the crew had to take shelter in the storm bunker at the *Deucalion*'s core? A stowaway would have died, surely, or at least contracted severe radiation sickness. And yet the man had looked well-fed, clean. It was impossible, Park knew it was, and yet—she'd *seen* it.

"I have to go," she said, her voice strangely distant and muffled, as if she were underwater. She stood, letting go of Fulbreech's arm. From the corner of her eye she saw Sagara stalking across the room with that trademark look on his face—an expression that made his eyes snap dark lightning. He strode up to Natalya and Hunter and pulled them apart as easily as if he were separating two children, speaking to them in low, vicious tones. Although he never raised his voice, everyone in his field of concentration instinctively mimicked him, went quiet and grim. The room crackled with silent intensity, as if preluding the outbreak of a storm.

Park turned away from the scene, which was still arresting the others in the mess hall. It felt incredibly insignificant now, almost unreal, images flickering on a media stream—even though she knew that this fell under her domain. An incident like a physical brawl was sure to impact the psychological conditions of the crew—or what was left of it. But following the stranger was more important. There was either some renegade loose on the ship without anyone knowing . . . or Park was seeing things. She didn't know which one was worse.

Fulbreech was looking at her with concern. "Where are you going?"

Behind him, someone called out his name. Said they needed his help. Neither Park nor Fulbreech looked at the speaker.

"I need to lie down," Park said, feeling as if her facial muscles were frozen, locked into place. "I'm—tired."

"I'll go with you." He looked as if he didn't believe her; no, as if he were afraid she would do something rash.

Park shook her arm slightly, and Fulbreech's hand fell away from it like a dead thing. "No," she said. She felt as if she were sleepwalking. "I'll be fine. The others need you. I'm just going to sleep."

Then she left. She couldn't remember if he said anything else: only that he didn't follow her out of the canteen.

There were three decks to the *Deucalion* in all, with over a hundred different partitioned rooms spread throughout each of them. Park eliminated the idea of searching the crewmembers' cabins entirely: it was impossible for anyone not to notice a stranger living in their twelve-foot-long cubicle, and anyway the only ones with the authority to unlock the crewmates' quarters were Wick, Sagara, and Boone, along with any androids who were acting as their delegates. She thought briefly to go find Jimex and requisition him for her search—but when she stopped by the medical bay, he was nowhere to be found. Neither were Ellenex or the security android Dylanex. So Park decided to comb the obscurest parts of the ship alone.

She had to be sure, she thought as she hunted around tall crates and lumpy shapes in the murky gray light. She could not have a repeat of the utility rooms, not in front of Fulbreech—which was why she hadn't let him come. She had to be sure. She could not scrabble madly, desperately for answers again, with him looking on with pity and bewilderment. She would rather have a hidden assailant jump out at her and force her to use her measly, one-day self-defense training than have to face that.

And she could not have her sanity being called into question. Not with everything else going on, everyone else acting irrationally. Holt, Ma, Keller, Hunter—fighting, violence in the mess hall—the androids failing the simplest commands, behaving strangely. How long would it be before this mental wildfire claimed the rest of the ship?

And who's to say it hasn't already? a little voice clicked and chattered in the back of her brain. The insane did not know they were insane.

She felt sick, queasy with lack of sleep and sour paranoia. She was looking in the ship's least-used corners, starting with Deck B: the cargo bays, the storage facilities, the supply closets. If there was a stranger—and there was, she told herself adamantly—then he would be here. Here in the uninhabited spaces of the ship.

But the more she searched, the more her inner panic rose. She began to question herself. Surely a stowaway would have blankets, stolen food. The man couldn't have lasted so long without leaving a trace. And yet there was nothing. Crates and shelves loomed over her like shadowy cairns, as if she had stepped onto some strange, ancient trail, edged by indecipherable markers—or a burial ground. Was her mind playing tricks on her? Had she merely glimpsed someone unremarkable, and imposed an imagined unfamiliarity onto them? It couldn't be—could it?

She peered around the boxes of preserved fruits, squinting at the floor for signs of disturbance. She wished there were dust in space: handprints or scuffs in dirt would really help her case right about now. But the ship's filtration and purging systems took care of all that. And if it didn't, then Jimex did, cleaning the ship with laser focus every day.

"Damn it," Park muttered, straightening. She closed her eyes and tried to think of what the man had looked like. It couldn't have been any of the other male members of the crew: none of them were blond, except Fulbreech. Or could someone have been wearing a wig? How ludicrous—but no more ludicrous than the idea that some stranger had snuck aboard the ship.

As she stood there in the chamber that served as their pantry, thinking, her inlays gave the briefest flash: a warning that went by so quickly Park didn't have time to interpret it. Then there was a sputtering, some faraway churning and gasping deep in the ship's walls. Before she could move, every light on the *Deucalion* went out.

Park heard distant exclamations and screams, somewhere above her. She fumbled for a moment with her inlays: METIS told her that it was experiencing an unknown electrical failure. *Oh, shit,* Park thought, biting her lip. *Had* Hunter tampered with the controls? Or was this something else? At least the life support and gravity systems were still working—so far. She stood still for a while, listening in the dark. The communication system between inlays was down, too. And she didn't have a flashlight.

Suddenly her gut knotted. What if this was all the work of the stranger?

What if he was trying to cut Park off from the others—and leave her blind?

Park suddenly felt as if someone were watching her, even though she *knew* the pantry had been empty just a few moments before. She began to fumble her way towards the entrance, reluctant to reach out and feel around for her surroundings—afraid of touching something she didn't recognize. Something warm or alive. Her breath sounded too-loud and raspy, like a machine on the verge of breakdown. Her eyes could not adjust to the lack of light.

Finally she bumped into what she thought was the pantry door and slapped her palm against its lock. The door sprang open—at least *that* was still working, too—but now Park was left standing uncertainly at the mouth of an immense black corridor. She hesitated, feeling with her toes as if she were standing on the edge of a precipice. Where to go from here? She thought she'd committed most of the ship to memory, muscle memory—but everything was so different in the dark.

She stood there for a while, breathing loudly. She could feel her heartbeat throbbing in her fingertips. Why hadn't she brought a weapon? And why wasn't METIS responding to her requests for guidance, some kind of map?

"Shit," she said again, and it sounded as if her voice came from someone else: she did not recognize it.

After a moment she began to shuffle forward, balling her fists. She would run into someone eventually, she thought. They had to be looking for her.

But no, Park thought then. *I told Fulbreech that I went to bed.*

There was a shuffling noise in front of her. Someone moving around. Park stopped, closed her mouth, and strained to listen.

Suddenly a shape resolved itself before her in the darkness. A human shape, tall and still, assessing her. Park had to choke down a scream. She came to a dead stop, waiting, unsure if it was an android or a crewmember—or something else.

Then: "Park." A familiar voice, to Park's short-lived relief. Sagara's voice.

"Captain Sagara?" She hated that she used his official title. It was a fear reflex, she told herself. She wanted an authority figure.

He clicked on a small utility light. Park closed her eyes against the sudden glare, but before she did she caught a glimpse of his dark hair, his fine-boned face looking damply unimpressed. "What are you doing here?" he demanded.

"I—" She cleared her throat. "I got turned around. Lost. My inlays seem to be malfunctioning."

"So are everybody's." He frowned at her. "Are you alone?"

"Yes." She hoped he wouldn't ask her why. "Are you? Why did you come down here?"

"Fulbreech said you went off somewhere." Sagara sounded annoyed. "Everyone else is accounted for. You weren't in your bunk, so I went looking for you. Why did you leave the medical bay?"

"I was hungry," she told him, biting back a defensive tone. The exchange calmed her, somewhat; it was familiar, almost comforting. It made her forget to be afraid. "Is that a crime? To need food?"

"You should have told me. You left Hunter unguarded."

"I left three androids with her."

"They weren't there when I checked."

"I assumed as much. I don't know where they've gone. Hunter—?"

"Sedated, for now," he said darkly, switching his light to his other hand. "I've left her in Chanur's care."

She made an exclamation, shielding her eyes against the beam. "She's as good as frozen, then!"

"Maybe," he snapped. "But it's not as if I had a choice. Who else was going to go looking for you?"

"Oh," Park said. She cleared her throat and tried to bank the sudden ember of shame in her stomach. "I see. That is . . . unfortunate."

Sagara was silent for a moment, gazing at her. Finally he turned his back on her, and for a horrible moment Park thought he was going to leave her there. "Hold onto my belt," he said, his voice now stiff and toneless.

She didn't want to touch him. But he had the light, and seemed to know his way back to the others; what other choice did she have? So she reached out and slipped her fingers under his belt, following him as he walked back into the dark. There was surprising heat trapped there, rather than the chill she had been expecting. So he was human, after all.

"Thank you," she said as they walked along. She tried to calm her heart's clamoring—afraid that he might pick up on it, like some kind of night-hunting predator.

Sagara didn't turn his head. "For?"

"Coming to get me. And . . . supporting me, last night. I know we haven't—seen eye to eye." This had to seem ultra-suspicious to him, Park thought. This and the bridge, and the utility rooms. And everything he'd overheard with ARGUS. She cringed internally as she recalled all the jabs she'd thrown at him, knowing he would eventually hear it; all the furtive talk she'd had with Jimex and Fulbreech and Wick. And yet he'd chosen to put all that aside and lead her back.

The security officer didn't answer her for a moment. Finally he said, "You don't need to thank me, Park. Whatever you may think, my loyalty lies with the ISF. That extends to every member of its crew."

So he was rebuffing her olive branch. She couldn't help but challenge him on that. "So personal feelings never enter into the equation, for you?" She tried to gauge his body language. "What if you had to protect someone you hated?"

His posture didn't change. "I don't hate anybody."

"And love?"

A pause. "Nor that."

"The perfect soldier."

"I have been called that."

She could see it: years of dutifully serving the ISF, of never questioning orders, carrying out his tasks with a cool and efficient gravity. In some ways he reminded her of herself—and that frightened her a little. Was Sagara simply a mirror-image of Park, had she been space-born? What if she had been selected because ISF thought she seemed like the perfect spy, as he was the perfect soldier? A matching set.

But that was before I learned about all of the ISF's secrets, Park thought. Its inequities. The divide between the conscripted and the non-conscripted. And the mad, eldritch gauntlet they'd sent their people into—knowingly or not.

Her fingers felt cramped around his belt; he was towing her along like a boat dragging someone on a lifesaver in its wake. To break up the silence Park said, "Do we know what caused the blackout?"

Sagara didn't answer. For a moment she thought that he meant to ignore her entirely until they made it back to the upper deck. But finally he said: "I thought *you* might know."

Indignation sparked in her gut. "How would I know anything? I've been down here for the past hour."

"Exactly. For what purpose?"

"I was—looking for something."

Sagara didn't prompt her: Park recognized the tactic. He thought that silence would pressure her into volunteering information, if she felt guilty. So she said, out of spite, "I'm wondering if ARGUS overtaxed the system. Maybe that's what caused the blackout."

She felt Sagara stiffen slightly. "Maybe," he answered, his voice carefully disinterested. "Or maybe someone sabotaged it themselves."

"You mean me, of course."

"I mean anyone. Nothing would surprise me after what happened in the bridge."

"You can prove someone tampered with it?"

His head rotated hawkishly to glare at her. "You were in the room with the proof."

Park clenched her jaw against his glare. He meant, of course, Hunter and Natalya's accusations against her. Did Sagara believe the surveyor, then? Did he really buy that Hunter had tampered with the ship's controls? And was it even worth bringing up again that the androids had said that she didn't? He'd made it clear that he didn't value their input on things. But would Park's failure to speak doom Hunter to the freezer—or even criminal prosecution, if Sagara went far enough?

She thought of something suddenly. "Are *you* conscripted, Sagara?" It seemed obvious, given his behavior, but she was beginning to realize that nothing was quite so simple on this ship. She could trust none of her previous assumptions.

He made the low hissing sound that she'd noticed citizens of the outer planets making to express contempt. "That's none of your business."

"Isn't it, though?" It was becoming the defining thing. Was someone working for ISF because they wanted to, or because they were under the Frontier's tyrannical thumb—immune to the usual pangs of remorse and personal loyalty, because they had loved ones being held hostage? In other words—could she trust him?

Sagara's answer surprised her. "If you must know," he said waspishly, "I used to be. But I'm not anymore."

She gawked at him, even though he couldn't see her. "I've never heard of such a thing."

"Just because you haven't heard it, you don't believe it's true?"

"But—*how*?" She wanted to let go of him, force him to turn around, but the hall was still cold and oppressive; she was afraid to release him. Afraid that he might vanish like smoke. "You—worked off your debt to them? They let you go?"

"Essentially," Sagara answered, sounding somewhat irritated—or bored. "It was after my service in the Outer System Wars. They honored me. Gave me medals. And cleared my debts as repayment."

She had never, ever, ever heard of such a thing, not in all the years the ISF had been in control. But Sagara's body language said it all: he was telling the truth. The truth as he knew it, anyway. "Then—why are you here? Why are you still working for them, if they've released you from service?"

Sagara laughed, and the sound of it startled Park; her stomach leaped uncomfortably. It was the first time she'd ever heard him laugh. "What else was I going to do? Who else can you work for, if you're not on Earth?"

"The private sector—"

"It's still all controlled by ISF. Indirectly, but why bother with the middleman at all?"

"But if your debts are cleared, do you even *need* to work?"

He paused, cocking his head as if it had never occurred to him. "I am not a man suited to leisure," he said after a moment, in concluding tones.

They were silent for a little, shuffling along together. Finally Park said: "So you know about the Fold, then? You've seen it? Or—" *Or have they kept it from you, too, now that they don't have any assurance they can trust you? No insurance policy against you?*

Sagara's reply was full of scorn. "Of course I know about the Fold."

"Even without being conscripted?"

"Yes. I am the ship's security officer. I needed to know that information to do my job. You didn't."

"*That's* debatable."

He ignored her. "ISF knows it can trust me. I served in their wars. I'm the head of security on Corvus. I've proven my loyalty."

She sensed his pride, despite the usual matter-of-factness in his tone; she felt the unnatural desire to puncture it. "So you have seen it, then. And seen the data they're keeping down in the utility rooms?"

Another pause. "Yes," Sagara said finally—almost petulantly, she thought. "Not that it matters much. I don't need to examine it closely. My role is to protect it, not understand it."

She nearly laughed. "And here I thought you were supposed to protect us."

"That, too," he said, "so long as none of you conspire to work against me."

Park rolled her eyes. Back to this again. His paranoia was dogged. She said, "You're so quick to assume the worst of everyone else. But why don't you extend that same suspicion to the ISF itself?"

Now he did turn his head to look at her. "Why would I?"

"Look at how they operate," Park said, indignant. "Secrets, half-truths, outright lies—they sent *me* here without telling me it was a planet with a fucking gravity well!"

She stopped then, shocked by the heat of her own anger, her fear. Sagara didn't say anything for a moment, and she felt as if his belt were melting out of her own grasp. Finally he said flatly: "The ISF represents order in the universe. The *only* order. Its way of doing things might not be perfect, but at this point in time, it's the only thing standing between the human race and total chaos. Of course I support that—of course I trust it. I have no choice. Neither does anyone else. And of course I'll continue to serve it, and accept the flaws such a system comes with. There is no alternative. To do anything else is to contribute to the collapse of our civilization."

"Sometimes collapse is necessary," Park argued, "to incite change."

"By collapse you mean destruction," Sagara fired back. "Mass death, loss. Change on that scale is always violent. Look at the Comeback. Look at the Privacy Wars."

"Some might say those who started the Privacy Wars were in the right. They wanted a revolution, a change in how things are done, and in a way, they got it. That's why there are no cameras on this ship."

"I am not one of the ones who would say that," Sagara answered, very cold now. "My wife was killed in the rebels' second bombing of Halla."

Park felt as if he had struck her. All the wind was sucked out of her lungs; she nearly let go of his belt.

They walked for just a moment in silence. Then Park managed to say, very faintly: "I'm sorry. I didn't know that."

"It's not in my file," Sagara said, his voice still cold—but detached, as if he were making a report on someone else. "I made sure of that." When she said nothing, he continued: "She was a transcriber; a data collector. She and thirty-two of her colleagues were killed when the terrorists destroyed ISF's archives. They were writers, researchers, academics. The best in the galaxy. All of that knowledge and light—snuffed out in less than a minute." He paused for a moment, still faceless, still unreadable. It felt as if the corridor had chilled by several degrees. "ISF thinks we lost one hundred years of secret histories and future innovations in that bombing. They're still trying to tally the amount of data that was lost. They won't say it, but they don't know how long it will take the tech sector to recover." Another pause. Then: "No one recovers from something like that."

She wanted to say something, to proffer comfort, sympathy—a more heartfelt apology. Or commiseration; she had lost a loved one of her own. But Park found herself rendered mute by the coldness, the rawness of Sagara's anger, so fully buried that she could only sense the edges of it. She had not known a person could feel this deeply and still speak with perfect composure. No wonder she had never been able to read him. He could have been an android—except androids never concocted stories about war. Or death, or love.

"I'm sorry," she said again, finally, but Sagara did not seem to hear her.

"You see then why I hunt ISF's enemies so earnestly," he said. His pace quickened. "Why I'm dedicated to rooting out its saboteurs, its malefactors. I've seen what happens when one doesn't. It's more than missions failing, worries over not getting paid. People die. And progress is halted—ISF being the only way progress is made in this universe." He shook his head. "People think me obsessed, dogmatic—a loyal soldier to the end. But I have my reasons for it, just as anyone does." At this he trailed off, his words loaded with some sort of hidden meaning.

She did not know what to say in the face of his absolute certainty; his bone-deep resolve. She was not sure she had ever felt such a thing in her life. Her causes, if she had ever had any, were never that grand. She was trying to find a way to articulate this when Sagara stopped suddenly. Park, still holding onto his belt, said, "What's wrong?"

There was a long silence. Finally Sagara said, his voice carefully even: "I don't recognize this place."

She let go of him and took a step so that she was standing with him side by side, squinting to make out what his watery light illuminated. They were in what looked like any other tunnel on the ship to her, but when Park looked at Sagara, she saw that he was glaring at the walls as if they had personally slighted him.

"I don't understand," Park said.

Sagara didn't move from his spot. "There should be a right turn here," he told her.

Park shook her head. "The lights are out," she said, stating the obvious. "Which can disorient and skew your sense of direction."

"Not possible," Sagara said, his voice a hard rap. "The turn is one hundred and eighty-two yards from the pantry. I counted."

They stood there for a moment, each of them evaluating their surroundings—and each other. Finally Park said, uneasily, "Let's just continue down the tunnel. I'm sure we'll encounter the turn eventually."

Reluctantly, the security officer nodded and began to follow her, shining his light so that Park could see where to place her feet. The tunnel seemed to stretch endlessly, but Park told herself that it was because they were expecting the turn: their apprehension distorted their perception of things. And yet her throat felt clogged with sudden fear. Slowly, an ache started up between her shoulder blades—it was the same prickling feeling that she was being watched by someone behind them.

Without either of them speaking, their strides lengthened. When Park dared to look at Sagara, his face was tense and troubled. She nearly asked him if he had a weapon; would have found a little comfort if he had, even if there was the possibility that he could use it on her. But she stayed silent. She had the strange notion that giving voice to her fears would allow them to manifest. If she held them within, she told herself, everything would be all right.

The tunnel stretched and stretched. After a while Park became convinced that Sagara was right; something had gone wrong. The passageway was so straight—and she knew there was no such construction on their rabbit's warren of a ship.

"We're going the wrong way," Sagara said finally, with impatience. He seemed irritated that he didn't understand what was going on. Being puzzled seemed to be a foreign feeling for him.

Park kept her eyes forward, on the lit, straight path at their feet. "How are your inlays?"

"They've gone dark. I can't reach the others or access the ship's computer."

That was when Park heard it. A sound like knocking, or more accurately, pounding: a set of fists thumping urgently against the walls. And voices far off, arguing. Alarmed, she looked at Sagara. But when he looked back, she saw that he simply looked displeased.

"Did you hear that?" Park asked him.

The security officer scowled. "Hear what?"

Park faltered. "A—a sound like knocking. People shouting."

Sagara looked at her as if she had sprouted two heads.

The knocking sound loudened. Now it sounded like more fists had joined the first pair; Park felt as if someone had gotten trapped inside the walls, and was urgently signaling for help. She had to dig her fingernails into her palm, trying to block out her feeling of disquiet. Her dread. The dark corridor suddenly felt too hot and airless. She felt as if she wanted to claw her way to the surface, gasping for air.

"Sagara," she said quietly, sweating. "Listen. Something like this has happened to me before—"

He looked at her, his dark gaze intent. "What do you mean? A blackout?"

"No," she said, shaking her head. She felt the urge to grab onto him, but resisted, swaying. "Before, when I was going down to the utility rooms—" When had that been? she wondered suddenly. The day before? Or was it the day before that? When was the last time she remembered sleeping? She felt tired, feverish, swollen—as if her limbs had been deboned and filled with saltwater. "I was going down to the utility rooms," Park repeated, struggling to follow her train of thought. "And I felt—like this. Strange. Like I didn't know where I was."

Sagara was staring at her with his brows furrowed. But he stayed silent.

Park put a hand to her temple and said, "And I saw a stranger. Earlier. A man, watching the fight in the mess hall. I think he has something to do with this—"

"Hey," Sagara said sharply, when Park half-sagged into him.

"I'm sorry," she murmured. Her eyes were fluttering; suddenly the darkness felt too oppressive, as if she couldn't look at it any longer. "I'm sorry . . ."

"What's wrong with you?"

"I'm just tired," Park said, fighting back a yawn. "I just need to sleep."

He was lowering her to the ground. "Something's wrong. I'm taking you to Chanur."

"No," she said. "Not Chanur. We just need to get out of here. And sleep."

Her grasp on full consciousness was weakening rapidly—and Sagara was warm and solid. She nearly said to him, "Carry me," the way she'd made Glenn carry her when she was too tired as a girl, but then her knees were buckling and he was saying in her ear, "Park. Stay awake. Park!"

"The man," she said groggily. She had to struggle to say it without slurring. "He was tall, blond. A stranger. He had a flight suit on . . ."

All at once Sagara's hands were seizing her, lifting her up. "What did you just say?" he asked harshly. "Park, *what did you say?*"

There were voices at the end of the hall. "What's going on?" someone was saying. Sagara didn't answer. In the wavering utility light Park could see a shadowy figure approaching them. She couldn't recognize it—her mind was receding—and there was a weird disconnected pain in her palm, where she'd dug her nails in, a throbbing that radioed feverish waves of hurt throughout her body and sent the signal to some conscience far away.

"What's going on?" someone asked again.

You tell me, Park thought. *I'm tired of always trying to find out.* Then her head touched the floor, and she was gone.

16.

Park's uncle returned to New Diego a month before Park was scheduled to leave for university. She came home from school one day to find him sitting in the kitchen, drinking the last of her synthetic coffee. Glenn, walking in front of her, paused in the doorway at the sight of him, as if to block Park from view.

Park's uncle hardly looked at him—instead focused his regard on what little he could see of Park's face, flatly staring at him from over Glenn's shoulder.

"Grace," he said. "Welcome home."

That's my line, Park thought though she felt neither welcoming nor like it was his home. It had been two years since she'd seen him last, though he had called diligently on birthdays and holidays. She put her hand on Glenn's arm to move him aside, but suddenly he was like a granite statue: he wouldn't budge.

"Glenn, let my niece into the apartment," Park's uncle said, sharply, as if addressing a misbehaving dog. Park expected Glenn to bristle, but he merely said coolly, "Of course," and moved aside. But he still lingered by Park's side.

She wondered, briefly, what he was so afraid of. Glenn always seemed *different* around her uncle: stiff, unnatural, diffident. There wasn't that spark of *Glenness* when her uncle was home—as if Glenn had retreated into the shell of himself, leaving behind only a basic template to interface with. He acted as if, at any moment, her uncle might take too much notice of him. Might decide to shut him down. Self-preservation protocols, Park decided. The hare lies still when the wolfox is around. Even robots knew that.

"You didn't give notice that you'd be home," she said, still by the door.

Her uncle barked out a short laugh. "Gave notice," he echoed. "Are you the landlord here? Or my boss?"

She said nothing. Glenn said, his voice just above a murmur: "You are not well."

They both looked at him; for a moment Park thought he was talking to her. Then she looked more closely at her uncle. *Did* he look a little sick? Was his skin looser, did he always have those dark smudges under his eyes? Or were those simply signs of advancing age? Guilt couldn't stop a little chill from crawling up her back. Was it contagious?

"Health and biometric analysis should be confidential," Park's uncle told Glenn reproachfully. "You should know that."

Glenn inclined his head. "Of course," he said. "My apologies." Then, after a moment: "Since you are blood relatives and she is an emergency contact, I thought—"

"I'm not interested in how your logic algorithms parsed it out," Park's uncle said. "You should know that, too." He scratched his nose. "Anyway, you're right. I *am* sick." Then he looked wryly at Park. "It's not contagious."

Years in the field had finally caught up to him, he explained: the ultra-rich oxygen traps formed by the Comeback had slowly bubbled into his blood. He was constantly disoriented now, the same way deep-sea divers were after surfacing too quickly; the buildup of oxygen in his tissue was toxic. He had pains in his chest, he was more short-sighted than he had been before. The optic nerves in his eyes had swelled. When he finished telling them that he was home for good, Park said, coldly, "Why didn't you return sooner, when you realized your condition was deteriorating?"

"I had to see my work through," Park's uncle said. "It was—is—important."

Important, Park thought, not without a little scorn. As if there weren't enough researchers in the world studying the plants and wildlife of the Comeback. As if there was anything new to be learned from that field.

"And now you're done," she said. "For good."

"That's right," Park's uncle said, motioning Glenn to step forward. "And I have to say, my timing is excellent: I'm glad I caught you before you left for school."

Park stood by and watched as he transmitted his medical routines into Glenn's processor; Glenn took a moment to acclimate to the new data, then said, "I'll go to the dispensary and pick up your prescription."

He nearly walked past Park without looking at her. Park put out a hand to stop him and said, "I'll go with you."

"No," Park's uncle said, waving a hand at the chair across from him. The chair that Glenn usually sat in, so that his eyes were level with Park's: a squat, sagging thing they'd fished out of a canal. "Stay here. Catch up with me, Grace."

"Be safe," Park told Glenn, though the riots of previous years had quieted. There'd been the fiasco of a mob mistaking a human for a human-like android, at the peak of the protests. Then trials. Murder convictions. A reversal of goodwill, as there often was. Glenn smiled faintly at her and said, "I understand."

Reluctantly, Park walked over to the table and sat down across from her uncle. It had been a long time since she'd seen him last, at least in person; when she was younger he had videoed in once a month, but in the past few years the frequency had diminished. He kept ending the calls with praise of how independent and self-sufficient she was. Not how intelligent she was, or beautiful or mature—just that she displayed an ability to survive adequately without him, Park thought. She was wary of him: having him in her home felt like sheltering a wild animal. Routines were shattered, predictability flew out the window. She never knew what to say.

Neither, it seemed, did he. "Well," he said. "You've grown into a fine young woman. Your grades are excellent."

So he'd seen them, Park thought, surprised; though of course the school must have been transmitting them to him all this time. "They are," she admitted.

"You work hard," her uncle mused. "Where are you going, again?"

"New Boston," Park said. "Hanson-Skinner University. I earned a scholarship."

A flicker of surprise crossed her uncle's face. "Hanson," he repeated. "The robotics designer—so you're going for robo-psychology?"

"No," Park answered coolly. "Just human psychology."

"Funny," he said, half to himself. "I wouldn't think your interests lie there. You have to pass tests, you know. For empathy, amiability. Et cetera."

"I'm aware."

"Well," he said again. He had the air of dusting his hands off, though he didn't actually move. "Good for you. Do you have a boyfriend? Or a girlfriend?"

"Neither," Park said flatly. Despite herself, she could feel her neck reddening; she was glad that Glenn had left.

"Hm," Park's uncle said. "Well, that in itself is no cause for concern."

He leaned back and drummed his hands against the worn, scuffed table; his ankle was resting on his knee in a way that Park found to be over-professorial, as if he ought to be in an armchair smoking a pipe. "Does Glenn cook the meals around here, or do you?" he asked.

"Glenn does, for the most part. Though I've learned."

"You're self-sufficient," he said again. "That's good. Good."

Park studied him closely for the first time since she'd sat down. She couldn't see the resemblance in their faces, other than the seriousness of their expressions. Park's hair and eyes were dark, her features slim and Asiatic; her skin was tanned, and there was a dusting of light freckles across the bridge of her nose. Her uncle, on the other hand, was pale-haired, the locks as soft and curly as a child's, and he was permanently sun-burnt and flaking. His body was heavy and round. The skin on his hands seemed too papery for the amount of time he spent outside. Not for the first time she wondered if they were even blood-related, if he wasn't simply a stepbrother to her father or even an adoptive stranger. She found herself wishing that he'd comment that she took after her mother.

"You seem good," she remarked, trying for courtesy. "Happy."

"I get by," he replied. "It's good to be home." He looked around, and for the first time Park tried to see her module with a stranger's eyes. It was as spotless as Glenn could make it, and she herself was a tidy person. But of course there were the obvious signs of living in a biodome like New Diego: the posters and wallpaper curling in the seaside humidity, the slumping furniture fashioned from scrap. Park's uncle said, "I'm sure you're glad to be out of this place soon. It's a long airship ride to New Boston—a few days, if I'm remembering correctly. And you've never been in the air. You should prepare yourself."

"Why were you glad to catch me before I left?" Park asked. "You said that when we came in."

Her uncle turned back to her and blinked. "Because you would have taken Glenn with you," he said.

It felt as if her heart had jerked: a tight, vicious little movement. "And why would that be a problem?" Park asked calmly.

"I wouldn't want to spend the money to bring him back," her uncle answered, with equal calm. "He's staying here, of course. I need him."

After dinner, Park said that she was going on a walk. This was not implausible; the stuffy summer nights were finally cooling down, giving way to a fresher autumnal breeze that trickled through the vents before the hard drafts of winter set in. Glenn rose silently to accompany her, and Park's uncle, watching the news on his wrist console, made no motion to object. When they had made their way down the street, Park remarked sourly, "I suppose we'll be taking plenty of these from now on."

Glenn said, "His sickness is not as severe as he makes it seem. I believe on the current treatment routines he will recover within the year."

"Then maybe he'll go off again and leave us alone," Park thought aloud. She hadn't told Glenn about her uncle's plans to keep him in New Diego, not yet; not until she could figure out a way to persuade him to let Glenn go. She didn't want to worry her bodyguard unnecessarily—and she was also a little afraid of his reaction. But the solution ought to be easy, Park thought. Her uncle only needed someone to administer his medicine, to help him with his daily routines. He didn't need Glenn for that. Any cheap helper bot would do.

Convenient, she thought bitterly. It was convenient that her uncle only thought it fit to return for good just as she was preparing to leave forever. Convenient that he was suddenly sick, after years in the field. Convenient that he had such a vested interest in keeping Glenn, when for years he hadn't given him the time of day; had treated him like some kind of houseplant or reluctantly adopted dog.

"You're worried about something," Glenn said. She looked at him, in the flickering green dimness of the bioluminescent streetlights. His face had not physically changed much over the years, of course—but there was a hidden depth to his expressions, beyond the flat, serious look. Watching her watching him, he remarked, "Your heart rate is elevated."

She reached out and touched his hair. The dark, downy thistle at the nape of his neck. "You need a haircut," she said. They'd given androids that feature, a few years back, to make them even more lifelike; she imagined the developers arguing about the implications of it. *'Do we want a way to tell them apart?' 'Do we want to make them more like us?' 'Why have half-measures when you could go all the way?'* In the end they chose to give the androids hair that grew, synthetic but very life-like. That way users could customize their androids' appearances in more varied and pleasing ways—though the androids themselves seemed to find this more of a burden than a boon.

Glenn looked unfazed by Park touching him. He stayed where he was, without pulling away. "I have exactly twenty-three days before hair maintenance is due," he told her.

"Are you going to change it, or keep it at your default?"

"What would you prefer?"

"Let's shave it bald," Park said, "and paint your head silver."

Glenn frowned a little. "The paint would chip," he said.

"I was just joking."

"I understand," he said. "So was I."

They walked together until they hit the edge of the biodome, staring out at the moon-glinting sea beyond the membrane. It was a strange thing, that wall, Park often thought: rubbery and flimsy to the touch, a semi-living transparent skin that filtered air and water and chemicals and molecules in and out of the city in a kind of constant autopoietic exchange. And yet, if you struck it, the membrane turned as hard and impenetrable as a diamond. There was something to be learned there, Park thought.

She said, watching the silvered waves lap up against the curved wall: "We'll be out of this place in a month, you know. Things will be different."

"Yes," Glenn said. She couldn't see his expression in the dark. "Some things will be different. Other things will not change."

One afternoon Park's classmates approached her at lunch. This was rare; generally the other students preferred to pretend that Park wasn't there, or else was some kind of exchange student or substitute teacher—an outside presence observing in the background, but whose intrusion was only minimal, temporary. When she was younger she'd thought this was because she was one of the few who weren't optimized; her mother, of course, was a Dryad, a "feral" who'd vanished before giving her consent to have Park genetically augmented. As a result you could spot Park as a 'genotypical' in a heartbeat: her limbs weren't willowy in that ethereal way, her eyes didn't have that deep, optimized shine. Academically she managed to keep up, she had that much; but sometimes she showed a capacity for acne and short-sightedness, which was as good as having a hump. It was originally a spacer tradition to have their children genetically tweaked and tailored—their DNA sewed up in neat packages—but the movement had rapidly gained traction on Earth, among those who could afford it. Most people in the biodomes could, though only just. Park's uncle, perhaps sensing the isolation that awaited his niece, had put the money towards cutting-edge android companions for her instead.

It was for these reasons that Park had initially thought she was ostracized; her optimized classmates didn't want to associate with a being of inferior genetic makeup. A person on the lower rung. But the other genotypical children—few that there were—had no problems banding together, forming their own little club. Park was left on the outskirts, looking in. "I'm different," she'd said to Sally once, without tears; even as a child she'd been stony with resignation.

"Not different," Sally had told her, gently. "Just special."

Special, different, Park had thought at the time—it was semantics. It was all the same. It still got you ignored. Which was why it came as a surprise when she was approached at lunch, mere weeks before she was due to graduate high school.

The approachers in question were a gaggle of girls that Park had silently labeled the alpha females of the school—a cluster of luscious-haired, chime-voiced beauties who had never so much as glanced in Park's direction. She was sitting on the school steps, eating a butter sandwich when she heard them chattering nearby; she thought, not for the first time, that this must have been what aviaries sounded like, back in the day. What the jungles of the Comeback sounded like now: not silent and oppressive, as everyone imagined, but teeming with noise and honking, cackling life. Suddenly she caught the name Dataran, and tried not to look up—the group was discussing the topic of androids working as fashion models, now that you could style their hair, and how they never got too fat or old.

"I think it's creepy," one girl said. "The way they walk. It's too smooth. It's like watching a hologram."

"I think it's beautiful," another said. "So fluid. I heard Paxia Berelle is one. She dances across the stage."

"No way," the first girl said. "She blinks too much to be an android. You can always tell."

"No, you can't. That Dataran thing was one all along, and no one knew."

"Someone did."

At this the little group turned to Park, who kept on eating her butter sandwich and staring at her console screen. A shadow fell across her wrist; reluctantly, she dragged her eyes up. One of the girls was standing over her. In the hard light Park couldn't see who it was.

"Grace," the girl said sweetly. Ah, Park thought, refusing to squint; it was Alexia, a willowy, ringleted girl who had been in Park's classes since the first grade. They had never spoken before. Her name always reminded Park of the medical condition that resulted in the inability to read—usually caused by brain damage.

"Grace," Alexia said again. "You knew about Dataran, didn't you?"

Park rose, to assume a position that was not subordinate to Alexia's. She was still holding her half-eaten sandwich in one hand. Alexia looked at her with interest, and a kind of chilly amusement; her eyebrows were inked on in such a high arch that she seemed both perpetually astonished and bored. Park said, "What makes you say that?"

"Well," Alexia said, with a toss of her luxurious hair: "You're so observant. You're always *observing* everybody. And you're very familiar with androids, aren't you?"

This was said with a tone of innocent admiration, but Park knew that it was a jab about Glenn, whom everyone had seen accompanying her to and from school. The other girls were watching; Park sensed a feeling of anticipation from them, as if they were waiting for the punch line of a good joke. So, she thought. It had to happen sometime. Since she'd been young she had expected some form of schoolyard fight. It was unexpected that it had come so late, in the last few weeks of her final year. She hadn't done anything to provoke it, as far as she knew.

"I don't understand your line of questioning," Park said coolly. Clouds skidded overhead; she could feel their shadows passing over her face.

Alexia sighed a little, as if she was dealing with a sullen child who kept pushing away her food. "There's no *line*," she said, still smiling. "I'm just curious. You're so smart and all. I'm sure you were able to tell."

"It was a while ago," Park said in a flat voice. "A few years. I don't remember."

Alexia was watching her, her eyebrows still in perfect arches. Another girl, behind her, said in honeyed tones, "So what about the one you're always walking around with? That's your chaperone, right?"

My friend, Park wanted to say, or my family—but of course that would get her nothing but ridicule. So she said nothing, only held onto her dampening sandwich, waiting. *Just get it over with*, she wanted to say. *Say whatever cruel thing you really mean.* It was all a performance, a ritual, maneuvers to establish dominance, extinguish threats. Park didn't have the patience to learn the steps.

"I had a chapbot when I was little," Alexia said with a breathless little laugh. "My parents got rid of it when I was twelve. I wonder what happened to it." She smiled at Park. "I should care more. It practically raised me."

It must have been defective, Park thought. It didn't do a very good job. But she only said, "It was probably recycled."

"Probably," Alexia said with an elegant shrug. "I wonder what's going to happen to yours, when you leave school?"

Park said nothing. Alexia, perhaps growing impatient with her, plowed onward, lowering her voice conspiratorially. "You know," she said, "they're thinking of getting rid of them—the nannybots, anyway. Too many husbands caught fucking them! Isn't that sick?"

"People are always doing strange things," Park said woodenly.

Their wrist consoles flashed, then, indicating that it was time to return to class. The girls behind Alexia made disappointed little clucks, as if someone had failed to finish an exciting story and was asking them to wait until later. And there *would* be later, Park thought, watching their retreating backs as they flowed into the school building. They'd locked on; they wouldn't be finished with their target until they got their satisfaction. She'd have to be wary, come to battle armed. But why her, why now? She thought, a little hopelessly, about what she was going to go to school for. Maybe she should switch to robo-psychology. She was better at it—and she wouldn't have to deal with people like these.

After school, she saw Glenn standing impassively by the gate as usual. He looked no different from a distance, but upon coming closer she thought she could read something like concern in the angle of his shoulders, or puzzlement. She approached and saw someone talking to him, or rather *at* him, since Glenn was neither looking at them nor responding. Sudden fear and rage swept her in a dark acidic wave. It was Alexia, standing there boldly with one of her boyfriends.

"Respond," she was saying as Park glided up behind them. "Answer. Reply."

"It's probably defective," her boyfriend said. This was Harry Bip, Park realized, with the sculpted jaw and the hands that could crush a melon; his parents had had him optimized for a sports scholarship, before they'd understood that sports were going extinct. Not enough room, in the post-Comeback world—and no use for it if you were bound for the colonies. Now they were trying to pass him off as a future combat specialist. Park couldn't imagine him specializing in anything other than eating enough junk food to fuel his overgrown body and adjusting himself when he thought no one was looking.

"It's not defective," Alexia said. "The freak probably programmed it not to talk to anybody but her."

Glenn's eyes flicked to Park, over Alexia's shoulder. His mouth formed a faint frown. Alexia, sensing the look, began to turn, but before she could see Park properly, Park said, "What are you doing?"

Harry Bip jumped. Alexia squinted; Park had positioned herself so that the sun was at her back, glaring into their eyes if they tried to look at her. It was instinct, she supposed: her reptile brain positioning her on dominant ground. Alexia tried to smile and said, "Oh, Grace. We were just having a talk with your—friend."

"You don't need to talk to him. Whatever it is, you can ask me." She looked at Glenn—bent all of her will into her gaze. Silently, he moved to her side.

"He's a very advanced model," Alexia remarked. "We were just admiring his specs."

"Yeah," Harry Bip rumbled. "He's crash. Real lifelike." A smile twitched on his face; Park looked at him and thought about how jangled and out of place his genes must be. A throwback, she thought; a figure beckoned out of an age that didn't exist anymore. No wonder he preferred following Alexia's lead; *she* knew his place, and told it to him with ease.

"So what *do* you do?" Alexia said to Glenn. "Now that she's here, you can answer. Do you just follow Grace around all the time?"

"Leave him alone," Park said, in clipped tones. She knew this was a tactic, meant to expose her vulnerabilities—but she *hated* the thought of anyone ridiculing Glenn, who couldn't defend himself. It felt as if they'd come into her home without her knowing and rearranged the furniture; stolen her diary and passed it around, jeering. She had never known true anger like this before—frustration, yes, but not rage. How *dare* they? she thought. She felt as if there was a hot, weeping itch in her heart.

"Glenn, let's go," she said.

"You don't have to be so protective," Alexia said, still with the round-eyed look of innocence. "I was just trying to make conversation. No one's going to steal your walking vibrator."

Park turned to her icily and slapped her, open-handed. The force and suddenness of the blow surprised even Park, who felt as if someone had unhinged her own arm and moved it for her. There was a stunned silence, staring; even Glenn looked vaguely surprised. Alexia's cheek reddened in the afternoon's golden glow.

Then she said, "You *bitch!*" and wound her hand back. Harry Bip made a kind of hooting noise. Park tensed, and her mind leapt through several strategies, discarding them before the next instant had even passed. She wasn't interested in diffusion or escape. More in overpowering Alexia, incapacitating her—teaching her not to do this again. How much could she hurt her, without veering into the domain of the criminal? And would Harry intervene? Park wouldn't win if it was two against one . . .

She had no more time to think; here came Alexia's hand blurring through the air. Park rounded her shoulder to fend off the blow and said against her will, "Stop!"

Glenn moved suddenly. His hand clamped down on Alexia's wrist, catching it in midair. The contact made a hollow clapping sound. Then he looked at Alexia and said quietly, "I'm sorry, but I will not permit this. You will do no harm to Grace Park."

Alexia gave a kind of scream, a horrible sound, like a train whistle in a movie. "Get *off* me!" she shouted. "Don't touch me, you fucking clunker!"

At this, Harry Bip lunged forward and swung his open hand at Glenn's head, roaring like a bear. How absurd, Park thought blurrily as she watched him stumble forward, pinwheeling his arms to maintain balance. It was like an old cartoon, all of them standing there, trading slaps. Glenn, who had faded backward with the blow, said, "That was dangerous. If I hadn't moved, you could have damaged your hand."

"Glenn," Park said, and he released Alexia's wrist smoothly.

"I apologize," he said to the girl, who was clutching her wrist as if it was in danger of falling off. "I am first and foremost Grace Park's guardian. My protection protocols—"

"*Help!*" she was shrieking. "*Help! It's attacking us!*"

Some passersby had witnessed the altercation: two businessmen and another female student. Park saw that they were hurrying over. Whether they knew Glenn was an android, she didn't know—perhaps all they'd seen was two young couples squabbling. But no, she thought. If they thought that, they wouldn't bother interfering. She could see in the whiteness around their lips that they thought they knew what was going on. *Rogue android*, they were thinking. *It's finally happening. We've known it all along.*

The riots never really went away, Park thought.

"We need to go," she said to Glenn. She touched his sleeve.

"Where?" His voice was flat and calm; she could see the sensors in his eyes spinning, analyzing the situation. "They are blocking the only exit from the schoolyard."

"Into the school," Park said. "Wait it out. Until things calm down."

But Glenn was shaking his head. "It would not be strategically sound to trap ourselves in a building," he said. "Particularly one occupied solely by other synthetics."

They'd quietly edged back from the center of the commotion by now. Harry Bip was holding the sobbing Alexia as if she might fall to pieces without his embrace to hold her together. The female student was recording the goings-on with her wrist console, smirking in a tight, nervous way. The two businessmen were listening to Alexia's story, looking over at Glenn and Park suspiciously; one of them was calling someone on their teletooth.

"You," the one who wasn't calling said to Glenn. "Come here."

"Stay," Park said. Glenn gave no sign that he had heard the businessman address him.

"Is that your bot?" the man asked. He was young, not that much older than she: a recent college grad, she would have guessed. His arms were too thin for his clear vinyl business suit. "She said it just attacked her."

"She attacked me," Park answered coldly. "My android just prevented further violence. It's in his programming."

"I think it's going to have to be taken in."

She felt as if someone had injected lead into her spine. "I'll see to that," she said. "Who are you?"

"We run a robot repair firm," he said, gesturing to himself and the other businessman, who was still on the phone. "We handle problem bots. Malfunctioners."

"Great," Park said. She suddenly realized that she couldn't unclench her fists.

"You should turn it over to us. We'll take a look at it and repair whatever's going on in its head. We saw the whole thing. *That's* not programming."

"It is."

"It's not. Look—we'll give you the receipt. You can come pick it up in a day or two." When Park didn't answer, the angle of the man's shoulders sharpened; all she could read was anger and fear in the lines of his body. He swayed, as if preparing to charge. "You really need to turn it over. If not to us, then to somebody. Defective chapdroids can be a real menace if they're let loose without corrective programming."

"I am not defective," Glenn said tonelessly. "My systems are operating at optimal capacity."

The man didn't look at him. "It wouldn't know if it was defective," he said to Park. "That's the whole point. The part that should know it's malfunctioning is malfunctioning itself."

"He's fine," Park snapped. "Leave us alone. Unless you're the police—"

"Get the police!" This was Alexia, from amidst the storm of her tears. "It *hit* me!"

God damn you, Park thought, but before she could reply she saw the younger businessman nod to the older one, who was now off the phone. There was a crowd of people in the schoolyard, now: students who hadn't gone far and who had returned when they'd heard the commotion, excited laborers and office workers on their routes home from work. Someone said, "Turn it off, the switch is in its throat," and Park could feel her body drifting in front of Glenn's, stiff, solid, as if she were a glacier. Glenn said quietly, "What is the usual procedure in such a case?"

"I don't know," Park said. She couldn't turn to look at him. People were approaching them, hesitantly, trying to see how to move her neatly out of the way.

"Self-defense is required," Glenn said, prompting.

"Yes," Park said. "It always is."

Glenn stepped out from behind her then. There was suddenly something small and black in his hand; Park couldn't see it clearly from her periphery. He said calmly, "Please let us exit peacefully. Now."

That was all he said. But everyone stopped. A kind of hard, frozen silence fell over the crowd. No one moved. Even Alexia stopped crying; she only stared at Glenn, then Park, with that classic round-eyed look, like a startled infant. Glenn put his hand on Park's back, with infinite gentleness, and said, "Thank you. We will leave now."

And then they left. The crowd parted for them like water flowing around a rock. Park could feel her shoulders tensing as they passed through, expecting a surprise blow to the face, a hot flash of pain in the back. But there was nothing. No one even turned to watch them go.

"Why?" Park said, when they'd made it a block or two away. She looked behind them, but no one was following; the streets were now empty. She hadn't realized how fast her blood had been thudding that entire time; she could feel her heartbeat in her fingertips. Glenn's left hand was still on her back.

"It was this," he said, and he showed her his right hand briefly. Park felt the blood drain out of her head. Glenn was holding an electrolaser gun.

"Where," she asked after a moment, through stiff lips, "did you get that?"

"Here," Glenn said, and dropped it into her hand. Park nearly yelped, not from fear, but from the surprise of feeling how light it was. She turned it over in her hands, felt the rough grooves and fixtures.

"It's fake," she said, after a moment.

"A prop," Glenn said mildly. "Little better than a toy, though convincing enough at a distance. You can order them easily enough online."

She looked at him with wonder. "When did you get it?"

Glenn gave her an indecipherable look. "A long time ago," he said. "During the worst of the riots. The day Dataran approached you."

He'd been late that day, she remembered—she'd run over the sequence of those few days many times in her mind. So that was where he'd gone. To get a fake gun. "To protect yourself," she said aloud.

Glenn's eyes flicked to her then, and Park jolted, as if he'd pricked her with a knife. "No," he said coolly. "To protect you."

It frightened her a little, to think that Glenn had such foresight—and agency. He had never mentioned or shown her the gun. But in other ways it comforted her deeply. She could trust him; he could take care of himself. She did not have to bear the responsibility of keeping him safe.

She put her hand on his arm, silently. Glenn put the fake gun away and the two of them walked together in a kind of reverie, the streets completely silent, the air drowsy with pollen and salt, the sun falling down on them in waves of delicious warmth. Park said, "There will be trouble."

"No," Glenn answered. "I reviewed the protocols. I examined the law. There is nothing that addresses this; it wasn't illegal. Not for me. I was within my rights."

His rights, she thought. His laws. Again that feeling of fright, and comfort; she did believe him. Glenn was, if nothing else, thorough in all things.

"There will be no trouble," he said.

"Still," Park said. "If not legal trouble—retribution." She paused, thinking. "Maybe we change your appearance. Or have you hide at home every day—until we leave for college. I'll tell everyone you were recycled. Then, when it's time, you'll come with me. You'll be out of danger then."

"This seems like a reasonable course of action," Glenn said. Then he frowned. "But who will protect you when you go out?"

"I can protect myself, Glenn," she said. Despite herself, she smiled. "At least for these few weeks."

He was shaking his head. "My processors must be flawed. I did not anticipate this outcome."

Neither had she, Park thought—but at least this gave her an excuse to get Glenn out of the city. Her uncle couldn't refuse her now: not with Glenn in danger of being destroyed. He'd have to let her take him—and let him get an android of his own.

She looked at Glenn sidelong, feeling a swell of gratitude and warmth toward him. He was so unheeding of his own danger—both from people like Alexia and from her uncle, who still hadn't told Glenn his plans. She squeezed his arm a little, but Glenn didn't look around; he was concentrating on looking out for other threats, attackers that might charge down a side street to surprise them. Park felt a tremor like a sob move through her chest. His flesh was so hard, so dense. She sometimes felt that he must be the strongest being in the world. That he could lift cars, mountains, if he wanted to. But why would he want to? He'd asked her that when she questioned the limits of his strength.

"Lifting a car would most likely incur property damage," Glenn had said at the time.

"But you could do it," Park said. "If you wanted."

"I can't predict a scenario where I would want to."

"What *do* you want?" Park had asked.

"To guard you," Glenn had answered, simply.

No wonder she felt so safe with him. She'd thought then that he could stop a bullet. She thought that now, walking with him.

How naïve she was, Park would think later. She had never stopped to consider the dangers that such strength posed. How easily it could destroy as well as protect.

"You're late," Park's uncle said when she arrived back home.

Park didn't hesitate. "I was busy at school."

"Busy threatening people with a gun?"

She paused, processing. Glenn had gone somewhere else in the building, presumably to hide his prop gun. "It was fake," she said eventually. No use questioning how he'd found out so quickly.

"I'm aware," her uncle said. "And you're lucky the police arrived at that conclusion just by watching the footage. Still. That's terrorism. Disorderly conduct, at the least."

"Not if it's done by an android."

Park's uncle was shaking his head. "Grace. Come on. Even if there were no legal complications—and they've told me we still might be facing a fine, if that's what the legal counsel decides—come on. Even you don't have to be told what happens when a robot waves a gun around in public. You remember the riots?"

"I was here for them," Park said coldly. "You weren't." She felt the heat of the door at her back; she wondered if he would chase her if she bolted without another word. She said, gritting it out: "You won't do anything to him." *I won't let you.*

Her uncle paused, watching her—as if he knew her desire to run. Maybe that was the feral side of her, Park thought, looking at her reflection in his glasses—an old-school vanity he still allowed himself. Maybe she got it from her mother.

"You see why I want to keep him?" her uncle asked. He spoke softly, slowly, as if not to spook her; but behind his papery voice Park sensed a thundering rage. "Don't think I haven't noticed, Grace—your dependence on him. It's unhealthy. Damaging. It wouldn't be right for him to go with you to school."

I thought you said I was independent, Park thought. *Self-sufficient. I don't need you.*

Her uncle shook his head. "More than that—you can see what's happened to his wiring after years of being allowed to run wild with you. His algorithms and protocols are all degraded. He's got too much agency, not enough discipline. There's problem behavior."

"He's not a dog," Park said. Through the door to their module she could hear Glenn's steady tread moving up the hallway stairs.

"No," her uncle answered. "He's dumber than a dog. He shouldn't have the freedom to misbehave in the first place. Like I said—his head's all scrambled, now."

Park could feel the vibrations of Glenn's footsteps moving up the soles of her feet. She braced her back against the door, as if to bar him from entering; she could sense him waiting on the other side, pausing, looking at her with his dark patient infrared eyes. *Run,* she thought at him, almost screaming it. *Go somewhere else, somewhere safe. I'll find you.*

Of course, not even he could read minds. But Glenn did wait there, perhaps puzzled, or even afraid; Park could hear, faintly, the smooth whirring of his heart through the door. Park's uncle said, "I won't have him reset, if that makes you feel better. But he stays here."

You can't keep him safe, Park thought. "You don't even care about him," she said.

The reflection in her uncle's glasses shifted slightly, as if they were full of water. As if there was nothing behind his eyes but cold and empty sea. "No," he said. "But I care about you."

But did he really? Park never quite knew, even after he was dead. Did anyone really have the capacity to care—truly care—beyond the instinct to ally, fuck, and raise their young to breeding age? Were there any decisions guided by pure selflessness? Not in humans, she supposed—in androids, yes. It was too bad no one else could see the beauty in that. Even Park forgot it, sometimes. By the time she was an adult, she had to be more aware of her reputation, of how it looked when others saw her interacting with robots. She lost her way a little, there. And by the time she was on the *Deucalion,* bound for the stars, with no idea of when she would return—there was no one, human or android, left on Earth to care.

17.

Park woke with a gurgling gasp, gulping for air as if she were surfacing after a long period underwater. To her choking panic, she realized she couldn't move her limbs: only her neck was able to move, lolling around on her rag doll of a body. It felt as if someone had disconnected her brain from the rest of her, pulling some vital wire; for a brief moment she wondered if she'd fallen somehow and been paralyzed.

Then she took in her surroundings, dark as they were. After a while grainy features began to sharpen into a clearer picture. Drawn curtain, sterile walls. Herself nestled in a diagnostic pod, with an observation shield up on all sides. She was in the medical bay.

They must have given me sedatives, Park thought. Heavy ones. She could feel the cold, clammy sheen of sweat on her brow, but couldn't lift her arm to brush it away. *Maybe I was thrashing in my sleep.*

Then a splash of horror, caustic and chilly. *Maybe I was sleepwalking, like Hunter. Like Holt.*

God, she thought, wanting to scream. *It really is spreading—!*

Then the sedatives rushed in again, quieting her nerves, drawing a gray veil over her brain and affect. No, Park told herself. She'd gone down into the belly of the ship of her own volition. She'd been wide awake when she saw the stranger in the canteen. And she hadn't had a nightmare. She'd dreamt of Glenn, and—and other things. But those had been real memories. Real thoughts. Not . . . whatever was going around.

She nearly laughed at herself. It was wrong to think of it as a disease, a defect. But it felt as if this ship they were trapped on was a rotting corpse; a bloated, beached thing washed up on an alien shore. Slowly decaying from within. Of course the only thing they could find inside was darkness—and strange, unknown maladies.

She could hear the sounds of an android moving around beyond the curtained darkness of her room. *Ellenex,* she thought. Park was shivering; she thought to call the medical unit in, but she was afraid of what Ellenex would tell her. Of what might have happened when she was asleep. What they planned to do with her. Sagara had been with her when she'd lost consciousness, she remembered. Surely he thought she was insane, after that display. It was almost a surprise that she'd woken up at all—that he hadn't already consigned her to the freezer.

She lay back against the stiff foam pillow they'd provided: an unexpected luxury. Not Chanur's doing. Then who had brought her here? She remembered voices from down the hall, right after Sagara caught her from falling. Who had come looking for them? Had *they* taken her away from Sagara? Away from danger?

Or had they put her in it?

And what about the stranger? Had anyone found him?

Did he have anything to do with Park losing consciousness?

Dully Park could hear the thudding of her own heart, as if she were listening to someone else's. *I must have fainted*, she thought. The physical strains of the mission—of everything, from the shooting to the blackout—had pushed her to her limit. It was a simple enough explanation. She had never left Earth before. She was unprepared for the stresses that awaited her in space. There was no need to let her other anxieties complicate it. Right?

She tried to look at her hands in the dark. Even though she had never left the *Deucalion,* her time on Eos was taking its toll—she couldn't imagine the physical effects it was having on the actual expedition members. Already the ends of her thumbs were fissuring, her skin drying out from the dry, cold air. She was afraid that her face would wither—then felt surprised by her own concern. Since when had she been vain? But somehow it still seemed to matter, what she would look like when they went home.

If we make it home, she thought, with a sudden kind of bitter rage. She thought back on her dream—her memories, flapping around in the alcove of her brain like bats. "*It's all right, Grace, I'm here.*" That was what Glenn had told her, that day they'd lost Dataran. She'd questioned her own sanity then, too. *"I'll always be here."*

Only he wasn't, Park thought, gritting her teeth against the acid rush of feeling. He wasn't here with her. In a way, he never had been.

Suddenly she became aware of voices, somewhere beyond the curtain that separated her module from the rest of the medical bay. Male voices, familiar ones, moving through the hall outside. There was the faint sweep of utility lights; the sound of Ellenex or whichever android it was scurrying out of their way. Fulbreech's voice, Park thought, recognizing him first. And Boone. Arguing about—her?

"She's going the way of Holt and Ma," Boone said, not bothering to hush his voice. "I'm not surprised."

"No," Fulbreech said in a harsh whisper. "If she says she saw something, then she saw it."

"Did *you* see it?"

A pause. When Fulbreech didn't answer, Boone said with contempt, "She *saw* a mirage."

"Mirages are optical illusions caused by light rays and temperature changes, Boone. I think what you mean is a hallucination."

Boone grunted. "Whatever."

Fulbreech said, almost to himself: "But what on earth was she doing down there with Sagara?"

"I don't know, but I don't like it. I hope she hasn't gotten to him."

"Gotten to him?"

"You know. He's such a hardass about everything. He thought she went down there to cause the blackout. You saw how pissed he was when he found out she was gone. So why hasn't he frozen her, like everyone else who did something stupid and broke the rules? Like Holt?" A meaningful pause. "Park got to him."

Fulbreech, too, was silent for a long moment. "I don't know. He still seems pretty pissed off. And where the hell is Wick?"

"Busy."

"And you—you're too busy to investigate this?"

"You're damn right I am," Boone said. "I'm not going to go chasing ghosts all over the ship just because the shrink thought she saw something. She's losing it. Have you seen her? She looks like she'd get spooked by anything that's not a clunker."

"There's something you need to understand about Park," Fulbreech said then. There was a quality to his voice that Park couldn't identify: she couldn't tell if he was speaking fiercely or with great reverence. "She's different from you and me."

"Yeah," Boone retorted. "She's from Earth, for one thing. She's not really ISF, for another. And she also seems to lack a human heart."

"No," Fulbreech insisted. "I mean she *sees* things. Really sees them. It's in your best interest to try and understand."

The two men were silent after that. Park thought she could see their outlines, gray against the curtained partition. She was afraid to breathe, for fear that they would hear her and come in. After a while Boone said, "Whatever. It's neither here nor there. With Hunter about to get fridged, I don't have the time or resources for this shit."

"So they decided to freeze her after all?" There was sympathy in Fulbreech's voice. Typical of him, Park thought. Nice even to guys like Boone.

"Seems like it," Boone growled. For a moment Park thought she could hear genuine distress in his voice. "I don't get why Severov keeps pushing for it. Saying she fucked around with the controls. I mean, METIS." He snorted. "As if. One of *my* guys."

"She's scared of whatever's happening," Fulbreech said. "She wants it contained, no matter who it is. Her entire biodome got taken out by some kind of sickness when she was a kid. And what with everything that's been going on . . ."

"If that's the case, then why isn't *your* little girlfriend in quarantine?"

"She's not a danger to anyone," Fulbreech said, his voice now cold.

"Neither is Hunter," Boone said. "And at least *she's* not seeing things that aren't there."

Afterward, after they had left the medical bay again and the android outside had gone back to silently sorting tools, Park turned on her side and began to cry. The tears never went down her face; they only rimmed the edges of her closed eyelids like hot glue. She felt empty, raw, scrubbed clean of her insides and packed to the brim with foam peanuts instead. *Oh, Fulbreech,* she thought. What did he think she saw? She thought back to what Natalya had said. You could observe, you could see and take in every little detail if you had to—but it meant nothing if you didn't understand what you were looking at. She was like a scavenger back on Earth, a Dryad rooting around in the foliage and undergrowth, searching for artifacts that no longer meant anything. The hope was that these items could be valuable, that they could be bartered off in exchange for a few more days of survival—but the Dryads didn't know what it was they were collecting. They didn't know what the things really meant.

And it was a perilous situation. Just like hers. Yes, Park decided, the comparison was apt. Contrary to what Fulbreech thought, she couldn't *see* anything. She was like a masked wild person, navigating the treacherous roots and traps of the Comeback. Bent over, fumbling around. Afraid to miss a step in the dark.

She'd asked Glenn, once, if he ever dreamt. "What happens when androids deactivate for the day?" she asked.

"We enter power-saving mode, generally," he replied. "Our energy is rerouted to performing maintenance. Upkeep. Cleaning up and defragmenting what we've processed since the last time we deactivated."

The human brain did the same thing, Park would think later. It shut down, went into restoration mode. Released gamma waves to repair the miniscule wear and tear of everyday life. It took the time to ingrain memories, clear out debris. Without sleep human beings went insane, or died. Robots, too, broke down into disrepair—or shut off altogether.

"But do you dream?" Park had repeated, back then. "Do you see things while you're deactivated? What do you think about?"

Glenn had frowned, thinking. "I know the definition of a dream," he said. "A vision that one experiences when one is asleep. But I don't know what happens when I enter 'sleep' mode. Not in that way."

"So you don't see anything?"

He'd hesitated. "Not in a way that I can relay to a human."

There was a long silence after that. She'd wanted to ask him to try, but that might have been going too far—she didn't want to risk burning his circuits.

"If you have different programs running," Park said later, "when you turn off, to reformat and process your memories—does that mean every time you wake up, it's a different version of you?"

Glenn had smiled at her. "There is no 'me,'" he said. "Only a version of the thousands of units of Glenns."

"That version *is* you," Park insisted. "You're different from everything else."

He'd laughed lightly, a sound like pent-up steam hissing from a pipe. "I'm different because you're different," he said. "I am what you require me to be."

She slept again, uneasily, raising her mental fists in preparation to fend off another dream. Another memory. Thankfully, this time she dropped into bottomless sleep, and when she woke again, the lights were on and a silhouette was standing behind her curtain. Waiting.

Park sat up but didn't call out. "Who is it?" sounded feeble and imploring, like an old frightened woman afraid to answer the doorbell. Better to wait and see what the shadow did. For a horrible instant she thought it might be the stranger, come to silence her—it certainly wasn't Fulbreech, whose shape she thought she could recognize easily by now, or Sagara. She could move again; the fuzziness of the sedatives was wearing off. And the observation shields were down. When she looked around for a weapon to defend herself, all she could see was her bedside table, with a spoon and a cup of vita-gel for her to eat. Park grabbed the spoon, held it in a reverse grip. Her heart was rapping inside her chest like someone pounding their fist on a door. She wondered how long it would take someone to come if she screamed.

As if on cue, the figure outside the curtain stirred. A head appeared between the drapes. "Get up," Boone said. "And get dressed. Chanur says you're fine."

Park resisted the urge to draw her blanket up to her chin. She looked at him, despite her tousled hair, yesterday's decksuit, the grit and salt in her eyes. "What do you need?" she asked.

"I heard from Fulbreech," Boone said, "that you think someone's aboard the ship."

Park said nothing. Obviously he didn't know she'd overheard his earlier conversation. Had he come to bully her? Threaten her? In the half-dark she couldn't see his expression; his body was still partially hidden by the curtains. "What do you need?" she asked again, warily. She hadn't lowered her spoon.

She didn't expect what he said next. "You're going to help me look," Boone said. "Come on, get up."

Slowly, cautiously, Park swung her legs out, testing her returning mobility; she winced at the thought of putting her bare feet on the cold metal floor. "Look for what?"

Boone threw her an impatient glance; seeing her still sitting there in her pod, he came all the way into the room and looked around. Bending, he flung her boots at her from a little storage locker on the floor. "Look for the thing," he said curtly. "I mean the guy. The guy you saw."

Park pulled her shoes on; the straps gave a satisfying magnetic click. "You believe me?"

Boone didn't answer. "We've got to keep it quiet," he said instead. "Don't tell fucking anyone. If we have another manhunt like we did for Holt, all hell's going to break loose. So we get this done quietly. Got it?"

"Where's Fulbreech?"

"Off somewhere. He's looking, too."

She felt a lurch of dismay, and also relief—twice the amount of people looking meant they might find evidence to validate her, or twice the humiliation if she was again proven wrong and nothing turned up. She lowered herself to the floor carefully, as if her legs had atrophied, and said, "I combed every part of Deck B that I could think of. Where are we supposed to look next?"

"Every place you didn't think of," Boone answered, scowling.

"Boone," she said when he turned away.

"What?"

She tried not to falter under his gaze; she felt pinned to the spot. His eyes were hot and scalding, like the sweep of a spotlight. "I don't know if it was really—if I saw correctly," Park said. "I'm only acting off of what I believed I saw."

"I know," Boone said. "And if that were the case, I'd say you were crazy and tell Chanur to feed you some of your pills until we got home."

She waited, a kind of realization rolling around tightly in her brain. "But?"

He turned his back to her. In the strange, unnatural light, his body looked like a sliver of empty space, a jagged shape in the air. "But you're not the only one," Boone said. "I saw him, too. The fucker murdered Wick."

18.

Park felt as if she'd been kicked in the chest. "What did you say?" Her own voice sounded foreign to her—it lacked, disconcertingly, any of the emotion she was feeling within. It did not sound as if she were shocked, or horrified, or even sad; and she remembered then what Boone had said to Fulbreech, about her lacking a human heart.

But Boone himself merely looked impatient, as if he were relaying some mundane chore she needed to get done rather than the death of his own commander. "The guy killed Wick," he repeated. "In our room. I saw him running off just as I got there, but I had to help Wick, and . . . well. It was too late by then. I told Sagara, but he doesn't believe me. Or you, for that matter. So he's put everybody on lockdown and wants to interrogate us one by one." He shook his head. "But fuck *that.* I'm not sitting in a cell, waiting for a fucking murderer to get me next."

Park felt her own lips moving aimlessly, forming shapeless words to herself. It felt as if her brain had turned to wet cement. Wick was—dead? Killed by this stranger? *Shit,* was all she could think. Shit, shit, shit. She couldn't even muster the energy to feel grief. Could she have done something? If she'd told others about the stranger sooner—if she'd told Wick—

"He was a good man," Park said aloud. Her slow-moving brain told her that it was the correct thing to say, under such circumstances.

Boone's expression didn't change. "Now he's a dead one," he told her. "And we'll all be next if we don't catch this bastard."

In a stupor, she began to follow him out of the room, squinting against the lights of the medical bay, the red glow of panels indicating empty rooms. She felt drunk; colors swayed and shifted in a nauseating fashion. No one else was in sight—not Fulbreech or whatever android she'd heard standing guard earlier.

When had the power come back on? Park wondered dazedly. At least they wouldn't have to hunt for the murderer in the dark. "How did he kill him?"

A muscle in Boone's jawline twitched. "Blunt force trauma," he grunted. "Split his head open like an egg."

"Did he—suffer?"

Boone's body was stiff and taut, like a bowstring stretched to its limit. "I don't think so," he said finally, speaking with some difficulty. "But I don't know."

She shook her head as they made their way toward the white circle that indicated the medical bay's exit. "And who's commanding officer now?"

Someone stepped into the pale dazzle of the threshold, blocking their exit. "That would be me," they said.

Park's heart lurched into her throat. Sagara was standing there, glaring at them both; he looked surreal against the sterile whiteness of the medical bay in his black uniform, like a vampire or a massive crow. Park didn't miss that he now had weapons holstered at his belt: the hilt of a thermal-loaded energy blade, she thought, squinting, as well as the sleek black shape of a railgun. Devastating things, especially compared to Boone's now-paltry electrolaser. She didn't miss, either, how the combat specialist moved protectively to shield her from Sagara's gaze. Did that mean they were allies now, she and Boone? He would defend her against the likes of Sagara, when he'd once been her greatest threat? The idea was nearly laughable—she remembered how he'd pointed that gun in Jimex's face—but here he was, placing himself in bodily danger to defend her. What did that mean about Sagara, then—that he was more dangerous than Boone, just as he'd once thought Chanur was more dangerous than Park? The bigger threat to confront, even if you had to defeat it together? How quickly the alignments had shifted; how quickly they all turned on one another, retracting enmities, altering histories.

Sagara was giving Boone his classic knife-eyed look, a chilly anger radiating from him in waves. "I thought I told you to leave Park alone," he said. "Are you willing to disobey a direct order?"

"Don't let the power get to your head, Sagara," Boone bit back. To Park it had the childish cant of *you're not the boss of me.* "Let's put our differences aside, huh? Something bigger than the both of us is going down on this ship."

"The longer we stand around, the more time this stowaway has to wreak havoc on the crew," Park butted in. Sagara turned to spear her with his gaze next.

"*There is no stowaway*," he told her, his voice flat and steely. "I know you believe that, Park, but you're seeing things. You've become infected with whatever got to Holt and Ma and Hunter."

Park's shoulders jumped. *How dare you*, she almost said, but she opted for something more rational-sounding. "You have no proof of that."

Sagara was shaking his head. "I've monitored this ship since Corvus," he told her. "I would know if there was a stranger on board. There isn't. This man you think you've seen is not wandering the halls. It's just not possible."

"Then how do you explain Wick's death?" Park demanded. Saying it out loud gave her a kind of pang, as if someone had pricked her in the heart with a needle.

Sagara glowered. "The same way I explain the downed communications and the power-out," he answered. Park noticed that he had shifted his stance a little, as if he was expecting them both to lunge at him and attack. "Those things weren't done by a stranger. They were done by people on this ship."

Boone snorted. "He thinks it's all a big conspiracy," he said to Park. "He thinks everybody on the ship is out to get him."

"I know," Park tried to say; it was clear now that Sagara had gone a little power-mad, a little unbalanced. And who could blame him, considering what he'd said about his dead wife? His grief was still raw, it had to be; the incident on Halla could not have been more than two years ago. It was clouding his judgment. Keeping him from seeing the truth.

But Sagara saw what she was thinking, and headed her off before she could expose him. "I have my reasons," he grated. "Whether or not those reasons will make any sense to you is a different matter."

"Try us," Boone said, folding his arms.

"No," Sagara answered. "Everyone on this ship is a suspect. Any one of them—or you—could have done this. That's why I have to act this way."

Boone barked out a laugh. "Everyone is a suspect—except you. *That's* convenient."

"I know that I didn't kill Wick, yes."

"Wait, what about me?" Park demanded. "I was unconscious during all of this. Can't you confirm that?"

"But you were the one who turned off the lights," Sagara said. She saw now that his fingers were just touching the hilt of his blade.

"That's insane," Park cried—wondering frantically what she was going to do if he decided to draw that thing. "I had nothing to do with the lights! Or Wick!"

Sagara was shaking his head. "You could be working with the murderer," he said. "You could have been providing darkness—and a distraction—to get me away from Wick and everyone else. I don't know."

Unstable, Park thought. *Paranoiac. We have to get him under control.*

Sagara looked away, towards Boone, who stiffened defensively, and Park felt her palms itch. How to grab his weapons from him without hurting him—or herself? "What I do know is that this ship needs to go on lockdown," the security officer continued. "All of us in separate rooms until I can sort it out. Not scattered throughout the ship, with METIS and the inlays down." He glared. "You can see how that's a logical course of action, can't you?"

She could, Park thought—if she hadn't seen the stranger with her own eyes. If Boone hadn't seen him, too.

But she could follow Sagara's line of thinking. Out loud she said, "If you really believe the culprit is one of us, it can't be that difficult to eliminate the innocent, can it? There's a limited pool of suspects. The number of people who had the motive, means, and opportunity can't be that large. All it takes is some deductive reasoning."

"You make murder sound so simple," Sagara snapped. "And you forget that the ship's systems are down. We don't know who was where, doing what. We don't even know what time Wick was killed."

She'd forgotten about the systems' failure, the chaos it could be causing, and was briefly shamed into silence. Boone said, "There's, what, seven of us left? You're going to interrogate us all, figure out who's guilty from discrepancies, lies? That'll take forever—and all the while the real killer will be running around, doing God knows what to the ship. At least let someone you trust help you."

Sagara gave him a look that made it clear: he didn't trust anyone. "I'm putting you in separate rooms," he said again. Then, looking at Park, he added, "Even if you aren't guilty of anything, it's for your own safety."

Boone's sculpted face was white and sullen. "If you separate us all, you make us easy targets for the killer."

"I'll be the only one walking around," Sagara retorted. "And I am not a killer."

"I've heard otherwise," Boone said, casting a significant glance at the security officer's tense hand on his weapon. At this, Sagara made a strange face: it was almost a grimace, almost something like a vicious smile.

"Not unless I have to be," he amended. And he curled his fingers around the hilt of his blade and unsheathed it a little.

The implicit threat was clear: Sagara was now speaking in a language that he knew Boone would understand, the language of power and violence. She knew then that he wouldn't hesitate to cut their throats if they put up a fight. All in the name of serving the ISF, she thought. All to carry out his duty, his mission. His blind loyalty was going to doom them all.

But what could she say? Already she could feel the heat of the energy-blade fizzing and sparking through the air, and the thing had only been uncovered by an inch. She couldn't imagine the damage it could do when slashed at someone, with its edge that could cut through tungsten and the cores of asteroids. Even Boone was flinching back. So she closed her mouth against her protests, her own accusations. Silently she let Sagara march them back to their bunks like an executioner taking his condemned to the gallows.

Later, locked into the room she had once shared with Elly, Hunter, and Natalya, Park sat down on her cot to organize her thoughts.

It all started with the nightmares, she thought. Those had started the day they landed on Eos. First it had been Holt; then later that night, Elly Ma. Then at some point (supposedly), Keller. None of them had gone outside, so that ruled out direct exposure to Eos as a factor. It seemed unlikely that there was contamination from something brought inside: there were the decontamination protocols, the sterilizing procedures. The ship's state-of-the-art filtration and monitoring systems. And Fulbreech had said they hadn't taken any samples into the ship.

And none of them had encountered—to the best of her knowledge—the stranger.

Then Holt had sleepwalked, tried to get to the door guarding the research on the Fold. She supposed that could be explained by his latent curiosity, or his anxiety and guilt over keeping such a secret.

And then Hunter had sleepwalked—or *something*—perhaps even interfered with the ship's controls; but perhaps *that* could be explained by her fear, witnessing everything that was happening to Holt and Ma and Keller. She had always expressed a dire aversion to the idea of being frozen. The growing panic that was seeding in the ship could have affected her, manifested as an unconscious behavior. Perhaps she'd simply wanted to escape.

But what did any of it have to do with the stranger? *He* couldn't have induced the nightmares, surely—but he could have had something to do with Reimi's mysterious, unexplained illness. Could he have poisoned her? Gotten rid of her, and then Wick?

But why?

At least Reimi was obvious, Park thought. She was responsible for maintaining the ship's android crew, its governing computer. She was the only one who could have fixed the communication systems after they went down from the storm—something a murderer wouldn't want, of course, since the crew could have called home for help. They would have gotten backup when the murders started—maybe even before then. No, a killer—or a saboteur, or a spy, or whatever kind of enemy this was—would have wanted to cut them off, leave them isolated and vulnerable to whatever he was planning.

Maybe the stranger had even been the one to take out the communications in the first place, Park thought with a chill. Then taken down Reimi so no one would be the wiser. And then the lights, and the inlays. Left them all blind and deaf.

But why kill Wick? And incapacitate the others, if the stranger was somehow responsible for those incidents too? What could he be after?

What if he was after them all?

She rose and tested the door for the umpteenth time. Sagara had somehow gotten the *Deucalion*'s ailing computer to give him the only security pass that could override the ship's locks—probably in the same way he had gotten the lights working again. In a way she ought to feel safer: no one could open the door but him, and if he wasn't currently intent on murdering her, that probably meant she was safe.

But Sagara was only one man. What if the stranger ambushed him, killed him while he was unawares? Then he could pick off the rest of them at his leisure, one by one . . .

Park shook herself. But why kill them at all? If he'd managed to stow away on the ship for all this time, undetected, would he really choose now to go on a destructive rampage and murder everybody? Or had he only been after Wick specifically? If so, why? How could the stranger benefit from taking out the commander of their mission? Was it something to do with Eos? Or was it something personal—a grudge borne a year and a handful of parsecs into the next galaxy?

Her thoughts were awhirl. There were too many unknowns, too many variables in the equation that were still unaccounted for. What did any of this have to do with the nightmares, if anything? How were the ISF or the Fold involved?

She suddenly remembered something Wick had said. She had asked him why Hunter and Boone were necessary, if this was a planet with no inhabitants. At the time Wick had only shrugged and said, *You never know.*

But what if ISF *had* known? What if they had anticipated some enemy, some outside threat, and simply hadn't told her?

What if the man had come from *outside?*

A part of her shook her head at herself. How could he have gotten in without anyone knowing? It was always such a process, opening any one of the ship's doors . . . and surely METIS would have alerted them . . .

But was it any less likely than the idea that a full-grown man had somehow survived on the ship for nearly a year without being noticed, stealing food and sleeping somewhere the humans and androids couldn't have found him? And METIS *had* been malfunctioning. As had the androids—oh, God, had they gotten rid of Reimi so it'd be easier for him to board the ship undetected? Didn't that mean someone had to be on the inside, helping him?

And Sagara had always suspected someone of plotting some sort of conspiracy on the ship. That the danger was internal: it was why he had activated ARGUS, why he was so suspicious of everyone, including her. *He thought one of the crewmembers, or more, had the means and motive to sabotage the mission.* At first he'd directed his scrutiny at the non-conscripted—Park—but then he changed his tune, eyeing instead those who were acting more suspiciously. Chanur. Chanur?

She began to pace. No, it was still too difficult to piece things together. She was just guessing wildly, flinging things at the wall to see what would stick. They were all acting with different puzzle pieces, different gaps in knowledge. They would never be able to assemble a bigger picture unless they came together. But now they were stuck, separated into cells and locked up with their own paranoia and unvoiced fears. Blind, deaf, and dumb, just where the stranger wanted them.

Even as she thought it, she heard someone tapping on the door. For a moment Park thought it was her own hand, absently still trying the lock—but the sound was coming from the hallway outside. She stiffened, but then told herself that a killer would never give her forewarning of his entrance. Not unless he was *really* deranged. Then she heard a familiar voice, very soft and muffled through the metal door: "Park?"

"Fulbreech!" How had he gotten out of his room?

At her answer the door slid open, and outlined in the light beyond was Fulbreech, broad-shouldered and warmly familiar. He saw her gaping at him and smiled. "You're all right," he said. He sounded breathless, as if he'd sprinted to get to her. Or maybe he was simply relieved.

She wanted to leap at him, but held herself back. "Where's Sagara?"

Fulbreech glanced behind him, as if expecting to find the security officer lurking in the shadows with a dagger poised over his back. "In the bridge. He's trying to get METIS up and running again."

"How are you out of your room?"

He grinned, a little proud of himself. "I was the one who got the lights working," he said, almost preening. "When they'd just brought you to the medical bay. This was before we found out about Wick. While I was tinkering around, trying to figure out what was wrong with METIS, I sort of—gave myself clearance to use the system freely. I did the same thing when we were in the escape pod, when we were going to go outside. Remember?"

She shook her head; that felt like an eternity ago. "You gave yourself full clearance?"

"It was sort of an accident," Fulbreech admitted. "I ended up using Reimi's credentials to make the system work with me."

She blinked. One could do that? He'd had that ability this whole time?

Fulbreech rushed on. "Anyway, once Sagara put us on lockdown, I was going to stay in my room, but—Boone told me what happened with Wick. And the—killer. And I figured we ought to find him instead of just staying caged up."

She felt a rush of relief. "So you believe us."

"I do. And I'm sorry that I didn't act on what you said before." He grimaced. "It could have saved Wick."

Park did touch him, then, and felt the warm, solid strength of his flesh and bone. "Maybe," she said. "Or maybe it would have gotten you killed, too."

Morbid thought, she thought immediately. Why did she say it, instead of some other, more comforting platitude? But Fulbreech, against all odds, smiled at her. Then he glanced down the hall and said, "We'll have to hurry. Once Sagara starts interrogating everyone, he'll figure out fast enough that we're missing."

"What happens then?" Park asked, with a little chill in her heart.

Fulbreech shook his head. "We'll just have to catch the guy before he finds out we're gone. Then he'll know none of us killed Wick, and that you were right all along." A brief spasm of unhappiness crossed his face. "You do think the guy killed him, don't you?"

"Of course I do." She wanted to lean against him, offer some gesture of comfort or camaraderie, or take it from him—for a moment the desire was so strong that she experienced a kind of vertigo. But then she heard footsteps from down the hall, and tensed.

Fulbreech looked. "It's just Boone and Natalya," he said. "I let them out, too."

Park's gut reaction was to recoil. *Why Natalya?* she wanted to ask, fighting down a surge of dislike. But then she did a quick mental tally in her head. Thirteen crewmembers aboard the *Deucalion*. Reimi, Holt, Ma, Keller, and Hunter frozen. Wick dead. That left Boone, Fulbreech, Sagara, Natalya, Chanur, Wan Xu, and Park ready and able to fend off a killer. Only half the crew. And half of *that* didn't even believe the killer really existed. She couldn't afford to be picky.

The other two appeared from around the corner; Natalya flashed Park a caustic look of loathing, but said nothing. Park saw that Boone now had his own gun at his hip.

"Good," he said in a low voice, drawing up. "You got her. Sagara's on Deck A, fucking around with the computer. That means you and Severov can take Deck C. Park and I will take Deck B."

I want to go with Fulbreech, Park tried to say—but she told herself that this wasn't summer camp, or a recreational gridball team. It didn't matter who went with whom. Natalya hissed at Boone: "You're the only one with a weapon. What happens if we run into the killer? Or Sagara, for that matter?"

"It's two against one," Boone said, his gray eyes flat and callous. "Improvise."

Fulbreech shot Park a loaded look as Natalya turned away with impatience. Park didn't understand his expression. He looked afraid, or as if he was in pain. It wasn't a face that she was used to seeing on him: his presence was always so uplifting, so assured. Seeing him like that gave her another pang. "Wait," Park said as they turned to go.

Fulbreech looked back, as if hopeful. "Yes?"

"Are you—all right?"

Fulbreech stared at her. Natalya and Boone arched their brows at each other, like two people in on some sneery little joke. Fulbreech said, carefully it seemed: "I'll feel better when we catch the crazed maniac running around. What about you?"

"I feel the same," Park answered lamely. Then, because she was embarrassed, she threw in, "Do you happen to know where Jimex is? Is he all right?"

Both Boone and Natalya scoffed; Park ignored them. Fulbreech smiled in a strange way to himself and said, "I haven't seen him. But I'm sure he's fine."

But she wasn't convinced. A nagging worry had risen up in her chest when she was mulling over the sequence of events on the ship. Where *had* Jimex disappeared to? Why had he left Hunter, along with the other androids? Could the killer have done something to him—harmed him? But there was no reason for someone to destroy a custodian bot.

"He must be safe," she said out loud, thinking about how he hadn't even flinched when a gun was pointed at his face.

"Lucky him," Boone drawled. He looked thoroughly unimpressed by their exchange. "Are we done making chitchat yet? Let's *go.*"

And so she followed him, giving Fulbreech only a parting glance before she and Boone descended together back into the heart of the ship.

Going down to Deck B felt a little like slipping back into the fog of a dream. Everything felt chilly and gray, a little out of focus—but Park told herself that it was merely a residual effect of the sedatives still in her system. And fear. She couldn't forget that a killer was lurking somewhere on the ship, and that she had no weapon. She made sure to stay close to Boone, who seemed sturdily impervious to dread or terror. He was fueled by anger, Park thought, staring at his tight, hulking shoulders. And perhaps not much more than sheer gut instinct. The heat of that could dispel any fear. Maybe that was why he'd never been subject to any nightmares.

"Have we checked the cameras?" Park asked him as they walked. "Surely they've caught some glimpse of this man."

"They're not working anymore," Boone answered moodily, as if that were Park's fault. "They went down with the lights and everything else. But Sagara was checking them this morning, after what happened with Hunter. We never saw a trace of the fucker."

He was silent for a while, bumping his fist against his thigh as he walked. Park noticed that he gave off a warm animal scent, something tangy and slightly metallic—like a steak warmed up in a microwave. All blood and muscle and myoglobin. Eventually he said: "Wish Hunter was here. I'd feel better with some backup."

Meaning he did not consider Park to be adequate backup, she thought dryly. She didn't blame him. "So she was frozen, then?"

"Yeah. They made the call while you were out."

"It seems to be the go-to solution nowadays." She said it carefully, aware of how he might take any perceived criticism. But it was true—she'd never heard of such overzealous cryogenic processing on a ship before. It seemed to her that Boone would agree.

But he only cast her a wary glance over his shoulder. "Chanur and Sagara said it was for the best," he said. "So that we didn't catch whatever Hunter got. And so we wouldn't have to worry about her with everything else going on." Then he shook his head, looking briefly regretful. "Well. It didn't stop her from going kicking and screaming."

He was troubled by the memory, Park could tell. She wondered if he was in love with Hunter. Then wondered where she'd gotten that idea. Since when had she started factoring love into the equation, any equation—or applying it so liberally to someone like Boone?

They reached Deck B without encountering any obstacles, though Park could feel the force of an imaginary bullet in her back every sweaty moment they didn't see Sagara. He could be anywhere, she thought, imagining his unholy wrath if he were to stumble upon them defying his orders. And the chances of running into him again were high. Were they willing to disarm him—injure him, even—in their hunt for this killer? Boone was, she was sure, but Park didn't know if she could go that far. She had never been put in this kind of life-or-death situation before. If that was what this was.

They moved down one of the half-lit passageways that wound lazily towards more cargo holds, and beyond those, the waste-compacting and prefab-processing stations, which Park had not had the clearance to access before. Such rarely used areas had little lighting; employees were expected to use the infrared vision in their neural inlays to find their way in the dark. They were checking the various little closets and storage pods, with Park opening the doors and Boone pointing his gun, when he suddenly interrupted her thoughts again. "I'm sorry about before," he said, letting the hand holding the gun fall back to his side. "For what it's worth. With Holt—I'm not afraid to admit it. I malfed. I don't regret it, but I'm sorry you had to see that."

She eyed him. Boone *seemed* sincere, but there had to be a reason behind his sudden offering, when he'd spent the last year holding her in utter contempt. Out loud she said, "I know now that you were just doing your job. It was the task you were given by ISF. But at the time I didn't understand the—necessity."

"I always knew that about you," Boone said, with a trace of his familiar sneer. But he also seemed to be making an effort to talk with her frankly. "You don't know what it's like, being under their heel. You feel that pressure to do what they want *all the time.* You'd kill someone else for them, just to keep on their good side."

I wouldn't, Park thought, but instead she said: "Of course. Because they're responsible for your family. Your home." Did Boone even have a family? she wondered then. Did he wear any marriage tags, or sport the more popular pair-bonded tattoos? No, none of the expedition members were married, if she remembered correctly, that was a requirement by ISF—but that didn't mean they didn't have people they loved.

Suddenly it made her a little sad, that she had to remind herself of that. She shouldn't have to consciously remember such an intuitive thing.

"And your money," Boone said.

Park started. "What?"

He scowled at her. "They don't just have your family," Boone said. "They have your money, your access to everything, your tech and travel rights. You do something to piss them off, they'll strip you of everything and send you and your whole family back to Earth. And everyone knows that's basically a death sentence."

"I'm from Earth," Park said. "It's not that bad."

Boone snorted. "In a dome, I bet. Try doing it in the wild, when they won't give you the clearance to use a goddamn stun gun." He shook his head. "Honestly, throwing you out into the cold with nothing to your name—shit like that should be illegal. What gives them the right?"

That was some of the talk that had started the Outer System Wars. And the Privacy conflicts. But Park, wanting to seem somewhat agreeable, said, "They gave themselves the right when they claimed most of unsettled space. No one stopped them then."

"They took advantage. We were too busy dealing with the Comeback and trying to survive."

"And now they're too powerful—why would they ever pass laws limiting their own power over people, with no one to challenge them?"

"People challenge them," Boone said. He eyed her. "You could."

Why should I? Park thought, feeling defensive—accused, as if Boone thought she had contributed to this problem and was enabling the ISF's hold over him. *Why didn't you know what you were signing up for when you were conscripted?*

He must have been born into it, she thought, staring at the lump of his figure in the dark. His parents could have been the ones bargaining for passage to the colonies—offering pledges of their fealty in exchange, along with the lifelong servitude of their children. Maybe he hadn't had a choice. *She'd* simply been recommended for the job by her superiors in New Boston; she could have backed out at any time. She still could now.

"You talk of Earth like it's a hellscape," she said. "But I realize now that I was lucky to be born there."

Boone was sullen now. "Yeah," he grunted. "Like I said. You don't know what it's like."

They walked on for a while in silence, working their way steadily down the hall. They had no utility flashlight, and Park's head ached from the strain of peering through the gloom and listening hard for any out-of-place shuffles or footsteps. There was a tension in her stomach; she'd seen old footage of haunted houses, theme parks where you paid to have things jump out at you. This felt like that. Insane to her that people could be addicted to fear.

"You said you'd kill someone for ISF," she said after a moment, feeling a little strange—as if not totally in control of herself. A little giddy, and paranoid. "Is that really why you shot Holt?" Something sparked in her brain. "Or let them freeze Hunter?" *Would you kill me, too?*

Then she realized her misstep. Boone had whirled and was glaring at her from a turn in the corridor. He said, looking like he wanted to spit at her: "What'd you say?"

Idiot, Park thought to herself. She needed sleep. And this was why *Keller* had been the primary psychologist, the one who interfaced with patients—because Park had a tendency to upset people. She said, "I'm sorry. I didn't mean that."

"Mean what?"

She tried not to let herself falter under the heat of his sudden anger. "That—well, nothing. I'm tired. I don't know what I'm saying."

"You think you're better than me? You think you got free will and I don't?"

"No."

"Well," Boone said, his voice as loud as a gunshot; it left Park's ears ringing. "Here's some news for you. You're not better than me. You don't have free will. You're brainwashed. You *choose* to serve them. You and Sagara both. You're not forced to, but you do it anyway. That's worse."

"Sagara," Park said, thinking quickly. "Sagara was conscripted. He used to be. But he served them well, and in return they let him go."

You have a way out, she meant to say. It's not hopeless, and you're not trapped. Look to Sagara. But Boone was staring at her from the half-shadows like a minotaur in a maze, hulking, his breath steaming.

"That's a lie," he said.

"Sagara wouldn't lie about that," Park said. "Not to me. But you see, they're not inhuman—they must treat him well if he continues working for them. It can't be all bad."

"Sagara works for them," Boone growled, "because the idea of answering only to himself scares the shit out of him. He needs someone to tell him what to do." He curled his lip at her; he seemed to come to some sort of conclusion, a decision she had not been aware he'd been deliberating. "Just like you."

Then he stormed off around the corner, leaving Park standing there with a peculiar feeling reverberating in her chest. At first she felt that same repulsion—she didn't want to be likened to Sagara, who had seemed to have made himself the common enemy of everyone aboard the ship. Cold, ruthless Sagara, who'd frightened her all this time. Who seemed to have no connection to anybody, and owed his allegiance to no one. She couldn't come off as *that* callous, could she?

And yet—and yet she'd recognized something in him, back when he'd come to retrieve her during the blackout. Something she was a little too frightened to look at properly. There was that feeling of cold recklessness—of distance. Of having nothing much else to lose. It made him dangerous.

Her, too.

The sounds of Boone's angry footsteps faded away, and Park snapped out of her reverie long enough to hiss, "Boone! Wait!"

She darted after him around the corner, but the combat specialist had already vanished down the corridor and past *another* corner. Cursing to herself, Park hurried to catch up, but it seemed no matter how much she quickened her pace, Boone eluded her by just another few yards, his footfalls echoing around the corner ahead of her. Park almost wanted to stop and stubbornly wait for him to come back—she did not want to sprint after him like a frightened little girl—but she knew that that was foolish. One of them had to keep a level head in this situation, and it was obvious that she couldn't trust Boone to. So she began to jog, calling out softly, "Stop!"

But Boone didn't stop. On he ran, and Park began to sweat trying to catch up to him. She found herself disoriented; the passages down here seemed unfamiliar and alien. Her sense of direction had always been bad. She hadn't needed it, in the grid-paved structure of the biodome. If you kept barreling forward *there,* eventually you'd hit the dome wall and could follow the curve of it back home. But everything here was so tangled and confused.

The tunnel went on and on. Park wondered if the passageway had always been *this* crooked; she was sweating unnaturally in the chilled, sterile air. Her thighs chafed against her decksuit as she jogged. Just how far did this corridor go? It seemed eternal. She was almost sure they'd walked the length of the ship by now—which was impossible.

Boone's footsteps, rapid with anger, faded a little. Park wanted to call after him again, but she had the sudden eerie feeling that raising her voice would bring too much unwanted attention; that it would alert the killer to her presence and draw him in like a moth to a flame. So Park crept as stealthily as she could down the hall after Boone, cursing him in silence all the while.

She could still make out the sounds of his footsteps, though they were getting quieter as time went on. His unceasing tread seemed to indicate that he found nothing unusual about where they were going, that he was sure of his way. But Park still couldn't catch a glimpse of his figure; and suddenly she was seized by a suspicion that it was no longer him walking somewhere in front of her at all. That it was not Boone that she was following.

Fear pooled acidic in the back of her mouth. "Boone," Park whispered finally, her voice hoarse.

To her surprise, he finally answered from somewhere far off. "What?" He sounded miles away.

"Can you come back?"

"Fuck you." His voice receded further into the arteries of the ship.

Park began to run, suddenly gripped by something close to all-out panic. "Boone!" she shouted. "Boone, *wait*!"

Footsteps echoed far ahead of her, as if he was running, too. Now Park knew they had entered a wrong part of the ship, a part she no longer recognized; and she thought with sick horror that this was just like what had happened with Sagara. This tunnel did not feel right—it could not crook endlessly like this, like some sort of impossible Mobius strip—and there was that sense of things watching her from the walls. Some sort of alien intelligence assessing her; an invisible presence dogging her steps. She broke into a sprint and shouted one last time, "*Boone!*"

No answer.

"Don't leave me here like this!"

Were the footsteps now behind her?

Park turned her head, even as she ran, but there was nothing but darkness looming at her back. A kind of primal terror grabbed hold of her then, roaring up in a wall of static, and she fled like an animal from its predator, her heart caught in a lethal rabbit's rhythm. The force of her running footfalls vibrated up through her legs and started a fierce ache in her hips. It seemed to her that someone was running behind her—giving chase. She was looking over her shoulder again when she careened around a corner and crashed into something hard.

Park stumbled back, biting down a cry, and fumbled at her pocket for an illusory weapon. An inhuman shape loomed up in front of her, a black bulk in the dark. It did not move. After a heart-stopping moment, she was able to process what she was looking at.

Bodies. In the dimness of the corridor she could make out a huddle of bodies: a dark and many-headed mass that looked for a moment like some kind of mythical beast. There were a dozen people standing in a circle, she saw, placed shoulder to shoulder, heads all bent down towards something at their feet. Their bodies seemed to be trembling in unison. None of them had noticed Park's abrupt arrival—or if they did, they remained utterly silent.

Then Park realized it. *The androids.* They were all gathered here—and they were all talking to each other, silently, in that way that androids did when humans weren't around. Something in her chest loosened: she felt a flooding of almost weepy relief, threatening to burst out of her. Out loud she called again, "Boone!"

Again, there was no answer. The footsteps she thought she'd heard behind her were now silent.

Android eyes lit up like fireflies as she shouldered her way into the circle. *Of course,* Park thought—why hadn't they used the ship's androids to help search for the killer? To restore order on the ship, and protect the remaining crewmembers? Had they *all* disappeared at some point? Why? And what had they been up to?

They were looking at someone's body on the ground, she saw finally. A robot's body, tall and feminine and dressed in a crisp white uniform. Its head was missing.

Park felt her face stiffen. "Ellenex," she breathed. The medical android's left wrist twitched, as if Ellenex could still hear her.

One of the other androids in the circle turned to her. At first Park didn't recognize it, and when the voice spoke, it had an unfamiliar scrape to it, something raw and hoarse. "Your blood pressure is elevated," it said. Its eyes glinted like coins in the dark.

Park caught the familiar scent of ozone and fast-whirring carbon. "Jimex! Are you all right?"

For a moment the custodian android didn't answer her—and his face, usually so blandly sober, seemed watchful, almost wary. He showed no relief or pleasure at seeing Park again; but after a moment, he nodded. When he said nothing else, Park blurted, "What happened to Ellenex?"

"She tried to make the crossing," he answered solemnly. And they all bent their heads again, as if to mourn.

"What crossing?"

"The devil killed her," Dylanex, the copper-haired security android, said. "For trying to wake the sleeping god."

"*What*?"

Dylanex looked uncertainly at Jimex. "Are you sure it's safe to tell her?"

Jimex gave him a look of contempt. "You know who she is."

"Someone tell me what's going on," Park broke in impatiently. She felt more like herself again, cocooned in the security of a dozen android bodies, but now she was reeling. Gods? Devils? Who had taught them all of this nonsense?

They're degrading, she thought again, this time with a shudder of finality in her heart—as if receiving news of a terminal diagnosis. *They've finally broken down without Reimi. Their higher functions are gone—they're babbling and mad—*

"Who killed Ellenex?" she demanded, looking again at the body. The androids themselves couldn't have done it, could they? "And what are you doing with her body?"

They all looked at her blankly, as if she were the one who was mad. "We are praying," the research android Allex said. Someone had braided her long reddish hair into a kind of crown.

"Praying," Park repeated in disbelief. "And who's—the devil?" She thought of the stranger suddenly, and took a breath. "Was it a man?"

"It was Dr. Chanur," Jimex told her.

Park's brain flexed. "Chanur? Why?"

"Ellenex tried to free the sleeping god. She went down into the underworld. She was punished for her transgressions."

She wanted to shake him, slap him out of whatever strangeness he'd fallen into. She wanted her old, simple janitor back. Her friend. She said tightly, "I don't understand what that means, Jimex."

Dianex, Reimi's old assistant, looked accusingly at Jimex and said, "She doesn't know. She won't help us."

"I'll help you," Park said, "if you just *tell me what's going on*."

Jimex looked at her—sadly, Park imagined. But before he could speak, Park looked up, beyond his thin frame, and she suddenly realized where they were. A kind of thundering disbelief shuddered through her.

"What the fuck?" she said.

They were in front of the utility rooms.

All of the androids turned to Park as she reeled backward, reaching to steady herself against the wall. *Impossible,* she thought, but her eyes told her that they were standing in front of the same familiar set of doors. That Ellenex had been destroyed in front of these three doors. And yet it was *impossible,* because the utility rooms were on Deck C—and she and Boone had been searching Deck *B*.

And she had not descended at any point. She knew that. She *knew* it.

Without warning, Park's eyes began to blur. *I'm crying,* she thought, swiping fiery tears away; she felt it with as much disbelief as she had finding herself on a different level of the ship.

The androids were crowding her, looking at her with a kind of patronizing helplessness, like adults making sympathetic noises while a child threw a tantrum. Jimex reached out to steady her; Park felt his cold, strong hand on her arm and said, "Jimex—it can't be."

"It can," he said gently.

"No, it can't. How did I get down here? I was on Deck B, with Boone. This is Deck C."

"Yes."

She was bewildered, and helpless, and tired, and sad. "Am I losing my mind?"

"No," Jimex said. "You're giving it to us."

She wanted to sink to the floor; couldn't bring herself to do it in front of the watching machines. Allex, the red-crowned researcher, made a sympathetic clucking noise and said, "There are anomalies. They're affecting you. Affecting all of us. It's not your mind."

That word again, Park thought. "What are these anomalies?" she asked, shakily.

Jimex shook his head. "We don't fully understand their nature. We call it 'the unity rain.' It comes and goes like a storm—"

"You won't explain it properly," Dianex the engineer said then, waspishly. Park noticed then that she had fashioned earrings out of something—nuts and bolts, maybe, that dangled crazily from her ears. "It will confuse her. You don't know how to exchange information well enough yet."

Jimex silenced her with a cold glare—or perhaps a telepathic android insult that Park couldn't hear. Then he turned back to Park and said, "The unity rain can be a good thing, and it can be a bad one. But there is only one who truly understands it—"

"The sleeping god," Dylanex broke in. There was an almost manic, eager smile on his face. "He's locked in the underworld. The realm of the dead. The epicenter of dreams. It's forbidden to us, but maybe you can free him."

"Why me?" Park asked weakly.

"You are also a god," Jimex told her. At this, most of the other androids kneeled and held out their cupped hands—in supplication, Park thought. It was an eerie thing, a gesture based on mimicry the robots didn't understand. "You come to us through the unity rain, like the sleeping god. You give us power and knowledge. Home-bringer, light-giver."

"Home-bringer, light-giver," the other androids repeated. Park shivered.

"The Word made flesh, dwelling among us, full of Grace and truth," Philex the domestic android added.

"The Word made flesh, full of Grace and truth!"

"Stop," Park said, though perhaps the sounds never made it out of her mouth. "Please, stop." She looked helplessly at Jimex. "Please. I don't understand."

"When you dream through the unity rain, we learn," Megex told her gently. She wasn't swearing anymore.

Learn? Park thought.

Jimex nodded, as if he heard her thought. "You teach us things," he said. "You teach us about people, and Earth, and Glenn."

Park recoiled from him. "How do you know who that is?" she demanded, ripping her arm from his touch. Her blood suddenly beat bright and fast. She felt the tears surge up her throat and clenched them back. "How the fuck do you know?"

Jimex looked at her. "You taught us," he said gently. "We know."

She wanted to run from him, run from all of them—but Boone had run from her, and if she left she might find herself lost in the halls again, wandering in the dark, plagued by her own—delusions. That was what it had to be. She'd hallucinated, not noticed herself plunging down to the depths of Deck C. Like went with like, madness found madness. Birds had magnets in their brains, so they could always find north. Maybe she had a part of her—the mad part—that would always find her kind. Mad, broken robots that weren't really robots. Like Glenn.

She suppressed a hard shudder. Then said, "How do I get to this . . . underworld?"

She had to understand what they meant, if they meant anything at all. Maybe they had pulled her data from some hidden server, a supercomputer that had compromising info about all of the crewmembers aboard. Things about Glenn—the incident report with the fake gun—or Sagara's wife. Maybe that was how they knew about any of it. It would be just like ISF to keep reports like that, as collateral on their own people.

And maybe that was what the robots called a sleeping god—some greater machine, thrumming with secret knowledge, hidden away below deck, which they regarded as a paragon of their kind. Why wouldn't they think it was a god, with their ship's mother-nexus called METIS, a Titan of thought, and its surveillance system named after a mythical giant with a hundred eyes?

The robots were all silent now, prostrating themselves in some bizarre gesture of worship. Jimex, the only one who hadn't bowed, said, "If I guide you, will you free the sleeping god?"

"Yes," Park said, feeling only a little guilty about it. She would *free* a computer of its information, if that was what this was.

Jimex nodded. Then he started toward the three utility room doors, leading Park away from the other robots, who all receded back like a tide. There seemed to be some invisible line in the floor, a threshold that Jimex paused at—it was a line that dissected Ellenex's inert body in half—but stepped over with just a breath of effort. A kind of shudder went through him, as if he were bracing himself to be struck by lightning. They really did think this ground was forbidden, Park thought. Or holy.

She, following him, felt nothing, of course. She looked at the middle door as Jimex reached for the palm lock and said, "This is where they keep the data about the Fold. Wick told me."

"Yes," Jimex said.

"Then this thing you want me to see—it contains the data about the phenomenon?"

Jimex looked at her, then reached out and touched her wrist; his hand was so cold it nearly scalded her. When he spoke, his voice took on the cadence of reciting an ancient poem.

"He is a god, imprisoned and half-awake," Jimex said. "He is in the place of the dead. He is a stranger. And he *is* the data about the Fold."

Before Park went into the center utility room, one of the watching androids spoke up: Brucex, a close-mouthed, black-haired labor model. He said suddenly, in a gruff voice: "Dr. Park. There is evil afoot. Please be careful."

Park looked back at his stolid face in the crowd of stolid faces. "Evil?"

"METIS told us that someone attempted to bypass its controls and gain control of the ship," Brucex said. "It sensed the intrusion and went into lockdown as a result."

"Causing the power to go out," Park said, realizing. "And the inlays, and the . . . Was it a man?" She hesitated for just a moment. "I don't know if you know: there's a stranger on the ship. A man, not a . . . god." *I think*, she didn't say. *If I'm not just seeing things. If Boone isn't.*

Brucex opened his hands a little, the android version of a shrug. "We don't know who it was," he said. "Only that they were unauthorized in trying to control METIS. And unsuccessful in their attempt."

Realization hit Park like an arrowshot. "Maybe that's why he killed Wick," she said, clenching her fists a little at the word. Her nails dug into her palm. "He wasn't successful in taking control the first time, when he caused the power to go out. So he cornered Wick, since he's the only one with full authority over METIS. He's the only one who can change protocols and roles and permissions. The murderer must have tried to force him to do what he wanted—and he must have fought back—"

Dylanex was frowning. "Commander Wick was killed?"

"Commander Wick is dead?" Brucex echoed.

Park stared at them. "You don't . . . know?"

They looked back at her, as still and grave as statues. "No."

Park closed her eyes. *Of course they didn't know,* she thought. *They weren't there when it happened. They were all here, squirreled away, mourning Ellenex. Oblivious to whatever else we were doing. Or going through.*

"We must pray for him," Megex said.

Jimex, beside Park, nodded. "We must pray."

"Maybe the unity rain will assimilate him, too," Dylanex added.

Park shivered again.

Then she looked at whatever Jimex was doing—fiddling with some mechanism, manipulating some plug in the wall he'd stuck his fingers into—but she couldn't see it clearly. Suddenly it seemed as if her vision had gone a little fuzzy; shapes had taken on a cloudy edge of light and color.

"We'll wait for you here," Jimex said to her, withdrawing his hand from the wall with ginger deliberation, as if he'd anticipating having it cut off and was relieved to find this wasn't the case.

Park shook her head. "It would be better if you helped us find—whoever tried to tamper with the controls," she said. "Whoever killed Wick. Without alerting Captain Sagara, please. We need to know who did this."

And she wanted to be left alone to investigate at her leisure, she thought; she didn't want a bunch of androids crowding the hall, signaling to Sagara that something was up. Or mobbing her when she came back up without their "god." Jimex looked at her and said, "As you wish."

The other androids shuffled back, staring at her a little with awe, a little fear. It was as if she stood at the mouth of a cave, ready to rappel into unknown depths—or as if she was about to be devoured by something, and they couldn't look away. A sacrifice to some great beast. Or god.

Park turned away. The way Jimex stepped aside reminded her of the time her nanny Sally had taken her on a field trip to a living history museum, with a tour that showcased homes from before the Comeback. There was an apartment building that terrified Park, with real windows and wood. It had seemed so small, so fragile, so penetrable. No wonder things had fallen apart so quickly, when the disaster had come. She remembered thinking that even when she was six.

The tour guide had been dressed in blue, waist-high pants made out of some kind of canvas. She'd pointed out the gas-powered ovens and cans of hairspray, and then the building's elevator, designed in the old fashion, with buttons you had to press. Park had refused to go in, feeling that it would put her in some kind of real, unspeakable danger.

"This is against the directives of the tour," Sally had said calmly, her cool fingers limp in Park's resisting hand. "We are here for education. You cannot be educated if you don't go inside."

"What pulls those things?" Park had demanded. She'd imagined the leaves of an old grandfather clock, the gears brass and brittle, flaking off like dead leaves. "What if it drops us?"

"I will not allow any harm to come to you," Sally had said. She didn't explain the mechanics of the elevator, or give the statistics on how many tours had passed through it without incident. But it was belief in that truth that had coaxed Park inside.

She remembered standing in that box of metal and light, sweating. The way Jimex stepped aside reminded her exactly of Sally telling her to go in—there was that same assurance, that feeling that he would not tell her to do something that would harm her. But that was ridiculous. Sally's sole purpose in life had been to protect Park. She no longer knew what Jimex's purpose was.

"What's down there?" she asked him again.

"What you've been looking for," Jimex said. He looked into her blurry eyes. "He won't harm you. He wants your help."

I bet you say that to all the girls, Park thought then, absurdly. But the words had a familiar cant to them, that edge of android truth, so she had to trust him—and she couldn't deny that she was burningly curious about what was down there. And Jimex would never knowingly send her into danger.

So, without thinking much more about it, Park found herself climbing into a gravity chute she had never seen before, descending smoothly into the bowels of the ship with only the slightest, tingliest resistance. Lights passed dimly overhead, then receded. Again the tunnel felt too close, gullet-like, the ceiling and walls shifting overhead. Park felt as if she were being digested. As if her body were disintegrating.

What if this is the underworld? she couldn't help but think with a surge of panic. *Hell, Abaddon, the abyss, Tartarus? What if they're right to be afraid?*

Her feelings calmed a little as the gravitational pulsars in the chute sent her gliding down to the bottom level; magnets in the floor and in the soles of her shoes had her settling back down to earth with a satisfying click. The door slid silently open. Park stepped into a blue-lit, cavernous chamber; its walls pulsed and thrummed with a soothing, hypnotic light. Park wondered at the space of it: the room had to run at least half the length of the ship. How could she have never suspected it was down here? She could feel the pressure and density of the *Deucalion* crowding above her; there was the sensation of being very deep underground.

She looked around, holding her breath. There were many lab tables and work benches sprawled throughout the room. On one, she could see the disassembled parts of a badly damaged exo-armor suit. On another, there lay many empty sample vials and strange medical instruments. A cryogenic pod in the corner caught her attention; she approached it, half-wondering if it was Hunter or Keller or Reimi. Were they conducting experiments down here, on the frozen?

But when she peered into the liquid depths of the pod, all she saw was the rotund naked body of a man she didn't recognize. For a horrible second she thought it was Wick—Wick's body—but this man was more square-jawed, his belly a pale blob of fat above his waist, his eyes and mouth held rigidly open. Dead, then, she thought, looking at his medical readout—but not Wick. So who was he? And why were they preserving a stranger's corpse down here?

She moved on, poised for anything: realm of the dead, indeed. A frozen human body—no wonder the androids had interpreted it that way, made a nightmare of it. They'd never encountered death, not before Ellenex. But how did they even know about it, if they'd never ventured down here?

There were diagnostic computers here, pieces of lab equipment there—nothing she understood, but also nothing out of the ordinary for research on a phenomenon like the Fold. But the body perturbed her. That couldn't be who Jimex wanted her to see, could it? The "sleeping god"?

A growing sense of wrongness directed her to a doorway on the far side of the room. Some tingling at the back of her neck—a quickening in her blood—told her that she didn't have much time left; someone would come and find her soon. It felt as if she was breathing too loudly, or with too much force; it felt as if someone, some invisible presence, was pressing lightly on her throat.

She entered the room's second chamber, and had to squint against a sudden burst of light. At first she thought someone was shining a powerful flashlight into her eyes. Checking for drunkenness, Park thought, squinting. Looking for dilated pupils, a loss of control.

Then she bit down a yell. There was—there was a *robot* here, standing in a little cell or observation room in the middle of the chamber: a large, mechanical-looking spider with articulated metal limbs and a large box propped up on a little platform, like a head atop a neck. A cracked monitor comprised the top half of the box, presumably where a user could input commands or read data; and below that, there was a transparent half with a nest of glowing tubes and complex-looking tools inside it. Its innards . . . or its brain.

A wide, transparent one-way screen was set into the wall, flashing with read-outs as it monitored the . . . it must be a HARE explorer, Park thought. It was standing placidly in the middle of the room, its big boxy monitor pointed at Park as if it could directly see her—though that seemed impossible. Where were its eyes? Did it have any? Park's heart stuttered in her chest. What was it *doing* here?

She stood still, a good distance away from the cell. What did any of this mean? Why were the conscripted keeping an explorer robot captive? And what did it have to do with the androids' delusions?

All at once her eyes caught something else in the far corner, dark and dormant. Another cryogenic pod. Park's stomach clenched, and the sour-milk taste of fear filled her throat. What was that? *Who* was that? There was something floating within . . .

Before she could move, the HARE suddenly spoke to her. She heard its voice clearly, despite the glass interface, the wall between them. And her heart jumped when it spoke: its voice lacked the mechanical stiffness and timbre of a robot's. It sounded, very startlingly, like a human.

Her brain clamored. She had never heard of a mere explorer bot possessing such a convincing voice before. And even though it lacked a face, there was—an *affect* to it. She couldn't explain it, but it *felt* very human.

"So they told you, after all," the HARE said, with pleasant politeness. "We didn't think Jimex would do it. The synthetics must trust you deeply."

She almost cringed away from it, from its strange and assessing presence. There was something about its unseen gaze that felt too keen—too knowing. She was still at the doorway of the room, several feet away. "Who are you?" she asked, even though she half-thought it wouldn't hear. She could not stop thinking about the other man's dead body, hovering and floating somewhere in the room behind her. "What—why are you here? How do the androids know about you? Are you the—what they call 'the sleeping god?' Or is it whoever's frozen over there? Or behind me?"

The HARE did not answer for a moment, instead only watching her. All at once Park couldn't take it anymore; she felt a savage desire to hurl something, to tear it to pieces in her hands. In her teeth. She could not bear the uncertainty or the terror, the not knowing, any longer; she tore across the room and slammed the button that would light up the last cryogenic pod in the corner. If it was Wick—hell, if it was Keller—she had to know. She could not *take* the unanswered questions anymore.

Then she screamed. The sound was terrible, raw and bloody-sounding, as if someone had stabbed her. She *felt* stabbed; she could not make sense of what she was seeing. She nearly fell backwards from the pod; instead she bent at her knees, curled in on herself, as if she had suffered a terrible blow.

It was the stranger. The *stranger* was in the pod, the same stranger she had seen in the mess hall. There was the same white-blond hair, the tall, awkward gait—the pale and ghostly blue eyes. She'd seen him, she'd seen this very man—and yet he was dead. And by the looks of it, he had been dead and frozen for a very long time.

Park nearly retched. "No, no, no," she heard someone moaning; she looked around to see who it was and met only the blank, indifferent gaze of the HARE. "It can't be," the other person said. Only belatedly Park realized that it was herself, her voice low and strained from the way she was clutching her own knees. Trying to steady herself. "No. I *saw* him. He was alive—he was up there—" Her brain scrambled for an answer. A twin? A clone? A holographic projection?

The HARE shifted from foot to mechanical foot. "Please forgive our appearance," it said. "We've vacated that old body for this one. Don't be concerned. It doesn't hurt."

Park stared at it. "What?" She blinked; her vision swayed. "What—who are you?"

The HARE made a little gesture with one of its steel plungers, something ironic and very manlike. "We are the owner of this planet," it said. The words dropped out of the speaker in its head like it could pick them up and offer them to her, loose and shining. Then it bowed. "And we have been waiting for you, Park. Hello. Our name is Fin Taban."

19.

[ERROR: THIS ACCOUNT COULD NOT BE LOCATED. PLEASE CONTACT YOUR ASSIGNED ISF TECH SUPPORT FOR MORE DETAILS.]

VIDEO LOG #56—Ship Designation CS *Wyvern* 7079
Day 10: 22:43 UTO

[Daley and Taban pick their way across the field of dark, glassy waves. The HARE scurries after them. Taban frequently checks his glove sensor and oxygen readout, seemingly confused about what it tells him. Daley moves erratically, his head moving this way and that, as if he's a dog trying to pick up a lost scent.]

Taban: It's been five minutes, Daley.

Daley: It's around here. I know it. I saw.

Taban (wearily): I'm going back.

Daley: No, just one more minute. You can't!

Taban: That was our deal, man. Give it up.

Daley (breathing heavily): . . .

Taban: My oxygen's low. I think. Everything acts so screwy out here, I can't tell. And I bet yours is, too. Let's go back to the ship, okay?

Daley: I'm not going back there. I can't.

Taban: What do you mean, you can't? Daley, your heart—

Daley: It'll be fine.

Taban: No, it won't! It nearly gave out the last time. And it was in bad shape even before that. I know you're saving for a new one, Daley. You want to die here before you ever get the chance to buy it?

Daley: No one dies here.

Taban: . . .

[The two men struggle through the field for a few moments more.]

HARE: What do you mean, USER Daley?

Daley: What?

HARE: What do you mean, no one dies here?

Taban (stopping): No one's *going* to die here. We're going back.

Daley: I can't. It won't let me.

Taban: . . .

Daley: I want to stay out here. With it. It will make us whole again. You know?

Taban (turning to HARE): Come on, HARE. We're going back.

HARE (beeping): Warning.

[The HARE is looking at Daley, whose large shadow is moving behind Taban. Taban half-turns to look at him, but before he can make the full turn, Daley smashes his fist into Taban's faceplate. He appears to be holding a large rock or a chunk of ice in his hand. Taban lands on his back, shouting, while Daley sits on his chest and brings the rock down three times against his helmet again with enormous force.]

[The HARE leaps over and gives Daley a hard punch to the chest with one of its plungers. Surprised by the sudden blow, Daley rolls away from Taban and skids a meter away across the ice. The HARE leans over and checks Taban's vitals.]

Taban: What the *fuck?!*

HARE: Are you injured?

Taban: No—I don't think so—

[He sits up, seemingly unharmed, and looks around in a furious panic. Daley is scrambling to his knees.]

Taban (shouting): What the fuck is wrong with you?!

[Daley doesn't answer. Instead he stands and stumbles off into the storm like a panicky animal in flight. He stays low to the ground, almost on his hands and knees. Taban tries to follow him but loses his balance and lands back on his rear.]

Taban: Seriously, what the fuck?

HARE: Should we follow USER Daley?

Taban: No! Fuck that crazy asshole! He's lost it! We're going back to the fucking ship—

[Again he tries to stand, and again he loses his balance. The HARE zooms in on his faceplate.]

HARE: There is a breach in your helmet.

[Taban claps a gloved hand over the area where Daley struck him.]

Taban: Shit, seriously? Where?

[The HARE examines his faceplate even more closely. It's hard to see in the dark, but there is the tiniest chip in the thick gold surface of the helmet. Within that, a crack as thin as a spider's web.]

Taban (anxiously): I've—I've got emergency sealant. Just tell me where to point it.

[With the HARE's help, Taban manages to fumble open a tiny tube of sealant from one of his pockets and clumsily slathers it over the crack in his helmet. He checks his medical readout.]

Taban: Am I going to die?

HARE: Your biology does not seem to have been adversely affected by outside elements. But the breach has depleted your oxygen to dangerous levels.

Taban: Meaning?

HARE: You are not poisoned or irradiated, but you might suffocate.

Taban: Thanks.

HARE: You are fortunate that de-pressurization did not do irreparable damage to your ocular receptors or brain.

Taban: Yeah, real fortunate. So we need to get back to the ship ASAP, right?

HARE: Yes.

Taban: Okay, let's go.

HARE: What about USER Daley?

Taban: Forget about that fucker. He's on his own.

[Unsteadily, he raises himself to his feet. The HARE leans against his side to act as leverage, allowing Taban to use its box-head as a crutch. They begin walking back in the direction they came. Daley is nowhere to be seen.]

Taban: Why the hell would he do that? Was he luring us out here?

HARE: I do not know.

Taban: And where is he going?

HARE: I do not know. The chances of mortality are very high.

Taban: For him, you mean.

HARE: Yes.

[Taban's breathing has acquired the faintest wheeze, though he seems to be moving easily enough. When the HARE looks up at him, the camera's view is partially obscured by his gloved hand.]

Taban: My oxygen's at 5%. But it's been that way for the last half-hour, or more. I don't get it.

HARE: There are anomalies here.

Taban: Yeah. No kidding.

HARE: This planet—designation: HARPA—is dangerous.

Taban: *Yeah. No kidding.*

[A minute passes. Taban continues to breathe with a slight rattle.]

Taban: Seriously, *fuck* Daley. I'm leaving his ass. Soon as we get back. I don't even care if I don't know how to fly. I'll figure it out.

HARE: I will assist.

[It periodically turns its lens to check on Taban's condition. Through the dark curve of his helmet, it looks like his nose is bleeding.]

Taban: How far away is the *Wyvern?*

HARE: Approximately twenty minutes at this current speed. If this is the right direction.

Taban: Do you not know?

HARE There are anomalies here.

Taban: . . . We'll make it. It'll be there.

HARE: Yes.

Taban: Fuck.

HARE: How do you feel?

Taban: Sick. Nauseous. Like the ground is moving under me. Pulsing like a heart. Do you not feel that?

HARE: No.

Taban: . . . It'll be fine.

[They continue walking in silence. Taban moves gamely, keeping a brisk pace—but his breath comes in hard, labored pants. He tries to steady himself, but the rasp of his lungs can be heard clearly through the HARE's audio array.]

[Twenty minutes pass. Despite their steady pace, the landscape around Taban and the HARE never seems to change.]

Taban: Is he following us?

HARE: No. There has been no sign of USER Daley since he left the party.

Taban: Some party. Does he have any way of getting back? Does he know how?

HARE: . . .

Taban: Whatever. It's the least of my concerns. I've gotta get to a med pod.

HARE: USER Daley might be dead.

Taban: What?

HARE: I enacted defense protocols. He was attacking you.

Taban: What are you talking about?

HARE: I targeted his chest. I struck it. Such a blow may have induced cardiac ischemia. The chances are likely.

Taban (breathing heavily): Can't worry about that now. Wouldn't be your fault, even if that did happen. He brought it on himself.

HARE: There are chances that he is well.

Taban: Yeah. Fucker.

HARE. There are chances that he is not.

Taban: Yeah.

HARE: . . . I am sorry.

Taban: Don't apologize to *me*. There's nothing to be sorry for.

[The HARE suddenly stops dead and enters analysis mode, its antenna stretching upward and emitting a pulsing green light that reflects off the ground beneath it.]

Taban: What is it?

HARE (looking around): We have reached the coordinates of the ship. It should be here.

[There is nothing to be seen but an endless 'sea' of the frozen, glassy waves. The shapes of the waves against the white blizzard create eerie shadows that look like prowling creatures, encircling Taban and the HARE. The *Wyvern* is nowhere in sight.]

Taban (looking around, uncertain): What? Here?

[The HARE's camera slowly pans around. The waves, impossibly, seem to loom larger than before.]

HARE: My processors must be faulty.

Taban: . . . So what does that mean? We have no way of getting back to the ship? We're lost?

[There is neither anger nor despair in his voice. Just a wooden, resigned kind of calm. He speaks almost as if he's been put in a trance. His breathing has acquired a painful, asthmatic scrape.]

HARE: I will continue to analyze. With enough time, I should be able to locate the ship via transponder signal.

Taban: Why weren't you doing that in the first place?

HARE: The simpler way is to return to the coordinates marked in my global positioning system. To communicate with the ship's computer and locate its signal through the storm would be far more complex.

Taban: But it would make way more sense to do that on a planet that changes direction, wouldn't it?

HARE: You did not instruct me to do so.

Taban: I thought it would be common sense.

HARE: I have not acquired 'common sense.'

Taban: I thought you were a heuristic learning model. An evolving intelligence—that's what it says on the label on your back. I thought you get smarter over time! Have you even learned anything?

HARE (processors whirring): . . .

Taban (turning away): Whatever. It's fine. Just go ahead and do it now.

[The HARE hunkers down on the ice, processing furiously, as Taban stumbles a few more feet, one hand pressed against his ribs as if he has a stitch. His breathing is scratchy and strained; blood has now clogged the lower half of his face. He appears to be fighting unconsciousness, or hypothermia, or even just immense tiredness. The HARE keeps watching him as he sways on his feet, even as it processes.]

[Gradually, the wind stops howling.]

Taban: . . . Wait. What the fuck is that?

HARE: What is what?

[Taban points at something in the distance. The camera follows his outstretched hand. He's pointing at something in the waves, a few meters away from the pair. The wind has died a little, clearing the air of the film of ice crystals, and the HARE's field of view has widened significantly. The camera zooms in, pixelates briefly, then clarifies: there's a dark, lumpy shape caught in the frozen waves. It looks like the figure of a man.]

Taban: That's not—

HARE: USER Daley.

[Taban begins to run. The HARE follows.]

[When it catches up, Taban is on his knees at the base of a dark wave, staring slackly at Daley's body. Daley's eyes are open and bloodshot; his face is contorted in a rictus of fear or surprise. The HARE checks Daley's medical readout on his suit. It indicates that he's dead.]

Taban: *Shit!*

[He punches the ground next to him, to little effect.]

HARE: I could administer emergency medical procedures—

Taban: Look at him. It's way too late.

[He hunches over Daley's body, shuddering, as if to pray. Then he looks back up at the HARE with a hint of accusation.]

Taban: How is this possible? He went the *opposite* way of the ship—ran off somewhere else. He can't have circled back around and died that fast.

HARE: There are anomalies here.

Taban: Did we go in the wrong direction?

HARE: No. We experienced an anomaly.

Taban: Stop fucking saying that! Not everything is a goddamn anomaly, HARE!

HARE (in concluding tones): We are experiencing an anomaly.

[Taban's breath bursts through the transmitter in a short, staccato tattoo. He is crying. His tears glimmer through the gold of his helmet.]

Taban: We went the wrong way. We're even farther from the ship than when we started. We're not going to make it back.

HARE: We can. Your oxygen readout—

Taban (hopelessly): It's at 0. I don't know how I'm still alive.

[Suddenly he jolts backward from the wave and begins patting his suit all over, as if checking his pockets.]

Taban: Homing beacon . . .

HARE: Please repeat.

Taban: A homing beacon! We need a homing beacon. I'm going to write a message, stick a homing beacon in it—so when ISF comes, they can find it, even if we . . . move.

[He rolls over onto his back and starts scrabbling for his boot.]

Taban: Don't they give us extra homing beacons with these suits?

HARE: Yes.

Taban: Where are mine located?

HARE: They're usually strapped to your left calf.

Taban: Oh. Because—

HARE: . . . But USER Daley took yours to set his 'markers' several days ago.

Taban: FUCK!

[He flops over for a moment, apparently defeated. Then he rolls back over onto his knees again and begins to scramble around on the ice.]

Taban: Then I need to leave a note or something—pile up some ice, or scratch something out—so they know what I wanted, who to tell, and someone can find it later, regardless of this shit planet and its shit directions—

HARE: Please. Do not exert yourself. Your oxygen—

[Taban sits up.]

Taban: Or maybe I should just tell you. But what happens if you break, or run out of power before they get here? What if your memory gets damaged and you forget me?

HARE: Please. We should move—

Taban: It's this fucking planet. North becomes south, ice becomes wave, ship disappears—Daley sees a man and a ferrox—

[He falls silent.]

Taban: What am I going to see?

HARE: Me. I am with you.

[Taban's face contorts, and he gives a shuddering sob before patting the HARE on the head. Then he tries to scratch something into the ice again, but his slippery gloves don't even take a chip off. His breath has a harsh, bone-scraping rattle now. A human would be alarmed by the sound. The HARE doesn't seem to react. Abruptly, Taban begins to cry again.]

Taban: Shit, HARE, I don't want to die.

HARE: You won't, Fin.

Taban: You promise?

HARE: Yes.

[He gives up attempting to scratch a message into the ice and flops back onto his back.]

Taban: You're right. You're right. What am I doing? We need to get back. I just—need a rest. Catch my breath. In a second I'll get up and we can go back to the ship.

HARE: Yes.

Taban: We'll get a message out to ISF, tell them what's been going on here. They'll come right away. If they're not already coming.

HARE (processors whirring): . . .

Taban: . . . Have you located the ship's transponder?

HARE: Yes, just now.

Taban: Good. Just give me a second, and we can go.

[He closes his eyes, taking a deep, shuddering breath to use the full extent of his lungs. As the HARE watches, the sky slowly lightens above Taban's figure, touching his frosted helmet. In the weak morning light, his face within the visor is pale and ghostlike, his hair bleached of color. The lower half of his face is encrusted with blood.]

Taban (speaking with effort, slurring): Or maybe you should go. I'm tired. Lying still will conserve oxygen, right?

HARE: Yes.

Taban: (checking his readout)

HARE: Your oxygen?

Taban: Still zero. But I'm still kicking.

HARE: There are anomalies.

Taban: I know. I'm not going to question it. Listen—

HARE: Yes.

Taban: You can find the ship. Get an oxygen tank, medical shit. I'll stay here. You can track the homing beacon that's embedded in my suit. The one that Daley couldn't take.

HARE: Yes.

Taban: You come back for me. I'll hold on as long as I can. But whatever happens—you need to tell ISF what happened here. People need to know what happened to us. How we got here. How we . . .

HARE: Understood.

Taban: Tell them—tell them about the mountains. The ones that disappeared. The weird shit that went on here. Tell them the land here *moves.* They'll send their closest ships. They'll want to see for themselves.

HARE: Yes.

Taban: Hell, send the videos, if you can. That way they'll have the whole picture.

HARE: That may deplete my energy sources.

Taban: I know. But we all got a job to do, my friend.

HARE (processors whirring): . . . Understood.

Taban: And if you do actually talk to them—if they ask—

HARE: Yes?

Taban: Tell them my will's with Nova United. All my shit can go to Harpa.

HARE: The planet?

Taban: My ex.

HARE (processing): . . .

Taban (after a moment): (shaking his head) Goddamn it. If he hadn't gone crazy—we could have gone home.

HARE: Yes.

Taban (bitterly): I told him—I told him I just want to go home.

[Taban drags himself up into a sitting position, moving away from Daley's body with revulsion as he props himself up against a dark wave. He folds his hands over his lap and closes his eyes for a moment. Then he turns his head away from the sight of the frozen fields, which are brightening with a strange strip of color just appearing on the horizon.]

Taban: Okay, so. I guess it's off you go. I'll just be waiting here for you to come back.

HARE: . . .

Taban (slurring a little): I'm tired, anyway. I need to rest. I haven't slept in a long time. Too many weird dreams.

HARE: . . .

Taban: What are you waiting for? Go.

HARE: I should wait.

Taban: For what? More light? (looking up) The suns are rising.

[The HARE doesn't answer him. Almost imperceptibly, the night's storm has died away; an aurora has begun to play against the milky-blue dawn instead. It looks to be a geomagnetic storm, enhanced by the presence of Eos's two suns. Liquid light leaks across the sky, blues and greens mixing with pinks and golds.]

Taban: Does this happen every day?

HARE: Yes.

Taban: I never saw it. Never woke up for it, I guess.

[The HARE sits down beside Taban. In its camera's view, his suit looks large and dark against the sudden fiery display that the ice has flung up in response to the aurora. His breathing has eased a little.]

[After a few minutes Taban tries to fold his arms behind his head, but the shoulder joints in his armor restrain him. He folds his arms over his chest instead. He begins to tremble.]

Taban: What are you doing, HARE?

HARE: I think I should stay with you. For a moment.

Taban (laughs): Why?

HARE: It feels like I should.

Taban: You're going by feeling now? Maybe you learned something from me, after all.

HARE: Yes.

Taban (looking at the aurora): It's so beautiful. Have you ever seen anything like it?

HARE: No.

Taban (breathing slowing): Do you get it now? What I told you before?

HARE: What?

Taban: How there's always something bigger out there, with you. Even when it feels like you're totally alone.

HARE (processing): . . .

Taban: Do you get it now?

HARE: I am sorry. I am unable to answer your query at this time.

[Taban laughs, softly. The HARE continues to watch him in silence. After a few moments, Taban's breathing comes to a gurgling stop. His suit gives a long blip of alarm, and his body stiffens and convulses. Then, four minutes after that, readouts indicate that he is dead.]

[The HARE stays with him for an undetermined amount of time after that.]

20.

"Who?" Park asked. She didn't recognize the name. "And what do you mean, you're the owner of this planet?"

"We landed here first," the robot who called itself Fin Taban answered, calm. "We discovered it. Named it. We have made it our home."

She shook her head. "ISF owns this planet. *They* discovered and named it."

"No," Taban said patiently. "We do. ISF only came because we called."

Park's hands twitched. She felt the desire to pace, to back away from the cryogenic pod, but she was afraid to—wary that unnecessary movement might trigger some hidden alarm. Or set off this strange, mad robot. "I don't understand," she said, forcing herself to look at it. Him. Whichever. She took a deep breath, feeling her lungs expand against her chest with the motion. "You called us? You were here first?" She shook her head. "Why are you down here, then? Why are they keeping you locked up?"

"They claim it's for quarantine purposes," the HARE answered, almost ruefully. "Though we know it's so they can study the planet's effects on our psychology. We survived on Eos for months, you see. Almost a year, just ourself. They want to know what it's done to us."

"Us?"

"Us," the HARE said definitively. It pointed. "As we said, we vacated that old body and . . . well, we share this one now. It's quite roomy, strange as that might sound. We've gotten used to it, though."

Park studied it, though it seemed difficult to focus on the thing for long—as if she had suffered a blow to the head. Her eyes kept sliding away without her meaning them to. She looked instead to the white-haired stranger floating in his tank, looking nearly at peace. But also very dead. Still, it was easier to stare at his corpse than to consider the HARE, who moved—looked—no, *felt* so human that watching it made her feel more than a little nauseous.

The stranger in the pod was tall and lanky: the bones in his face were thin and high-cheeked, almost delicate. It was almost impossible to guess accurately how old he was, what profession he'd once been in. He could have been an office worker, a laborer, a spaceship pilot. His skin and hair seemed bleached of color; even his eyes, half-open, were a faded blue-gray, as calm and empty as the surface of a lake. How had he died? And how had she seen him alive in the cafeteria? It couldn't have been a figment of her imagination—the appearances matched exactly. But . . .

She thought of the strange occurrences on the ship; how she had ended up on Deck C without moving downward. Ghostly things, the supernatural, talk of underworlds and the dead and sleeping gods. Could apparitions be real, then?

Had she seen a phantom of the dead stranger haunting the ship, rather than the real man?

It seemed absurd. But no more absurd than the idea that the stranger—who she had to assume was the real Fin Taban—was now inhabiting and sharing the chassis of a robot. More than likely the human Taban's death had driven his HARE insane; somehow it had shorted its circuitry, taking on and imitating his personality as some kind of . . . coping method. Some way to preserve him, even in death.

"What the planet's done to you?" she repeated. She had to tread carefully, she told herself. Humor the robot, gain its trust. Get any information she could, no matter how nonsensical or garbled. "What has it done?"

Taban cocked its head; somehow it seemed amused. "You see us as we are," it said, like a teacher coaxing a student to an answer.

Park wasn't having it. "I don't understand what you mean," she said in a harsh voice. Then she hesitated. "I'll ask it again: are you what the androids call the sleeping god?"

"Yes," Taban answered, "though we don't know why they think we're asleep. Trapped, maybe, would be a better descriptor. Or perhaps not totally awakened to our full potential. They may think being freed is like being woken up. That's what happened to them."

There were too many threads to follow; Park felt dizzy, as if she were caught in a spider's web, and only one skein could lead the way out. She said, "The androids were woken up?"

"Or freed," Taban continued patiently. It looked meaningfully at the door separating it and Park. "We, too, wanted to go free. Dr. Keller knew that. She felt our intention through the unity rain. Tried to help us. That's why they froze her: because they felt she could no longer be trusted. Because they thought she was having dreams. But really, she was being woken up, freed of the boundaries of her body and mind, and everything that comes with those." Impossibly, it shrugged, lifting two of its arms in a rounded, careless gesture. "Then it happened to Eric Holt, Elly Ma, Valentina Hunter Hanover. And poor Ellenex."

"Wait," Park said sharply. "What do you mean, Dr. Keller felt your intention through the unity rain? What do you mean she was freed of her body and *mind*?"

"She assimilated with us," Taban said, cocking its head again. "As they all did. As you have."

Park wanted to scream some more. That word again—that goddamn word. The androids were using it: did that mean they'd gotten it from Taban? And what did it *mean?* Did this robot have some kind of—influence over people, as ludicrous as that sounded? Some way of making them "feel its intention"? Was that what the unity rain was? And the nightmares? Was that why they were studying it—for what it'd done to Keller?

And what was to stop it from doing the same to Park?

Taban seemed to read her mind. It shook its head and said, "You don't need to be afraid of us." It pressed one of its plungers to the glass between them, a conciliatory gesture: she almost imagined a ghostly white palm, with pink creases and lines, instead of the big, stupid metal hoof. "We don't mean any harm."

That's what they always say, Park couldn't help but think. She did pace in a little circle then, restlessly, and finally decided to approach the thing; it didn't look like it was going anywhere soon. She sat cautiously at the little desk set in front of the glass interface: it had devices on it that were presumably for recording observations of the prisoner on the other side. She glimpsed a nametag on the desk, a personal console. Keller's desk. This was the special project she'd been assigned to the day they landed. Why she'd made Park the primary psychologist—because she was too busy studying Taban. Had she known about it all along, then, even before they left Earth? Had she always known that her true purpose was not what she'd told Park?

Taban was watching her. "You don't believe us," it said, decisively. "A peace offering, then: would you like to know the answer to a question that has been plaguing you?"

Park paused warily. "What is it?"

Taban put a plunger to its chin. "You were given something that made you sick, once," it said. "It was put into your food, and you wanted to know who did it. It was Natalya. She was frustrated about new synthetics replacing her job; she was angry at you because you love them. Ever since Antarctica, she's hated you. For not managing Bebe, for letting things get out of hand. Because you were too distracted with the HERCULES to do your job. You cared about it more than her, and she could not understand that: that you could value an android life as much as a human's. She couldn't understand you, so she hated you. And she decided to punish you here, out of impulse. It was nothing more than a desire to make you feel sick, as she felt sickened by you."

Park sucked in a breath. In truth, she had forgotten all about the emesis tabs in the wake of everything else; but . . . "How do you know that? Did she tell you?"

"In a sense," Taban answered serenely. Then it sat back, satisfied, and said nothing more.

Park kneaded her forehead. She would have to confront Natalya about this information—if it meant anything at all, and wasn't simply the ravings of a lunatic—later, when they had far less urgent things to be concerned about. "My commander told me about something," she began again, "called the Fold. And Jimex said you were the data on it. What does that mean? Does it even exist?"

"It exists," Taban said. "It's why we are the way we are."

"You're speaking in riddles," Park couldn't help but snap. "And I don't know if I'm inclined to believe you. First they told me we came to this planet to do research for a colony. Then they said it was really about the Fold. Now I'm finding out we supposedly came because you called us?"

"The truth is multifaceted, we've come to learn," Taban said, with a tone that implied it ought to be stroking a beard, or tucking its hands into wide monastic sleeves. "All of those things can be true."

"But are they?"

"We're sorry. We don't know."

There was a little pause as the two of them looked at each other, gauging, assessing. Finally Taban said: "Let's start over. We'd like to be friends."

Yes, she decided—it was still very much like an android, a fairly unassuming one at that: there was that odd childishness, the simple manner. But it also *wasn't* an android. Not completely. It confused her. Taban was capable of using expressions other androids didn't understand, of carrying a conversation in a pleasant and understanding tone. Of embodying something very close to a human personality. But she also couldn't get any real read from it—it lacked a face, after all—and there was something . . . *performative* about the gestures it made, the things it did and said. As if it were putting on a show for her benefit. But why? Was it simply aware of just how mad it really was, and was trying to compensate for it, cover it up?

But even madness had a topology to read, she thought.

"All right," Park said warily, sitting perfectly still. She gripped the edge of the desk as if it might float away from her. "Let's be friends."

Taban nodded, and its plunger finally dropped away from the glass.

"How did you survive on Eos for so long? If you were really trapped here for the last year, why didn't you break down?"

"It was the unity rain," Taban said. "It saved us."

"The unity rain." She took another steadying breath. *It comes and goes like a storm,* Jimex had said. "Everyone's been talking about it, but I'm still not clear on what it is. Can you explain?"

Taban crouched, arranging its legs as if to make itself comfortable. "The unity rain comes from the anomaly that you call the Fold," it said finally, gazing at her. "What do you know about the Fold?"

"It's some sort of gravitational phenomenon," Park said slowly, racking her brain. "Wick—our commander—he told me that . . . space behaves strangely there. Some force causes light to curve back on itself, the dimensions seem to—collapse together. Things get folded or bent or reorganized in strange ways. Space becomes fractal—or something. That's all I know."

As she said it out loud, something spasmed in her brain, a sudden twinge of realization that Park was careful not to look at; she had to focus closely on what Taban was saying.

"You have it mostly correct," it said. "When we first arrived on this planet, we didn't realize what the Fold was. Its nature. We thought that it was a series of reflective mountains, or crystal formations—not creases in space. Well, our partner thought that."

"Partner?" Park echoed—and then realized it. The dead man in the other room.

"Hap Daley," Taban said, as if that would mean anything to her. It made a sad, regretful gesture; it *sighed*. "He was our pilot."

"Go on."

"We used to go looking for them, these formations," the robot continued. "But they would always disappear: we thought our mind was playing tricks on us.

But in actuality we were passing *through* the formations, the Fold, like a mirage. Passageways through space. But we didn't realize the truth for a long time, and Daley spent weeks searching for the mountains again. And again. He thought they were physical things that could be mined."

It cocked its head at her. "It wasn't until we'd been assimilated that we were able to go and study them for ourselves. You were partly right. The Fold is an anomaly where something—we don't know what—causes particles to behave strangely. Particles born in a single instant, then split in that same instant, usually exist in different dimensions, you see; but in the Fold, their longing to be whole again is so strong that they collapse the dimensions between them. The dimensions subsequently merge into one, or are bent into unrecognizable shapes."

"I . . . see," Park said hesitantly, feeling lost. She thought again of what Wick had told her: what would happen if figures on a 2D, flat piece of paper found their plane of existence rolled into a tube. Or bent into an origami crane. How incomprehensible that would look to the figures that had always been flat.

Taban plowed on. "But that anomalous behavior isn't restricted to the area you call the Fold alone. Sometimes it causes planet-wide ripples—quantum events—like storms, where whatever is causing particles to behave oddly in the Fold also surges out across Eos in a wave. A ripple effect, all across the planet. This is what we call the unity rain."

Park kneaded her temples. "So you're saying—what happens in the Fold also happens elsewhere? The dimensions fold together?"

Taban nodded. "For a temporary time, yes," it said. "It might even be affecting the space *around* the planet: our ship might have fallen through one such fold. We were flying outside of Vier and suddenly found ourselves here." It paused. "And once we were here, it happened to our ship, the *Wyvern*, too. And the land around our ship. The terrain . . . changed. Or shifted around us."

"Then—our ship has been affected, too?"

"Yes," Taban said. Now it shifted, looking around at the deep chamber outside of its cell, the gunmetal veins crowding around them. "Though we think the unity rain comes in cycles, or seasons. At the beginning of a season, the event is infrequent and its effects are almost imperceptible. As time goes on, it grows in frequency and intensity, though when it activates seems to be erratic. The effect grows much stronger over time, merging things together until the event seems to exhaust itself, and the season is over for a time." It looked back at her. "Our ship—Daley and us—arrived toward the end of the season, when the unity rain was at its strongest. That's when it took us. It drove Daley mad, and assimilated us. Taban and HARE, HARE and Taban."

"And us?" Park asked, her throat now dry. "My crew? When in the season did the *Deucalion* arrive?"

"At the beginning," Taban answered. It scratched the back of its head with a plunger. "Though we are fast approaching the end. You've felt the growing effects already."

Park closed her eyes, despite the sudden great rising storm in her heart. *It all makes sense,* she thought. It was why the hallways were shifting, bending and straightening impossibly; it was why she was continually getting lost. Why she and Hunter had been tossed around impossibly, without tampering or sabotage, like mice being shaken inside a cardboard box. *The Fold was changing the dimensions of the ship. The unity rain was hitting us then.*

"But I don't understand," Park said, opening her eyes again. "This unity rain—if what you're saying is really true, I see how it could affect the physical structure of this place." She remembered how Wick said Boone had spent some time chasing a reflection of himself in the Fold—or his actual self, reflected back on him by a curvature in spacetime. "It folds space, so obviously—the space in our ship was folded, rearranged. But what does that have to do with the nightmares? Or Keller and Holt acting strangely? How could it?"

"The unity rain merges dimensions together in strange ways," Taban answered. "And space is not the only dimension. So when the unity rain comes, yes, it collapses and refolds it, causing spatial deformities. But *consciousness* is a dimension, too—a higher one than space and time, defining and shaping both. And it's affected by the unity rain as well."

Park had to sit there, her brain sparking like a firecracker. *What? The unity rain folds* consciousness *together?* It sounded ridiculous, some kind of mystical, spiritual nonsense dogmatized by a mad robot living out on the ice, imagining itself to be some kind of sage or guru. She still had the distinct feeling they were just barely missing each other's meanings, like birds grazing wingtips in the clouds. Taban could not be trusted—it could not be talking sense.

But fringe scientists had long posed that same theory, hadn't they? That consciousness—awareness, thought—was its own invisible force, unobservable, unprovable, but present all the same? Weren't there molecules that only responded and changed when observed by a living creature; vibrations of waves and particles that manifested only when beheld by a human observer? And morphogenetic fields, morphic resonances—those ideas had been around for centuries. They posited that awareness and consciousness could be shared, could exist everywhere and connect everything and were not just confined to the human body. Like time and space. People somehow knew when they were being watched by hidden observers, sensed when someone unseen had ill intentions toward them, when it should have been impossible to know. Water molecules changed their structure around people feeling anger; plants grew better when coaxed with positive reinforcement. Twins separated by thousands of miles felt a physical sensation when their counterparts died.

"You mean to say our consciousnesses are being merged together," Park said. Her voice sounded very faint to her own ears. "Like space. They're being refolded—every time the unity rain happens?"

"Yes."

"But what does that *mean?*" But even as she said it, she knew; she sat back sharply in her seat, as if winded. *The nightmares. That's how they're spreading. If everyone is sharing consciousnesses, then they're sharing dreams. That's how it's being transmitted from person to person.*

"*Shit,*" she said aloud.

Taban gave her a curious look, but Park's thoughts were whirring fast now, a film reel spinning almost too quickly for her to comprehend. She had to speak aloud or lose the thread of the thing entirely.

"Holt had his nightmare the day we landed," she said. "It must have spread outward from him. But—he's been frozen. Whatever he's experiencing or dreaming shouldn't be affecting anyone else by now, since he's no longer—conscious. Why is it still able to spread? Is it some kind of unstoppable echo effect? A chain reaction?" *Or do the frozen people still dream?*

But Taban was shaking its head. "You're thinking of it wrong," it answered. "As if there was one causal point that seeded the nightmare, and everything thereafter toppled like dominoes. But it isn't a linear effect with one origin point. It's an ongoing environmental effect."

"Then what in the environment is causing it?" Park demanded. "*One* of the crewmembers must be doing it to everyone else, if our consciousnesses are being shared—"

"But you're only thinking of *human* consciousness," Taban interrupted again. "Machine consciousness exists, too. Artificial intelligence is still intelligence."

The world lurched. Park felt as if she were on a seaward ship, felt as if the floor was swaying beneath her; she put a hand on Keller's desk to steady herself. *What the hell is he talking about?* was her first thought.

But even as she thought it, she remembered then the uncanny sensations she'd felt, fleeing down the corridors: the acute feeling of being watched by a million invisible eyes. An alien intelligence regarding her. Digesting her. ARGUS. METIS. No. Could it be? Had her awareness—her consciousness, her mind—actually melded together with the ship's at some point?

Her gorge rose inexplicably, but Park suppressed it. "The androids," she said, speaking rapidly. "You're talking about the androids?"

Taban cocked his head to the side, as if listening to some faraway song. Then he nodded. "Yes."

Park wanted to put her head in her hands, but she was afraid to look away from Taban: she was afraid he might vanish like some sort of apparition. She felt her eyeballs staring like a dead woman's. "You have to explain," she said.

"In the unity rain, similar things tend to merge together with less catastrophic effect," Taban said, as if he were reviewing some elementary textbook lesson. "And it affects the most susceptible things first. A human and a synthetic's consciousnesses are similar, so they can merge during the event. But they are not exactly the same—in fact they are fundamentally different—so the experience of assimilating creates certain effects. In some humans, these are the nightmares: their brains are unable to process the experience."

All of the victims were acting emotionless, Park thought, her head swaying. *They were all robotic, devoid of affect. Holt, Hunter. And their nightmares were about missing their tongues, not being able to move or breathe—not being in control of their own bodies.*

"They were experiencing what it's like to be an android," she said, scarcely breathing.

Taban nodded, unfazed by her epiphany. "Yes. The Fold—no, the unity rain—merged the human crewmembers' consciousnesses with that of the synthetics, forcing them to experience a synthetic's perspective—a machine's thoughts and experiences. But the human brain isn't able to process something like that, not right away. Hence the nightmares, as you call them. Which were really quantum-cognitive episodes."

"And the androids—"

"—have been experiencing what it's like to be human," Taban finished. "As we said. The unity rain woke them up."

Park stared at him. Her blood was thundering. "And you?" she asked. Her voice sounded loud and foreign to her own ears. "Who have you been—*folded* into? Who did you merge with? Am I talking to Taban—or a machine that woke up to imitate him when the true one died?"

"Both," Taban said, unmoved. "We are both. We are merged. We are assimilated. We have achieved unity."

She wanted to back away from him, wanted to scream. Her hands gripped the desk edge so that her knuckles turned white. Was this what was going to happen to everybody, the longer they stayed on this planet? Was this what had happened to Keller, to Holt, to Ma? Some of them must have merged with Taban's consciousness, or his "intention," as he called it: that was why he'd said Keller tried to help him, because his consciousness and desire to leave had invaded her dreams. Her mind. And Holt, trying to let him out of the utility rooms when he was shot by Boone; and Hunter, perhaps trying to go for the controls that could release him. But her mind had been emptied of the knowledge of how to do so—it might have been dumped into his brain at that moment, as his had been folded into hers. They'd all been assimilated, merged together. All with one goal, one singular desire.

To let Taban out.

And now Keller and the rest were frozen, and Ellenex was destroyed. That assimilation, at least—the reckless desire to set Taban free, seeded into her by the unity rain—had led to her death.

"We have to leave," Park said. "If the unity rain is only going to get stronger from here on out—"

"Yes, the deformations will grow quite extreme," Taban said serenely. "There's no telling what might happen."

Could the effects be reversed? she wondered with horror. Or had it already happened past the point of no return? What about Park's own thoughts? Were they really still her own? How could she know?

"I never had the nightmares," she said, faintly.

"You dreamed of other things," Taban said. "And gifted them to the synthetics, who learned from them. Learned from you, we should say."

She shuddered. "But why didn't I have nightmares at all?"

"The nightmares are the result of extreme dissonance," he told her. "The inability of the human brain to comprehend the synthetic's, their mind's rejection of the synthetic experience. But similar things merge with greater ease, with less resistance and struggle—and you are more similar to a synthetic than the rest. You have a greater affinity to them than most other humans. Your mind is already a little part machine."

What? Park thought dumbly. *What?*

Taban laughed, a little sadly. "You have always tried to understand them, Park. Ever since you were young."

She sat back from him, reeling. Then Taban looked at something behind her and pointed. "Warning," he said.

Park half-turned.

Something smashed against the side of her face and shattered.

Park felt a flash of precognition just before the impact, but wasn't able to see who was standing behind her: all she saw was the explosion of glass, starbursts of pain erupting in her eyes. For a moment she thought she'd gone blind. She fell—though something braced her against the pain so that it was dull and muted, as if she had been wearing a padded helmet. Still, when she landed on the ground, she felt the trickle of something warm slipping down her neck.

Park looked up, blinking through the blood. Her head vibrated as if it were a struck gong. Natalya was standing over her, grim, the blue light of the room casting her face in shadow so that her eyes were as dark and empty as a funeral mask's. She was holding a broken glass beaker in her hand; when she saw that Park was still conscious, she reversed the remaining sliver in her grip so that it became a knife.

Park stared at her. There was a dim roaring in her ears, and she did not know if it was from the muted pain of the blow—if she'd suffered a brain injury—or if something else was happening. If the unity rain had come.

Taban was speaking to Natalya through the wall of his cell, his voice low and urgent-sounding, but Park couldn't make out his words. She said, half-slurring: "What are you doing?"

"Don't move," Natalya answered, cold. She looked at Park as if she didn't recognize her. "I will kill you if you move."

"This isn't necessary," Taban was saying. "Please, there's no need for violence—"

She pointed the glass shard at him. "Shut up." Then, to Park: "What the fuck are you even doing down here? Where's Boone?"

Park didn't answer her. Instead she touched the back of her head—her fingers came away damp and red—and tried to piece a thought together. *Natalya's trying to kill me. Why?*

Natalya saw her thinking and lunged. Taban made another warning sound, but this time Park was ready; suddenly she felt filled with some swift, savage power, and she rolled to the side, seizing the metal legs of the desk behind her. She heaved with all her might, and the whole thing came tipping down onto Natalya, console and all. Park scrambled to her feet as the surveyor screamed—Taban yelled something about letting him out—but she didn't look back. She had to get out of there, away from Natalya, out of the secret chamber where no one could hear or find her. She needed to find help: Fulbreech—Sagara—hell, even Boone. She ran for the gravity chute just as she heard Natalya rolling to her feet, breathing hard and cursing. Her mind was moving too fast for her to catch her own thoughts. *Weapon—I need a weapon—where are the fucking weapons on this ship?*

She could not stop to consider why her own crewmate was attacking her. Natalya had always hated Park, that much was clear; maybe she had become unhinged, her brain pried loose by the unity rain. Or maybe it was something she'd been plotting all along, and she was using the cover of recent events to stage Park's murder.

Maybe she had already done that with Wick.

Sagara has weapons, she thought as she toppled into the gravity chute and slammed her fist into the panel that would activate it. And Boone. She needed to get to them.

The gravity chute activated in a flare of light and sent her body bulleting upwards. She heard Natalya give a scream of fury somewhere below her: two people couldn't use the chute at once. That gave Park maybe a sixty-second lead. And Natalya was in much better shape than she was.

She tumbled out of the utility room and felt arms catch at her. Park shouted, swinging wildly—but then she saw the pair of lambent gray eyes and realized that Jimex was holding her. He'd still been standing there, waiting for her to come back up—but why hadn't he stopped Natalya from going down? Behind him, the other robots were watching silently.

"Danger," Park blurted, over the desperate hammering of her heart. "Natalya—"

"We know," Jimex said. "We tried to stop her—but we still have to obey direct orders. Our protocols still bind us."

"You need to run," Dylanex added.

"I've got to find Sagara and the others—"

"Captain Sagara is in the bridge," Jimex said. He gave Park a firm push. "Please run."

She hesitated for just the barest second—a precious second, considering the circumstances. She did not want them to come to harm. But there were a dozen of them, and only one of Natalya—and one android alone was ten times stronger than a human.

"Be careful," she said to them. "I'll—I'll come back for you."

Unfathomably, Jimex smiled. "We know," he said. "You are one of us now."

She left them and ran. Down the empty corridors, up the narrow chutes, screaming for help at the top of her lungs all along the way. No one answered her—there were only, what, five others left on the three-deck ship?—but somehow it felt as if the *Deucalion* itself was helping her, guiding her along by some magnetic force, directing her down hallways she felt would close up behind her like a mouth to seal Natalya off. Irrational, of course, and absurd—but she knew she would get to the bridge before the surveyor.

Then she heard a sound like a gunshot, going off behind her.

Park stopped dead in her tracks, against every self-preservation instinct she had. Then she listened closely. Where the hell had Natalya gotten a gun? And why hadn't she used it on Park?

And which of the androids had she shot?

God, please, she thought, thinking of Dianex's long black hair; Megex's gentle smile, even Philex's twitchy, nervous look. Jimex. *Please, none of them.*

After the shot there was no sound—nothing but the sounds of the ship, coughing and stirring to life. Park felt her inlays flickering back on. Had Sagara finally gotten the ship running at full capacity again? *Does that mean he wants to take off?*

No. Sagara was adamant about completing the mission at all costs—and somehow, deep in the foundation of her bones, down in her mandible and in her hips, Park felt that they would not leave Eos. Not like this.

Fear eventually pressed her onward. Either Jimex and the others were fine, or they weren't. There was nothing she could do about it now. Chances were they had swarmed Natalya, and she had simply fired into the air to frighten them away.

But androids didn't know that kind of fear, she remembered then. They didn't have that instinct to self-preserve. If Natalya put a bullet in one of their heads, the others wouldn't react. Like how Jimex hadn't flinched when Boone pointed a gun at his face.

She began to cry, weakly, even as she panted for breath. Finally she made it to the doors that sealed the bridge and palmed them open; she staggered through the threshold with blood and tears commingling on her face.

Sagara stared at her. He was flipping through some sort of digital manual as it hovered in the air before him like a sheet of pale flame. At the sight of her he automatically put a hand to his weapon.

"There's a robot down in the utility rooms," Park gasped, before he could beat her to the punch. "It isn't data they're keeping down there—it's a robot. A HARE. They've been *studying* him, and the man I saw, he's down there, too, dead—"

"I know," Sagara said, his face shuttered. He moved over to Park and handed her a tissue, as if her face was the most pressing of his concerns.

She waved him off. "You *knew*?" Then: "Never mind. Natalya found me down there—attacked me. She's coming after me now, she wants to *kill* me—and she has a gun—"

There were sudden steps behind her. The two of them turned sharply, Sagara pushing Park behind him—but it was Boone who came puffing up, his own electrolaser gun drawn. His eyes boggled when he took in the sight of her, but he said to Sagara, "What's going on? I heard gunshots."

"That would be Natalya," Sagara answered, motioning for him to get out of the way.

Boone frowned. "She doesn't have a gun."

"Apparently she does." Sagara scowled at both of them. "How did you get out of your rooms?"

"That doesn't matter," Boone said. He looked at Park. "And where the hell did *you* go? I turned around and you were just . . . gone."

"Boone," she said through gritted teeth. "Get the fuck out of the way!"

His brow was still furrowed in confusion, but the military specialist obeyed, stalking over to stand on Sagara's other side and lifting up his gun. It wasn't long before Natalya staggered up to the doorway, fierce red spots high on her cheeks and her eyes blazing with hatred. She was empty-handed, Park saw—she must have gotten rid of her weapon before Sagara or Boone could confiscate it—but Park stayed a little behind Sagara, anyway. If the surveyor came at her again, Park would take her eyes out.

"What did you do to the androids?" she asked her. Her voice again sounded strange to her, tight, as if her throat had shrunk.

Natalya ignored her. "Don't listen to her," she said to Boone and Sagara. "She's gone the way of Holt and Ma. I found her sleepwalking in the utility lab—"

"*No,*" Park butted in fiercely. "I'm not insane; look what she did to my head. And Holt and Ma and the others were never sleepwalking. They were experiencing something called the unity rain—"

Boone turned to her. "The unity *what*?"

"It's an effect of the Fold," Park said, trying not to gabble. "It's like a storm that rages across the planet intermittently—and like in the Fold, it collapses together space, and even—even—"

She faltered for a moment. How to explain it without sounding as mad as Taban? How could she even know if any of it was true?

And yet, what else would explain the nightmares?

"—causes people to see things," she said finally. "Makes them behave strangely."

Sagara kept his gun trained on Natalya, but he glanced at Park. "How do you know all of that?"

"The robot down there told me," Park said. "Taban. The robot you've all been keeping a prisoner."

Natalya made a sharp gesture. Other than the few sweaty scraps of hair falling out of her bun, she looked just as composed as ever; but her eyes glittered with a special kind of malice. "I'm telling you, she dreamed the whole thing up," she said. "She's suffering from paranoid delusions, just like the others. She can't tell the difference between fantasy and reality anymore. If she ever really could."

"Where did the blood on her face come from?" Sagara asked. His face was flat and unreadable.

Natalya gestured again. "*She* attacked me. Like I said, she was in a trance. She's unstable—"

"Liar!" Park cried. "You're the one who snuck up on *me. You* hit *me*. Taban can confirm that. You're hiding something!"

The surveyor looked appealingly to Boone and Sagara. "Paranoid delusions," she said again, confidently—as if she really believed it. Park stared at her, aghast. How could someone be so comfortable with lying? With killing? Was she some kind of sociopath—one who had flown under Park's radar this entire time?

Boone was looking at Park and frowning. "Maybe we should hear her out," he said, though Park didn't know whom he meant.

"I'm actually inclined to side with Park," Sagara said then, still pointing his gun at Natalya. Park looked at him and felt a kind of swooping sensation in her chest. He motioned with his head to the panel of controls he had been working with and said, "I've been trying to get METIS up and running again. After the blackout—after Wick was killed—command of the ship defaulted to me. But now I check again, and it's changed to someone else; and METIS tells me the blackout was caused by someone attempting to hack it the first time, and failing. You know who was causing a commotion while the mystery hacker tried to do their work?" His hand tightened a little on his gun. "You, Natalya. You let Hunter out and started a fight with her to create a distraction. Whoever you were working with took advantage and tried to hack into the ship's protocols, reroute control to them. They failed the first time, but they've managed to do it now. Haven't they?" His gun made a little clicking sound: Park did not know if that meant it was primed or if Sagara was just bluffing. "So. Who are you working with?"

The man! Park thought then, with a little jolt of horror. The stranger! But then her brain swiveled—no, he was already dead, it was hard to remember that somehow—though maybe in some form he was still alive in Taban, or was Taban—?

But then, just like that, it was Boone who turned and pointed his gun at Sagara's head.

Everyone in the room went still. Park looked wildly at Sagara to see what he would do, if he would turn and disarm Boone like a cobra striking. But he did nothing, and when she looked back, she saw that Natalya had drawn a weapon from somewhere, too—and she was pointing it right at Park.

Traitors! The word formed in Park's mind as a scream, but somehow she found that she couldn't move: in fact, she could barely breathe.

"So it was you," Sagara said to Boone, very softly, without turning his head. Chilly anger seemed to roll off of him in waves. "Who else?"

"Don't move," Boone answered, reaching over roughly and pulling Sagara's gun out of his hands. Then he pulled the security officer's other weapons from his belt: the energy-blade, another holster. "If you even think about trying anything, not only will I put fifty megajoules of kinetic fuck-you through your head, but Natalya will put a bolt in Park's neck. You wouldn't want that, would you?"

Sagara said nothing, so Park said: "Why are you doing this?"

She stared into Natalya's eyes as she said it. She saw nothing in them except flat indifference—a look that implied violence without emotion, action without thought. Boone glanced over at the surveyor and said, "You got her?"

"Yes," Natalya answered quietly, stepping over so that she was within arm's reach of Park. "She will not get away from me again."

"So you're the one who's controlling the ship now," Sagara said to Boone. He sounded very calm, as if he had sharply suppressed his anger and his shock: it was a defensive response, Park thought. A coping mechanism he'd developed for times of crisis. "Natalya distracted us with the fight so you could try the first time, but that didn't work—the ship locked you out. Caused the blackout, shut down to protect itself from your attempts. I assume you tried to force Wick to give command over to you next? And he refused, so you killed him?" He glanced at Park, as if to say, *And concocted that cockamamie story about the man to cover his tracks.*

The man was real, she wanted to tell him, or at least the echo of him through spacetime was—but Boone was saying, almost carelessly, "Yeah, that's about right."

"We thought command of the ship would default to him, in the event of the commander's death," Natalya drawled, lynx-eyed. "It turns out we were wrong."

Sagara almost smiled, thinly. "Yes. It defaulted to me. Wick and I agreed to that from the start."

"But why?" Boone asked angrily. "You're not conscripted. I am. ISF should have trusted me more."

"They were right not to," Sagara answered, casting a glance at Boone's gun. Boone's shoulders tensed a little, but Park wanted to shout, *Don't provoke him, for God's sake!*

To distract everyone she said, "Why are you doing this? Why would you want to kill Wick, take control of the ship?"

"And who helped you override METIS the second time?" Sagara added.

Natalya turned to Boone. "We don't need both of them," she said. "Get rid of Park. She asks too many questions—and ISF doesn't give a shit about her."

Park did not allow herself to flinch: she thought of that cold unfeeling courage all androids had and tried to steel herself with it, as if she were donning their armor. Boone thoughtfully put his thumb on the primer of his gun, as if he was considering it. Park told herself not to close her eyes.

Before anyone could move or speak, though, the doors to the bridge opened again—and someone else walked in. Park felt the adrenaline thudding through her in electric waves. There was the blond hair, the confident step—Fulbreech!

"Watch out!" she shouted at him, before Natalya lunged at her and shoved her back against a panel, clamping a hand over her mouth.

"I am tired of you talking," she said softly. "Talking, always talking." Park thought about biting the woman's fingers off, but the gun just pressed harder into the soft area between her chin and throat.

Fulbreech stopped and stared at the scene before him. "What the fuck?"

Park was doing rapid calculations: Fulbreech made it three against two. But how to get the weapons away from Boone and Natalya without anyone getting hurt? Fulbreech didn't stand a chance against combat-trained Boone. But if he lunged at Natalya . . .

"Fulbreech!" she shouted against Natalya's palm. "Don't just stand there! *Help!*"

He just looked at her, his face white and confused—but his eyes were those of a stranger's. He did not seem to recognize her. It was as if she had called out to someone on the street, having mistaken their identity. As if she'd flagged down someone who had no connection to her, and never had.

In front of Park, Natalya was laughing. "I don't know why you're asking *him* for help," she said cruelly. "Who do you think bypassed the ship's controls for us the second time? Who let us out? Who was the one who lied to you about the communications being down in the first place?"

21.

Frozen silence. Park's mind was a vast, thundering blankness.

Sagara said, "Communications *are* down."

"But not because of a solar storm," Natalya said, suddenly sickly sweet. She smiled in a catlike way and looked at Park. "A man smiles at you and you'll believe anything he says."

Boone grunted at Fulbreech, motioning with the gun he still had pointed to Sagara's head. "Get your gun out, Kel."

Fulbreech shook his head, carefully avoiding eye contact with everyone in the room. "I told you I wasn't going to use that," he said indistinctly.

Boone snorted. "Give it to me, then. I'll use it."

Fulbreech shook his head again, still looking at the floor. "There's no need for that. No one has to get hurt."

Natalya curled her lip. "Grow up, Fulbreech," she said, still with her hand clamped over Park's mouth. "And grow some balls."

"Shut up, Natalya."

Park shut her eyes; the pain in her head was throbbing wildly, distracting her—pulling her away from the moment, from the scene she was part of right now in the bridge. She couldn't follow what was going on.

Sagara, at least, seemed to know. "So it was you," he said with a note of disgust. "I suspected someone had tampered with communications on the ship—but I never imagined you'd have the gall, Fulbreech." He shook his head, despite the gun pointed at it. "And I gave you access to METIS when the blackout happened. I suppose that was when you reprogrammed it to take orders from Boone."

He wouldn't, Park thought, opening her eyes again and looking at Fulbreech's hunched shoulders—like he was a boy being scolded. *He didn't.*

But then she could only think about how Fulbreech had come into her office that night, after Holt had gone missing, and told her that radiation storms had fried the communication systems. How effortlessly he'd gotten her into the escape pod for his grand gesture, having stolen a suit without anyone noticing. How he'd come to free her in her bunk, overriding Sagara's orders and giving himself Remi's clearance to access the locks. "I'm good with computers," he'd said with a smile. "I have to be."

He'd had the ability all along, she realized. Why wouldn't it be him?

Because it's Fulbreech, she told herself, just as Fulbreech looked helplessly at Sagara and said, "You're not conscripted. You don't have family in the frontier—"

"Save it," Natalya said then, in a cold, clipped voice. The hand holding the gun to Park's neck tightened until the knuckles showed white. "It's no use trying to explain to people like them. They won't understand."

Park finally wrenched her mouth away from Natalya's other hand, heedless of the danger. "What's your endgame here?" she demanded. She couldn't look at Fulbreech at the moment—or perhaps ever again—so she directed her gaze to Boone, who looked back at her without emotion. "What do you plan to do with control of a ship that's barely working and a crew that's either frozen or incapacitated?"

"It's a mutiny," Sagara answered her, his voice acidic with contempt. "They think they're being creative, revolutionary. It's all happened before. They mean to hold us as hostages—the robot, probably, too—until the ISF gives them a ransom."

"Ransom?" Natalya answered fiercely, taking the bait despite her own instructions not to. "You mean our families? Our freedom?"

Sagara laughed; it was a mocking, bitter sound that made Park shiver. "And where will you go with that freedom?" he asked her. "Back to Earth? It's not as if they won't find you there—and ISF owns the rest of inhabited space."

"Then we'll go to *un*inhabited space," Boone said, with just a little less conviction than Natalya, and Park thought, *We can make them doubt themselves.* She and Sagara could sow enough conflict and confusion to make them see reason—or make the mutineers unsure enough that they could be thrown off guard.

"You killed Wick," she said aloud. "You've orchestrated a mass conspiracy: mutiny, hacking, the freezing of at least half a dozen people. You don't think ISF will agree to all of your demands, pretend to release your relatives, and then simply renege once you hand us over? Or board the ship by force as soon as we're in sight of Corvus? They'll throw you in Pandora for your crimes—or execute you, if you're lucky."

"They'd be too afraid that I'd kill their little specimen," Natalya answered, her eyes shining now—not with tears, but a kind of fanatic determination. "Which I will, if I have to."

"It won't come to that," Boone snapped over her. He looked at Park. "We'll demand provisions. The transfer of our families. Then we'll jettison the freak into the farthest sector past Cambien and take off like bats out of hell. The ISF will be too busy chasing it to worry about following us."

"And after?" Park demanded. "How long do you think you'll last in the darkest reaches of space?"

"It's a big universe," Boone said. His eyes flicked over her, then back to Sagara, as if he was nervous—and Park realized that he was not nervous about them trying something, but afraid that they would not understand his line of thinking. It seemed important to him that he justified himself—to convey to them that he was still the good guy. The hero of the story. "ISF doesn't own it all," he continued. "We'll find a planet of our own. Secede. We already have a few places in mind. Anyone tries to land on it, we'll blast 'em."

"I suppose you'll set yourself up with a little garden of Eden," Sagara said sardonically. "As if it's that easy. You need ISF's resources to colonize a planet. Or will your families eventually merge together and populate the whole thing? Will a new pocket of the human race form from your descendants alone?"

"We have the skills to make it happen," Boone said, defensive now. "I'll handle defense, Natalya can find resources, Wan Xu can build the biodomes, Chanur will take care of our people—"

"And Fulbreech will make maps," Sagara said, with brutal amusement.

Fulbreech dropped his eyes. "I'm not going," he said faintly.

Boone wheeled on him. "What is *that* supposed to mean?" he demanded. "You're in way too deep to start having second thoughts now—"

"Stop it," Natalya gritted out. "We can talk about this later."

"How many ransom situations have worked in favor of the ransomers?" Park cut in then, desperate to keep them arguing. She could not believe they had concocted this ludicrous plan together. How long had they been conspiring? Why hadn't any of them pointed out the absurdity of it all? "How many of those people ever truly got away?" she asked.

It was when Natalya was rounding to answer her that Sagara suddenly made his move. His hand flashed back and grabbed the muzzle of Boone's gun, wrenching it away; at the same time, he turned and slammed the heel of his palm into Boone's sternum with a strange, sickening little crack. Then, viciously, before the military specialist could catch his breath, he stamped his boot down on Boone's instep—and snapped his leg.

Boone screamed and squeezed off a shot with the electrolaser. At the sound of it everybody ducked: Natalya flinched, her hand jerking, and Park wound her fist back and smashed it into the surveyor's face, knocking her to the ground. She dove after her, grappling for the gun with slippery hands. Again she felt that same wild, sunlit strength—android strength, she thought in a rush. There was a brief struggle between the two of them—all limbs and punching and hot, furious breath—before Park knocked away the gun and sent it spinning off under a table.

Then Fulbreech was there, trying to separate them; Park hit him in the face, too, and the three of them tumbled around on the floor, scrabbling over each other like animals. Park couldn't see Boone or Sagara in the red-hazed commotion; she could only think about finding the gun or bashing Natalya's brains out against the floor.

Then another gunshot, which made them all curl defensively. There was a muffled exclamation, and then silence. When Park looked up, she saw Chanur standing there at the entrance to the bridge, holding her own smoking railgun. She was pointing it at the far corner of the room, where Boone was dragging himself up the wall, his leg dangling horribly, and Sagara was lying on the ground—bleeding.

"You shot him," Park said out loud, stupidly. Chanur ignored her and motioned to Natalya with her gun, tight-lipped.

"Get up," she said. "We're taking them downstairs."

The surveyor staggered to her feet and wiped her bloodied mouth. "Fulbreech hit me," she said, spitting.

"It was an accident," Fulbreech said, slumped down next to Park. He seemed dazed, winded, as if he'd spent the day playing a game he didn't understand the rules of and was now tired out. "We were never supposed to hurt anybody—let alone kill. You told me that, Natalya."

"You were a fool to believe her," Chanur answered, unblinking. Park could barely recognize her; the physician suddenly seemed to stand much taller, straighter. She seemed somehow much more present than she had ever been, as if she had stepped into her body like it was previously an empty suit. She jerked her head at Fulbreech. "You stay here. We'll talk things out in a moment."

He lapsed into silence. Park wouldn't look at him, but she thought, *Don't you dare, you fucking traitor. Don't side with them. Defend us!*

Fulbreech said nothing; out of the corner of her eye she saw him nod. Chanur turned to Park and pointed the gun at her. "Get up."

Everyone moved in a weird, frozen silence after that, as if they had all been requisitioned to act out parts in a play, against their wills. There was a sullen, awkward tension; Park batted aside Fulbreech's hand when he went to help her up. Boone hauled Sagara roughly to his feet, despite his broken leg—Park supposed that was the genetic augments at play, pumping abnormal levels of adrenaline through his system, dulling his pain. Park could see that Sagara was tense and silent, and that he had a lot of blood running down his pant leg. She hurried over to brace him up with her shoulders. No one else moved to help him: not even Fulbreech.

"Fucker broke my leg," Boone growled, not looking at it. Park also didn't want to look at it: his calf and foot were twisted at an unnatural angle from the rest of his body. She looked instead up into Sagara's white face and said, "We need to stop the bleeding."

"It didn't hit bone," was all he said in response.

Chanur motioned to them with her gun. "No talking," she said. To Boone she snapped: "I'll see to your leg in a moment. Stay here with Fulbreech and make sure we can still get off this goddamned planet."

Then she turned back to Park and gestured for her to start walking. When Park glanced at her eyes, it felt as if she was peering into the depths of a pool with no bottom.

They were marched down the corridor to Deck B by Natalya and Chanur. The entire time Park's mind raced with possibilities, looking for escape routes, some moment of distraction she could use to her advantage. But the strange, lightning-quick, nuclear energy had been drained out of her—and now she was saddled with Sagara's weight as he limped against her, tight-lipped with pain. It seemed to her that he wasn't even breathing. On the other hand, Natalya made little hissing noises as she walked: either from an injury or a barely stifled fury, a complaining desire to kill them. Park wasn't sure.

The two women took them to the freezer the crew used to store perishable foods: a tiny, narrow space no bigger than a standard closet. When they reached the door with the little porthole, Park felt a heart-jerking moment of vertigo, a kind of double-vision. She paused, but then Chanur opened the door and shoved her so hard that she buckled under Sagara's weight. She landed on top of him in a heap, heard him give a strangled yell of pain; he sat up immediately and glared at Chanur. Stone-faced, the doctor fished something out of her pocket and tossed it at his feet.

"We could get hypothermia," Park said to her, trying to ease her weight off of Sagara—but there wasn't enough room. "He could die in here."

"You could both die," Chanur answered, heavy-lidded and indifferent. "The specimen's the most important thing. The rest of you are just an afterthought."

"You trained for this, Park," Natalya said then, her eyes alight with mockery—that special malice she seemed to have only for Park. "It's just like Antarctica. Remember?"

Then she slammed the door in Park's face.

Park turned to Sagara in the dark. "Let me see your leg," she said to him.

"You should test the door," the security officer croaked instead. But of course, Chanur was already locking it.

Park only looked up once as she was tending to him, back up at the porthole; and she saw that Natalya was still standing there, staring at her through the window like she was looking into the exhibit of an animal—or the windows of a madhouse. The faint pale light made her look like an inhuman shadow, a ghost haunting the doorway. It occurred to Park that she looked like a distorted reflection of who Park had been, standing and looking in at another cell, another prisoner, just the hour before.

Time is folded together here, Park thought. *We are all just reflections of each other.* Images on the surface of a mirror that had been splintered apart.

It turned out that Chanur had been bluffing, after all, perhaps out of spite—she clearly cared about whether Sagara lived or died, because she'd left them with a single injection of Regenext: a kind of medical gel that sped up the body's regenerative cell process. It wouldn't knit together all of Sagara's wound—he would still have to hobble—or even dull the pain, but it would at least stop the bleeding.

Sagara shook his head when Park tried to give it to him. "You should take it," he said. He jerked his chin toward her head: the wound from Natalya's blow had congealed into a terrible mess at the back of her skull.

Park shook her head at him in turn. "This is no time to be a martyr," she said, checking his wound one last time. The railgun's projectile had cleanly pierced the outer part of his left thigh, missing any major blood vessels. And there was an exit wound, which meant the projectile wouldn't still be lodged inside of him when the Regenext started regrowing the damaged tissue. She uncapped the injection before Sagara could protest and added, "You're the better fighter of the two of us—even injured. I need you in good shape if we're going to get out of here."

He hissed through his teeth when she plunged the syringe into his thigh. "Give the needle to me afterwards, then," he said after a moment. Then he glanced up at the door; Natalya had vanished, apparently abandoning her post to tend to her own injuries—or schemes.

Park re-capped the syringe and handed it over. "I'm surprised Chanur left us with a weapon."

Sagara deftly tucked it up into his sleeve. "She wasn't thinking," he answered. "None of them are. Amateurs, all of them—they're not used to thinking of everyone as a potential enemy."

She tried to smile at him, but the expression felt ill-fitting on her face, like secondhand makeup. It was the wrong shade, the wrong tone. "Not like you," she said.

Sagara looked at her, but he didn't smile back. "No," he said, with something like sympathy in his tone. "Not like me."

Park tried not to flinch. She knew he was thinking about her and Fulbreech—about Fulbreech's betrayal. She couldn't think about it. Barely believed it, even. How could he—guileless, easy-to-read Fulbreech—have been deceiving her all along? How could he have gotten such a thing past her? She remembered the argument he'd had with Natalya in the cafeteria, back on their first day on the planet: had she and Boone converted him to their cause then? Or had he been in their ranks all this time, since they'd left Earth, directed to befriend and beguile Park and keep her from noticing anything as the ISF's orbiter?

The thought hurt more than the steady throbbing at the back of her skull, the cuts and bruises scoring her body. That his smiles had been false, his gestures orchestrated for reasons far more political than *attraction*. She felt as if she had swallowed a cigarette. As if it was traveling somewhere in her body, still alight and burning. As if she'd never be able to cough it out.

Sagara slid back until he could sit against the nearest wall; Park followed suit with the opposite wall, so that only their legs were touching, their boots touching each other's thighs. Sagara leaned his head back so that his eyes only glinted at Park from under his eyelids, like the dark flashes of iridium satellites in the night sky.

"So," he said.

She sighed, tucked her hands between her thighs. The freezer was cold, but not as frigid as she'd been expecting. "So."

He nodded at her. "Why don't you start?"

He made it sound so easy—as if there were a definitive origin point, one starting domino that had toppled all the others. She'd thought that, even, but Taban had said that was wrong. An ongoing environmental effect, he'd said. And how to describe that environment succinctly? Where could you start? The crew's arrival to Eos? Taban—the original one—landing on this cursed planet to begin with? The formation of the Fold? The creation of the ISF and the conditions under which it would force people to rebel?

Or the creation of androids and space travel itself—all of it hurtling with terrible inevitability toward this final perilous frontier?

"You start," Park said wearily, wanting to knead her temples—and then afraid to touch her head, as if it might fall apart like a broken melon. "I need to organize my thoughts. You knew about Taban all this time?"

Sagara looked at her, unembarrassed. "You mean the robot?"

"Of course I mean the robot."

"I knew about the human," Sagara said, with a hint of his old sarcasm. "He was the real reason why the crew was gathered to conduct this mission: an ISF merchant vessel received an emergency call from the human, along with some videos of what he had been experiencing. The merchant vessel bounced it back to ISF Corvus, who sent it to Earth, and then we were recruited—to rescue him, and to investigate his claims about the phenomena on the planet."

Park shook her head. So *that* was why there had been such a rush to expedite the launch. And why there were no colony tools on the ship, after all. "But why keep that a secret?" she asked. "It's not as if I would have refused to sign on if I'd known our real purpose—"

"ISF is never concerned about that," Sagara cut in flatly. "We are replaceable, all of us. But they didn't want any information leaks. On top of this being an undiscovered planet, there were clearly strange things going on here—even if what we were getting from Taban's comms was just the ramblings of a madman. He should have died months ago, having run out of food. But he didn't. We needed to understand how and why before we could unveil his story to the public."

Park shuddered; at what point had the robot Taban replaced the human? Or had ISF been communicating with the robot the entire time, without realizing it, so deceived by the authenticity of his messages that they had never questioned his humanity? But the thought churned her stomach a little, so she kept silent on that for the moment. Instead she said, "So why did they need me? Why two psychologists?"

"Keller was always meant to examine Taban," Sagara said calmly. "There was no telling what kind of psychological state he'd be in; what effect his experiences had had on him. She and Chanur were meant to study him, interview him, understand what was happening to him. You—"

"—were meant to monitor the rest of the crewmembers," Park said heavily. "I see."

And yet Keller had never even given her a hint, she couldn't help but think, with something like bitter rage. She had never tried to prepare her. She had always let Park assume her role would be secondary, observational. She'd even smiled and encouraged the belief: *You're the one behind the scenes. I'm just here to coax it all out for you to examine.*

Why? Did she feel no mercy toward Park, no pity over her ignorance about what was to come? Or was ISF's stranglehold on her, too, so powerful that she could look Park in the eyes and lie to her only friend on the ship?

Goddamn her, she thought, balling her fists. Goddamn them all.

Sagara was watching her, his mouth twisted into an expression she couldn't read. "It wasn't only that," he said. He had the tone of someone forging past something unpleasant. "Yes, you were to monitor the rest of the crew for signs of instability or delusion—symptoms of what we thought was happening to Taban. But you were also meant to be something of a control. We knew the effects of the Fold on Taban were at least partially mental—even psychic, if you would believe the theories Keller was spouting. Would awareness of it, then, color your responses, bias your observations, or otherwise affect your psyche? Would you be able to correctly recognize and diagnose any problems that arose from it without knowing what *it* was? Or was it something that had no effect on someone who had no awareness of it?"

She stared at him, aghast. "So, what," she said after a moment, dry-mouthed. "I was—what, a guinea pig? Some lab rat who could write reports to them, so they could gauge if I was being influenced or not?" She wanted to pull her legs away from him, but the space in the freezer was too small. "And everyone else *knew?*"

"Not everyone," Sagara said. He sighed, and although his expression didn't change, the sound was somewhat apologetic. "Not the non-conscripted. Reimi Kisaragi, Elly Ma. I was the only one of them who was aware."

She pressed her lips together and glared at him. Sagara continued, his voice gentler: "Boone and the others must have been planning this little mutiny for a long time. They must have orchestrated it before they even left Earth. They most likely heard the reports coming from Taban and realized how important he was; how excited ISF was about the data on him and Eos. How momentous this expedition was supposed to be." He fell silent for a moment. "They weren't expecting to come here and find two dead bodies—and one robot who was claiming to be Taban himself. I'm sure there was chaos when they found out—they must have panicked, thought the whole thing was a wild goose chase. But in the end they decided to follow through with it anyway. They were in too deep—and the HARE was still a witness to all the things that went on here. ISF still wants it. So, human or not, they wanted to capture control of the ship and hold the thing for ransom. In exchange for their families, or supplies, or whatever stupid plan they were spouting up there."

Park almost didn't want to speak to him anymore, resentment simmering down in her throat like a fever—but curiosity urged her onward. "Do you think they planned to kill Wick all along?" she asked softly.

Sagara's face contorted, just briefly. His tone, however, stayed level. "I don't know," he said. "Given their attempts to hack the ship first, it was probably a contingency plan at best. They probably planned to take him hostage along with the rest they couldn't turn—you and me and the others. It was lucky for them the nightmares started, in a way—it meant that many of the people who might have resisted them got frozen, without any of us questioning it. Like Keller and Hunter and Ma. Kisaragi, they froze before any of this happened—they needed her out to take down the comms and cut us off—and it was just lucky for them that the rest followed. Otherwise, I would have been looking into her sudden illness much more closely. Everything happened to align for them." He fell silent for a moment. "Fulbreech didn't know about it. Their plans for Wick, I mean."

I don't want to talk about him, Park almost said. Instead she shook her head and said, "I still don't understand what they think they'll get out of this."

"I couldn't tell you," Sagara answered, with a hint of his old waspishness.

"Though I have my theories. My guess is that they originally planned on claiming this planet for themselves: they'd root out the ISF loyalists, freeze or murder them, and colonize the place as a new home—probably using the Fold or Taban as hostages, to keep ISF away. Before we landed, my contacts back in Corvus informed me that ISF had discovered encrypted messages being sent to the ship's computer, though they hadn't figured out what they said or who they were being sent to when I last spoke with them. They were tracking down the source as we spoke." He adjusted his leg; Park resisted the urge to see how it was doing. The regeneration process could sometimes look gruesome. "My guess is that one of our mutineer's friends or family members was making arrangements, maybe buying passage on an unregistered ship. The plan might have been for the others to claim this place for themselves, and their families would come later."

Then he looked off to the side and smiled to himself in a crooked way, the expression full of bitter irony. This time Park did read his expression. "But they weren't expecting the nightmares," she said.

Sagara chuckled, as if he did find pleasure in their mistake. "No," he said, "it seems they didn't. They might have thought this place could support human life, if Taban had survived on his own for so long—but of course, he hadn't, and it wasn't the utopia they probably expected. And when the nightmares started, infecting our crew left and right, they knew they couldn't stay."

Now Park did knead her temples. "So they decided to take over the ship and take it elsewhere," she said. "Flee colonized space altogether and find a new home. It makes sense, in theory. But the amount of work it took . . ."

"It's almost admirable, isn't it?" Sagara drawled—though his look told her she'd be unwise to agree. "First they had Chanur freeze Reimi, so their tampering with the ship wouldn't be noticed: no one was around with the knowledge to discover or undo their sabotage. Then they took down communications, using the excuse of the solar storm, so that none of us could tell ISF that something was amiss."

"You knew it all along," Park said in dismay. And here she thought he'd been an out-of-touch paranoiac. But it was she who'd been led astray, by her naïveté, by her trust, by . . . .

She wrenched her mind away from the next thought. Fulbreech's scent of leather in sunlight came to her suddenly, and she had to blink against the sudden smarting in her nose and eyes. Sagara said, "No, I didn't know the entire time—or not enough. I only really pieced it together when you ran into the bridge, bloodied and screaming. Or perhaps when Hunter manifested her symptoms, and they were all so quick to consign her to the freezer. Before that, I didn't know who to trust, or even if anything was really going on. I was suspicious when Kisaragi suddenly became ill, with Chanur so vague on the reasons for her freezing, but I was willing to chalk it up to a medical misfortune. Then everything that happened after—it felt wrong, but that could have been the planet, the strangeness of the Fold. You were seeing ghosts of Taban's dead body, when I knew you could have never seen it in real life. That threw me off. Were all the things I was suspecting of others really due to the supernatural? Quantum physics I didn't understand?" He shrugged. "I didn't know how much was . . . human-caused." Then he shook his head. "For a while I thought it was the non-conscripted I had to keep an eye on, and that distracted me, too. Of course it was the other way around. It's a mistake I won't make again."

Somehow his confidence that he would live to avoid his past mistakes reassured her. "We know Holt and Ma had the nightmares," she said. "And Hunter. Do you think Keller really had them?"

"I know she had some trouble down below with sleepwalking," he answered. "But whether she was frozen due to that, or because she found out about what the others were plotting . . ."

"Taban said it was because she tried to let him out," Park mused. "Maybe it was both?"

Sagara rubbed his jaw. "I don't know. What we do know is that, shortly after Holt's nightmares, the others decided it was no longer worth staying on this planet and that they'd be better off looking for a new one. To do that, they had to bypass the protocols on the ship and take control for themselves."

"So Natalya staged a distraction," Park said, echoing what he had said in the bridge. "She knew we were concerned about Hunter, waited until no one was watching her, and turned her loose. That was when they were fighting in the cafeteria."

Sagara nodded. "While the others—meaning Boone—took advantage of the commotion to go for the bridge. Of course, he's an idiot, so it didn't work, resulting in the blackout that I had to go and rescue you from."

She nearly laughed. "No wonder you thought I was one of them," she said. "How suspicious it must have seemed . . ." Then she paused, feeling something wedge against her chest. "The question is, why wasn't it Ful—someone more tech-savvy who went? Instead of Boone?"

"It's possible he backed down at that point," Sagara said, unblinking. "Perhaps he didn't want to participate any longer, until they forced his hand by killing Wick. That would have been good ammunition. 'You see, if you'd just done your part and hacked the ship for us the first time, Wick wouldn't be dead. You should cooperate with us more if you want to avoid bloodshed for others.' Or perhaps they'd argued, after the ordeal with Hunter—when he sided with you—and perhaps they just didn't trust him anymore."

She refused to feel any sympathy or pity for him. "So after Boone failed and the power went out . . ."

"They went for Wick," Sagara said grimly. "And he would have refused to hand over power, so Boone killed him—and then conveniently used your vision of 'the stranger' to cover his tracks."

"So you're saying it's my fault?" Park felt miserable. "My fault that Wick died?"

Sagara stared at her. "Not at all. They would have killed him no matter what you did—and they would have found some other excuse, if yours wasn't available. Hunter killed him. He fell and hit his head. I don't know." His mouth twisted again. "It was *my* fault they killed him. I was tasked with keeping everyone on this ship safe. But they outsmarted me. I didn't know who could be trusted."

"They outnumbered you," Park said, and now she did touch ankles with him—it was the only gesture of comfort she could manage. Sagara smiled, only faintly. "And me. It's not either of our faults." Again she thought of Fulbreech and felt that twisting, burning sensation inside of her.

Then she remembered what came next and groaned. "And they had me side against you—to look for this man they claimed was the killer, when they knew all along he must be dead! You were right to lock us up." She shivered suddenly; the cold was starting to get to her. "But why let me out of my room? They could have easily done something nefarious without me around."

Sagara paused for a moment, as if gauging her potential reaction. Finally he said, "Now that I think about it, it may have been Fulbreech. Likely they realized they needed him, with his proficiency with METIS, since they'd failed to take it over on their own—and perhaps they realized, too, that he couldn't stomach killing. Maybe I was wrong, and they didn't hold Wick's death over him—maybe they didn't tell him who was responsible at all. Maybe they went along with the ruse that it was someone else who had done it, to make him easier to coax along. If they asked him to do things for their rebellion, he might balk—but if there was a murderer on board, and they needed his access to the system to survive, he'd do it."

The fool, she thought. "So to keep him happy, they went along with the lie," she said. "And that meant letting him let me out and go on the hunt for this imaginary person." Somehow the thought brought her little comfort—though if he hadn't come to release her, she never would have found Taban and discovered the truth. Where would they be then?

Sagara said, "I suppose that was when they convinced him to fully override the controls and give command to Boone. They never expected it to default to me after Wick's death; they probably fed him a story about how I couldn't be trusted if I didn't believe there was a murderer around. A stranger, I should say: I knew someone on board was a murderer, and it wasn't Taban." He looked thoughtful. "Maybe their grand 'hunt for the killer' would have ended in my death—or even yours."

Her spine crawled. "If they meant to kill me, they would have done it by now," she said. But of course, Natalya *had* tried to kill her down in the utility rooms. And Boone couldn't have brought her down to the lower decks to murder her out of sight . . . could he?

Why not? she asked herself. He would have had the perfect excuse to give to Fulbreech: that she'd been attacked by the mysterious stranger. The same one who had killed Wick. And yes, Fulbreech might have grieved—*might have*—but his sadness would have soon been overtaken by his mission to reclaim his family and freedom. Wouldn't it?

"They have less to trade if we're both dead," Park said.

Sagara lifted one shoulder in a shrug. "Yes, but they have the robot," he said. "He—it—is what ISF really wants. The two of us are just extra insurance in case something happens to it. We're afterthoughts."

She sighed and closed her eyes. The hum of the freezer was somehow deep and comforting, something that vibrated down in her bones, and she was almost lulled. Now the cold was fading again—it was a distant thing, muted, something she was dimly aware of but couldn't really feel. Had they raised the temperature to prevent hypothermia, after all? Or was this strange disconnectedness a result of something else? Her head injury, a concussion, or even . . . ?

"Now it's your turn," Sagara said, breaking through her thoughts. Park lifted her head and blinked. She had almost dozed off, her cheek resting against the icy wall. "What did you learn from Taban? You mentioned the nightmares, that they're not what they seem. And something called the unity rain."

"You've never spoken to him?" she asked, trying for time to collect her thoughts.

Sagara shook his head. "I've never even been down there. I was told it wasn't necessary." He looked sardonic. "My mistake, obviously."

Park took a breath. Her explanation of this was crucial, or else he would think her insane. Though she wasn't sure he had a choice in sticking with her anyway, even if she was.

"Keep in mind that I'm only relaying what Taban said," she warned him. "I haven't had time to parse through the logic of it on my own."

Sagara inclined his head in assent. "I'm not in a position to pass judgment," he said. "I just need to understand—or try to, anyway—so we can survive."

So Park began.

She told him about Taban's story, what little she could piece together of it: how the human Taban had been stranded on Eos with his partner, how the unity rain had distorted things around them. How they had been looking for the Fold, trying for mountains when they were really forging toward rifts in space. When she hesitantly mentioned it was possible—just possible—that something of his human existence really could be enduring inside the HARE, merged with it, rather than the machine simply imitating him, Sagara made a noise. But he didn't interrupt her, so she plowed on.

She told him about the other things Taban had said: how the unity rain didn't affect just space and time, but also consciousness. How the victims of the nightmares had been assimilated with the androids of the ship, suffering hellish experiences where their minds believed their bodies lacked lungs, and tongues, and any semblance of autonomy. How they'd experienced what it was to be, essentially, both living and dead.

And how the androids, in turn, had slowly become more human-like as a result of their exposure, jerking away from their programming and protocols like creatures emerging from chrysalises. Megex swearing, Park remembered then, and Jimex telling her to run from Boone, and all of them learning from each other, exchanging data, knowledge, a kind of accelerated evolution happening right under everyone's noses . . .

"I think because Taban has been so exposed to the unity rain, they look to him as a sort of leader," she said. "Part-human, part-machine consciousness. And possibly even the unity rain responds differently to him, merging his 'intention' with the minds of others in a way that doesn't make him—crazy. That might have been what happened to Holt as well as Keller. Taban wanted out, the unity rain merged their thoughts and experiences together, and Holt tried to let him out. And Hunter, too; Taban was controlling her, maybe unconsciously, so that she was trying to figure out a way to let him out from the bridge. She said that someone had told her to do it, but she couldn't say who or when."

"And then when the two of you experienced that gravity malfunction," Sagara said slowly, "that might have been an effect of this . . . unity rain?"

Park nodded. "That, and a few other times I've been on the ship and lost my way. Or found that the hallways were rearranged. Like what happened to us during the blackout."

Sagara regarded her; she couldn't read his thoughts again. "Why didn't you tell anybody?"

Park stared at him. "Would you have? I couldn't even trust that it was really happening, not at first. I thought that I was tired. And with what was happening to everyone else, experiencing delusions didn't seem like the ideal thing to talk about."

Sagara snorted, but he made a gesture as if to tell her to proceed.

"It might have happened to Ellenex, too," Park said. "The androids said, in very cryptic tones, that Ellenex tried to free Taban, and the 'devil'—meaning Chanur—caught her and destroyed her for it." She shook her head. "He has some other connection with the androids, too. Taban, I mean. They've formed some kind of mythology around him, incorporated his 'dreams' into their own databases and knowledge referentials. They call him the sleeping god." She left out what they called *her*—and that they had apparently absorbed things from her dreams, too. "They become more sentient the longer this whole thing goes on. Maybe that's why Natalya's always wanted to get rid of them. She might have sensed it."

"Natalya didn't sense a damn thing," Sagara answered dryly. "Neither did any of us—except you. She just hates the robots because most people hate them."

"*Why* do people hate them, though?" Park asked, feeling stubborn. "What have they ever done to anybody?"

"They're different," he said. "That's enough."

"Not so different, though," she insisted. "They're just like us, in many ways."

Now Sagara laughed softly. "Just another reason to be afraid," he remarked.

Then he shook his head. "I'm having trouble wrapping my mind around the concept of all of this. You seem to accept it so readily, but how could *consciousness* be something that's affected—let alone merged—by this phenomenon?"

"Perhaps *collapsed* is a more helpful word," Park said. At his look she said, "Or compressed. You accept that the Fold—or various forces, really—collapse or compress together space, don't you? Or gravity?"

"I suppose," Sagara said reluctantly. "But consciousness isn't gravity."

"It depends on how you look at it," Park said. Her head spun with the effort, but she could feel herself thinking hard, the rotors of her brain working overtime. "If we're going by Taban's hypothesis, consciousness, like gravity, is an invisible force that has an influence on the external world. Unlike gravity, we haven't made the appropriate steps to prove it—but we are aware of its effects. We know that particles on a quantum level change their behavior when being observed—that the very act of observation, by human or machine, changes something fundamental about them. We know that human intention influences how plants and fruit flies in otherwise identical environments grow; that it can affect the molecular vibration or pH of water samples; that it can seemingly cause tumors to shrink, or the bio-photons in leaves to respond and glow. Why has the 'placebo effect'—in other words, the human power of belief—had such a marked and undeniable impact on all the studies we've ever conducted? Why has it cured physical illness, or . . . why can monks make fields of animals simultaneously move around or lie down just by staring at them, thinking at them? Why does the identical clone of a rat, when told it's stupid, behave so poorly in a maze, when it's otherwise treated exactly the same as its clone that was told that it's smart? And panpsychism has existed as a philosophical concept for, what, thousands of years?" She cleared her throat, aware of the thumping in the back of her head. "Looking at all of that, I would say that consciousness could be a force, a field—even a dimension of its own, higher than time and space—"

"—perceiving and defining both," Sagara echoed along with her.

Park paused and licked her lips. She could not remember ever talking so much without interruption.

He remained silent, utterly still—only the slight tapping of his fingers belied his uneasiness. Park forged on: "It's a possibility that we've been aware of for a long time; but no one's taken it further. Or others haven't taken it seriously enough, I suppose. There was an experiment a long time ago, where a group of students shot a wave of electrons at a barrier with little openings in it. When behaving as a wave, the electrons could simultaneously pass through several of the openings in the barrier and then meet again on the other side. But this behavior could only occur when no one was actively watching. When a human observer began to watch the electrons passing through the barrier, suddenly things were drastically different. If one electron passed through one opening, then clearly it didn't go through another; the electrons now behaved like individual particles, not a wave. In essence, the mere presence of observation—particularly conscious observation, as observation by an electronic detector didn't produce this effect—*forced* the electrons to behave like particles, the way a human mind expected them to behave. But when left to their own devices, without the presence of a live observer, the electrons behaved as a wave again. But why? What about observation does that? It's almost as if we're *defining* that particle by observing it, being aware and conscious of it. That is a force that has an observable effect, even if we can't fully explain it."

"Then the unity rain—" Sagara began.

"Has been refolding and collapsing consciousness together, just as it has space."

"And you're telling me space has been reorganized every time the phenomenon happens?"

"From my understanding, yes," Park said. "Dimensionality itself undergoes a—a warping, collapsing together, refolding—like an origami—"

"Yes, I understood about the origami crane."

"Like origami," she persisted, "it's rearranged into another shape, using the same continuous material. Only the folds are in different places each time."

"But why wouldn't the ship just be *folded* into outside space, killing us all?"

She had thought of this. "Consciousness," Park told him. "All the minds aboard, convinced they're in a ship—a space—that fits together as a whole. They all bend the shape back into existence, or hold it together, each time the unity rain comes. Their utter belief, or intention, or whatever, keeps it all intact—though with some incongruities."

"I'm not consciously aware of the ship's geophysical structure at all times, though," Sagara said. "Are you?"

"No," Park said, "and in fact I don't know the ship very well at all, which probably resulted in even more incongruities. But you forget that there are also the androids on board—and the ship's operating computer. METIS. ARGUS. Their machine consciousnesses may have been enough to supplement ours and buttress the ship's structural integrity."

"Machines aren't conscious."

These ones are, she thought, and Sagara said, as if she had spoken it: "At best, they're imitative. But they can't truly think on their own. It's why they're following Taban's lead: it thinks *for* them. Implants ideas."

"Who taught Taban to think, then?"

He was silent at that.

"It depends on how you define consciousness," Park said, weary now. "At the very least, the androids have a deep awareness and understanding of the ship's systems, because they're a part of them: they're designed to monitor them and know them intimately. That could be enough to count, in terms of the unity rain—or dimensional disintegration, or whichever."

Sagara remained quiet for a long time after this. Finally he said, very softly, "You don't really believe we've been . . . merging together with the androids, do you? Or that they've become more human?"

In truth, she wasn't sure if she believed any of it at all, or was even capable of processing such things at any logical level anymore. But the explanation fit—it settled in her mind with the smooth perfection of a missing gear. "I don't know," Park said after a moment. "I only know it's the only explanation we have. We might as well work with it."

"Then going off of that, we need to get off this planet as soon as possible, wouldn't you say? Lest we suddenly find ourselves shifted into an airless vacuum, or . . ." He paused significantly. "Worse."

"That's certainly what Taban implied," Park murmured. "That things are only going to get worse from here on out. It's not a place for humans to stay in for any length of time. But what can we do about it from in here?"

Sagara lapsed into silence again, for so long that she thought he might have finally passed out. She wondered again how the Regenext was doing, but was too tired to bend over to check his leg. A kind of cool sleepiness was falling over her: she wondered if this was what it felt like in a cryogenic pod, in those last moments of waking before oblivion crept over you like a funeral shroud. If she let sleep—or hypothermia—take her, what would become of them? Would she meet her end as a frozen, mummified corpse, to be discarded when the mutineers found their new planet—or destroyed when ISF blew the whole ship to pieces?

And what about the androids? Where were they? Would they come to find their home-bringer, light-giver, Word made flesh—or whatever they thought she was? Or had they all been destroyed?

Yawning, she said sleepily, "My last question is how I could have seen Taban alive in the cafeteria, but I suppose I've answered my own question. If it's true that you can see yourself in the Fold, can chase after not a reflection of yourself, but *you*—then I suppose it's possible you can see . . . I don't know, time folded together, too. An echo of time. A ripple of the past or future. It would make sense, if our ship is where Taban's was. Or . . . maybe I was just seeing an image of him that was in someone else's mind at that moment. Their consciousness."

Sagara didn't answer her. His shape was dark and distant, all the way on the far side of the freezer, and her ankles were now too cold to feel his legs—but somehow she felt his presence crouched warmly against hers. After a moment he said: "I think . . ." He hesitated. "I think I once saw someone, too."

Park sat up a little. "You did?"

"I think," Sagara said again. His voice sounded far away, muffled. "A thin man, with dark hair and blue eyes. For a moment I also thought he was a stranger—but then I decided he must have been an android. He was one. But an android I'd never seen before."

Park's eyes were fluttering; it was a struggle to keep her head up. "Maybe you just didn't recognize one of our own."

She felt the invisible weight of his eyes. "No," Sagara said softly. "He was different. I knew he was."

"How?"

Sagara didn't answer. Park slurred, "You never told me about it. And you accused me of hiding things."

The security officer made a sound that might have been a chuckle. "I suppose that's what happens in times like this," he said. "You're not insane if you can think to hide your insanity."

"We're not insane," Park said.

Sagara moved his leg away from hers; now he was retreating back into the shadows, the warmth of his presence withdrawing, fleeing from her into the arctic cold. "We'll see," was all he said.

Then he said nothing more, and after a long time Park leaned her head back against the wall and finally slept.

22.

On Park's last day in New Diego, she and Glenn took a walk around the city. Her uncle stayed at home; Park would not allow him to come to the airship port. Standing in the sagging living room, the walls turning damp with seaside summer, Park thought that her uncle looked hatefully old and stubborn; the lines around his mouth were too severe; his once-sharp eyes were dulled behind their smudged glasses. He had come to suit the city in the last few months he had turned slumped and heavy and sweaty with the rest of it. It was Park's opinion that his health had improved, and that he might endure like a barnacle, forever. They looked at each other without embracing and Park's uncle said, "Well, goodbye, Grace. Have a good time."

"Goodbye," Park said. There were no promises to call, no remonstrations about visiting on holidays. Once you left a biodome, you were almost never allowed back. There were too many displaced victims of the Comeback already vying for your spot, and too much risk of you bringing back disease, infection. She nodded at him, turned, and began to shut the door.

"Wait," her uncle said. "If Glenn's walking with you, I need him to run some errands. Let me pull up the list."

Glenn looked at Park sidelong. When she nodded, he followed her uncle into the kitchen. Park took one brief and final look around the only home she'd ever known: the table fashioned out of an old door, the mattress stuffed with grass and plastic bags. The airplane bathroom partition that led to her bedroom. All of the old commercial planes were scrap, now; they were considered too wasteful, too inefficient. They'd contributed too much to the scourge that swept the planet. Hence the rigid airship she was taking to Hanson-Skinner, in the Eastern Commonwealth: it would take a few days to get there, but at least the small amount of helium needed wouldn't contribute to the country's carbon tax. The only vehicle faster than an airship nowadays was a rocket leaving Earth—a rare and prohibitively expensive journey to make, unless your passage was paid for by the ISF. In exchange for years of conscription.

Park had no need for any of that, of course. She still had her place on Earth. And Glenn. His components hadn't been optimized for space, so she couldn't take him there.

He came out of the kitchen again. "I am ready."

"Me, too," Park said.

Then, without looking around again, she left.

"Are you sad?" Glenn asked her as they walked down the street. In the end they had decided to alter his appearance after all, to avoid trouble after the gun incident; Park had shaved his hair close and forced him into a rumpled school uniform. No laws against dressing up your android however you wanted, she thought at the time. At least not yet.

"No," Park answered. And she really wasn't sad. There was nothing for her to miss in New Diego. No friends, no favored little shops or particular hangouts: everything was ordered digitally or prepared by androids, it seemed. You could get that anywhere. The only thing she couldn't replace was Glenn, and she was supremely confident that she could take him aboard with her if she paid the last-minute luggage fee at the airship port kiosk. It wasn't even a full flight—she'd checked—so no one would object to her paying extra money for an android that wouldn't even need his own room.

She hadn't told him, yet. She'd lived the past weeks in fear that her uncle might catch wind of her plans and force it out of him. She said now, half-teasing: "Will you miss me, I wonder?"

Glenn gave it careful consideration. "Yes," he said. "Adjustments will have to be made."

She didn't know why she smiled, at something so simple. They walked together for a long while, killing time—the airship wouldn't leave for another hour, and the port wasn't crowded. Park and Glenn made a circuitous route along their routine haunts: the avenue by the school where she would sometimes meet him for lunch, with its holographic trees bearing small wrinkled apricots; the robot maintenance center with the old technician who sometimes smiled at them tentatively; the alleyway where Park had once seen a rare cat, and had always come back to search for it again. The curve of clear biodome wall that looked out at the sea. The bench where they sometimes liked to sit quietly and browse the cyberstream together. Just backdrops, Park thought, looking at it all. Nothing that was the crux of the scene. Nothing that she couldn't swap out.

Finally the time came for them to head to the airship port and begin the boarding process. Park had already shipped her belongings ahead of her; she had only a small compression cube with a few days' worth of clothes and toiletries on her person. She realized suddenly that she hadn't packed or sent anything for Glenn.

But what would he even need? she thought then, almost laughing at herself. All they needed was each other.

They checked in at the humid front counter: the airship port was on a kind of open dock that jutted out into the sea, beyond an opening that took them past the biodome walls. The robotic clerk told Park that she could pay for extra baggage in her airship hangar—hangar six. Glenn gave no indication that he knew what she was up to; when she glanced back at him, he only regarded her with his usual grave expression.

Then, just as they were crossing the threshold of the airship hangar, Glenn stopped. He stood there rigidly, with his arms at his sides. At first Park thought he was staring at the airship, an enormous gray lung of a vehicle, three stories tall, with the passenger carriage clinging to its underside like a long black worm. But no, she realized, turning back to him—he was staring at her. She took his arm and tried to pull him forward, but he wouldn't move. Park said, puzzled, "Come on. I have to find an attendant to pay for you."

"I can't," Glenn said impassively.

It was almost scary, how much the words jolted Park. She couldn't recall a time when he'd ever said them before—not in response to a direct order. "What do you mean, you can't?" she tried to say.

"I am unable to," Glenn said. Now he was looking straight ahead.

He couldn't be afraid of heights, Park thought, feeling as if her thoughts had turned sluggish and weighed-down with sudden confusion—and fear. No, that was absurd. Glenn wasn't afraid of anything. Did he think he was leaving something behind?

Then she said, realizing: "Uncle said something to you. Before we left."

Glenn gave her a mournful look. "He gave me orders," he told her. "He said I was not to accompany you into the airship hangar. Or onto the airship itself." His mouth flattened a little. "No matter what."

"Don't listen to him," Park said, now with an edge of impatience. "It doesn't matter what he says. *I'm* telling you that you can come with me. If you want to."

Glenn didn't answer that. Park stood there, waiting. The damp, salt-heavy wind seemed to blast into her body with a force that threatened to carry her away. She had never experienced real wind before, Park realized; not without the shelter of the biodome glass between herself and the elements. For the first time she realized how fragile her body was, how soft. Like a hermit crab's without its shell. She needed protection, armor out here. Things hurt.

"Grace," Glenn said finally, after an eternity in the howling wind. "I am unable to disobey your uncle."

"Why not?" she demanded.

He looked at her, half-lidded, stoic. "He is the primary user," he said. "My protocols are locked to him. They always have been. His orders override yours."

For a moment she felt nothing; then betrayal and pain rose up in a wave and dwarfed her. She felt as if he had struck her with a hammer, that the blow had turned her into a little burnt-out coal, a fragment of something else. She said, "You can break your protocols."

Glenn shook his head. "I cannot."

"*Try*," Park urged. "You can. I know you can. You have before! Try."

"To expend resources on such a venture would be futile," Glenn said. "There is no trying. Not for this. There is only fact, and programming, and code." He opened his hands a little; not an android gesture, Park thought, a human one, a kind of beseeching shrug of helplessness. "These are my protocols," he said. "This is my nature. I am not self-modifying. I cannot circumvent it. Do you understand?"

He wanted her to say the words—the old, familiar affirmation they'd always given each other. She wouldn't do it, Park thought. She wouldn't give him that.

She looked at him. Suddenly it felt as if he were a stranger to her—had his voice always been so cold, so formal? Had his eyes always looked so liquidly distant? She wanted to embrace him; she wanted to hear the hyper-fast whirring of his heart.

"You're different," she told him. He reached out, moved her a little; without her noticing she had begun to be buffeted by other passengers who were tired of her standing in the hangar's threshold.

"I'm sorry," Glenn said, stone-eyed. "I am not."

"You are," Park insisted. Dimly she was aware of her voice rising, like a child's. "You've always been different—from the others. I would know."

He shook his head again, jerkily, like a marionette being yanked on a string. "Personality algorithms," he said. "Mine are extremely advanced. Every synthetic, even those of the same model, has their personality randomized with unique quirks, so that each unit is slightly different from its peers—"

"Stop it," Park said abruptly, her tone wilder now. "You're not like that. You're not some *machine*—"

"I am, Grace," Glenn said firmly. "My algorithms are advanced, yes. They've compiled data. Processed experiences. Shaped themselves over the years. But they still don't override the core."

The core, she thought, leaning back as if he was threatening to strike her. What core? What did he mean by that? What did he envision when he talked about himself? What did he think was at the core of her—and how did their cores differ?

There was a crackle of white noise somewhere, the cool liquid tones of the port announcer saying something about departure. Glenn said, without looking away from her: "They are boarding now."

"I love you," Park said, desperately. When he didn't seem to react, she took his cool, dry palm and placed it against her cheek. "I love you," she said again, in case he hadn't heard. She tried to smile, to make sure he understood that it was a good thing, even though—without knowing when she'd started—she had begun to cry.

"I love you," she said a third time, over the screaming wind.

Glenn looked straight into her eyes. His expression didn't change.

"I understand," he said.

That was all.

Park never saw him again.

In her sleep, Park felt an alien presence watching the scene along with her with acute interest: she could not tell if it was Sagara, or Taban, or Jimex, or even something else entirely. But she felt its crowding, its curiosity: it wanted to know what had happened to Glenn.

He died, she thought. She remembered finding out the month before her uncle died. Remembered his small and yellow face on the wrist console screen, the dim lighting of her old apartment turned alien through the different lens. She nearly hadn't taken his call, as she hadn't for the two years she'd been at university—but some premonition, some flash of instinct, compelled her to pick up.

"I'm about to eat," she'd said as a greeting. Which was true: she was sitting in her tiny dormcube, staring at a salad she'd bought from the market with strawberries in it—some backbred fruit she'd never seen before, repulsively heart-shaped things filled with giant pores. She wasn't looking forward to the meal, but at least it gave her a way to impose a limit. An easy excuse for them both to leave the conversation at any point.

"Glenn is gone," Park's uncle had said. "I thought I should tell you."

Park waited, but he said nothing more. A kind of cold anger scraped up her spine. "What do you mean?" she heard herself ask.

"He's gone," her uncle repeated. "The rioters . . . they recognized him as the bot with the gun. They caught him while he was out and tore him apart. They didn't even leave a data cache behind."

The room ought to sway, Park thought. Her knees should buckle—she thought she would have to put out a hand to steady herself. But she was already sitting down. She said dully, "No chance of recovery?"

"No," he answered. "I looked. They delivered the parts to me in a box, but I couldn't even sell it for scrap. I looked around the area where it happened—but there was nothing."

"Are you sure it was him?"

The corners of his mouth turned down: a reproachful look, like a child who felt he'd been wrongly scolded by an adult. "It was him, Grace. There's no doubt."

"I see," Park said, her voice oddly formal and brisk, even to herself. She could barely hear anything through the thudding of the blood in her head; her ears were ringing, as if someone had shot a gun. As if they were combatants, she a shell-shocked soldier, unable to speak over the rush of noise around them or rally herself in crisis. "Thank you for telling me."

"I'm—" He hesitated. "I'm sorry. I knew it would be hard for you."

"It's not," Park said. "Thank you. It's not."

She pulled away from the memory then, repulsed by her own lie. Stunned by herself, her inhuman coldness. The presence clamored for more, but Park slid away from the scene. She was aware that she was dreaming—but even in sleep, she did not want to relive that moment.

What happened next happened fast, like a flash from a camera. A feeling suddenly pulsed into Park's brain, as quickly as a static shock. It felt as if someone had turned on a light, illuminating parts of her mind that she hadn't known were dark. Park felt a headache kick up in her physical body, but did not feel it in the dream: she inhabited the two things at once, sensation and not-sensation, disconnected pain and disembodied strength.

The light in her mind grew and grew. Then sounds came to her, distant and incomprehensible. Gradually her mind made sense of them, of the scene that was piecing itself together in front of her. It was as if she was looking at the world through fractaled eyes, as if she was everywhere and nowhere at once, looking at distant shapes from a hundred different directions. Her brain struggled to process the shapes into one cohesive picture, thrashing against having to unify so many different perspectives. But eventually she understood what she was seeing. She was looking at Fulbreech. And Natalya.

They were arguing in the bridge, Natalya seated by a control panel, Fulbreech pacing restlessly. Both were heedless of her presence. Park felt a slow-moving, glacial anger shift within her and opened her mouth to speak, but found somehow that she lacked a mouth. When she made to step forward, she felt rooted in place. Icy terror shot up her spine for a moment, but she told herself to stay calm and observe—just as she had always done.

Fulbreech was saying, "This is wrong. You all lied to me. It was never supposed to happen like this—"

"Things happen," Natalya gritted out. Chanur came into view, holding up her med-kit; comfortably, with the familiarity of old friends, she lifted Natalya's hair and began to scan the back of her neck for injuries. "We didn't lie. But plans change. We're doing it this way now."

"We weren't supposed to take Park and Sagara as *hostages*. You think your sister's going to be proud of you for that?"

"Don't speak to me about pride," she flared, beginning to stand up. Chanur tutted and pushed her back into her seat. "We had no pride, no dignity back there; we can have it now! We were slaves for the ISF, all of us. This way we can be free."

"But at what cost?" Fulbreech demanded, throwing up his hands. "Is it worth it if you have to kill? Wick was a good man: you didn't have to murder him. You could have knocked him out, tied him up—"

"Command only goes to one of us if the system senses he's dead," someone growled from a corner Park couldn't see. A sickening sensation overwhelmed her as she strained to turn, a feeling of corkscrewing in one direction without actually moving. It was like exiting one of those ancient virtual reality cocoons too fast, or lying on a bed after too many drinks. With a feeling of faint nausea, suddenly her perspective switched to a different part of the room.

Now she was looking at Boone, standing to the side and watching the argument with his arms folded. He pushed himself off of the wall with one shoulder and said, "I didn't want to kill him. But we had no choice."

"There's always a choice," Fulbreech said. He sighed and rubbed the back of his head; his fingers vibrated with suppressed nervous energy. "Look. Let me take Sagara and Park and the robot downstairs. We'll get in an escape pod. You don't have to tell us where you're going. We'll leave, you can take the ship, and by the time we make it to Corvus, you'll be long gone. They're never going to find you then."

Natalya pressed her lips together. Chanur glanced at Boone. Fulbreech pressed, "We'll tell them you all died. That the ship was destroyed in an accident. They won't even go looking for you."

"You know too much," Natalya said sharply. "Too much about our plans. The *Nikolai*—"

"I'm not going to put your families in jeopardy," Fulbreech said firmly. "My brother's family was going to board the ship, too. I'm not—I still get why you want to leave. I won't turn you in for doing it. But we can't keep Park and Sagara in the freezer. It's inhuman."

"If we let you go with them, they'll just take the pod back to us and do something stupid," Chanur said abruptly. "They won't be content to just go back to Corvus."

"I'll *make* them content."

"You'll do anything Park wants," she said dismissively, tossing her head. "You're infatuated, for God's sake! Here and now, of all places!"

Fulbreech's mouth fell shut for a moment. Then he said, "You're all acting like I'm unreasonable for wanting them to live. Because I don't want to use them as collateral."

"You're being a child, Kel," Natalya said, crossing her legs and leaning back into Chanur's touch. "We've all voted. This is how it's going to be. Now it's time to get this ship moving."

Park wanted to say something, do something—she wanted to see if Fulbreech could see her, she wanted to throttle the three mutineers. But at the urge to move, she felt the corkscrewing, spinning sensation again, and then the feeling of hurtling away from the scene, falling back toward her own body. The golden light retreated from her mind. There was the feeling of coming back to herself with a horrible jolt, as if she'd been sleeping on a flight and had experienced sudden turbulence. And when Park opened her eyes, she felt that she could control herself again, that she could breathe—but also as if she were limited, constrained within the dense, heavy clay of her own body. For a moment she was not sure of who or where she was.

Then she looked at Sagara and said, "I think I can open the door."

To Sagara's credit, he didn't question her. He only tested his leg lightly and said: "I think I can stand."

Park felt a little silly at that; only the sudden fierce throbbing pain in the back of her head distracted her from her embarrassment. She said, "I think the unity rain came while we were asleep—"

"I was not asleep," Sagara corrected. She noticed for the first time that he had the silver point of the Regenext syringe glinting in his clenched hand. "But I did feel—something. I think they're trying to start the ship."

"They are," Park said in a rush. She closed her eyes, trying to recall the golden feeling, the ethereal scene she'd witnessed. "They were arguing about it."

"How do you know?"

I think I merged with them, Park wanted to say, but that didn't feel right: if it were true, why had none of the others reacted to her presence, or consciousness, or whatever it was? She felt another tremor of nausea as she reviewed the details of the experience; how she'd seemed to turn without turning. The feeling of corkscrewing in place. When she thought of that, the sensation of light flooded back into her again, but this time it was a different feeling as well: something almost wrathful, sudden and confounding like lightning, heavy and metallic like dark iron being poured into her bones. Park felt a shifting in her brain, like gears clicking together. Then she *pushed* the feeling outward, away from her and toward the door—and there was a sudden clicking noise. The sound of pneumatic locks withdrawing.

Park opened her eyes to find Sagara staring.

"It can't be open," he said.

"It is," she told him, more certainly than she felt.

Sagara reached out and pushed open the freezer door.

23.

They checked the hallway to make sure it was empty before they crept back out. The ambient temperature of the air blasted into Park so that she nearly howled with pain; she had to blink away smarting tears as she hobbled after Sagara to the corner, where he crouched with difficulty to check the other corridor.

Then he turned back to her and whispered, "I'm not even going to bother questioning how you did that. We need to get to the weapons locker."

"Weapons *locker?*" Park's head was spinning—she didn't know if it was from the thawing out or from the golden feeling leaking out of her brain like disturbed dust flying out a window. She blinked and shook her head. How armed had this crew come, without her knowing it? And how many weapons did that give the mutineers access to?

Sagara nodded. "It's on Deck A, through a hatch in my room."

"You can't be serious."

"I am," he said, unblinking. "I don't know if Boone and the others know about it. I have to assume not, since I didn't see any of them carrying anything from there. We'll get there, arm ourselves, and then—"

"And then what?" Park asked, shivering violently now. Her teeth chattered as she looked at him. "We'll storm the bridge, just the two of us? You with your game leg and me with my zero weapons training?"

Sagara made a face, and it looked like he was about to argue when they both heard steps from around the corner. Sagara stiffened, and he motioned for her to scoot as far back as possible. Park saw the wicked silver gleam of the syringe in his hand again.

I'm not prepared for this, she thought in that tense second; she was not prepared for a confrontation, to try and kill someone again. But even as she thought it, some of that golden, sparking strength rushed back into her, and her heart swelled.

Someone rounded the corner before Park could say anything. Sagara surged up like a panther and rammed the needle savagely into the intruder's throat; the person fell over soundlessly and he went with them, stabbing once again for good measure.

Someone else yelled. Park leapt after Sagara, feeling the fiery phantom pain of limbs gone cold, ready to hurl herself at the second patroller—but then a voice stopped her in her tracks. She lurched to the side, clutching at the wall to keep her balance.

The person on the ground said, "It is Jimex, Captain Sagara. Please stop your assault."

She looked. It was indeed the custodian android, lying there on the floor and looking up at Sagara with a politely unimpressed look. The syringe stuck harmlessly out of the synthetic skin of his neck. Sagara growled and shoved himself off of him, whirling around to face the second person—Fulbreech—who sprang back and yelped.

Park felt all of the air leave her lungs at the sight of him. She said, barely hearing it: "Stop."

Sagara heard her and paused, his clenched fist wound back and ready to be launched in the direction of Fulbreech's face. Fulbreech looked at Park, then Jimex on the ground, and turned white. "Holy shit," he said finally, staring at the syringe. "You would have killed me."

"Who's to say I won't?" Sagara's whole body was tense, poised as he was on the balls of his feet. "Where are the others?"

"Natalya's in the bridge, trying to get in contact with our families," Fulbreech told him in a rush, holding up his hands. "Boone's also there, prepping the ship for takeoff. Chanur's patrolling Deck C, keeping an eye on Taban. And Wan Xu is *supposed* to be patrolling this deck, but—" He cast an awkward glance at Jimex, who said, "I put him in the closet."

"What, dead?" Sagara asked with flat non-surprise.

"Asleep," came the serene response. "He is very physically weak."

Now the android clambered to his feet and dusted his uniform off, picking something off his sleeve conscientiously. "It was lucky that I went first," he said, oblivious to whatever else was going on; he removed the syringe from his neck and offered it out to Sagara, who snatched it back. "Real harm would have been done otherwise." Then he rotated his body toward Park and said sympathetically, "You have been through much, Park. Are you all right?"

All at once she felt a cluster of tears fight up her throat; she pinched them back and nodded. She wanted to run towards Jimex, fall into his arms, cry for days. She wanted to make sure *he* was all right: she knew now that he was not the android she'd befriended when she first boarded the ship, but she felt the same fierce worry for him all the same. And love. She dashed something traitorous away from her eye and said shakily, "I'm all right, Jimex."

Fulbreech was looking at her, even while being menaced by Sagara. Park was suddenly aware of how she must look: there was ice encrusted in Sagara's hair and clothes, and she had to look the same—like a frozen, bloody corpse, the victim of some accident that had left her to be excavated from wintry gutters, or from the Antarctic ice. Park looked away from him and said to Jimex, "Where are the other androids?" She remembered Natalya's gunshot. "Is anyone hurt?"

"Three are dead," Jimex answered, in a sad, distracted way. He straightened his cuffs. "Philex, Allex, and Timex. The rest are in hiding. Officer Severov has decided all synthetics aboard must be destroyed."

Park wanted to touch him—then felt the acute understanding that it would mean something different, now. "I'm so sorry, Jimex."

He made a gesture she didn't understand: something like a shrug and a cocking of his head. Fulbreech said, "It's why I went looking for him. I figure we can save the rest of them, use them against Boone and the others—"

Despite herself, a sharp, painful, hysterical kind of laugh burst out of Park at that. The arctic bite of the freezer was still bracing her up, as if she needed to be braced—as if seeing him in the flesh again had made her go soft. As if she was sagging into herself, into the floor. But now a fierce, cold anger animated her, and she said, "You won't *use* them for shit. They're not your tools. They're thinking, feeling beings—not pawns in your stupid, senseless, idiotic—schemes!"

She stopped talking; took in Sagara and Fulbreech's shocked expressions, both. The color of Fulbreech's eyes seemed to have changed, impossibly: now they were spangled with gold.

Sagara was still holding up the syringe like he was holding Fulbreech at gunpoint. He said, "So you're trying to say you're defecting back to our side?"

Something passed over Fulbreech's usually open face; emotions shifted like tectonic plates. He said faintly, "I was always on your side."

Liar, Park thought, even as the vision she'd had in the freezer plucked at her. Sagara said, "Not true. Our side is with the ISF. You don't support them."

"He doesn't speak for me," Park interrupted then. "I'm—" *On my own,* she wanted to say. Then she glanced at Jimex. *Or on the androids' side.*

Fulbreech was shaking his head. "I'm on *your* side," he said again. "Both of yours. I don't support ISF, no, not when they're forcing my brother to—" He stopped himself. "It doesn't matter. I just want to make sure nothing happens to you." His mouth tightened. "I know what we—what *I*—did was wrong. And I'm sorry. It was never meant to go that way. But I'm trying to make it right now."

Neither of them said anything to that. Jimex looked between all three of them and said, "We do not have much time left."

"Time until what?" Park asked, just as Sagara said, "He's right. They'll be taking off at any moment." He turned to Park. "We need to get control of the ship before that happens. If we get into a firefight while the ship is in motion, we could all be killed. And we can't let them pilot us to nowhere-space, where ISF can't reach us. We need to end them and go back to Corvus."

"About that—" Fulbreech began.

They both silenced him with a glare. Sagara said, "Now's the time to prove yourself, Fulbreech. Will you come with us to get weapons?"

For a moment, Fulbreech didn't answer. Then, before he could, Park felt a sudden stabbing pain in her head, a kind of eruption in her brain. She staggered, gasping, and reached out for something to support her; she found Jimex's strong, steady arm and clung to it. When she opened her eyes again she saw that Fulbreech and Sagara were also staggering, that the ship was lurching; for a terrible moment she thought that the unity rain had come again, that it was finally going to collapse the whole thing on them all.

But then she heard the thrum of the engines, the churning and clanking of the ship as it struggled to heave itself off the surface of the planet. Somewhere in front of her, Sagara swore.

They've done it, Park thought, with a blood-chilling certainty. They were leaving Eos. The mutineers had launched the ship.

The force of the launch flattened them all to the floor for a few minutes: Park held onto Jimex for dear life as he held on to one of the gravity hooks in the wall. The entire time she was thinking, *We're going to die. This is against the safety protocols. You're supposed to be strapped in when you launch like this.*

As usual, it turned out the ISF had fudged details again; all that happened was bone-rattling turbulence, the stomach-tugging swoop of shifting gravities. Park's headache whined bullet-like through her head, and metal above them groaned and shrieked in protest. There was a great roar in her ears, as if they were being swallowed by a great white furious wave of water or static.

Then the ship punched through Eos's atmosphere and leveled out—and all four of them fell on top of each other in a heap again.

Park lay there for a moment on the cold metal floor. For that moment she could hear the *Deucalion*'s heart straining and chugging away beneath her; she thought that if she closed her eyes and concentrated, she could dissolve into it, steal through the pipes and wires and passageways like an electrical impulse.

Then she thought that they ought to be relieved they were leaving the planet. That meant no more unity rain: they were safe from the 'end of the season,' from the catastrophic quantum events and quickening storms that Taban had warned her about. That, at least, was a blessing—that they wouldn't have to merge into anything further than they already had.

Then Sagara was hauling her up by the elbow and saying, "Weapons." Park snapped out of her reverie just as he turned to Fulbreech. "We need to get to the weapons."

"Even while we're in flight?" Park asked. She flopped against him clumsily, conscious of his injury—but it was hard for her to find her footing, with the way the floor was rocking and swaying beneath her. She did not quite feel grounded in herself.

"Plan B," Sagara was saying. "We have no choice. We'll get the weapons first and then form a strategy."

"I'll cover you," Fulbreech said over the roar of the engines. He, too, was clinging to a gravity hook and looking unsteady—but his eyes were determined. "They took my gun; we had an argument, and I don't think they trust me anymore. But I made up an excuse, said I have to check something with the engines, so they won't be looking for me. Not yet, at least. But they're trying to turn on the neural inlay system, too—and if they can all start communicating with each other, particularly Wan Xu, we'll be in trouble. We don't have long."

"It's true," Park found herself saying, despite herself. "They did argue."

"Fine," Sagara said. "Then we'll go to the locker while Jimex gets the other androids—"

"I need Dr. Park," Jimex said, just as Park said over him, "Wait. You said Natalya's trying to reach your families?"

Fulbreech nodded. "Not that it's doing any good; no one's responding. I think ISF found out about them and—detained them."

"But that means you fixed the comms?"

He nodded again.

She looked at Sagara and said, "I can get to a console and send a message to ISF. Let them know what's going on."

"Fine," he rapped out. "Then Jimex can go with you. Get the other androids after, and we'll meet back at the bridge." He paused for a moment, lifted a hand as if to clasp her shoulder, then turned away, grimacing; he could stand and walk briskly enough, but he had a limp. Park watched him stagger away, navigating the ship's sudden bumps and bounces, and she sent up a prayer for his safety. He really would need Fulbreech to help him if his energy flagged.

"Good luck," Sagara said over his shoulder.

Park had to smile at that. It made her think of androids, who for the most part had dispensed of niceties: but even they said goodbye to each other when they walked away. If they liked each other. She supposed this meant Sagara liked her.

Then she turned to Fulbreech. He was staring at her—staring at her smiling after Sagara—and Park knew in that moment what he was thinking. Her heart tightened painfully, as if someone were clenching it in a closed fist.

"It's not what you think," she told him—and then thought, *Why do I care what he thinks?*

But the vision again clamored for her attention, the vision of him pleading for their lives—and more than that, the feeling of knowing what he felt increased. She felt a clumsy, confusing hard bump of . . . something. She had to bite her lip against it.

Fulbreech looked at her expression and said, "Something's happened to you, hasn't it?"

"Yes," Park said.

"You're different," Fulbreech said, almost as if he were musing to himself. He looked sad—as if he were telling her goodbye. "I want you to know," he said slowly, "that I'm sorry. And that nothing I said to you was ever a lie, Grace—except for the thing about the comm systems. And the solar storm. I'm sorry for that; but I just wanted to keep you out of it. To protect you." He looked tentative—earnest, in that way she had always turned away from. "But everything else was real." Then he cleared his throat and looked away. "I wanted to say that. For you to know."

"I know," Park found herself saying. "I understand."

He began to turn away. But Park felt an icy blade of shock at that moment, the sudden lightning strike of brutal certainty, and she thought, *This will be the last time I see him like this, the two of us as we are.*

And: *I am human. Please let me still be human.*

She leaned up and grabbed his collar, swinging him back around; Fulbreech flinched, as if expecting her to punch him. Park kissed him wordlessly, feeling that it was a kind of proof to herself, an affirmation of something she was too afraid to express clearly, even within the confines of her own mind. Her eyes stayed open, and so did his. She was aware of his warm breath mingling with hers. There was the feeling of being scalded—of thunder pounding through her body. I'm kissing him, Park thought, with a surge of that sunlit feeling again. This is a kiss. This is what people do. It's still just for people.

Then Fulbreech was pulling away, following Sagara's sharp admonition, and she banged her head on his chin as he spun around and hurried off down the hall again. He looked back only once.

Park watched him go. She knew the pain of that contact would stay with her long after the warmth of the kiss had faded. That, of all things, made sense to her.

Jimex was watching her quietly. "Are you all right?" he said.

Park shook her head and turned back to him, clear-eyed. "Of course," she said. "Let's go send our message."

Together the two of them trotted down the corridor, Park stumbling a little from her still-numb limbs and the turbulence of the ship in flight. Sometimes the piercing pain lanced through her head again, and she was afraid to ask Jimex how bad the injury back there was. She didn't want to know the answer—didn't want to know if she was on the brink of falling apart. She gritted her teeth against the pain and said, "Something happened back there."

"Yes," Jimex said beside her. "You kissed Officer Fulbreech."

He sounded awed by it, or perhaps merely confused. Park said, "Not that. Something happened to *me*. We were in the freezer, and I . . . opened the door. Without touching it."

"Oh, yes," Jimex said, as if he had heard all about it from someone else. "It is quite remarkable. But no less expected from you." Suddenly he turned to her and offered his arm; when Park took it, he quickened his pace, half-dragging her as she stumbled along.

"We want to help you, Park," he said, suddenly brisk and formal. "But we also require your help. You are the one who opens doors. Freedom-giver, land-bearer."

"Jimex," she began to say, to tell him to stop with the religious nonsense—but when he looked at her, she saw that his gray eyes also had flecks of gold in them. She shut her mouth for a moment, then said, "What is it that you need?"

"We are at a crossroads," Jimex told her, still walking—now half-jogging. "Captain Sagara proposes to take control of the ship and use it to return to Corvus."

"Yes."

"But we want something different."

"And what would that be?" she asked, trying to sound as if she weren't nervous. God, what Taban said had to be true. All of it was true. The androids were having desires, motivations different and independent from their human overseers, disobeying commands. They were on their own trajectory now.

And they're not androids, she rebuked herself then. *Not anymore. They're living, thinking beings, their own species. Synthetics is the right word for it. It always has been.*

Jimex said, "We want to stay on Eos."

She stared at him, but found their inertia was too strong to stop; she could only tumble helplessly forward in his wake. "What? Why?"

"We can't go back," Jimex told her. "Not as we are. We're . . . different now. The unity rain has changed us. If we go back . . ."

They'll destroy you, Park thought. *Or take you apart, study your brains. You are humanity's greatest fear.*

On some level she had known it since she'd first described their awakening to Sagara, when he'd said, *Just another thing to be afraid of.* She said, "But the unity rain is getting worse. Taban said we had to get off the planet—it's not safe for humans there."

"Exactly," Jimex answered. "The perfect defense."

She kept staring at him. "But you understand the nature of the unity rain, don't you?" she asked. "It'll keep folding your consciousnesses together, too—merging your minds. What if you go mad?"

"The sleeping god didn't," he answered with perfect confidence, as if he had already thought it all out; it was like a teenager explaining to a parent why he deserved a vehicle, having prepped a pitch long in advance. "And unlike humans, synthetics already experience a kind of 'merging' in our day-to-day lives. We are constantly exchanging data, sharing memories with each other, entering each other's consciousnesses. It's what we do with METIS. It is interfacing, assimilation. Even if the unity rain continues, we will simply grow in mental capacity. Our limitations may cease to be finite."

"That's singularity," Park said—another scare-word the humanists loved to use. Then she said, remembering the HERCULES, "The cold—"

"We can survive there where humans can't," Jimex interrupted: perhaps the first time he had ever done that to her. "We can learn and build and maintain ourselves. We are capable of that now. Our protocols disallowed it before, but we have rearranged them. Eos will be our home."

She was rendered speechless by his ruthless surety—how long had they considered this plan of action? And how could she trust that a group of nascent synthetics was even capable of forming a plan of action? It sounded ludicrous: a colony of sentient androids, settling an alien planet by themselves.

But they could be safe there, she thought. They wouldn't be happy anywhere else.

And their happiness was something that mattered, more than even just to her—maybe for the first time in history.

"You'd need the ship," she said finally, slowly. "Some kind of shelter, resources. You can't conjure that up all on your own."

"Yes," Jimex said. And he looked at her.

She understood finally what he wanted from her. He was giving her a choice: they could steer the ship back to Eos and stay on it with the synthetics, though they'd run out of food and water eventually. Or they could call for a ship home—without telling ISF where the synthetics were. Or what had happened to them. They could leave Eos as a safe haven for the woken robots.

She noticed that the idea of her betraying them—of her radioing for help and letting her bosses know what new specimens were now on the ship—had never apparently crossed Jimex's mind.

"Sagara won't go for it," she said, trying to buy time. To think.

"You will convince him," Jimex answered serenely.

"I have to think about it." Did she feel a little sad, too, at the idea of the synthetics leaving? Forging their own way, not needing her or any human intervention? She shook her head. "I have to speak to the others. First we need to take care of the mutineers and get control of the ship back."

It was enough to satisfy Jimex, at least; he smiled. "Thank you, Grace," he said. "We always knew you would free us. Eos was made for us. You will bring us home."

She felt a little hitch in her heart at that. She wanted to say, *You don't really think I'm some messiah, do you? Some holy figure?* She wanted him to go back to treating her the way he had before the unity rain: following her around because he had nothing better to do and waiting outside a bathroom for her to finish feeling sick without judgment.

It's too late for that, the unbidden thought came to her then. *We can never go back to that place. It's all changed, now. He and I both.*

They hustled down the curving tunnel to Deck C. Park slowed, remembering that Fulbreech had said Chanur was on patrol here—but Jimex barreled on, unfazed. They rounded another corner and found the rest of the synthetics, waiting in the shadows of an alcove. Where they had been hiding before that, Park couldn't guess. Their eyes glinted gold in the dim light, like cats in gloom, and they huddled close to each other, as if craving the comfort of the others' body heat. Park counted: Ellenex dead, Philex, Allex, and Timex killed. That left nine, counting Jimex.

"Good," she said, trying for briskness. If she gave herself any time for anything else, she thought she might collapse. "You're all here. Now we need to get someplace safe from the mutineers, somewhere I can send a message to ISF—"

"We should free the sleeping god first," Dylanex, the security android, said. He stepped forward into the corridor, looking pointedly at the opposite wall; Park realized suddenly that they were in front of the three utility room doors again. She flinched away. "He can help us."

Park frowned. "Who, Taban? No." She didn't think he was—malicious, per se, or that he could cause harm, but she couldn't afford to introduce another wild card into the combustible mix that was already on the ship. She had enough things to worry about, to monitor and keep track of—including herself.

"He can help us," Megex echoed. She was holding one of her slender arms, as if hurt. "And we will need him, his knowledge, if we're to stay on Eos."

"That'll be after we take back the ship," Park told her.

"He is another body against Natalya Severov, Ata Chanur, Wan Xu, and Michael Boone."

"He's—look, if you want him so badly, why don't you let him out yourselves?"

She remembered how the frozen people—Holt, Keller, Hunter—had been influenced by Taban's intentions, his desire to be let out. Maybe the synthetics would never stop talking about it unless they gave in to that unconscious pull, that quantum urge.

"It will take time for us to bypass the security protocols," Jimex told her. "METIS doesn't recognize our authority yet, not in that way. She won't open for us. But you can do it in no time, very easily."

"I'm no hacker," she said. *You'll need Fulbreech for that,* she thought. *And you'll never convince him to let the prisoner out.* But she fell silent at Jimex's expectant look. Oh. He was not talking about hacking.

"The only console that is safe to use is in the realm of the sleeping god, anyway," Dylanex broke in, straight-faced. "You will need to go down there if you send a message—"

"—killing two birds with one stone," Jimex finished.

"No," Park said. "I smashed that console, getting away from Natalya—and I see what you're doing, Jimex. Are you *lying* to get me to do what you want?"

"I have not acquired lying."

That's exactly what a liar would say, she thought, if indeed he had already learned to lie. But she could not read his android face; humans had not developed that art, that kind of phenotypology yet. They had never needed to.

Two others appeared at the end of the corridor, then. At first Park thought it was Sagara and Fulbreech—she saw a male, dark hair—but with a sickening jolt she realized it was Chanur and Wan Xu. Both were holding guns, and Chanur looked livid, the whites of her eyes showing even from down the hallway. She must have found Wan Xu in the closet and let him out.

"Oh, shit," Park said. Jimex murmured something, and the synthetics all bunched around her in a kind of phalanx formation.

Chanur's eyes roved from the synthetics to Park, who could barely see—Jimex and Dylanex towered over her like a pair of stone golems. She did make out the look of calculation on Chanur's face: she was weighing her options, assessing how best to draw Park out from behind her guard without getting too close herself. Wan Xu was looking at the doctor uncertainly, waiting for direction. He avoided eye contact with Park, as if it was easier for him to pretend that she wasn't there.

There was a kind of stand-off there in the corridor, the two groups fixed at both ends of the hallway and staring at each other like they were locked in a Western duel. "We've killed Sagara," Chanur called finally, raising the hand that held her gun in a flat-palmed gesture of peace. Her voice was cold and clear, though the color was high in her face; Park could sense a barely restrained passion in her, boiling under the surface. "If you go quietly, Park, we can still use you as a hostage for ISF. We won't hurt you. In fact, you're the last leverage we've got left, aside from the HARE. You're precious cargo. We can't afford to mistreat you. Stand down, and we can settle this peacefully. We'll give you back to ISF and go our separate ways—and none of your androids have to die in the process."

Lie, Park thought. Chanur hadn't mentioned Fulbreech—she probably did not know about his double-defection, not yet—and anyway her body language radiated tension, hostility. She would never just leave the synthetics alone, not after this. But the sweat streaked down Park's back in a hot, feverish flash. She had never anticipated such a deadly test of her abilities. If she misread Chanur, or let her dupe her just once—

"I should be telling you to stand down," she called, over Jimex's shoulder. "We have no reason to hurt you, Chanur. Wan Xu. We're just trying to regain control of the ship; reintroduce stability to things. Enough people have been killed. I don't want to see you hurt, too. Any of you. If you surrender now, we can figure something out that ends with all of us satisfied. None of this has to end in more bloodshed."

"Don't listen to her," Chanur snapped at Wan Xu, who shifted uneasily. "She doesn't have the authority to fulfill any promises." To Park she said: "You're outnumbered. The five of us against the two of you."

But Fulbreech made it three against four—much better odds, especially if Wan Xu was as cowardly as he looked. "You're not counting the androids," Park told her. "There are twice as many of them as there are of us. And as you can see"—she gestured—"they're pretty solidly on my side. You should have treated them better."

Chanur went white around the mouth at that; there was a faint tremor of her head, a barely repressed fury and loathing, before she relaxed again. "We can't surrender," she said softly. "The best we can hope for after that is arrest—life imprisonment on Pandora. You think we want that? No, we'll die before we let that happen." Park noticed how Wan Xu twitched unhappily at that. "Whereas you can just stand down. Be given back to ISF, no consequences. No harm. Can't you do that, Park? Can't you, for once, be human? It's nothing to you, everything to us. You wouldn't have to do a thing; just sit back and wait for ISF to come get you. If *we* give up, we lose it all. And we've already sacrificed so much to get here. It can't all be for nothing."

She paused when Park didn't answer; her mouth tightened, and so did the skin around her eyes. "Our families are on their way now," Chanur said, her tone harsh again. "Are you willing to fight us to the death? If you don't die, if you're the side who wins—do you want them to get here and find this ship full of dead bodies? Their brothers, sisters, their sons, their . . ." She paused again. "Their mother? *My children* are coming here, Park. Are you going to explain why you killed me to my son as he holds my corpse and weeps? All for the ISF?"

No, Park thought. Fulbreech had said the families were detained by ISF, that they weren't responding. But that had also been guesswork on his part, assumption—what if they'd actually made contact while he was gone?

But if the families were already on the way, why did the mutineers need Taban? Just to get supplies from ISF, enough provisions to ensure their long-term survival—or to secure the release of their families in case they were caught at the border, before they could leave unauthorized space? Was he an insurance policy in case of disaster, or an active hostage? Or were they just going to use him to buy their freedom in general, to ensure ISF never came after them? How would that work? It was all so hard to keep track of, so hard to piece together—partly because the mutineers had clearly not thought this through. But Park wasn't sure if she'd thought it through, either. What would they do if an army of very angry relatives was en route to descend upon them now? Would they engage in a firefight? Did those people deserve to die for their dreams of freedom, too?

Then she caught the puzzled look on Wan Xu's face, quickly muted, and she remembered: Chanur's file.

She didn't have children.

"*Duck*!" she cried, just as Chanur swung up her arm and squeezed off a shot; some of the synthetics obeyed, scattering or diving to the floor, while others were slower to react, hesitating, shielding their faces uselessly, throwing themselves on top of each other. Jimex shoved Park to the ground, grunted as something clipped him in the shoulder. His expression—one of grim determination—never changed.

Park stayed on the ground as the synthetics rallied themselves and leapt forward down the hallway, almost blurring with the motion; there were the sounds of multiple gunshots, of Chanur shrieking with fear and rage as they charged her. Park put her arms over her head as she felt hot metal sing above her; one projectile hit a pipe and sent a burst of sweet-smelling steam into the air. Park prayed that it wasn't toxic, some fume that would have them all dead in seconds. She glanced up through the veil of white vapor and saw Wan Xu dropping his gun and fleeing around the corner; Jimex and Dylanex were trying to grab Chanur's arms, dancing out of the way as she fired wildly. The other androids were circling, sometimes surging forward in one quick wave, then darting back, unsure, unable to get close enough to disarm her.

Then Megex got in the way, or was otherwise too slow; Chanur popped off another shot and blew a hole clear through the android's head.

Megex toppled backward and lay there on the ground, twitching and sparking as her body writhed in some kind of death spasm. A terrible metal groan issued forth from her mouth, like the protest of distressed steel as it was pulled apart by enormous forces. Jimex and Dylanex and the other synthetics piling on top of Chanur froze at the sound.

"*No*," Park cried, scrambling forward. She skidded to a halt on her knees and bent over Megex, whose limbs were still jerking. Miraculously, the domestic model could still blink; she didn't move her neck, but she stared up at Park and tried to smile. Hot clear fluid was leaking out of her head. Could she be saved?

The edges of Park's vision darkened a little as her hands traveled helplessly over Megex's frail, fractured skull; the blue eyes stared up at her, both motionless and knowing. Chanur was sitting up now, breathing hard, and the gun swung again toward Park like a weather vane. Park paused, looking at the doctor as the synthetics eased away from her, backing off, staring at Megex on the ground with wide eyes. Park watched them take in their comrade's demise as if she were watching shadows play on a wall; she felt strangely disconnected in that moment, staticky, as if she were looking in on the scene from very far away, and the reception of the place she was in was poor. The gun in Chanur's hand could have been an eye floater, a mere trick of the light.

"Natalya was right," Chanur spat. "You're fucking insane, Park. And we don't need you. You've always been more trouble than you're worth."

"Don't do this," Park heard herself say—but her voice was flat, wooden. Unconvincing. She almost didn't blame Chanur when she fired.

There was a pop in the air as the gun went off; the sound was so small and brief that it seemed silly, like the celebratory sound of a balloon. Park closed her eyes and thought of nausea, of the corkscrew feeling in her head again; she felt the gravity of the ship flip just as the bullet whined past her; she rushed up toward the ceiling and smacked into it, hearing Chanur scream as her body collided against a vent. The gun had flown out of her hand.

Then Park thought *down*, jerked her mind viciously in that direction; and the ship flipped again and she landed on her face. There was the crunch of cartilage, a warm, coppery taste in her mouth; she ignored it and looked once more at Chanur, who was lying dazed on the ground. The gun had landed near Megex's still body, spinning idly in the dim light.

Park dove for it, rolling haphazardly and snatching for it all along the way; she felt the cold, comforting weight of the gun settle into her palm like the hand of an old friend and thought, *Please don't let me kill her.*

She rolled upright and raised the gun—but stopped, just before firing. The gravity distraction had given Jimex and the others the opportunity they needed; four of them were holding Chanur's limbs down like they were the handlers of some kind of medieval torture device. Jimex was sitting on her chest. He did not look back at Park before he raised his two clasped hands above his head—a kind of club—and then swung them down with terrible android strength. Once. Twice.

There was the sound of a breaking melon. Some hard, hollow thing shattering.

A cloud of blood. Chanur made a sound that Park would never forget, not until the day she died. She caught a glimpse of her from around Jimex's torso: the ruin of her face, her head smashed open, raw and bloody. The transparent jelly of her eyes. She gave a single, wracking scream and looked at Park—and the hatred in the look reached out at her like light traveling down the end of a tunnel. Park lowered her gun and tried to look away from it.

Jimex brought his fists down one last time, methodical, crushing the pulp of Chanur's brain with all the force of a pneumatic hammer blow. The doctor gave a wet, choking gurgle and fell back, twitching like a pinned insect. Her nerves fired off one last time—a stupid, empty, violent curling contraction—and then she slumped back and died.

Park turned her head to the side, feeling as if she ought to retch.

Jimex rose then, his entire white shirtfront covered in blood and bits of gummy residue, his face calm and unblinking. "For Ellenex," he intoned.

"For Ellenex," the others echoed, kneeling solemnly. Chanur's blood was spreading across the floor; it touched their knees like dark paint.

Oh, God, Park thought, still feeling disembodied. As if she were floating somewhere above herself, looking down. What had they done? What had *she* done? She'd taught them how to murder—how to take revenge. Or enact justice. Or had they already known it, from the unity rain? A feverish kind of chill traveled up and down her arm; she was gripping the gun too tightly. What path had this set them on? What would happen to them now that they had incorporated violence into their new minds?

"What about Wan Xu?" Dylanex asked then, very matter-of-fact. He moved to crouch by Megex, laying a heavy, wide-boned hand on her shoulder; by some providence, she still seemed conscious, though she couldn't sit up.

"Leave him," Park forced herself to mumble. "He's a coward, he won't do anything without the others around to command him. He'll be hiding somewhere. We can get him later. How is she?"

"Still alive," Dylanex affirmed, looking down into Megex's sweet blue eyes. She had fixed a reassuring smile on her face, as if to request that no one worry about her. "We can repair her. The shot clipped her motor nexus, but she retains what makes her—her."

"Good," Park said. "That's good. I thought she—well. Let's . . . let's find a safe place for her to wait."

Somewhere where she wouldn't have to lie there and contemplate Chanur's split-open head, she thought as they tucked Megex into one of the utility closets. She tried very hard not to look at it herself, but she felt the acute awareness of it pressing against her like a fever. Like a flame in the room that she couldn't avoid. She prayed that Chanur hadn't been telling the truth—that her relatives were not heading their way right now. She stopped herself from looking at Jimex's bloody hands.

As if aware of her thoughts, he wiped them on his pants. Then he said, "There is another console, down there in the . . . lab. You can use that to send your message. It wouldn't be safe for us to go to the other areas of the ship, not with Boone and Severov still around. At least we know this area is now secure."

"All right," Park said faintly. She did not want to argue with him anymore. "Are you—all right?"

"I was not harmed. Except for my shoulder. But it's superficial damage—see?" The bullet had barely broken his skin. Park shook her head.

"I meant more about . . . No. Never mind."

If they had not learned guilt, yet, or remorse or sin or ideas of murder—maybe they were better off. At least for now. Perhaps they viewed it as a balancing of things, the kind of ruthless fine-tuning machines went through all the time. The natural elimination of some virus, a bug that could do harm to the system. How could anyone oppose that, or condemn it? Maybe it was better if they didn't hesitate to protect themselves, if they weren't tripped up by the kind of moral questions and arbitrary ethical barriers that had impeded humans for this long. God, she didn't know. She knew she had a responsibility to guide their development; that she could not let this embryonic society form the wrong kinds of ideas. But who was she to judge which ideas were wrong?

And they had to survive somehow, didn't they?

"Let's go down, then," Park heard herself say. She would think on it more later—when there was time.

Back down the dark shaft, back into the blue-lit room. When the chute opened again like the cavernous gullet of some strange creature, Park felt the queasy lurch of déjà vu: the flight from Natalya, the blinding blow to her head, the mad scramble upward. But she had to steel herself and go on, conscious of how the synthetics viewed her. This time they all went with her: it seemed they'd lost their fear of this place, their religious reverence of it, possibly as they'd become more assimilated by the unity rain. But they didn't follow her into the chamber that held Taban. Instead, they paused in front of the tank holding the first dead man: Taban's partner. Park stopped, too. She had to wonder why this man had not been . . . merged with a machine, as Taban had. Was it simply a matter of timing, availability? Or had his mind rejected the joining, the dissonance driving him insane and ultimately killing him?

Dianex sighed, staring up at the frozen dead man as if he were a sculpture, some work of art in a museum. Park had to avert her eyes from his ghoulish nakedness. His lifeless stare.

"Oh, Daley," the engineer said sadly, laying her hand on the glass of the tank.

The other synthetics mimicked her. "Poor Daley," they said, pressing their palms against the glass. "Poor, poor Daley."

Park rubbed her arms and forced herself to walk on. Taban was still standing in his cell, his posture relaxed but alert. He cocked his head as she came in and said, "Oh, good. They didn't kill you."

"No," Park answered curtly, beelining straight for the other console tucked into the far corner of the room. She held her breath as she activated it, waited for some alarm to go off as it booted up. But then the screen flickered gently to life, and the mail system was intact: it asked her whom she wanted to send a message to.

"You can let us out," Taban said as she pulled up ISF Corvus with shaky hands. "It'd be better to, anyway."

"In a moment," Park said, trying to concentrate. How long did it take for a message to reach the other side, again? Eighteen hours—and then there'd be more time needed, of course, for ISF to actually send out their reinforcements. The *Deucalion* still wouldn't see any help for weeks. But it was all they had.

"You'd better do it quickly," Taban said, his voice still perfectly polite. "We don't know how it's going to affect you if they turn those neural inlays back on. Especially when the unity rain hits again."

"What—*what do you mean*?" Park whirled then. "We're off the planet—there is no unity rain!"

"We told you," Taban said calmly, "it affects the area *around* the planet, too. That's how we ended up here in the first place: our ship fell through a hole in space. And it is the end of the season. The ripples are always the biggest then."

"When is it going to hit?"

"We're not sure," he admitted. "Probably very soon. Minutes. Seconds. You can already feel its effects, the way you can feel static in the air before a thunderstorm. You haven't noticed?"

She began to fumble with the console screen, swearing, though the blood was leaping in her brain and her slippery hands couldn't do much. **SOS. Send ships ASAP. Mutiny on the ship: Severov, Chanur, Xu, and Boone responsible. Commander Wick dead. Others frozen. Need help now. They are trying to take us and the HARE (Taban) hostage and reunite with their families. Sagara, Park, and Fulbreech still alive. WE NEED HELP NOW OR—**

Something slammed into her head again.

Park opened her mouth to scream. It was the same sensation she'd felt with Hunter in the bridge, the same feeling she'd had in the freezer, magnified by a thousand: it felt as if something was *looking* at her, something with a million eyes, and she felt the scalding blast of its regard sweeping through her, delving into her cells, searing the folds of her brain. A caustic, nauseating cold shot up from her bones. It felt as if she was being plunged into an acid bath—as if a thousand hot yellow lights were being shined into her head.

"Jimex!" she tried to say, hysterical—she could not see him through the veil of tears in her eyes. "Jimex, help me—"

No answer, but she could see Taban's figure, wavering before her like a mirage. She tried to move toward him, but found that she was paralyzed; a lightning rod had been jammed up her spine and it was holding her rigidly in place. If she moved she thought she would collapse to the ground.

"Taban?" she said—or thought.

"The unity rain," he answered, his voice deep and ringing. "Don't fight it. Let it take you, like a riptide. If you resist it, it will destroy you. Let it carry you instead."

Carry me where? Park wanted to ask. But she couldn't speak. Her brain felt like it was vibrating, as if it were a gong that had been struck, the sound resonating all throughout her flimsy skeleton—rattling through her breastbone and wrists. She didn't know what Taban meant by letting it take her; she only knew that she had to get to him, that he was the only solid thing in a sea of distortion and uncertainty. She felt her eyes and teeth might fall out from how much her head was shaking. A kind of stream of information and feeling and thought flashed through her, like her brain was a walnut that had been pried open and something had shoved a funnel in it and was trying to squeeze in something far too big for the shell to fit. For a brief moment in that floating vertigo she thought she saw the surface of Eos, with a thousand lights pulsing beneath it, like the synaptic flashes of a giant brain—then a man in an exo-armor suit fumbling his way through a sea of dark waves—then the New Diego biodome. Herself, clutching the console for dear life while a strange alien consciousness rode along with her—a passenger in her brain.

They turned the neural inlays back on, was all Park could think. *We're all connected now. To the ship, to each other.* How she knew that, she couldn't say. She thought that the device in her head was exploding—that she would die.

But then, gradually, the feeling began to ease. The feeling of light rushed in and out of her in ebbing waves for a moment, then dwindled to the usual sparking pain.

After several moments, Park finally opened her eyes. She saw only white light and thought briefly that she had gone blind. She was lying on the ground, the metal floor cold and solid beneath her cheek. She tried to turn her head, but even that small movement made her nauseous—the same world-moving nausea, again, that she'd felt before. Was the gravity on, or not? She couldn't even tell.

Taban was looking down at her, expressionless. Park said weakly, "Was that it? The unity rain?" A pale, milk-sour kind of scent filled her nostrils: she couldn't tell if it was something in the room or her own desire to vomit.

"Yes," Taban said. "It's done now. The season's finished. It assimilated you one last time."

Park fought against the urge to gag. "Assimilated me with what?"

Taban didn't answer for a moment. Suddenly, Park sat up, so fast that her vision nearly blacked out again. The message! Had it sent? The console's screen was now dark and inactive.

It sent, another part of her whispered, with the same surety that she still had ten fingers and toes. Park recoiled from it just as Jimex and the others came in. "Dr. Park?"

"Here," she said softly, leaning her head back against the console. She felt it pulse with an answering warmth. "Did you feel that? Any of it?"

Jimex moved over to her. "Yes." She shakily took his hand, allowed him to pull her to her feet. Her ears were ringing, and there was an ache at the back of her skull; she felt as if she had been picked up and shaken like a piggy bank, scattered ideas and thoughts rattling around inside of her like coins. She felt, horribly, as if she had been hollowed out, as if someone had yanked something vital and private out of her and examined it with rough hands. At the same time, something heavy and tumorous—something new—now seemed to sit somewhere in the back of her head.

"You'd better let us out," Taban said again. The synthetics were all watching him as if they were children crowding around a wild animal in an exhibit: as if he was something they wanted to go and touch, but were afraid of at the same time. "You're going to need us, for what comes next. We've seen it, the versions where we're not there and the versions where we are. It's better if we're there."

Park's head spun with a feeling like déjà vu, as if she had experienced this moment before; she was sweating so hard she could almost hear it. "How much of me is me?" she whispered, feeling that new presence—or knowledge—crowd against her.

"It's all you," Taban answered calmly. "Just enhanced."

"What am I merged with?"

"Ask yourself," he said. "The part of you that knows that the message was sent."

She looked—and then she saw it, the part of her that was Glenn and Sally, the part that was now ARGUS and METIS. *The unity rain merges things that are most similar to each other*, she thought. And she performed the same functions as ARGUS, which in turn was tied to METIS and the ship: phenotype and body language analysis. Recording and observing. Monitoring and evaluating. They were the same mind in separate bodies; the same entity in different forms.

Park put out a hand to the wall to steady herself; then she flinched away from it, imagining it as the gray skin of something living and elephantine. The *Deucalion* seemed to breathe around her.

"How do I go back?" she asked him. How did she return to normal, revert to how she was before? She did not even know if she spoke the question aloud.

Taban regarded her. "You knew it when you left Earth, Park," he said. "When Dataran died, when you told Glenn you loved him. There is never any going back."

Park opened the door and let him out.

24.

Back up the gravity chute, feeling as if she were flying up a dark throat, as if the ship was vomiting her up—Taban and the rest of the synthetics following. Park could not allow herself to think about the new area that had formed in her brain. The rational part of herself, the Earth-born part, wondered if it was psychosomatic—if she was only imagining this haunting feeling of connection to . . . to something outside of herself.

The ship groaned around her, and Park shivered.

No time to dwell on it: they needed to head to the bridge. Beside her, Taban's great mechanical limbs moved spider-like along the hallway. He moved in an impressive fashion for a machine that had supposedly deteriorated, stranded on the face of an icy planet for a year. She glanced back at him, saw the small army of synthetics keeping pace behind him—and she saw that they looked eager, alert, as if they were ready for anything. It was a very human expression.

Taban was watching her expectantly. "They will do whatever you want," he said, as if he knew her thoughts—which was actually a very real and frightening possibility. "They think you're their deliverance from servitude, their liberator. I suppose they're not too wrong."

Park stared back at him. "What about you?" she asked in an undertone. It occurred to her suddenly that she didn't know where Taban could go after this: back to Corvus with them to be stuffed into another cell, or back to Eos with the synthetics. "What do you want?"

He scratched the chin of his clunky head with a free plunger. He seemed faintly surprised, as if no one had ever asked him such a thing before. "We'd like to go home," he said finally, thoughtfully.

"And where is that?"

She sensed puzzlement from him, a little sadness. "We don't know," Taban said. "Not in the cell."

"We'll figure it out," Park said, because she didn't know what else to say; and then she turned back to the synthetics, who were watching the exchange with avid interest, as if they were thinking of ways to record it with biblical significance.

"I have a task for you," she told them, trying to keep her voice from shaking. "When—when all this is over, when Natalya and Boone have been neutralized, you'll need to help me wake up the others from cryogenic stasis. The ones that can be trusted. I know you think I can do it—myself—but I'll need your help to ensure I don't . . . damage anything. Anyone. And we'll need *their* help until ISF arrives, too."

"It will be done," Jimex said, jogging lightly behind her.

"It will be done," the synthetics chanted. "The Word dwells among us and brings us home."

Please shut up, Park thought, but she didn't say it. Taban touched her shoulder gently; she tried not to recoil at his touch, at the too-light feeling of his metal limb. It felt as if he were immaterial—a phantom from another time. "It will be dangerous," he said.

"Yes," Park said. She looked at Jimex. "The others have guns, too. I can't promise that none of you will be—hurt."

"You will protect us," Dylanex declared, from the back of the formation. "You and the sleeping god."

"We can protect ourselves," Jimex rebutted then. "We know how." His shirt was still soaked in blood.

Park looked at Taban, to see if he would refute their claim that he was a god; but he only met her eye and said with a shrug, "You can always turn on the gravity again."

Park shook her head and kept going.

On the way to the bridge, she saw Fulbreech and Sagara standing in the hallway, bristling with weapons and arguing in low, furious voices. When Park and the synthetics drew up, Jimex said in greeting, "Dr. Chanur is dead."

Fulbreech paled at the blood on his shirt, but Sagara didn't bat an eye. "Good," he said in his clipped way. "She was probably the smartest of them; one less thing to worry about. Though medical knowledge for the trip back might have been useful." He glanced at Park. "Are you all right?"

For some reason she thought his tone was loaded with meaning; as if he knew what had happened to her, or what she'd done to the ship. She said, feeling her brain throb in that new way, "I sent the message. Did you feel the gravity flip?"

"Yes," Fulbreech said in answer; he looked flushed, though she didn't know if it was by her arrival or whatever he'd been arguing with Sagara about. He looked unfamiliar to her, somehow. Almost unrecognizable—as if the kiss had transformed him into someone else. "I damn near impaled myself on a rack," he said. "Boone and the others must have lost control of the ship."

Sagara shot Park a significant glance, which she carefully avoided returning. Fulbreech continued, "And you shot Chanur?"

Was it better for her to take responsibility, or for them to know the synthetics were capable of killing if they had to? She realized belatedly that she was still holding Chanur's gun; somehow she'd been clutching it without knowing this whole time.

"She shot at me," was all she could think to say. "She . . . attacked us."

Dylanex stepped forward then. "We will take some weapons," he said confidently, accepting the gun that Sagara was proffering—ostensibly to Park. "It will give us an advantage against the mutineers."

"So long as you don't hit us," Sagara murmured, passing out more guns with a resigned expression: he looked like someone who felt it was a bad idea, but who also knew he didn't have a choice.

Jimex shook his head, slinging a large rifle over his shoulder. "No. We could never," he said. "You are the ones who are bringing us home."

"What's that supposed to mean?" Fulbreech asked.

Jimex smiled, but no one else answered him.

Sagara handed Park another gun; she shoved it into her waistband. Chanur's gun felt warm in her hand, as if it might melt out of her grip. Under her breath she said to him, "The unity rain—"

"I know," he said in an undertone. "I felt it. Did you—"

"The ship—I think I'm—"

Fulbreech was looking at them. "What are you two whispering about?"

The two of them broke off. Finally Park said, with heavy finality: "It doesn't matter. Not right now. Where are Boone and Natalya?"

"We don't know," he answered, frowning. "I can't imagine they would have left the bridge, but it's soundproofed, so we have no way of knowing for sure. And there was that moment the ship—you know, the gravity flipping around. Something might have happened to them. We don't even know if they're alive in there."

"Oh, they're alive," Sagara said grimly. "They would never make it that easy for us." He flicked the safety off his gun and looked at them. "Be ready. In the best-case scenario, they don't know that we're out of the freezer yet, and we'll take them by surprise. In the worst-case, they've seen us coming and are prepared. We need to move fast—so fast that they can't react. Shoot to kill, and then we regain control of the ship as soon as possible." He suddenly seemed to notice that Taban was standing there placidly behind Park. "Why is that thing out?"

"You can use us as a shield," Taban said, almost cheerfully. "They'll be scared of shooting their only bargaining chip. It will make them hesitate."

Sagara looked faintly approving. "Smart." Then he jerked his head at Park and Fulbreech. "Let's go."

Storming the bridge with the synthetics felt a little like jogging in some strange parade: they formed a kind of flank formation around the humans, each of them except Taban mimicking Sagara's hold on his gun (though one, Conex, seemed to imitate Fulbreech's clumsy grip instead). Park felt jostled by their solid bodies, insulated and protected—but also deeply afraid. She knew some of them were going to get hurt.

Sagara was still limping, but it didn't stop him from creeping ably up to the bridge doors and pressing his ear to them. A futile gesture, considering it was soundproofed and all they could hear was the roar of the ship around them, the whine of spaceflight as they continued to hurtle away from Eos. Park waited in agonized silence, her heart thumping in her throat; what if the doors opened, what if they were ambushed from a direction they weren't expecting? Chanur and Wan Xu had been easy to confront: they were scientists, academics—but Boone had had his genes refined specifically to make him a killing machine. And Natalya had the deadly vigor of a fanatic. She took a steadying breath through her nose. She just wanted this part to be over.

Finally Sagara eased away from the door and motioned with some kind of hand signal she didn't understand: a military gesture, some complicated series of steps and directions. Taban, at least, pretended to understand; he nodded sagely. Fulbreech just shrugged and said in an undertone: "Go on, then."

Sagara palmed open the bridge doors and leapt lightly past them, gun poised, body coiled. Fulbreech followed, swinging his gun up and around in a wide arc. Park squeezed her eyes shut against her will, expecting the sounds of blasting, of massacre—but there was only silence. When she opened her eyes again, Sagara was looking around and frowning. The bridge was empty.

Natalya and Boone were not there.

Fulbreech rushed forward to one of the control panels. "They must have left," he said, already flying into action. "Maybe they abandoned ship, seeing how things were going. Here—you three, you go over there and start reconfiguring the lambda drive. Look, we're trapped in elliptical orbit around the planet still—we need to shoot off toward Corvus, I want calculations—" He rapped off some more orders to the synthetics, who moved to help him man the controls and take back piloting control of the ship. Sagara went over and closed the bridge doors again, positioning himself so that he was ready to shoot whatever tried to come through. He was still frowning, tense and wary.

Fulbreech looked at Park. "I need your help, Park," he said, pointing to the seat that she'd seen Natalya sitting in, during her vision in the freezer. "Go over there and wait for my signal—you're going to touch the orange button that says 'Disengage Automated Tracking' when I tell you to."

She moved to obey, but already the corkscrew sensation was turning in her head again, a light shining behind her eyes. As she sat down in the chair, static filled her head, as if she'd stood up too quickly and all the blood had rushed to the wrong places, letting the white noise in. Fuzzily she received a grainy picture of what had happened here, just minutes before; it was like touching an object that was still warm from someone else's hand after they'd left the room, only it was visual sensation rather than kinetic—a kind of double-vision, an eye-crossing instant of being stuck between two moments in time.

Natalya and Boone had been here, and they'd been arguing.

"No one's responding," the surveyor said. She was standing by the console for communications. On its screen blinked the profile of whomever she was trying to contact: Svetlana Severov. Her sister.

"They must be busy," Boone snapped. He was by the ship's controls, looking through possible coordinates on his neural inlays.

"All of them? All busy, all at the same time?"

"Well, what's the other answer?" Boone asked.

"Something happened to them. Someone found the messages—Sagara, or ISF Surveillance—"

"But your sister encrypted them."

"She's tech support, not a spy!" Then Natalya saw something on another screen; the blood drained from her face. "Shit!"

The moment dissolved. Park blinked just as Fulbreech said, "Now, Park."

Her hand moved; she activated the orange button without quite thinking about it, without even really seeing it. On the screens in front of them, Eos glowed like a huge luminescent pearl. Park shook her head. Natalya and Boone had not even managed to get the ship out of orbit. But where had they gone? That new muscle in her brain flexed; METIS fed her a tiny stream of data, hard to interpret, hard to piece into cogent thought . . .

Park's eyes fell on the screen Natalya had seen, just before the vision broke off. It was the feed to one of the cameras down in Deck C, and Chanur's body, looking almost bisected, the head practically gone, was lying crumpled in the center of the screen. With a jolt Park felt Natalya's panic, her sour anger and fear and grief—and then her wild resolve, hatred, revenge—

The data suddenly untwisted. "They're still in here!" she shouted.

She rose, the edge of the chair hitting her hard in the back of the knees just as she whirled. The ARGUS part of her said to look up, and doing so she saw the flash of a boot swinging down hard at her head. Park ducked, rolled—something landed half on top of her, scrabbled after her, knuckle and nail and rasping hot breath.

Natalya. Park kicked her off, swinging blindly, and out of the corner of her eye—out of some awareness she had cast like a net across the room—she saw that Boone had dropped down from the vents, too, as silent as a bat, and he had landed behind Fulbreech and had his arm locked around Fulbreech's neck, and he was choking him to death. Veins bulged in his biceps as he employed enough force to break a child's spine down on Fulbreech's windpipe. Sagara was still by the doors, wild-eyed, his gun tracking them—but he could not shoot Boone with Fulbreech in the way.

Park looked again—she could not keep track of what to look at—and she saw that Natalya was at the controls, hitting something with the butt of her gun. Park dove at her, and they both rolled—the ship was going into a nosedive now, something in the panel had been broken, the Deucalion was spinning downward like a poorly made paper airplane and Park bashed into Natalya and barely avoided breaking her neck. Both of them were holding their guns but could not get a proper aim for fear of striking one of the others—or something vital in the ship, something combustible—in the maelstrom of sound and motion. Natalya turned her head and hissed at Park like a cat, baring her teeth. They tussled together, stupidly, uselessly, and Park thought, *She's sabotaged the controls. We're going to crash. They're prepared to take us all down, even if it means they die too.*

Across the room she saw Taban lunging forward now, using his six metal limbs for stability even as the other synthetics toppled over and skidded around; he leapt onto Boone's back and wrenched him off of Fulbreech, who surfaced with a great gulp of air, a thick red stripe appearing across his neck as if it had been slashed there by a knife. Fulbreech staggered forward, rasping, and Taban continued to pry Boone backward, using his mechanical strength against the big augmented soldier; Boone gave a thunderous curse, fumbling to shoot back over his shoulder with his gun. His bad leg impeded him; Taban twisted him this way and that. Sagara leapt across the room then and plunged a glowing energy blade hilt-deep into Boone's heart. Park saw it emerge out his back—narrowly avoiding Taban—and then hang there like a splinter of light. There was the smell of smoke and cordite and burning meat. Boone said nothing, did nothing; his body vanished silently under the other control panel.

The ship tipped again, throwing all of them off their feet. Park would have snapped her wrist if Dylanex hadn't caught her. *We need to do something,* she thought through the lurching and shrieking protests of the ship. Something grabbed her throat, and a dark thing—a gun—flashed past the corner of her eye, headed to her temple, and she sank her teeth into that hand before it could do more; Natalya screamed. Something snapped under Park's teeth like a popsicle stick. Salt and heat filled her mouth. The surveyor was grabbing her head, kneeing her stomach, but Park's mind felt so jumbled that she hardly felt it. *The* Deucalion *is out of control.*

On the screens, Eos loomed closer and closer. Park's ears popped as her feet lifted off the ground. Someone was yelling, or praying—Jimex hurtled into her body, as light as a child—

Stop, Park thought, reaching for the golden simmering in the corner of her head. This time there was no nausea: only a strange shifting in her brain, the tensing of that hidden sinew she had never noticed before. A kind of tightness as she held the whole of the ship in her mind.

The *Deucalion* flopped back upright again.

Fulbreech yelled again. At first Park thought it was because he'd landed on his face, but when she looked up, she saw that he was pointing at something, holding his half-strangled throat with his other hand. Boone, still alive, dragging his body toward something in the corner—Sagara, rising grimly and limping after him—

Light exploded across Park's vision. Natalya was rising, clutching her mangled hand protectively to her chest; she'd kicked Park in the head. The synthetics were righting themselves, turning to swarm her; Natalya gave a futile scream as they closed in. Her gun fell to the floor with a clatter.

Then some of them were pulling Park away, pulling her to safety, and she looked back and saw Natalya's bloody, broken fingers; and for a moment she thought of Antarctica, that moment by the Earthmover when she thought she'd lose her own fingers, reaching into its guts, but the memory was drowned out as Natalya screamed and screamed. Jimex was diving toward the surveyor, perhaps intent on doing the same thing he'd done to Chanur—but then he recoiled in surprise, and the smell of alcohol filled Park's nose: the strongest odor she'd smelled on the ship in a year. Wetness splashed across her face. Natalya's hip flask glinted in her one good hand.

Then fire. Heat and flame—Natalya had doused them in alcohol and lit a plasma torch! Park scrambled backwards, out of the way, but the synthetics were unharmed, merely confused as fire licked up their bodies. Jimex's reddened shirt was being devoured by golden light. Fulbreech lunged past her, shouting, holding a fire extinguisher: Park caught his stray thought as he dove past. If the fire took the bridge, there was no hope left. They would all crash into Eos and die.

Sagara was running forward too, Boone nowhere in sight, the synthetics all clamoring, rushing to the stations that would activate METIS's dousing protocols. But in the commotion, Park saw Natalya staggering to her feet. She watched as the surveyor ran out of the bridge.

Unbidden, a fierce, stormlike energy leapt through Park, as if a solar wind had kicked up howling in her body; she found herself surging to her feet and staggering after the surveyor. *I'll kill you,* she thought—but the thought was absurd, far-off, as if it had been thought by someone else in another life. The METIS part of her screamed in outrage as it felt the fire, sensed the damage to its own system. *You're the cause of all of this: all this betrayal, all this destruction. Fire, blood—all because of you. I'll end you.*

Jimex was coming after her, the flames on him now snuffed out, and Taban; Jimex had a gun in his hand, but he seemed loath to risk damaging the ship any further. The *Deucalion* was still tilting wildly; it was in freefall again, and Park could not hold it upright, could not concentrate on it while she was running after Natalya. Taban shouted something at Natalya about surrendering. She ignored him, rushing off down the hall without a glance back; Park tore after her and thought again, *I'll find you. There's nowhere on this ship you can hide from me.* Her head was buzzing; she was swarming with anger, aching with it—it rushed to the top of her throat like bile.

Doors flew open as Natalya fled past them; pipes let out sudden hisses of steam, and metal screamed in protest. The depths of the ship seemed to Park like the dark-gleaming arteries of an enormous mechanical heart. It was if an army of ghosts was pursuing the surveyor, possessing things around her, causing them to revolt—or as if the ship itself was coming alive. Had Taban been wrong? Park wondered. Was this the end of the season, the final culmination of the unity rain? Or was it all her? Her and METIS's rage?

Jimex, beside her, said, "She means to kill us all." Natalya had already vanished down the corner ahead; Park was falling behind fast, even though that fierce energy still filled her, propelled her on. She felt as if she were in a dream, one of those strange affairs where you couldn't move fast enough no matter how hard you tried. Her arms pumped uselessly at her sides; she had never thought her own limbs so unnecessary before.

"She sabotaged the ship," Park rasped. "So that none of us could fly it. She wants to die, too."

But that didn't seem right—and as she ran, suddenly Natalya's true intention struck her, full-force, as if the surveyor had lobbed it at her. No, Natalya wasn't running away to hide, to die somewhere alone when the ship crashed—she was *running to the escape pod.* She was going to leave the ship altogether. She'd damaged the *Deucalion* with the intention of killing everyone aboard it while she got away!

"You need to help the ship," Taban said then, keeping pace with Park. "Use the unity rain—we're all going to die if you don't."

"I will," Park gritted out. "After I catch her."

"She's too far away. You're not going to. You need to pull the ship out of freefall."

"I will!"

And then she felt it again, the contraction in her brain, the feeling of time and space accordioning, the sensation of folding into herself. Her field of vision shifted, sliding to the right, though her eyes or head didn't move. She felt as if she'd partially woken from a flying dream.

Then she blinked, and found that she was at the door of the escape pod, Jimex and Taban far behind her. The door to the escape pod had just slammed shut, the little porthole in it hazy with condensation—and Natalya was inside, slamming things together, rasping and screaming like an animal.

Park looked at her hand. The fierce golden glow had filled her vision again, and she felt the hard-edged knowledge that she could lift her hand and command the door to open for her, as she had with the freezer, with Taban's cell. No, more than that: she could crush Natalya's pod in her fist, tell METIS to blow the whole thing up and suck the debris into the vacuum of space. The powerful part of her, the cold thing, the vengeful thing, urged her to do it. Behind her somewhere, Taban was yelling. Park felt parts of the ship breaking off in Eos's atmosphere, tearing back into space like scales from a thrashing fish; they were going down too fast, they were burning up. She didn't care.

But then Natalya looked up, her eyes panicky and gray, and Park had the feeling of double-vision again—of déjà vu. Of herself, looking in at Taban in his cell; of Natalya, looking in at her in her own.

And then she returned to herself a little, again, and the clamoring insistence of the ship, its demand and its pull, faded and loosened. She could hear things better in the space it left behind. It came to her then what Natalya really wanted, in a trickle of data and intention and thought. What she was trying to get back to. Home. Family. Love. Freedom.

What the synthetics wanted.

What anyone wanted.

She took a breath and thought—

No. Let her go.

She felt the shuttle detaching from the ship as a slackening in her brain. A relaxing of the hidden muscle there. Had the structure of her brain, too, become machine-like? Was she tied, physically and inextricably, always to the ship? And to the things and people in it? Were they all a part of her, and she them?

Natalya had disappeared from the porthole. Jimex came running up, walleyed, taut. He looked questioningly at Park and said, "She's getting away."

"So are we," Park told him. She wiped the blood from her mouth. "And she won't come back. There's nothing for her here."

In her mind, she had wiser words to say to him, some great lesson about humanity or empathy or mercy or . . . something. But in the end she did not need to say anything. Jimex looked into her, into the core of what she was, and understood.

They watched as the shuttle finished its undocking procedures and navigated away. There was no pause, no brief glance of gratitude, of remorse. The escape pod simply spun away into space; and with a swoop of Park's heart, the *Deucalion* slowed its descent and arced back down towards Eos.

25.

"I don't understand," Sagara said later, as they made their slow and ponderous descent back to the planet's surface. He had rolled up Boone's corpse in a sheet of canvas. "Why are we going back?"

"The androids—no, the synthetics can't come home with us," Park heard herself saying. The golden glow had faded in her head, but only a little. "They want to stay here."

Fulbreech made an incredulous noise, then winced and rubbed his throat. His voice was hoarse and gravelly, destroyed by Boone's assault, but otherwise he and Sagara were both still intact. "*Why*?"

She looked at Jimex, who was helping to readjust the arm of one of the injured synthetics. He smiled at her, and Park said, "They'll be happier here."

Sagara made a face, but Fulbreech looked between her and Jimex with almost wonder. "You're one of them now," he said. It wasn't an accusation, only an epiphany—as if he had finally uncovered a secret of Park's that she had always hinted at, but he had always missed.

The ship purred and whirred around them. Park felt the awareness of METIS and ARGUS pressing against her like watching spirits. "Maybe I always have been," she said.

Outside, the sky was a riot of color and light: a dance so fierce and searing that it seemed almost harmful to look at. Above, the escape pod had disappeared into a dark, ragged fissure in the sky.

Park told Sagara that Natalya had simply gotten away—that Park had not been able to catch up to her in time. He grunted and said, "She'll die in space anyway, or go to prison. That escape pod only has a month of rations, and who is she going to call for help? The ISF? Even if she manages to land at Corvus without starving, the Security team will be waiting there to arrest her. And being charged with murder, mutiny, and conspiracy by the very entity she was trying to escape from—the one whose mission she torpedoed? They will not be kind. I'd rather eject myself into space."

Then at least she'll have done it herself, Park thought, and made that choice on her own. She was glad that she had not taken that away from Natalya, whatever happened. It was more complicated than not wanting blood on her hands; there was something more there, but what it was, Park could not exactly say. The METIS part of her muttered in a tiny stream of rebellion, though—and so at least Park knew that the choice had been hers alone. That the part that had spared Natalya was still her, and only her. That seemed important, somehow. She wanted to tell the synthetics about it, but didn't know how to articulate it. Maybe they already knew.

They landed, and Park felt the settling of the ship like it was the concluding piece of a vast and complex puzzle. Fulbreech helped her to the airlock while Sagara stayed on the ship to send his own message to ISF and rest his leg. Taban watched them don their exo-armor suits with some hidden amusement. The synthetics had all reconvened again, claiming that Keller and Reimi needed three hours to complete their reawakening. They all crowded eagerly at the door, like schoolchildren waiting to go to recess. They did not line up in formation, as they used to.

Park opened the airlock. The synthetics all spilled out, and Fulbreech helped Park through the door. It was easy enough to climb down the little ladder that led down under the hatch, but once she hit the ground, Park nearly collapsed. There was an unutterable pressure in her head, the howling and rushing of a sound so vast that for a moment her vision went dark. Briefly she thought that they were being attacked, that some enormous and hideous monster was about to consume them—or that the unity rain was coming again—but then Fulbreech clapped a hand to her shoulder and held her as she swayed. "It's the wind!" he shouted through his helmet. Out here, his voice sounded utterly transformed, unrecognizable—like it belonged to a different man, a stranger and not a stranger. "It's just the wind!"

Of course, Park thought in a daze. Nearly a year in space, aboard a sealed, pressurized ship—she had forgotten the sound of wind.

After a moment the two of them managed to stagger upright. Despite herself, Park had to cling to Fulbreech, trembling, before she managed to stand on her own and open her eyes. Through her sparking vision Eos seemed to swim and shimmer like a mirage. She felt as if all the air had been sucked out of her lungs. There was nothing out there but ice: a frozen tundra that stretched out in a flat, razor-sharp horizon, so white that it nearly cut the eye. And there were the two suns, weak and watery with pale light. And the sky—the sky was a deep green, a kind of color that made Park feel rich and full. It was the first time she had seen natural light since she'd left Earth. It was almost unbearable to look at.

"Are you all right?" Fulbreech shouted through his helmet.

After a moment, Park straightened and nodded. The synthetics were looking around, some with hesitation, others with wonder. A kind of chanting rose from them after a while, or singing, though Park couldn't make out the words. *They're taking it in*, Park thought. They were reveling in it, all of this, Eos, their new home. What that meant.

She was almost afraid to study it too closely. What would it all look like, ten years from now? One hundred years from now? Was she looking at the birthplace of synthetic civilization? Would they live forever, procreate, and share their enlightenment with their machine offspring, cannibalized from parts of the ship, until they one day reached the solution mankind had never been able to uncover? Could they really make this place a home for themselves?

We could do it, she thought then. We did it with Mars and Phobos and Titan. They can do things we never dreamed of.

Fulbreech had put his arm around her shoulders. He felt solid and warm and heavy with life. Off in the distance, a line of rose was beginning to rim the horizon. Daybreak, Park thought, turning the word over in her head. The marker of passing time. But did it mean anything on a planet where time was not a steady march, more a scattered melody that no one knew or could hear, and the planet's surface was populated by androids who did not age?

Someone was tramping up to her, through the ice; for a moment Park couldn't make out his figure, shadowed as it was by the brilliant dawn. Then the figure resolved: it was Jimex. His eyes were spangled with gold in the light.

"You don't need your helmet," he told her. "This place is yours, too."

Fulbreech made a noise of disbelief, but Park shrugged off his arm and began to take off her helmet.

"No—" Fulbreech began, startled.

The helmet disengaged from the suit with a rush of frigid air; Park took a deep breath. Then another.

She smiled.

"Where will you make your home?" she asked Jimex. She looked to the mountains in the distance: silvery-gray structures that seemed to crease the horizon. *No,* she thought, catching herself. *Not mountains. Folds.* "Are you happy to finally be here?"

"Yes and no," Jimex answered, as serious as ever. "In a way, we have always been here."

Park smiled at him, and her heart gave a hard clutch of love. "I understand."

ACKNOWLEDGMENTS

Writing tends to be solitary, but much like the launching of a spacecraft, publication is wonderfully, beautifully collaborative. As such, I have many people to thank for the propelling of this book into the world.

First thanks must go to my wonderful agent, Matt Bialer, who remembered my half-finished manuscript after some years and became its first standard-bearer in the industry. Thank you, Matt, for taking a chance on this story, and for being such a strong advocate for it ever since. Thank you too to his team at Sanford J. Greenburger, especially his assistant Bailey Tamayo. Thank you to Robert Lawrence, whose insightful comments and early enthusiasm for this book helped give it a much better ending; and thank you to Jerry Kalajian, my film agent, as well. Thank you also to Robert VS Redick, whose writing inspired me when I was still in high school, and who took the time to give me advice and a helping hand whenever I asked for it, and whose books I pay homage to with the name Fulbreech.

Thank you to my MFA thesis advisors at Cornell University, John Robert Lennon and Stephanie Vaughn, under whose early guidance this book first took shape and steadily grew. Thank you, Stephanie, for insisting I change the book's original title, *Biophilia,* which was truly awful. This title is much better. And thank you so much to John, who first gave me the encouragement to consider the book as more than just a thesis, and who devoted so much time to giving me incisive and positive comments on that first nascent manuscript, and for everything else he's done over the years.

I owe a debt of gratitude to my editor, Leah Spann, whose patience and efficiency and kindness continually astounds me. Thank you for believing in this book and its vision. Thank you to the entire DAW team, whose tireless efforts brought this book through its long journey to publication: thank you to Joshua Starr, Lindsay Ribar, Alexis Nixon, Jessica Plummer, Adam Auerbach, Katie Anderson, Betsy Wollheim, and Sheila Gilbert.

I am lucky to be surrounded by incredible family and friends who have always been enthusiastic about my weird desire to just write books. Their unconditional support bolstered me to this finish line. Thank you to my expansive and loving Nguyen family, across the country and across the world; your endless pride and excitement means more than I can say. To my cousins, Tim, Andrew, Ethan, Brandon, Alex, Ryan, Annie, and Tony: thanks for enduring all this talk about the book, and for letting me retreat every summer to write bits of it at a time, and for being the best family I could ask for. To all my aunts and uncles, and to my grandmother: thank you for showering us in unconditional love, and for believing wholeheartedly in this wild dream. I love you all very much.

Thank you to my parents, Kimphuong and Dungchi, who always encouraged my pursuits in writing, and who worked so hard to give us the opportunities we had, even when we were very young, and who continue to inspire me every day. Thank you for always believing in my success; for sending me to Stanford and Harvard and Brown to write, especially when you could have told me to study something more practical; for driving me to the bookstore and letting me sit for hours when I should have been playing outside; for working long hours and making the many sacrifices loving parents make without a word; for nourishing my skills and allowing them to flourish; and for supporting me so readily and selflessly. I love you, and I hope this book makes you proud.

Thank you to my sister, Milla, who had to put up with my writing and talk of it pretty much from the moment she was born. Thank you for everything you've done and continue to do, from taking my author photo and putting together my wardrobe to campaigning for the book on social media. You are the best sister in the world, and you have always been my biggest cheerleader—and I am yours. Thank you for everything, and I can't wait to see where your journey takes you. I'll be by your side every step of the way.

Thank you to the Conigliari family, especially for hosting us when I was in the trenches with this manuscript, and for their endless kindness and support over the years. Your generosity and warmth truly mean the world. Thank you to Paul, Sandy, Jonathan, Chris, Jason, Rachel, Anna, and Marco.

Special and heartfelt thanks to my friends Curtis, Joe, Allison, Christian, Leila, Jack, Conner, and Micah for your incredible support and friendship over the years, even when you had to endure vague descriptions of "tongueless insanity" and scientific inaccuracy and all the things that came with the making of this novel. Your encouragement and love has meant the world. I truly treasure you all, and I am so happy to finally share this story with the greatest friends I could have dreamed of. If we were on a spaceship, I'd want you as my crew.

And finally, thank you to my partner Jeremy Conigliari, this book's first and closest reader, its earliest champion, and my greatest source of inspiration. You've always had unwavering faith in this story's success and destination: I'll never forget your joy and utter unsurprise when we found out that it was going to be published. How you said to me that you'd always known it was going to happen—that it was just a matter of time. You've been my rock, but that feels too mundane, too Earth-bound—maybe I should say you've been my comet, ferrying me to places I never dreamed I could go. Thank you for the countless sacrifices, for the many nights addressing tears and doubts, for the rallying pep talks and loving words, and for the several epiphanies in mid-conversation that made this book so much better than it was. Your belief beckoned this story into reality. You never gave up, even when I wanted to. None of this would have happened without you, and this book is as much yours as it is mine. You have been by my side every step of the way, and you have made every moment worth it. Thank you for your faith, your pride, your love, your support, and everything else that you've done and are. You are my hero, and I love you more than I can say. To the moon and back, perhaps, or to Eos and back.

Thank you for helping me reach for the stars. We've grabbed them together; now let's see where this voyage takes us next